MURDER

 on the

CLIFFS

MURDER

on the

CLIFFS

A DAPHNE du MAURIER MYSTERY

JOANNA CHALLIS

Minotaur Books ⚓ New York

This is a work of fiction. All of the characters, organizations, and events portrayed in this novel are either products of the author's imagination or are used fictitiously.

ISBN 978-0-312-36714-5

DEDICATION

For Michael O'Regan, my everyday hero, and for three ladies who made it happen: Kim Lionetti, my agent and friend, and Laura Bourgeois and Hope Dellon at St. Martin's. Thank you.

Thanks also to April Hearle for her Latin translation.

MURDER

on the

CLIFFS

CHAPTER ONE

The storm led me to Padthaway.

I could never resist the allure of dark swirling clouds, wind-swept leaves sweeping down cobbled lanes, or a view of the sea, its defiant nature stirred up. The sea possessed a power all its own, and this part of Cornwall, an isolated stretch of rocky cliff tops and unexplored beaches, both enchanted and terrified me.

It is not a lie to say I felt drawn out that day, led to a certain destiny. As I shut the gate to Ewe Sinclaire's cottage, I was struck by a sensation of expectancy. For what, I did not know.

Walking with the wind, I allowed it to determine my direction. The grassy coastline, pointing toward the southern headland, formed my corridor. Along I went, mesmerized by the rising, angry ocean, its snarling waves lashing against the shapeless boulders.

I soon came upon a cove. A beautiful, magnificent, dangerous cove. The steep decline down did not deter me, nor did the advancing treacherous tide. Danger only energized me.

Groaning thunder gripped the sky and the rain began to drizzle. The drizzle transformed to droplets and the droplets to pelts. Undaunted, I headed toward my target—the largest boulder at the end of the cove—and walked quickly to beat the incoming tide.

And then I heard it.

A scream of terror . . . up ahead.

I hurried on, glimpsing a girl not far in the distance, a body sprawled at her feet.

Reaching the sight, I forced back sickness. A young woman lay there, her abundant black hair splayed across the sand, eyes wide open . . . still, lifeless. Waters lapped about her, wanting to draw her to the sea. Shutting my eyes, I fought the urge to run.

I squinted at my silent companion, the salty spray stinging my eyes. "We have to move her," I shouted. "Or else . . ." I gestured to the fierce waves behind.

The slight girl, fifteen or so, nodded, frantic. Directing her to the feet of the woman, I took the arms and together we dragged her up the beach.

Lightning danced and thunder roared across the sea. My companion screamed again, shoving her hands over her ears.

"We've got to get help." I pointed to the body.

The girl stared at me, new fear haunting her pale, thin face.

"What's your name?" I asked, checking the body for a sign. My attempts were futile, for no life stirred within the chilled veins, the diamond ring on her finger a grim reminder that she'd been loved. Dressed in a cream nightgown, the only hint of the woman's identity rested with the girl who struggled to find her voice.

"Lianne," she managed with a deep swallow. "Is she . . . truly dead?"

"It appears so." I brushed wet sand off my shaking hands and charged up the embankment.

Lianne followed. We had to find shelter from the rising storm, and quickly. Spying a rusted, broken-down boathouse a few yards up, we ran to it and once under its meager protection, Lianne and I gaped at each other. We'd shared an experience, a horrifying experience, and I felt compelled to speak first. "Did you know her?"

From her look, I suspected she knew the victim quite well.

"Your sister?" I prompted.

"No!" came the quick denial.

The wind rattled the tin roof. Pulling Lianne into the safest corner, we kept our gaze focused on the roof, hoping, *praying* the vicious wind would subside. The surging sea . . . the lightning . . . the whipping, whistling rain flashed its sequence before us. "I can't believe it." Lianne shivered. "I can't believe she's dead. . . ."

Banishing my own horror, I put my arm around Lianne. "I know . . . it's dreadful. Who is she?"

"They'll blame me, I suppose. . . . They always blame me. . . ."

"Who always blames you?"

"Oh." She flicked a piece of damp stringy hair off her face. "Them at the house. It's not fair. I don't want to go back."

She shivered again and I drew her closer to me, gently patting her back. "It'll be all right," I whispered.

Lianne gazed up at me, her eyes full of hope.

"I promise," I smiled, gently squeezing her hand.

We waited out the remainder of the storm in silence. When finally the winds abated and the customary calm set in, I guided a still apprehensive Lianne outside.

"See, it's over."

Lianne nodded but something about the pallor of her face suggested a new terror had begun.

Her eyes were fixed on the body.

Sensing her desperation, I held out my hand. "Don't worry. I'll do the explaining. My name's Daphne."

Relief replaced some of her fright. "You won't . . . leave me?"

"I won't, but you must tell me who she is . . . the woman on the beach."

Swallowing hard, Lianne nodded. "Her name's Victoria Bastion. She was to marry my brother."

"Your brother? What do you think happened to her? Why was she dressed in her nightgown?"

Lianne turned away. "I don't know. I never liked her. She was a kitchen maid, you know. They do odd things."

A kitchen maid to marry Lianne's brother? The way she said it inferred her brother's status well above an ordinary kitchen maid. Curious about her family, I asked a few more questions but received only monosyllabic replies.

"You'll see," Lianne said. "The house is this way."

We walked a little way before she paused suddenly to squeeze my hand. "Daphne . . . that's a funny name."

"Yes," I agreed. "I don't particularly like it."

"I don't like mine either."

"But Lianne is a beautiful name."

A little smile settled on her lips. "Nobody's ever said that to me before. Thank you, Daphne."

She was an odd girl. A queer innocence enshrouded her, like a child adopting the persona of a saint. I asked her the way to her home.

She lifted a brow in surprise. "You don't know it?"

"I'm a stranger here," I confessed. "I'm staying with my mother's old nurse, Ewe Sinclaire . . . in the village. Perhaps you know of her?"

Lianne shook her head. "I'm never allowed to go to the village."

"Why?"

"It's forbidden," she said simply, skirting past me.

Heading south across the cliff face, we reached an area I hadn't yet explored. By now, the eye of the storm and its deceptive calm surrounded us. The rain had ceased to the faintest drizzle, and though a muggy heat persisted, I shivered. I kept seeing the face of the dead woman.

Down a narrow valley and over a succession of steep hills, we labored on in silence.

And then I saw it.

Resting beneath the rise of the next headland, the grand lady stood. An Elizabethan mansion . . . sprawling . . . wild . . . unforgettable. A crumbling stone tower crawled up the cliff at one end, its ivy cloak bleeding into the house while morning sun waltzed across the hundreds of glazed windows, mirroring the warm honey-red tones of the bricks.

The sacred beauty of the house took my breath away, creating a pang in my heart, a yearning. I fancied her calling me, luring me to my destiny.

"Come on," Lianne said, strutting away.

My feet refused to obey me.

Lianne tapped hers and the urgency of the situation returned to me. Here I was lost in my own little world, mesmerized, when a woman lay dead.

The front door loomed ahead. I imagined it opening solely for me, and still in a daze, I almost collided into its heavy oak embrace as Lianne struggled to push it open.

Lianne rushed inside, crying, "Help! She's dead!"

An airy parlor greeted me, dominated by a huge red-carpeted staircase leading off into various paneled wings of the house. A great silence ensued. In the background, a clock ticked away. It was not a merry sound but strangely foreboding, and I found myself shivering from head to toe.

"*Who* calls?" a voice demanded above. "Out of my way, Trehearn. I shall deal with this directly."

Lianne paled at the voice.

"Has my lord been summoned?" the advancing voice continued. "Summon him at once. At once, I say."

I stood beside Lianne. Her gaze remained prisoner to the staircase, and within seconds her ladyship of the voice swept down. Tall and regal, with a hardened face bearing remnants of beauty, she tightened the tie of her yellow satin morning robe and frowned.

"What's this nonsense I hear? Who's dead?"

"We found a body," I answered, "at the cove."

Her ladyship slowly absorbed this news. "At the cove, you say?" Settling a bejeweled hand on the gilded knob of the staircase, she glanced up at the approaching footsteps. Her eyes were filled with cold composure.

"We have news," she informed the stern-faced man coming down the stairs.

"What's she done now?"

Ignoring his gentle, amused scold, Lianne rushed into his arms. "Oh, David . . . David, it's horrible, horrible! It's . . ."

Strong arms encased her. Tall and lithe, her brother's handsome face turned to her, the lower part of his jaw straining to make sense of her blubbering words.

"I . . . I don't know how to say it . . ." She shuddered. "But it's dreadful. Truly dreadful!" Squeezing her eyes shut, she clung to the inside of her brother's brown tweed coat as though wanting to bury her face forever in its green satin folds.

David, much older than his younger sister, in his late twenties I suspected, clasped her face in his hands and laughed. "It cannot be all that bad. What have you done now? Lost a purse? Stole a candy from Mr. Frankie?"

"No," she shook her head, her tone dropping to a whisper. "It's much worse. . . . It's . . ."

She appealed to me with her eyes.

Not wanting to intrude on this intimate family scene with the dire news, I hesitantly stepped forward, remembering that sometimes it is best to learn of something tragic from the mouth of a stranger.

"I am new to the area. I was out walking when I discovered . . ." Feeling Lianne's mother's intense scrutiny, I directed my gaze to David, for I felt the news must go to him first. "I'm so sorry to be the one to have to break this to you, but Victoria is dead."

"Victoria!" her ladyship gasped.

David's face froze. He staggered a little away, steadying himself by seizing one of the huge staircase columns. Sagging down, he leaned his head against the balustrade, dazed, his shell-shocked eyes massive orbs reflecting disbelief. "She's . . . dead?"

He posed the question to me for confirmation. I nodded, bestowing upon him a compassionate camaraderie.

Her ladyship sagged down beside him on the steps and Lianne followed, leaving me to stand there in front of the three of them. Somewhere in the background, I fancied another presence watching, or perhaps more than just one pair of eyes. Curious servants, overly interested housekeepers . . .

"Forgive me." Her ladyship recalled me. "What was your name?"

"Daphne. Daphne du Maurier," I said, and replied I thought it best to leave, considering the great shock.

She nodded with a vague comprehension. "Yes . . . it is best. But . . . will you come back? There will be questions and—"

"Of course," I promised. "I shall return tomorrow."

I turned around and made a quick exit, staring back at the great house, now cloaked in a veil of mystery.

CHAPTER TWO

The humble cottage of Ewe Sinclaire failed to engender the same response in me as the mysterious house on the cliff.

Hopes of stumbling upon such a grand house were partly the reason why I'd come to this remote part of Cornwall, to explore the abbey records and the great houses, churches, quaint villages, old manors, and medieval inns—anything of historical value or interest. In truth, I had far too many interests to possibly hope to study in a mere life of sixty or eighty years, but I had decided to begin here.

My family thought me mad. Why should I give up a London season for a holiday in the country? And not even for a grand country house party, mind. I'd been to plenty of those, but unless the invitation included a castle, house, grand estate, or something of historical value, they left me feeling bored, depleted, and wholly dissatisfied.

When I'd read the article in *The Times* of the lonely abbey on the Cornish coast bearing magnificent records dating back to Charlemagne's era, I had to visit. On my own, at my insistence.

My mother gaped in horror at the suggestion.

"You'd *skip* the season to do what? Crawl through dusty old records? Daphne, Daphne, however are we to snare a husband for you when you're forever poking into ancient things?" Shivering, she raised her eyes to the drawing room ceiling of our London house. "No. I demand you speak to your father at once. This notion of your going *on your own* and *staying at an inn,* I won't have it. It's not right, nor is it proper."

Proper. I hated heeding protocol. It was nineteen twenty-eight! I wanted to shout that we'd been through the Great War and that the world had changed. Life was no longer the Victorian stringency of the past—bomb blasts and death killed the old world's romanticism, thrusting everybody into a bleak reality. "Mama, Heidi Williams went to Crete by herself last year—"

"But she was meeting friends," my mother despaired. "You propose to go off camping like a gypsy." She raised her hand, signaling the end of the discussion.

Discussion, thought I, glum-faced as I left her to seek out my father. It wasn't a discussion but a flat "no."

I found my father where he always was at this time of the morning: in his study, preparing papers for the theater and busy packing his bag. He always had a soft spot for me, the dreamer, the silent adventurer in mind and spirit. I was different from my sisters, and he sensed the difference whereas my mother did not. My father and I shared a sacred bond.

Sir Gerald du Maurier, who loved the theater and all its theatrics, listened sympathetically to my need to escape this particular London season.

"But Daphne, my darling, you're *twenty-one.* Time to find a husband!"

"A husband," choked I, abhorred by the notion of becoming solely dependant on a man.

"Yes, a husband," my father continued, observing me rather curiously. "Don't you want one?"

I considered it.

"No, not really."

He lifted a startled brow. "But it's not as if you don't have admirers. . . ."

That was true. I did have, considering the circles we moved in and my father's great and influential contacts. The "admirers" he referred to were largely oversized, overrich, divorced, or too full of themselves to care for a wife. What they wanted was a showpiece, and I certainly was not going to become any man's showpiece.

Upon further discussion, he agreed to my plan, intrigued at the prospect of my digging up something "exciting" at the abbey.

"You never know"—he winked—"might even find something to use in a play."

My father, an actor and stage manager, and a large bear of a man, eccentric and lovable, understood art in all of its forms and wasn't afraid to take risks.

He waved me off with a jovial hand, my mother, still disapproving, by his side, having consented only on the basis of my staying with Ewe Sinclaire—an old nanny of hers who lived in a village not far from the abbey.

"She's a dreadful old gossip, that Ewe," my mother warned. "But I know you'll be safe with her and do promise to write, won't you? Your father and I will worry."

"I will, Mama," I promised, looking forward to meeting this "dreadful old gossip."

As I arrived, Ewe Sinclaire, a large robust woman bearing an enormous bust and bustling similarities to the character of Mrs. Jennings in Austen's *Sense and Sensibility,* huffed at the white picket fence gate.

"Well, there you are, dearie!" She paused to catch her breath and fan herself. "I've been waiting *all* day. What took you so long?"

I blushed, not wanting to confide I'd been drinking a cider at the local pub to absorb the atmosphere. "Oh, the train took longer than I thought."

I lowered my gaze. I didn't lie very well, did I? I'd have to work on correcting this failing, for the shrewd little sharp dagger eyes of Ewe Sinclaire devoured and conquered everything in sight. Wiry charcoal hair framed the merry rolls of her white fleshy face where a squat nose dwelt amongst twitching lips that seemed forever amused.

I liked her at once.

"Welcome to My Little House, Miss Daphne. My! How like your mother you look, though she were *real* pretty, Muriel Beaumont. Not saying that you're not, but you're different in your own little way." Appraising me again with those shrewd eyes, she nodded, as though silently satisfied with my appearance, and grabbing my bag with a large brusque arm, she bounded down the path.

The tiny stone path was lined with all kinds of florid overgrown flowers, shrubs, and midsized fruit trees. I paused a moment to savor the wild abandon, lingering in the wake of Ewe's windstorm, wanting to appreciate the gentle afternoon light enchanting the little whitewashed cottage with its signature thatched roof. A peaceful place, warm and inviting, even if it did appear, upon first entering, to be full of defects.

Stepping over a partially broken wooden floorboard inside the front door, I heard a tap dripping somewhere and a clanging pot sound in the distance.

"Oh, that *stupid* kettle!"

Waddling into the first room on her left, Ewe pushed open the door with an almighty shove. "Here's your room. There's the lounge and kitchen over there. I've got a small parlor, too," she said, and nodded, proud, dumping my bag on the tiny framed bed. "Not much room in here, but you're no snob-nose from what I've heard, are ye?" Her keen eye interrogated me. "Bookish type by the looks of it and you're pretty, which is a good thing, for it's not nice for a girl to be ugly or *plain,* as they used to say. Or was it unhandsome? Handsome! Why ever did they use that word for a woman when it belongs so obviously to men?"

I smiled. I could see the days ahead . . . no escape from the ramblings of Ewe Sinclaire's mouth until she fell asleep. Did she wake talking, too, I wondered?

Hovering at the door after instructing me to wash and change for tea before dinner, she asked me how long I intended to stay.

"Well, you can stay as long as you want or as short, if you fancy. I don't mind. I don't really *do* anything. I used to do things, useful things in the community, but now I'm practically a . . ." she considered at length, "*busybody.* Yes, that's what I am. I just go around and drink tea all day. Busy myself in other's affairs because they're a great deal more interestin' than my humdrum old life."

"Did you ever marry?" I thought to ask as we sipped tea in her tiny parlor laden with everything lace: lace curtains sweeping back from the murky panes of the two cottage windows, lace borders sewn around photograph frames, lace doilies on the coffee table and skinny mantelpiece, and lace-edged cushions on the three-setting burgundy couch she confessed had been a splendid buy from the proceeds of Treelorn Manor. "Did you ever marry, Mrs. Sinclaire?" I repeated the question, since she seemed to have drifted off into a world of her own.

"Oh, bless ye, dearie," she squawked. "*Me? Marry?* Who'd marry a silly duck like me? Tho' there was one or two fishes . . . but they slipped away into the moonlight. Married other girls. I got left on the shelf. Not that I mind—I've seen too many *disastrous* marriages to care—if a man weren't man enough to take on Ewe Perdita Sinclaire, then that was his fault. Not mine."

I set down my tea, examining the faces of the children in her photographs.

"Oh," she beamed, "they're my sister's. *Angels,* aren't they? They're like my own and they come to visit from time to time. My sister married a good fellow of Dorset—he works in a men's store, a manager really—and my sister and he have a charming little place of their own in town with their two angels."

"Any other family?"

She reflected, an unusual serious shade pulling over her merry eyes. "Yes. Always. I've been a nanny since I were eighteen years old. Every house I've served . . . every child I've reared . . . they've been my family. That's what we nannies are like. We *become* part of the family. It's just how it is."

"But you're retired now?"

"A retired busybody," she chortled, staring into the cracks of her ceiling. "But what interests me, Miss Daphne du Maurier, is why are you really here? You can't expect me to believe a young gel as pretty and as connected as you would bury herself down here for the holiday unless you intended to meet a young man?"

The question hung in the air, her incessant winking compelling me to snort. "No! You'll find I'm not like the others. I'm different. My parents can't believe I want to be here, rummaging through old abbey records instead of ensnaring a husband. Husband! Who'd want a man? They all expect servitude and I have too much to accomplish to be trapped in a prison."

"Ha!" Ewe exploded. "When love takes ye, dearie, it will take you with a *big fall*. Mark my words now, but you enjoy yourself while you're here, under my roof, delving into these abbey records of so much interest to you. But beware, you never know what lies around the corner within these silent parts."

I should have heeded her words.

However, the following day I blindly set out, early, before she rose, in search of the first glimpse of the ancient abbey.

I walked through the village green and into the woods, a luxuriant forest bearing new green leaves heralding the spring, the bark smelling of fresh rain, rejuvenating and tantalizing to the nose.

Discovering an ancient path by a gigantic cypress, I trudged my way through the thick shrubbery and out toward the sea.

I hadn't expected Ewe's home to be so close to the sea. Hidden on the borders, resting beside the village green, the cottage reminded me of the one in the fairy tale *Hansel and Gretel*. It possessed a quaint aura about it and I knew I'd love living here for a time.

No signpost existed for the abbey. I half hoped an old piece of timber nailed to a tree would guide my way, but the roaring ocean invited, and grinning, I abandoned my search for the abbey and headed toward the spiraling cliffs. Down and down I went, the windswept long grass tickling my legs, and eventually, I made it to the beach.

There was something very soothing about a stroll on the beach, the rush of the water about my ankles. I'd just jumped at a sudden wave when I heard the scream.

It was the scream that led me to Padthaway.

Though I'd accompanied Lianne to that great house and delivered the bad news on my meander back to Ewe's, I still questioned whether the event had actually transpired. They say shock takes hold of you, and dazed, I stumbled into the village, shivering at the remembrance of that beautiful face resting in the silent repose of death.

"Looks like you've seen a ghost," Ewe remarked, asking me if I preferred cucumber to ham or egg for noonday sandwiches.

I sat down on the stool inside her kitchen.

"What? Find a dead body?"

"Actually, I did," I heard myself say.

Chuckling, merry, she shook her head. "Ye mother said you were a dreamer. Dear girl. There's not been a dead body found here in Windemere since 1892, when Ralph Fullerton, a sailor, was found washed up in the cove. 'Twas a horrid sight by all accounts. Bloated up like a puffer fish!"

"Ewe, I did *really* see a body today."

"And you know," Ewe went on in her blithe fashion, "he stunk out the church for a whole week 'cause that's where they carted him before burial. There's an account of it in the abbey. You should look it up if you're interested in bodies."

"I daresay I will," I sighed like a heroine in a melodrama before sliding out of my seat and placing my hands firmly on her shoulders. "Ewe, please *listen* to me. This is no fabrication. A young girl and I found a body out there . . . the body of a woman, washed up on the beach." I paused, my face no doubt a visible white.

Comprehension slowly dawned upon Ewe. "A body? Who? What? Where?"

"By the cove." Shuddering, I summarized what had happened and my brief visit to the great house, sinking into the welcome support of the kitchen bench.

"My goodness gracious me."

Slinging a tea towel over her ample neck, Ewe shepherded us both to the parlor. "My, my, this requires more than a *cup of tea,* I reckon. Glass of sherry?"

Without waiting for my answer, she saw that I was settled, reminiscent of a doting grandmother, and raided the tiny glass cabinet on the opposite wall where she displayed her finest few precious pieces of china. Taking out the crystal decanter and two matching, highly polished glasses, she poured the drink and we sipped in silence.

"Victoria Bastion . . ." Ewe murmured, meditative. "Drowned, do you think?"

I tried to recall the details of the body. "She *seemed* intact. . . . She might have fallen from the cliff and broken her neck."

"Were there bruises about her neck?"

"Not that I saw. She just looked beautiful, even in death. And it can't be suicide for why would she give up," I blushed, "a handsome fiancé, a *magnificent* estate soon to be hers, and—"

"And?" prompted Ewe.

"Well, great prospects. Imagine being mistress of such an estate. She had at her fingertips what most girls only dream of; it doesn't make sense."

"How did they react at the house? Glean anything there?"

I shook my head with a faint laugh. "We are not detectives, but shock, I suppose."

"Genuine or nongenuine?"

"Genuine," I surmised, thinking of David's collapse onto the steps and his wretched emotions raw along with his mother and sister.

"Lady Hartley? Don't trust her. *She'd* be happy the gel's dead. She won't have to give up her place now, will she?"

That was true. But it didn't prove her ladyship's guilt.

Somewhere in the house a cuckoo clock chimed. Listening to its chirp in the aftermath of this news felt morbid.

"Well, you're invited back there, aren't you? You're a witness; they'll have to question you. You ought to call there in the morning. Sir Edward, hmmm, yes, he'll be summoned there, he's our inspector, half retired . . . oooh! A *real* murder mystery! Who'd have thought it'd ever happen here in quiet little old Windemere Lane."

CHAPTER THREE

Led to a wrought-iron chaise lounge, propped up with faded green tasseled cushions, a middle-aged woman cloaked in the deepest and severest navy commanded, "Wait here, Miss du Maurier. I will inform her ladyship."

My entry into the great house of Padthaway this time exuded all the polite correctness one associated with the aristocracy. Last time, Lianne and I had stumbled in, our shoes still bearing sand from the beach, our hair unkempt and our mouths unsure of what to speak. The ill news thus having been dispensed and absorbed over the course of a night, I had felt a little more comfortable following the stern, slim figure in navy to the open-aired courtyard down and off to the right of the main hall parlor.

The grim-faced housekeeper left, and I sat back to appreciate the beauty of the courtyard. It was quite a large area, and I rested upon the recliner beneath one of the many arched trellises bursting with jasmine and wisteria. All around, water trickled from a series of white Greek mythological fountains, the dark stone cobbled flooring winding itself through a maze of massive potted plants placed at strategic points for circular harmony. The effect created its own internal garden circuit, charmingly Roman and unlike anything I'd seen before.

The rattle of a tray heralded the return of the housekeeper.

"They will not be long, madam."

Madam! Did I look so old? Helping myself to the tea tray, I had just finished pouring when the rustle of a blue dress appeared from behind an anguished statue of Apollo.

"Sir Edward, Trehearn?" Her ladyship addressed the housekeeper, her quick eye detecting me.

Mrs. Trehearn inclined her head. "He has arrived."

"And my son?"

"Has been called, my lady. Miss Lianne, as well."

"Very well, Trehearn. Thank you. That will be all."

Though I'd witnessed this mistress-housekeeper relationship countless times, here it differed. I couldn't isolate the reason for the impression, but I wondered if Mrs. Trehearn regarded the house as her territory beyond the standard occupation.

"Thank you for calling," her ladyship addressed me, choosing the head armchair facing me. "It must have been quite a shock. My daughter is not coping with the horror of it all. You see, we saw her alive last night and now she is . . ."

"Dead." Making her appearance from behind another statue, Miss Lianne Hartley chose to sit by me, snuggling a little into my shoulder and pleading with her huge eyes. "Oh, Daphne. I couldn't sleep! Did you? How can anyone sleep after seeing something so dreadful."

I held her tighter, wanting to protect her from the memory of our traumatic discovery. "We must do our best. Is Sir Edward . . . ?"

"He's the local magistrate, if you will." Sighing, Lady Hartley waved her hand to my offer to pour tea. "He should have joined us by now. . . ."

Restless, she began pulling at a lone thread on her expertly cut blue silk dress. Upon closer inspection, it seemed more of a peignoir. Fitting, perhaps, considering it was the morning after—how did anyone recover and resume normal events when tragedy struck? I remembered the ones we lost to the war and how we'd moped through the house in mourning clothes. "It's a difficult time; I don't know what to say."

And I didn't. What did one say? *Was it suicide or murder, do you think?*

"Sir Edward will need his questions answered, if you are well enough to oblige him. I did send him a note for Lianne—"

"Oh, I'm fine if Daphne's here."

Drawing her blue eyes up to search mine, I interpreted her silent plea. She'd found the body first but she didn't want to speak, perhaps for fear of being blamed. Talking about it terrified her. Not surprising for a young girl of fifteen.

"I don't think the questions will be extensive today," Lady Hartley served to reassure us both.

Lianne looked at me again and I realized I had a decision to make. For some reason, she didn't want them to know she had found the body first. Should I tell the truth or should I protect Lianne from censure? Sir Edward, a short, rotund man with wiry gray sideburns, arrived and claimed the chair nearest Lady Hartley. I settled on a compromise when he began his questioning, saying I'd met Lianne on my search for the abbey, and we'd discovered the body at the cove. I described the event in detail, and as I rambled on, I sensed another was hearing my story, told under Sir Edward's intense gaze.

I was right. David Hartley loomed in the shadows.

I swallowed my tea, uneasy. There was something hanging in David's demeanor, like an unfinished thought. Did he believe me? Or did a shade of doubt exist behind those cynical gray eyes?

"Du Maurier," Sir Edward mused, flicking out his little notebook and pen. "I've heard of the name. You're not related to Sir Gerald, are you?"

"Yes, Sir Edward."

"And he coproduced *Peter Pan*?"

"Yes."

"How extraordinary." Lady Hartley beamed. "We've a little celebrity in our midst."

"Oh, I wouldn't say that." I colored.

"But you are, my dear. Sir *Gerald* du Maurier of *Peter Pan*! We've all heard of him. Oh, my dear, you simply *must* call me Lady Flo—"

"Mother!" David marched across the courtyard. "It hardly matters. Victoria is dead!"

The lukewarm tea stuck in my throat. He had seemed so cool and composed only a moment ago. We sat stiff in our seats, glancing surreptitiously at one another.

"I'm going down there," David announced, snatching his coat. "Down to where they found her. Miss du Maurier, will you show me where?"

Sir Edward's brows shot up. "We'll all go. I've got my car in the drive."

David's jaw clenched. "No, I'd prefer to walk."

Half-standing to my feet, I glanced at Lady Hartley before hastening toward the front door.

The door stood open and Mrs. Trehearn's hand rested on the latch, as though she'd been listening to the courtyard conversation and had rushed ahead to open the door for Lord David.

"It's absurd." Lady Hartley's cry echoed outside. "The rain's coming . . . and there's nothing left to see."

Lianne joined my stride behind David, her mother's attempts to call her back unheeded.

I thought David might have sent her back but he didn't, striding ahead, the man who suffered the most. He'd just lost his fiancé, the woman he planned to marry, to terrible circumstances. No reasoning or logic worked in such times.

As the rain began to pelt upon my face, I lowered my head, struggling to keep up with his long, determined strides. Fortunately the wind remained at bay as we continued across the headland. Another secret path, I thought. Imagining Victoria standing at the edge of the headland.

Lianne gripped my hand. "Thank you," she whispered.

She reminded me of a frightened kitten. What was she afraid of? Did she know something about Victoria's death? Perhaps she'd witnessed the crime . . . is that why she wished to hide behind my façade?

Wait, I was getting ahead of myself.

It would likely turn out to be an accidental drowning. Such things often occurred in the summertime. The bride may have decided to go for an evening swim or stroll upon the beach.

Yet for some reason I didn't think so.

CHAPTER FOUR

Sea spray foamed at the mouth of the restless sea.

"Where?" David croaked. "Where? Where did you find her?"

Catching my breath, I pointed to the curve beneath the cliffs. The water had covered the area. Seeing the pain reflected in the taut lines of his face, I walked toward the very spot, through the dashing icy waters that saturated my skirt until it clung wet and heavy to my legs.

The rain pelted down and I shivered in the cold.

"Sorry," David mumbled. "But I must see."

I nodded, finding the place where we'd found her, gesturing as to how she had lain and wishing myself far away. I had no business being there, sharing his grief in companionable silence.

He turned and his eyes hardened at the sight of Sir Edward and Lady Florence standing under an umbrella at the cliff top. "Blast! You'd think they'd leave me alone. Can't a man have a moment of peace?"

"Well, they're not likely to come down here," I said, and then, to fill the seemingly interminable silence between us, I asked, "Did she often go swimming?"

"She did not drown."

He had just confirmed what I suspected: that this girl had been strong and healthy, a beauty, and if she'd gone for a foolish late-night swim, she had enough wits to see herself out of danger.

"Then she err . . ."

"She's dead," he croaked again, looking like a lost little boy. "There'll be no wedding . . . no—"

Burying his face in his hands, he sank to his knees and sobbed, the waters rushing around him, carving a tragic picture.

I sank to my knees beside him.

So did Lianne, who'd crept up behind us.

"Oh, Davie," she whispered. "It's so awful. I'm so sorry . . ."

She flung her arms around his neck but he brushed them off.

What comfort dare one attempt to give? There was none. Death was death. One had to live it.

I got up and started back up the path to Sir Edward and Lady Hartley. Lianne followed and we huddled into each other to avoid the lashing rain, a futile endeavor for we'd no umbrella and our drenched clothes provided no protection.

Staggering up the sandy trek, I glanced back to see David still sitting in the tide, hugging his knees. The vision so inspired me, I felt guilty. The urge to write, to capture what I'd seen, was overwhelming.

Sir Edward's conscientious observation barely flickered as we reached the top of the cliff. His stern gaze remained fixed on the beach . . . on the lone figure in the sand.

"Ah, Sir Edward." Lady Hartley shook her head. "I *warned* her not to go swimming down at the cove, but did she listen to me? No. These young ones think they are invincible, but who can tame the tide?"

The tide reveled in its intensity. Forced to move, David roused himself, dragging his limbs mechanically up another route.

"I suppose questions are going to be pointless today?" Sir Edward's murmur hung ominously in the air.

Adjusting her umbrella, Lady Hartley turned on her heel. "Who knows where he'll go now. If he doesn't ride back with us, he may go off to the pub. It's a great shock. A *great* shock to us . . . all."

She headed to the motorcar and Lianne and I, shivering and hovering under Sir Edward's massive black umbrella, joined her. Inside the safety of the spacious car, the rain raked hard welts across the windows.

Sir Edward shook his head. "He'll catch cold. It'll be the death of him. I can barely see the road!"

"We should try to find him." Tapping anxious fingers on the door handle, Lianne peered through the glass. "There he is! Over there!"

"What? Go cross-country? In *this*?"

"I don't think Lord David will appreciate being hunted like an animal," Sir Edward seconded Lady Hartley's protest. "He's a man in mourning. He needs to grieve."

Navigating slowly through the rain, we soon reached the grand house. Helping myself out of the car, I pinched myself. Had I truly stumbled upon this adventure?

"Miss du Maurier," Sir Edward summoned. "I shall drive you home. I have questions to ask."

Lianne pulled me up the stairs to the house.

"Stay with me," she urged.

Having entered the house without a backward glance, Lady Hartley had assumed I'd follow, but Sir Edward had a different plan.

"This is a murder inquiry, Miss du Maurier," Sir Edward pressed. "I'd like to ask you a few questions."

Lianne's mouth opened wide. "A *murder*?"

Sir Edward ignored her.

"But she drowned! She often went swimming at night!"

"Victoria Bastion did not drown, Miss Hartley. Ask your brother if you do not believe me."

"I will."

Lianne thundered into the house and I hurried around to the passenger seat beside Sir Edward. I'd never driven a mile with a policeman before, and the prospect quite excited me. This was not a drama of the stage, but a *real* life drama. What had my father joked? *You never know. Might even find something to use in a play.*

I kept a lookout for David Hartley, not wanting to leave him, or the silent mansion alone in the rain. "Is this the largest house in the area, Sir Edward?"

"Yes. Grand old place, isn't it?"

"It's beautiful. How long have the family lived there?"

My teeth chattered and Sir Edward despaired he did not have a shawl to offer me. "For generations the Hartleys have ruled Padthaway. Hartley's not a Cornish name, note."

Yes, I had noted.

"They inherited the estate in the sixteenth century through their Tremayne cousins, and have lived here ever since." He turned into the village, his windshield wipers slashing through the rain. "I can drive you as far as the end of the lane and then perhaps we can seek shelter in the cottage. I am very keen to ask you questions as you are the one who discovered the body."

A tremulous sensation tickled the back of my neck. "Yes, I understand. If you want to wait while I change, I'd be happy to answer any questions you may have."

My voice sounded so calm, it even fooled me. I did not feel calm. In fact, I felt entirely the opposite. I shouldn't have agreed so hastily to support Lianne Hartley. Why should she fear finding the body first unless she knew something about the murder case?

A murder case.

As Sir Edward and I clambered down the muddy lane, dodging minute rivers and into Ewe Sinclaire's warm and dry cottage, my heart began to palpitate. I hadn't come here to involve myself in a murder. Ewe's inherent sense of duty, despite her love for gossip, would compel her to inform my mother posthaste. What would my parents think? They'd demand I return at once.

Leaving Sir Edward to manage his wet umbrella and coat alone, I presented a dripping image to Ewe. She twirled around in the kitchen, her fry pan flying out of one hand to the other.

"Mercy me! Don't frighten me like that!"

Settling the fry pan to the safety of the stove, her hands hugged her hips. "A drowned cat is what you look like. Didn't they even offer to drive you home? Those snub-nosed no-good Hart—"

"Sir Edward's here," I blurted, quickly summarizing the rest. "I've got to change and I'm sure he'd like a cup of tea."

"Sir Edward! *Here?*"

I thought she'd have a heart attack.

"Yes," I whispered. "And I must beg of you to speak of this case to no one. *Not* even Mother."

I ran off before she had a chance to reply or recover from the shock of having the local magistrate, the grandee, descend upon her humble parlor without due warning.

My years of rapidly changing school costumes into day wear bore fruit. I had on dry, fresh clothes within an instant and returned to the parlor to save Ewe Sinclaire from smothering Sir Edward with vociferous attention.

Thankfully, the kettle called her back to the kitchen as I seated myself across from Sir Edward.

He'd already taken out his notebook in preparation, his sternness apparent while rereading over prerecorded notations. "Miss du Maurier . . . you're in the area to conduct research or on holiday?"

"Both, Sir Edward."

"How long do you intend to stay?"

"That depends on what interests me here."

A grave brow crossed the center of his face. "As witness to this case, I'd ask you not to leave the village without advising me. Will you promise to do so?"

"Yes."

"Good. Now, if you will relay, in your own words again, exactly how you happened upon the body."

Uttering the near-truth under Ewe's watchful and sympathetic gaze combined with Sir Edward's methodical recording proved a challenge of the highest degree. Guilt consumed me. Lianne may have been there a long time before I arrived; she may have even pushed Victoria to her death.

"Did you examine or touch the body, Miss du Maurier?"

I cringed at the reminder of those icy cold veins. "I checked her throat and wrist . . . for a pulse. She was so cold . . . so cold . . ."

"Did you see any bruises on her? Anything unusual or suspicious?"

Ewe's rounded eyes remained intent upon me, encouraging and supportive. "Go on, dearie. You just say all you saw. Don't be afraid, now."

"Afraid," I echoed.

Sir Edward's mouth drooped to show his compassion. "Seeing dead bodies is not an easy thing, whether family or strangers."

"I've seen both during the war," I said, ending the upsetting discussion.

"So you're not afraid of bodies and death, Miss du Maurier?"

Lowering my eyes, I seethed beneath my skin. I didn't like the inference of Sir Edward's tone, and there was something about the man himself I didn't like either. Some unexplained instinct warned me of a coldness in his character, perhaps a natural condition for one in his occupation. "I saw no bruises on her neck . . . she may have had bruises around the back of her neck but I only felt for a pulse. I moved her only to protect her body from the incoming tide. She just looked so peaceful . . . so beautiful. It saddened me. So young, with such promise in life! Why . . . *why?*"

"The why is the answer to any mystery," Sir Edward replied. "I'm treating this as a suspicious death. As you say, the girl had everything to live for. She was about to marry Lord David—the wedding invitations had all gone out and my wife and I were among the guests."

I recalled the ring on her stiff finger—the diamond glistening, sparkling in the daylight.

"Where've you put the poor girl?" Ewe dared to ask. "In the church like Ralph Fullerton?"

Sir Edward flicked his notebook cover down. "There's no mortuary here so the church has to suffice. Vicar Nortby is in charge and I'm keeping the Bastion family away until we've had time to fully examine the body. I'd appreciate, ladies, if you kept what you know private for the moment. It's a small town and there's bound to be talk."

"Oh, ye can't keep this one under your hat, Sir E," Ewe piped. "It's the *Hartleys*. Those papermen will come down from London like hornets."

"Yes, I'm aware of that." Standing, Sir Edward shook out his coat while consulting the time on Ewe's cuckoo clock. "Blast! I should have been at the church an hour ago."

Ewe and I saw him to the door, Ewe unable to resist asking the likely verdict at this stage. "It's murder, do you think? Or suicide? Don't sound like she was strangled if there's no bruises. And a lovely white little neck like hers, the bruises would show up . . . maybe they'll show up in the next few days, mind. You got one of them body experts coming from London, Sir Edward? I don't suppose we've got any here in town, have we?"

"That's whom I am to meet," Sir Edward divulged, opening his umbrella and sauntering off down the path. "Good day, ladies."

"Well." Ewe shut the door behind him. "What a to-do! And you, a *key* witness. Even if I don't tell ye mother, she's bound to find out, y'know."

"I'll write them. *Please,* Ewe."

"Please what?"

"Don't say a word."

She chuckled, her copious chin rumbling a little. "Keeping secrets from parents, eh? I've done that before. Quite skilled at it."

"It'll be *our* secret." I seized her hands. "I'll only say in the letter what terrible event occurred upon my arrival. They never need know I am involved or else they'll whisk me away and I can't bear to leave this place now I'm here. 'Windemere Lane,' " I mused to myself aloud, " 'a beautiful bride washed up at the cove.' Oh, what inspiration!"

"Inspiration, my foot," Ewe mumbled. "Now, why don't you inspire me and cut up some potatoes?"

CHAPTER FIVE

As promised, I'd sat down and composed a letter to my parents. This appeased Ewe and set her mind to rest, though she expressed her disapproval with my wording of the incident.

"They'll see it in the papers," she warned.

The death of a beautiful young bride was bound to cause a sensation anywhere. That the affianced groom should prove to be Lord David Hartley, known throughout town and abroad in his earlier years, quadrupled the sensation.

I loved the sensation. I knew I shouldn't, but a feast for the imagination had greeted me at Windemere Lane.

I soon remembered that I'd stumbled upon Victoria's body during my erstwhile search for the abbey, an abbey I'd since abandoned.

For my second attempt, Ewe gave me the directions. "You'll get lost easily in these parts, winding narrow lanes galore, but if you follow what I've mapped out for you, you'll find the Grand Dame up there nestled in what we kids used to call the Dark Grove."

"The 'dark grove,'" I sighed, chewing on the edge of my pencil.

"Children went missing there years and years ago," Ewe went on. "It's a creepy old place. Too silent for my liking and run by a bunch of nasty nuns."

"Nasty nuns?" I laughed. "How could a nun ever be nasty?"

"Pious old birds. Too pious for my liking. Keep themselves away and think themselves above all of us mortals below. Oh," she wrinkled her nose, "they never set foot in the village. Oh no. They send their lackeys down to get their supplies, just like they used to do in the old days."

Deliberating whether or not to take an umbrella for my excursion, I decided on caution. One could never predict the weather. Thanks to Ewe's hot composts, I had not caught a cold from following David Hartley out into the sea.

"If Victoria didn't drown as Lord David says," I queried Ewe before I left, "then how do you suppose she died?"

"I haven't a clue, but I wouldn't trust one word out of the mouths of them Hartleys. They've got the talent to lie. Born with it, like all the richies. Sir Edward will have his work with them."

"He may be ill equipped to handle the case."

Ewe shrugged. "We'll find out. Well, off to the abbey you go and don't be finding any more bodies on the way. Oh"—she stopped me, placing a few pennies in my hand—"could you go to the drugstore on ye way back and pick up me powders? Mr. Penford knows the one."

I set upon my journey, my thoughts full of David Hartley. His grief seemed too genuine to fault. He'd fallen stunned, sagging to his knees out there in the waters, unable to believe she was really gone.

It was a tragic scene and one I itched to write, somewhere out here in the wilderness, in my own little notebook not unlike the one Sir Edward carried. Dare I make my own notes about the murder?

The mischievous notion appealed to me. Why should I not conduct my own murder investigation? My interest in people, potential characters, and their motivations demanded I at least try; what had I to lose? Nobody need know.

The hour-long walk to the abbey gave me ample time to absorb the innocence of early summer, the still-budding flowers from a late spring, the evergreen growth, the whisper of the morning breeze through the silent trees, their swaying branches drinking in the few glimmers of sunlight. A fine day for a wedding, I thought.

How had she died? I tried to think of her face, the way her body had lain there in the sand. There were no defining marks, no marks of strangulation or even a look of terror to denote murder. On the contrary, her face appeared so peaceful, so . . .

Suddenly, through the trees, the stone abbey arose, piece by piece, a towering monument, gothic, medieval, aloof. Around it, the deeply cut grass shone, as though a satin mat for its masterpiece.

Spying a lone nun powering across the green, I approached. "Hello, there. Is the abbey open today? I've come to look at the records and I have a letter of introduction by Bishop Rogers."

It always helped to have useful family friends and upon hearing of my interest in the abbey, Bishop Rogers had readily written a letter to the abbess.

The nun, a severe-looking woman of some forty years, accepted the letter from my hands and silently guided me inside the abbey.

Whenever I entered such ancient, quiet places, I experienced immediate peace. I understood how the church became a sanctuary for so many through troubled times.

"Wait here," the nun instructed, and I spied a nearby pew, one of twenty or so, and sat down to gaze up on the huge vaulted ceiling and admire the arched curves. Fairly quickly the nun returned.

"Miss du Maurier, the abbess will see you now."

I followed the nun into an inner sanctuary, a room devoid of anything but a desk, two chairs, and some kind of bookcase serving as a filing cabinet piled with handwritten notes groaning out of antiquated folders.

The mysterious nun closed the door and suddenly I imagined a heroine with no name. Could one write a whole book without naming the heroine, I wondered.

"Bishop Rogers is my cousin. I am Dorcas Quinlain. Welcome

to Rothmarten Abbey, Daphne du Maurier," the Abbess murmured from her desk, reading my letter. "We don't often welcome visitors with illustrious connections."

Behind her nun's weeds burned a bright face with very fine eyes, porcelain skin forever youthful, or so was the illusion, and a helpful spirit. "We don't often open all of the abbey's records to one so young, but on such recommendation, I would be pleased to show you what Rothmarten has to offer. However," she said, and paused, examining me closely, "first, I must ask you what your intentions are. We have many sacred documents."

"The Charlemagne scrolls interest me mostly," I replied. "I'd like to study them and perhaps write a thesis on what I find. I intend, if I am successful, to publish them in the *London Journal*. Hopefully, the article will inspire many to pilgrimage to Rothmarten and even donate a modest contribution to the safekeeping of the records entrusted to the abbey."

My answer pleased her.

"We have many interesting records in our library, which you will see, Miss du Maurier. I am impressed one so young is so interested in such things. I do so hope and pray there is no ulterior motive in your coming here?"

"I'm afraid not," I laughed my reassurance. "My family thinks me mad wanting to immerse myself in ancient scrolls instead of enjoying the delights of a London season, and in truth, Abbess, I am also here to escape."

"Escape? Whatever from, child?"

"From marriage and men."

She smiled with me, guiding me to the library where I imagined nuns or monks hard at work on their elaborate manuscripts centuries before.

The library commandeered one entire section of the abbey, closed to the public by a fretwork gate locked by the abbess. Rattling the key, Abbess Quinlain opened the gate for me and invited me to make use of one of the three stool desks like those employed in the dark ages.

"The records are in some disarray," she began by way of apology. "Sister Agatha and Sister Sonya were attempting to catalog them . . . that is when the discovery of the older scrolls were found. You'll find everything in the pigeonholes and there's paper and pencils in the drawer of the desk."

I thanked her, promising to work quietly.

"Take as long as you like," said she. "We have no fixed assembly today, but I should like to be the first to see whatever you discover. We've no Latin scholar here and Victor Martin, the writer of that piece in *The Times,* came by way of recommendation, too."

"Oh." I attempted, and failed to hide my embarrassment. "I'm no Latin scholar, but I do seem to stumble upon things elusive to others." I blushed, not sure whether to mention the body of Victoria Bastion or not, and then decided I may as well be honest and shared my recent discovery.

Abbess Quinlain turned very pale. "Have you seen death before, child?"

"Yes, once or twice. But this is very different . . . a *murder,* Sir Edward thinks."

"Sir Edward," the abbess sniffed.

She said nothing more but I detected a faint hint of disapproval. "What kind of man is Sir Edward, Abbess?" I asked, innocent and childlike. "He . . . er—rather frightened me."

"Sir Edward," she paused, sighed, "is a *bully* and not to be trusted. I know him from school days. Don't be frightened of him, Miss Daphne. He has friends in high places to whom he is indebted, but I've always predicted that one day he'll come down with a crash. *Pride goeth before the fall,* so scripture says."

And with that, she left me to ponder her dire prediction.

Sir Edward? Untrustworthy? I thought of his great sideburns and stern brow. One never knew a person, did they? Even those in authority could not always be trusted. If he had friends in *high places,* there could be none so more than the Hartleys, and if any of the family had killed Victoria, would he choose to conduct the case to their mutual benefit?

I confess the abbess's denunciation of Sir Edward interfered with my first day's investigation of the abbey records. I also confess the murder case would not leave my mind. Who wouldn't be obsessed? It was natural. I'd never been involved in a murder case before and the fact thrilled me.

The silent, stiff, and beautiful face of Victoria haunted me, daring me, taunting me, *hoping* I could find a way to "illuminate" the truth.

"Oh, er, miss, are you finished now with that one?"

I found myself staring into the face of one grumpy nun old enough to be my grandmother. "Oh, yes. And," I stood, taking my paper and pencil, "I must be going. I forgot I have to go to the drug-store to pick up something for my mother's nurse."

"Drugstore," the nun repeated, almost fainting.

I steadied her arm. "It's all right. It's just medicine."

"Medicine," she frowned, watching me flap away.

I breathed a long sigh of relief when I exited the abbey. If ever I'd entered a primeval place that was it. It seemed alien to the world, untouched and horrified by any reminder of reality. The abbey had escaped the Great War, and had remained virginal, something apart and unpolluted.

"Ah, the *sleeping* draught for Miss Sinclaire," Mr. Penford at the drugstore beamed at me, caressing his mustache into a fine, smooth line.

I inwardly shuddered. A desperate male, desperate for a wife. Not me, I vowed. Not me, not ever. "Thank you ever so much, Mr. Penford," I responded, gracious and correct. "I shall be sure to inform my fiancé of how *useful* a person you are should we ever think of moving to the area."

There, I'd said it. A white lie.

My mother would be incensed. A true lady never lied, even out of desperation, but I didn't care.

As I darted out the door of the shop, David Hartley stopped me in my tracks.

"Miss du Maurier," said he, suave, sophisticated, expertly dressed, and genteel to the bone atop his horse.

"My lord," I stammered, "I didn't expect to find you here."

"No?" He smiled. "Dare I ask where you'd expect to find me?"

"Oh, I don't know. On some . . ." I was about to say "stranded beach" and the ridiculous notion was instantly inferred by David Hartley.

"I see," he said coldly, resuming his air of indifference. "I bid you good day, Miss du Maurier."

He tipped his hat and trotted off.

"Did you get my powders?" Ewe pounced upon me as soon as I returned home. "And what d'you make of the abbey? Meet old iron face, Abbess Quinlain herself? What did she say? What happened? Did you find anything?"

I grinned in spite of myself. Ewe Sinclaire was, in one word, *incorrigible.*

And I loved her for it.

"No great revelations. But I did manage to see Lord David on my way out of the drugstore, and he was very out of sorts."

"Out of sorts? What kind of out of sorts?"

"I don't exactly know," I murmured, "but I know this: Abbess Quinlain does not like Sir Edward. According to the abbess, Sir Edward is not to be trusted. The more I think of it, the more I reason that each Hartley had a reason to kill Victoria. Only which one and *why* remains to be seen."

CHAPTER SIX

"Well, you've a chance to start your investigations now."

Ewe smiled, handing me the note.

"My, my," she twittered. "An *official* card invitation."

Swapping the card for the powders, I ran my finger over the printed crest. Not since my grandmother's house had I seen such a rare and wondrous thing, a reminder of yesteryear.

> *Miss Du Maurier,*
> *Please call at the house between nine and noon.*
> *Lady Florence Hartley*

"Must be old house stationery," Ewe remarked. "Aren't *you* lucky!"

Lucky. I didn't think myself lucky to be summoned for interrogation under the guise of a pleasant cup of tea, but I did look forward to returning to Padthaway.

"Will Sir E be there?"

"I don't know. I imagine so."

"Better get dressed then. You can't show up in *that*."

"Oh, Ewe," I teased. "You're such a frightful snob. Whatever is wrong with my gardening frock and boots?"

I enjoyed teasing Ewe, but I exaggerated. I had made a little effort, out of respect for the abbey and its occupants, but a frock and boots were not appropriate for a summons to the Big House.

Thankfully my mother had the foresight to pack extra clothes. I selected a smart black skirt, thin waist belt, and a pale lemon blouse. The lemon blouse sported pink buttons, adding a dash of color to an otherwise plain outfit.

I ran a comb through my hair and pinned up two sides, curling the ends. I wasn't beautiful, but I *was* attractive, though I hated my nose and my thin upper lip. I always wanted to have lips like the movie actresses had . . . full of pout and perfection. *Le Grande Femme Fatale.*

"Lovely," Ewe approved when I exited my room, slipping my arms into the sleeves of my best black coat.

"Pity you have to hide under your coat. What if they try and take it at the door?"

"Since I am a stranger," I pondered aloud, "it could be construed as presumptuous if I wore all black."

"You're not intending to *walk* there, are you?" Ewe's face exploding into a fierce scowl.

"I'll be fine." I waved cheerily, tapping the umbrella under my arm.

I weaved my way through the village and down the lane, admiring the quaint and slow village life. Simplicity. That's what appealed to me, myriads of minute lanes, stacks of cottage houses tumbling one upon the other, everywhere greenery and flowers, the old man walking the dog, the grocer stacking his vegetables outside his shop, the schoolmistress marching down the street to the post office. Up ahead, sunshine bathed the glorious contours and skyward steeple of the old church. Gothic structures like these dotted every nook and cranny in England and I rejoiced, for here in Windemere, I had three buildings to explore: the abbey, Padthaway, and the church.

Upon passing the church, I thought of the cold body lying inside awaiting her funeral. Having been examined by a "body expert" (I had to smile at Ewe's term), I wondered if Sir Edward intended to deliver the verdict as to the cause of death at Padthaway today.

Locating the long winding drive leading to the Big House, David Hartley's face, full of anguish, rose to mind. So many had lost fiancés, husbands, wives, fathers, and mothers during the war. One expected death from war, but not death by murder.

As I mounted the front steps of the house, I noted the fair weather, and wished I'd come to tour the house instead of as a witness in a suspicious death. I loved nothing more than exploring such treasures, and this one exuded its own unique personality. Half mansion, half restored castle, it dominated the flat cliff-head where it rested, a huge structure, old stone melded with new, shining glazed windows, arches and turrets, west wings and east wings built around a central tower dripping with ivy.

A young maid opened the door. Bobbing, she took my umbrella, and as I shook my head to the removal of my black coat, Mrs. Trehearn exited from a western corridor.

"Please come to the Drawing Room, Miss du Maurier. They are awaiting you there."

Following her through the expansive house, I yearned to count the corridors. The house looked like a museum. It'd take many days to become familiar with all of its inward pathways and rooms.

A beautiful set of Florentine doors guarded the most revered room in grand houses: the Drawing Room. This one was opulent, possessing quality furnishings, from Rembrandt oil paintings mounted on rose gilded wallpaper to cabinets filled with endless objets d'art that were undoubtedly priceless; the sweeping burgundy and gold drapes framed the windows and the marble fireplace bore its own selection of jade ornaments in the French salon suite setting. Amongst the pomp, Lady Hartley stood proud by the window in a black silken gown, her bejeweled hand fixed to her hip.

"Ah, Daphne," she acknowledged. "Do sit down and make yourself comfortable. Sir Edward is here, as you can see."

"Er, yes," Sir Edward coughed from a far corner of the lounge, decidedly uncomfortable.

Whilst taking a seat nearest Lianne on the upright tapestry-covered salon suite, I spied David hovering in a far corner of the room, slipping his hands in and out of his pockets. His entire demeanor screamed his annoyance.

"Miss Daphne." Sir Edward's bland smile failed to strike a harmonious chord. "I am quite certain *Miss Lianne* discovered the body before you did. Is this true?"

Lianne turned motionless beside me. She clenched the side of my leg. The action, however, only served to discredit her in my opinion. Why should she be so keen that I should find the body at the same time as she? Had she murdered Victoria?

"That is true," I said quietly, under my breath, wondering how Sir Edward reached the conclusion. "I am sure it was only *minutes* between . . ." I broke off.

"Then why did you lie and say you found the body at exactly the same time as Miss Hartley?"

"Because . . . because . . ." I glanced at Lianne's fearful face. "Because . . . I must have stumbled upon the body shortly after, and the *horror* of seeing a dead body and all . . ."

I left the remainder to interpretation.

And Sir Edward interpreted.

"It's understandable. A shock like that can obscure the facts. Thank you for your honesty."

I felt feverish, clad in my black coat in the French salon suite. I hoped Lianne did not hate me for telling the truth. It was important to tell the truth, even if we didn't want to, and I prayed she understood.

I dared not face her. I felt she was innocent but I also felt she knew something about Victoria's death.

A belief I intended to explore somehow.

"Thank you, Miss du Maurier. If you and Miss Hartley would excuse us, I have further questions for Lady Florence and Lord David."

CHAPTER SEVEN

"Quick, come with me!"

Evading the all-seeing eyes of Mrs. Trehearn, Lianne swept me into the next room. "From here," she whispered, "we can hear."

"What, eavesdrop?"

"Shhh!"

The room she'd ushered me into appeared abandoned, for white sheets covered the furniture. It may have been a small ante-chamber at one point, used to screen visitors prior to entering the Drawing Room. It was a system that belonged to those pretentious enough to heed protocol. "Do you often do this?"

"Always." Grinning, Lianne pressed her ear to the thin papery side of the wood paneling, inviting me to do the same.

I was not one to dispute when given such a rare opportunity . . . an opportunity to hear the whereabouts of Lady Florence and Lord David on the eve of Victoria's disappearance.

"When did you last see Miss Bastion?"

"At dinner," Lady Hartley answered, cautious, direct. "I've told you this before."

"It's important to get the facts correct," a dismissive Sir Edward chided. "Why do you believe your daughter lied about finding the body?"

"She was terrified. And she's really just a child, Sir Edward. She made no sense when she ran back to tell us. If it weren't for Miss du Maurier . . ."

A notable silence ensued and I imagined Sir Edward jotting down his notations.

"Lord David. When did you last see Miss Bastion, your fiancée?"

"At dinner" came the same reply.

"You, er, didn't go up to her room or wish her a good night? You said she left the table early."

"Yes . . . and, no, to your question."

"So you remained here the whole evening at Padthaway?"

"Yes. In my room."

"Asleep?"

"Oh, what is the point of your questions, man! If you have something to accuse me of, then accuse me!"

"David, darling," Lady Hartley tried to soothe. "Sir Edward is only doing his job."

This wise counsel had its proper effect. After a minute or so, Lord David asked if Sir Edward had any more questions.

"I know this is hard for you, my lord, but the young lady's death has baffled even our expert from London. We are as yet unsure as to the cause of death—"

"When *will* you be sure?" Lady Hartley interrupted without a qualm. "For there can be no other verdict than death by her own hand."

"Suicide, my lady?"

"Yes, *suicide*. Or perhaps a silly fall off the cliffs? Or perhaps she *drowned*. How will we ever know what truly happened? Can this expert of yours tell or not tell?"

"He is studying the nature and pattern of the bruises. Some only become apparent after a time."

"Oh, how interesting," Lady Hartley remarked.

"This is *preposterous*," Lord David cursed. "Bruises! I saw her. There were no bruises. She died painlessly. I have to think she died painlessly."

The abject emotion muffling his breaking voice sent a shiver down my spine. He loved her, so passionately, so dearly. He couldn't bear to think of her as dead or suffering in any way.

"My lord," Sir Edward said after a long pause, "you have to consider the possibility your fiancé was murdered."

Exchanging a wide-eyed glance with me, Lianne pressed her ear harder against the wall.

"Murdered!" Lady Hartley laughed. "Oh, please, it must be her family saying so. The girl had no enemies; who'd want her dead?"

I envisioned Sir Edward's great eyebrows rising and him thinking, *What of you, my lady, and your loss of position?*

"Miss Bastion began as a housemaid here, did she not? In the winter of last year?"

"You'll have to confirm the date she started with Trehearn," Lady Hartley replied, matter-of-factly. "She engages all the staff here. I have nothing to do with it."

"How many do you employ here, my lord?"

Through the paneling, I pictured David's frustration. "I have no idea. Twenty or so? Mrs. Trehearn keeps it all in her books. Staff doings, I mean."

He answered the question but it did not seem that his heart was in the room, in the conversation, or even, I hastened to conclude, in his present life. His heart remained cloaked in mourning, black and dismal and beyond consolation. To mourn one so dear . . . and to be accused—

"You were due to be married, was it, Saturday next? How do you feel, my lord?"

"How do I feel?" he echoed bitterly. "How do I feel? Shall I tell you how I feel?"

I closed my eyes. I imagined him chest to chest with Sir Edward, fierce, yet each retaining a dignified distance.

"I . . ." He suddenly broke down in gutted desolation. A man who cried, unafraid to show his emotions, ranked high among the elite, in my opinion.

"It's all right, darling." Lady Hartley's consoling motherly affections washed over the noise. "You don't have to do this today."

"Today? Tomorrow? Next week, next month? Does it make any difference to me? Victoria is *dead.* Dead!"

"Yes, well, we needn't exhaust the facts. Let us put them to good use."

"What do you mean?"

"Let us find her killer . . ." Sir Edward continued, "if she was indeed *killed* by nefarious means, we should do our utmost to finish the business."

"Yes, yes," he said upon reflection. "You are right. A *full* investigation. Yes! Nothing less than she deserves. Delve, Sir Edward, *delve,* into the inner recesses of this mystery. Solve the murder. The crime. Give me peace for my soul for it can never rest until I know the truth."

"Oh," I sighed, unknowingly aloud, as Lianne stared at me.

"Forgive me," I said. "It's just so *tragic.* I feel your brother's pain and his despair. Do you think there is something we can do to help?"

Lianne considered and I registered all the troubling emotions flooding her young face, which seemed so innocent and naïve.

She outstretched her hand and gave it to me in silent accord.

A solemn handshake.

An agreement to find the killer.

I needn't have worried for an opportunity to begin my investigations, as it seemed Lady Hartley had taken a singular interest in me.

I knew it was solely due to my status as Sir Gerald du Maurier's daughter, and because of my family's illustrious connections. Sometimes it went that way, and who was I to discount it?

As I took my leave, she invited me to dine at Padthaway, and I graciously accepted.

"An invitation to dine at Padthaway," Ewe cooed, "how . . . *divine.*"

I replied that I didn't think divinity factored into the equation.

"You're a key witness. *You* discovered the body. And that sets you right in the middle of this whole drama. Are you ready for it? It's going to be *big*," she emphasized with those shrewd eyes of hers. "Miss Daphne du Maurier found herself in the midst of a *murder* scandal in Windemere Lane. Oblige me, would you?" She chuckled, continuing on, "And oh, what a scandal! A young bride . . . found dead on a beach. Her handsome fiancé unable to accept the fact. He mourns her but is he truly innocent? And then there's the sister, who is said to be unstable. Not to mention the *mother.* Oh yes, *she's* the *prime suspect.* Lady Florence Hartley . . ."

"What's her history?" I asked Ewe. I couldn't imagine Lady Hartley anything *but* aristocratic.

Ewe grunted. "Lady Florence Stanton, she were, and come no prouder. An earl's daughter; brought money and her own title with her. Little good it did them with ol' Lord Hartley gambling it away. Oh dearie, I wonder how they'll handle this one? Can't closet up the body of Victoria Bastion! Mrs. Bastion, Victoria's mother, will be in a fine rage, mark my words. She had her heart set on her girl bein' the next lady of the manor."

"Victoria's mother," I echoed almost silently to myself. "How she must be suffering . . ."

"Oh, sufferin' a great deal, losin' out on all that money! She were set for life, were Mrs. Bastion, and lordin' it over all and sundry in the village."

"Victoria was a housemaid, wasn't she?"

"Not for long," Ewe quipped. "A too pretty housemaid in a grand place like Padthaway with Lord David roving about, fresh from his 'abroad' adventures and keen to try new discoveries—if ye get my meaning, and it ain't scandalous to your young, innocent ears."

"My ears may be young," I replied, "but they are not unhinged by scandalous doings. In fact, it's quite inspirational for me and my writing. Oh yes," I sighed, deciding to include Ewe in on the secret, "I've come to Windemere Lane at the right time. For a reason."

"A reason?" Ewe barked. "Well, I'd put my two bob on you more than Sir E in solving this case. I reckon one of those Hartleys did it—her *ladyship* more than likely. But Sir E, he's a stickler for the old and rich. He may seem to be investigating, but he'll never betray them, not ever."

"Even when . . ."

Words failed me, but Ewe made up for it. "Even when he ought to be doing his *duty* and not being bothered about *pleasin'* or makin' considerations for the Hartleys? Hmmm, a tough one."

"Then he shouldn't be conducting the legal case," I said.

"Oh, my," Ewe laughed. "If I were Sir E, I'd be worried about you."

"Me?"

"Yes, you, Miss prim and proper Miss Daphne du Maurier wanting to be a writer of great novels." She paused. "You've come to Windemere because you wanted adventure, and adventure met you halfway. You wanted inspiration, well, a real live murder case could be no more inspiration needed. I say so, even tho' I've never attempted to write anything in my life apart from a shoppin' list. Too wordy and too much effort, them novels, for my likin'."

She was right. I'd stumbled right in the midst of murder and mayhem.

In Windemere Lane, of all places. I intended to shake things up and solve the mystery of Victoria Bastion's death.

It had become my mission.

And nobody could stop me.

CHAPTER EIGHT

Exhausted by the morning's events, I retired to my room.

During my first few days, I had seen a dead body, visited a house that lingered like an elusive lover in my soul, and made a rather bizarre acquaintance or two.

Inspired, I lay on my bed to daydream and record whatever reflections came to mind.

I conjured up a grand production just as I'd seen countless times at the theater—a dramatic death, a murder, a house—a man, a woman, a mystery.

"Come on, sleepy head!"

Ewe poked her ample face right in the middle of my daydream.

"We're goin' to call upon Perony Osborn, the schoolteacher."

"What?" I blinked. "Schoolteacher?" I vaguely recalled seeing a school madam march down the lane. "Why do I have to go? Is she a friend of yours?"

"No," Ewe smarted. "But she's been here for nigh on twenty years and she's *full* of information. Might be worth it."

I couldn't deny it, or Ewe's conspiratorial winking eye. Rousing myself, I washed and tidied my hair and in little less than half an hour, Ewe and I crossed the green. I had intended to rest the entire afternoon before I was due to dress for the evening at Padthaway but Ewe's enthusiasm prevailed. She was as interested as I in this murder case, and was adamant that we explore every avenue available to us.

"How do you know Miss Osborn?" I asked, a hair's breath before we reached the unobtrusive tiny little town house cottage.

"We went to school together. Mind your *p*'s and *q*'s. She's a terrible snob with the English language. She attended a *grand finishing school in Switzerland*. Not like me. I finished me schoolin' and straight into the nanny business. Perony, after serving a family or two abroad, came back here to take up the post as local schoolteacher. She's always been a *local* girl so the role suits her. She's been here so long nobody can budge her. *And,*" Ewe grimaced before we knocked on the door, "she *taught* Victoria Bastion. I hear she even tutored the girl after hours with her English and the like."

The knock resounded.

A razor-sharp face belonging to one Miss Perony Osborn came to the door. She seemed annoyed to have been interrupted, from what, I could only wonder.

"Oh, Ewe, I wasn't expecting anybody."

"Well," Ewe said as she bustled her way inside, "I brought freshly baked muffins, so put on the tea, there's a good girl."

Poor Miss Perony Osborn had no choice. I watched her rushing about her tiny little house, setting everything to right, chairs, cushions, kettle . . .

"And this is Miss Daphne du Maurier," Ewe announced in grandiose manner. "She's the daughter of *Sir* Gerald du Maurier, yes, *Sir Gerald du Maurier,* who has a theater business in London. Perhaps you've heard of *Peter Pan* and such?"

Now Perony Osborn began to take an interest in me. Her absurdly thin eyebrows raised a fraction and her thin lips pulsed.

"Miss du Maurier, please do take a seat. I shall bring round the tea."

She appeared unused to visitors and I raised my eyebrows to Ewe, and Ewe winked in return. I trusted her superior wisdom.

Unexpected guests, we waited and I examined the small living parlor of Miss Perony Osborn. Devoid of family photographs, nothing betrayed the personality but for a selection of books set on high reverence within the china cabinet.

"Oh, Alexandre Dumas," I cried in delight when she came forth, bearing the tea tray. "I do so love *The Count of Monte Cristo*. Is that one of your favorites?"

"*The Rise and Fall of the Roman Empire* is my favorite," Miss Osborn replied, dour, while correctly transporting the tea tray to its "correct" position.

There were too many things "correct" about Miss Perony Osborn, I decided. "But surely," I enthused, "*The Count of Monte Cristo* far surpasses any depressing thesis on the Roman Empire. The Roman Empire, while intensely fascinating, is *dead*. Whereas, Dumas lives in all of us. *The Count of Monte Cristo* is an epic saga and a love story. And such stories abound to eternity."

"There you have the soul and heart of a romantic storyteller," Ewe declared. "Miss Daphne likes to write, you know, Perony, tales of love and woe. She came here to Windemere to research the abbey records. Why ever such a young pretty girl should *bother* is beyond me! *Charlemagne* . . . I mean, he's been dead for centuries!"

"Perhaps, Miss Sinclaire," Miss Osborn replied "correctly," "you underestimate the power of Charlemagne and his legacy."

"Miss Perony," I piped in, "have you yourself explored the abbey records? That's really why I've come to Windemere. I read the article in *The Times* and I've been interested ever since. My mother's nurse lived here," I smiled fondly at Ewe, "so here I am, and unfortunately, I've found myself in the midst of another great travesty."

"Oh?" said Miss Perony. "You mean the murder?"

So, she'd heard, as I expected she might. News traveled fast in a small town. Especially news of this nature. "So, do you really think it's a murder?" I asked, wide-eyed and all innocent.

"You had her at the school, didn't ye?" Ewe launched ahead. "Oh, Vicky Bastion," she crooned, "never a prettier girl were seen."

"Was she pretty, Miss Osborn?" I blushed. "Forgive me for being candid. I only saw her out there . . . on the beach. It was awful.

I cannot describe it, and I cannot help feeling sad for the girl and her family. Do you know her family well?"

"Very well."

Having effectively drawn out Miss Osborn by my admission, she began a confidence. Not a woman, I suspected, who easily gave out information to those of unfamiliar acquaintance. Even her good friends, I imagined, benefited little from her fierce privacy. A guarded creature, our Miss Perony Osborn, and one requiring time to thaw out to complete fruition.

"Mrs. B suffers cruelly. I saw her on the street after she had to identify Victoria. Connan went with her. Connan is Victoria's brother, Miss du Maurier."

"Oh please, call me Daphne," I insisted.

She smiled in turn. "It's a good thing Mrs. Bastion has Connan, Daphne."

"I'll say," Ewe supported. "Such a *good-looking* lad . . . and resourceful. He keeps the family goin' since their pa died."

"Mr. Bastion died several years ago," Miss Osborn relayed. "In the shipping trade, as many of us are. You'd understand that, coming from Fowey?"

I see Ewe Sinclaire had divulged my circumstances to the entire village community.

"My family have a house in Fowey and in London."

"They're gypsies!" Ewe nudged me, helping herself to another piece of lime cake. "Gad about from here to there. And now she don't want her family knowin' she's got herself into this mess."

"No," I pleaded to Miss Osborn. "I intend to remain here and complete what I started. I only managed to see a *glimpse* of the abbey records. It'll take *months* to get through them all."

"You should offer to help catalog them," Miss Perony suggested. "I know Sister Agatha. She's a cousin of mine. I could ask her . . . ?"

"That is *so* kind of you, Miss Perony! I confess I felt awkward poking into those pigeonholes with the dagger eyes of . . . is it Sister Theodora? . . . watching my every move. Sister Sonya is lovely . . . very learned."

"Oh, dear," Ewe chimed, "is that the time? We'll have to leave shortly, for she's to dine at Padthaway this night."

The news unsettled Miss Perony Osborn.

A crisp pallor crept into her cheeks. Was it concern?

"The Bastions are convinced Victoria was murdered, aren't they?" I whispered. "I want to ask you, Miss Perony, for I found the body with Lianne Hartley and the girl has taken a liking to me. Since I'll be in the area, I think I may become a regular visitor to Padthaway and as the saying goes 'forewarned is forearmed.' "

My openness and asking her particular opinion worked wonders on Miss Perony.

"I am not sure if I should say this, but as you are new to the area and are unaware of its history, I would be very careful." She stood up to arch her back, her small hand resting on its middle, denoting she endured some sort of pain there.

"I can only advise . . ."

"Advise what?" I prompted.

"The Hartleys reign supreme here. Their influence controls the village, the lives of the townsfolk, the livestock, and almost everything as it did hundreds of years ago. Little has changed since then."

"Do you mean," I hastened to assume, "their wealth and prominence precludes them from murder?"

"We are not that prehistoric," Ewe defended. "There is the *law*, mind. Nobody can escape the law."

"But they do," I breathed, and related a case I'd read in a newspaper in London. Exactly the kind to which Miss Perony Osborn referred: a rich aristocratic family, a murder, and the suspected murderer getting away with the crime due to "lack of sufficient evidence" despite the jury believing otherwise.

"Daphne is right," Miss Perony confirmed. "And such families have friends in high places."

She meant Sir Edward.

I didn't bring the name to attention.

But Ewe did.

"I hope Sir E will hold true! He must . . . for Mrs. B won't rest. She'll call the papers. Sir E has to do his job."

"Even if it means losing his tenancy on Castle Mor?" Miss Perony asked.

My eyes rounded and Miss Perony smiled her wan smile. "Yes, I can see castles and history do interest you, Daphne."

"Not only interest me," I cried. "They are my *love,* my passion!"

"Her inspiration for writing," Ewe translated.

"As are murder cases?" Miss Perony inquired.

I heard the undertone of her inquiry. She could see me walking straight into trouble, danger even.

I embraced it.

"I think," Ewe said, "and I do *think* a lot and I never keep my thinking to myself, as you know, so here's what I think now: Miss D will keep Sir E on his toes and Mrs. B will call the cavalry."

Miss Perony and I shared a grin.

You couldn't help but love Ewe Sinclaire.

"What happens next?" I inquired.

We listened to her humming deliberations.

"I think . . . we can rely upon you, Miss D, to work *that* out."

CHAPTER NINE

Ewe and I returned to the cottage to find a note slipped under the door.

"Tch tch tch." Bending her copious backside to sweep up the note, Ewe bustled through her house reading aloud the note.

"It's from Sir Edward," she announced in passing. "And it's for *you*."

I hurried after her.

"If it's for *me*, then may I have it?"

I held out my hand.

She reluctantly conceded it, peering over my shoulder. "He's got neat handwritin', I'll give him that, even if ye can't see it for the length of a whistle!"

"It says . . .

> *Miss Daphne,*
> *I shall have the motorcar waiting at the end of the*
> *lane to take you to Padthaway this evening.*
>
> > *Yours etc.,*
> > *Sir Edward*

"Sir Edward," I mused aloud, "does this Sir Edward have a last name?"

Ewe was about to tell me when I stopped her. "No, don't. I think I shall prefer to think of him just as Sir Edward. Do they call me Miss D now?"

My teasing came to an end when Ewe forced me to consider the time and I raced off in a frantic flurry.

What to wear! I pondered the eternal question as I rummaged through my assortment, stumbling across a dress my mother must have snuck in before closure. A shell-colored pink evening gown with a few rows of fringed tassels. "Perfect!"

Whilst rolling the sides of my hair in a fashionable upward style, popping one pin in my mouth and sticking the other in the hairstyle, I felt a sense of excitement. To dine at the Big House! To dine amongst a den of murder suspects, in the perfect position to monitor events as they unfolded. My mind was full of racing thoughts.

I should really not involve myself in the affair.

I should really just concentrate on the abbey records, write my findings, and return home.

I should really not wonder if Lord David liked my dress or the way I'd pinned up my hair.

And I should really *hurry,* for was that Sir Edward knocking at the door?

It sounded like a thump more than a knock, and I grabbed my handbag, coat, and slipped on a pair of modest heels. I had no time for jewelry and makeup; perhaps a wise dilemma, for the dress needed no jewelry and if I made the error of wearing too much makeup, people might arrive at the wrong conclusions. *Lord David had just lost his bride.*

I was a single woman of notable family in Lady Hartley's eyes, and if she disapproved of her son's last choice of wife, it was not out of the question that if I was not careful, she might see me as a possible new candidate for the vacant position.

The thought made me uneasy, especially when Sir Edward began the conversation by asking, "You are a young lady of Victoria's age, Miss du Maurier, would you be terrified of such a prospective mother-in-law?"

I blinked my astonishment. I had not anticipated such a direct question after a perfunctory remark on the weather. "It's hard to answer. Miss Bastion and I are very different people. We come from different backgrounds with our own principles."

"Morals?"

I lowered my gaze. True, I'd been raised in a fairly liberal household, but a strict moral code still prevailed. Victoria, young and impressionable, may not have lived by the same code.

"Do you think Victoria Bastion would have been a girl of relaxed morals?" Sir Edward pushed further.

I dreaded the deliberation. My immediate instinct said "yes," but what did I know of the dead girl on the beach? What did I know of her private live? Her aspirations? Her loves and passions?

"You think my question out of turn?" Sir Edward drove into the darkened drive leading to Padthaway. "But let me remind you, Miss Daphne. This is a murder inquiry and no stone can be left unturned."

"How did she die?" I asked in the smallest voice I could muster, gazing up at the lights of the great mansion ahead.

Sir Edward frowned as we arrived. "There is evidence to support she did not die of natural causes, but as yet such evidence is inconclusive."

Attending to an open button on my coat, I accepted Sir Edward's arm to escort me into the house. He'd not betrayed a single shred of information and I suppose I had to respect him for it. If I were a detective, I'd keep all my cards close to my chest, too.

I tried not to show my annoyance. I tried to smile at the maid opening the door, at the figure of Mrs. Trehearn clad all in black. I tried to behave as a dinner guest should behave.

The house at night breathed of wonder. Though kept moderately lit, I pictured how magnificent it would look with every light ablaze. As a young girl, I once attended a dinner party at a country mansion in Devonshire, and the spectacular sight of the house awash in light had arrested my sisters and me to the point at which my father had to snap his fingers twice to regain our attention. These empty corridors of Padthaway begged to be filled with gaiety and laughter and light, not the dour repercussions of death.

"Here we are." Mrs. Trehearn's skeletal-looking hand gestured to the right. "You will find the family down the hall."

"This is not the usual room," Sir Edward said, waiting for me to go first. "The family usually dines in the Queen Anne room. It's never changed."

"Why do you think that is, Sir Edward?"

"I honestly don't know. There have been deaths and bad times here before—"

"Perhaps something occurred inside the Queen Anne room?"

The notion dawned on him as we located the family seated at a circular walnut table with places set for five.

"Pity Lady Beatrice is so ill she can't join us, Sir Edward," Lady Hartley exclaimed, modish in her deep blue evening gown, her hair dressed high and sapphires sparkling from ears to neck, as she twisted the huge ring on her finger.

A chill swept over me as I thought of the ring on Victoria's dead hand.

"What a lovely dress, Daphne!"

Lady Hartley's eyes appraised me. "I do so approve of the new pink. I trust your replacement is adequate, Sir Edward?"

"I need a pink dress like Daphne's," Lianne sighed, placing her elbows on the table. Her mother gave her a deadly frown and she immediately placed her hands in her lap.

Dinner commenced, hot and cold dishes carried to the table by two maids. Sir Edward lured the silent and grave Lord David out in conversation about local land matters, with Lady Hartley occasionally venturing into the fray.

"Vicar Nortby should be replaced. He is far too old. *Deaf*, even. I can barely hear his sermons on Sunday."

"Not that you regularly go to church on Sundays, Mother," Lord David snapped.

"I do . . . attend regularly enough," she replied. "What of your family, Daphne? Do you plan to go to church whilst you are here? You're staying with Ewe Sinclaire, are you not? For how long?"

"My plans," I said, glancing down at my plate to avoid the intense scrutiny, "are unfixed. I can remain for as short or as long as I wish." I then mentioned my interest in Rothmarten Abbey.

Lord David's jaw twitched. "You are not a fool for scything through the relics of Rothmarten, Miss du Maurier. There's not many women I know who appreciate what we have here in sleepy old Windemere."

"It's not going to be sleepy for much longer," Lady Hartley put in gravely. "Will it, Sir Edward?"

"I'm afraid not, my lady. As I said to you and Lord David earlier, there are . . ." His gaze flickered over Lianne Hartley.

"Don't worry if Daphne and I hear it." Lianne picked up her fork to tap her forehead. "I mean, we're going to hear all of the *terrible* news anyway. Isn't it better we hear it now rather than later?"

Lord David sprang from the table. The action was so unexpected, we all jumped.

"Surely this can wait till *after* dinner," he exclaimed before stamping out of the room, leaving the rest of us to ogle one another.

"He detests the suspicion and the scrutiny the most." Lady Hartley eventually broke the silence. "And I daresay you heard he ran into Connan Bastion yesterday afternoon?"

"No." Sir Edward wiped his perspiring forehead with his napkin. "And I worked very hard to prevent that catastrophe."

"Well, it didn't work. Connan can't stay away . . . nor can David. They both gave Vicar Nortby a heart attack, from what I hear. He and your London person had to restrain the two from killing each other."

"Oh dear." Sir Edward wiped his forehead again, this time using the hanky inside his coat.

"More than 'oh dear,'" her ladyship warned. "They're bound to kill each other. Nortby came running here to tell me. 'I'll not have another body at the church,' he vows. 'Somehow, they *must* be kept apart.' The answer is clear. Connan Bastion shall have to leave the village and seek work elsewhere."

"But his family are *dependent* upon him," Sir Edward emphasized.

Lady Hartley shrugged. "My concern is chiefly for my son, of course. Need I remind you, Sir Edward, that my son rules the county. Connan Bastion and his ilk are merely subordinates. Therefore, it is Connan Bastion who must go."

"His mother . . ."

"Shall never agree, I know." Lady Hartley poured herself another glass of wine. "But I am in the position to see that she does."

A gloating smile tinkered across her lips.

"Bribery, my lady?" Sir Edward flushed. "I cannot approve . . ."

"Oh save your conscience for confessional. It has no business here . . . nor in my son's case."

CHAPTER TEN

Sir Edward and I drove back to the village.

"You are wise, Miss Daphne," he advised, "to speak of all of this to no one. Not even Ewe Sinclaire and *especially* not to any newspapermen who may knock at your door."

I knew he was right, but I wanted something from him before I agreed to his plan.

"I can be trustworthy," I began, knotting my fingers together in my lap. "My big ambition is to write stories, you see . . . and to write stories, one must *live* in the present, one must *absorb* the surroundings, study the people and their motivations, so, Sir Edward, I beg of you, if I am to remain silent, could you not share just a little information with me? I promise it shall go nowhere. My mother once called me the 'brick wall.' And a brick wall I am, silent and trustworthy."

If I'd startled Sir Edward, he didn't show it. He whistled under his breath.

"You're an unusual girl, Miss Daphne, if I may say so. Lord David was right to praise your curious spirit, but whether he is right on the whole is yet to be seen."

Hearing David's name mentioned sent a tingling excitement through me. "His mother is convinced of his innocence, Sir Edward. Do you doubt it?"

"His mother," Sir Edward coughed, "is the only true ruler of this village and its county. She rules in her son's name 'tis true, but everybody knows 'tis she, Lady Florence, who is to be obeyed."

"Perhaps she did it then?"

Sir Edward stopped the motorcar near Ewe Sinclaire's cottage. Turning off the motorcar's lights, Sir Edward turned to me, the downward turn of his mouth somewhat timorous.

Her ladyship had spoken of Vicar Nortby and Connan Bastion, but she also held precedence over Sir Edward, and I dared not think who else. "You lease Castle Mor from them, don't you? Was the castle in the Hartley or Lady Florence's family, Sir Edward?"

His silence answered me. It seemed he leased Castle Mor directly from Lady Hartley. "Is everybody scared of her?" I whispered whilst organizing my coat and handbag for departure.

"Yes," Sir Edward admitted. "She's a force to be reckoned with."

"Even in a murder inquiry?"

"Even in a murder inquiry."

I slipped out of the motorcar. "It is sad, don't you think, that this girl lies dead while her killer is very much alive? I do so hope you find her killer!"

"I am not so sure murder can be proven," he admitted. "Lord David is our prime suspect, but I fear, oh, Miss du Maurier, I fear his mother is *largely* involved. She may have even done it, but I may never be able to prove it. *Proof* is all that matters. We can know the identity of a culprit but to *prove* it is entirely another thing."

I murmured a good night and shut the door to the motorcar.

I wandered up the lane to Ewe's tiny dull-lit cottage. She was awake, as I expected. "Hm," she yawned, opening the door, "how goes it? Was the food good? What news? What news of the murder?"

I had to chuckle that she asked about the food before the murder case. "It's very odd . . ." I began, and went inside to start our usual deliberations.

I heeded *some* of Sir Edward's advice.

I didn't tell Ewe Sinclaire everything—just *almost* everything.

"*How* interesting," she crowed, seeing to the poached eggs for our breakfast.

"The eggs are done . . . and so is her ladyship. I foresee the 'end' of her domination here—oh, how delightful!"

"Delightful?"

"You shouldn't defend her, Miss D. She don't care for any of us. She only cares for herself, always has done. It's her way."

"And her children blindly tramp down this path?"

Crinkling her nose in thought, Ewe reassessed. "Lord David, I'll vouch, has shown himself apart from her in the last while."

"The last while?"

"In land matters and such."

"So he's exerted his independence and she—"

"Disapproves."

"Disapproves?" I croaked. "I'm sure she *loathes* it!"

"There's the writer speakin'," Ewe raised her eyes to heaven. "And I am not sure I approve of you wrappin' yourself up in this no-good affair. What good shall it lead you to?"

"It fascinates me," I said, to which Ewe sighed long and hard.

I couldn't wait to escape the house.

Her words accompanied me out the door, through the cottage gate, and down the lane. I hastened toward the beach. I'd go to the abbey afterward, I decided, but first, a morbid curiosity compelled me to revisit the murder scene.

As I walked, I imagined myself the beauteous Victoria, about to marry the handsome Lord David. She must have been ecstatic with her good fortune. Why had she slipped out for a midnight walk? Couldn't she sleep? Did she often stroll along the beach in the moonlight? Had she been alone?

Or maybe there was a simpler explanation. Suicide. I had difficulty believing it. Why would a young woman who had everything: beauty, a handsome fiancé, and a full life ahead of her kill herself? It didn't make sense.

As I pictured her wandering the shores bathed in the moonlight, I remembered doing something similar once on a Greek island. Granted, I had worn a shawl over my nightgown and took shoes, for the rocks were sharp. *The rocks were sharp.* Victoria had not been wearing shoes when we found her body!

If she'd gone for a walk or intended to go for a late-night swim, wouldn't she have removed her shoes somewhere along the beach? And why would she have gone swimming in her nightgown?

Why had Lady Hartley been quick to point out Victoria's love of swimming? She did not approve of Victoria Bastion, a former servant in the house, but would she commit murder? And what did Lianne fear? What did she know about Victoria's demise?

Images of the dead girl in her cream satin nightdress filled my mind. I saw her there, on the cliff, staring down, down . . .

I closed my eyes.

I pictured an aggressor, sneaking up behind her, pushing her over.

My feet took the path to Padthaway, a foolish expedition as I had no business being there. Pity I hadn't thought to leave behind a glove. Mrs. Trehearn answered the door. "Miss du Maurier." Astonishment, the briefest kind, shadowed her stony face. "Are you here to see . . . ?"

"Miss Lianne Hartley," I smiled. "May I come in?"

I pushed my way into the house, for she didn't seem eager to permit me entry.

Mrs. Trehearn proved a reluctant escort to Miss Lianne's chamber.

Severe displeasure clipped her mouth as she informed Lianne of my arrival.

"Oh, Daphne! How wonderful of you to visit me. Mrs. Trehearn," she giggled, sweeping me inside her sanctuary, "probably thought you came down the chimney!"

I asked why she thought this so.

"No one visits us, and I mean *no one.* You can't count Sir Edward or Vicar Nortby as visitors. I don't know why. When we're in town, *everyone* visits, but here . . ."

She directed her troubled gaze out her bedroom window. "I suspect it's because of Papa's death."

"Your father? When did he die?"

"Many years ago."

I nodded. Her room, I noticed, faced the old tower. The highest and remotest part of the house, the attic suited her eccentricity— open wood-beam ceilings, creaky floors, random old trunks stacked in varying corners, an eighteenth-century dollhouse, a Thonet rocking chair, a Victorian tea suite by the double-glazed full windows, and a modest collection of white semi-modern furniture all adorned a vast area of oddly slanted proportions.

White and lavender were her colors. They gleamed everywhere, from the sprigged lavender bed-quilt to the oil painting of a heather field on the wall.

A tiny smile played on her lips. "So, you came. I'm glad. Did you see Mummy? What did Mummy say to you?"

"I didn't see her," I replied, recognizing her mother's control over her. "Does she monitor your visitors?"

"No!" Lianne laughed. "But Trehearn does. Isn't she *positively dreadful*? I call her Old Crow. Don't you think the title suits her?"

"Very much so," I smiled.

"Aren't you scared of her? Most people are."

"No. It would take a great deal to scare me."

"Oh, I wouldn't be too keen to say that round here," came the swift warning. "This house *breeds* tragedy. My father . . . Victoria . . . and so many others . . ."

"Others?" I echoed.

"Over the years. Windemere is cursed. We'll never rest until the Rothmarten Abbey records are restored to their true resting place."

"What resting place is that?"

"A remote village in Italy. I keep saying to David they ought to be shipped there, but he refuses to do it. He could, you know, *force* the abbey to give up their precious treasure and return it to its rightful place."

"Does your brother truly have power over Rothmarten?" My question was filled with disbelief.

"Oh *yes.*" Lianne stared at me as if I were a mad person. "The Hartleys of Padthaway have always held precedence over Rothmarten since *centuries* ago. We've financed and seen to their protection. Now, they're not in need of 'swordlike' protection but still protection nonetheless. You ought to talk to Davie about this. Rothmarten was his favorite passion growing up. Do you know he donated quite a sum to restore those records you are so keen upon studying?"

My experience led me to recognize the importance of the phrase "quite a sum" among the rich and titled. Indeed, Lord David Hartley had benefited the abbey in a considerable way and I wondered if Abbess Quinlain kept her association with the Hartley family to a minimum because of this debt to a family of such prestige and influence.

"My mother is quite interested in *you,*" Lianne stated sheepishly.

"Oh . . ." I feigned ignorance. "Why?"

"She likes to build connections. And you, dear Daphne, are worth building. How amazing! I never thought someone who looked like you would belong to such a family . . . such a family of *interest* to my mother."

Poor Lianne. Once her mother learned I'd called at the house of my own volition, she'd draw on the acquaintance. It was the way of the aristocracy. She seemed to have wholeheartedly despised Victoria's presence, but she'd welcome *any* female with superior connections into her intimate circle.

"Do you think my mother likes me?" Lianne's face hardened. "Sometimes, I think she despises me. You see, I'm not smart like other girls. I'm different. I don't think she likes me to be different. I think she'd like me to be more like . . . *you.*"

"Me? Then you're both at a loss, for I'm *very* different. My mother says so. All families have their ups and downs. I've caught my mother saying things about me before. I'm the black sheep, in a sense. My elder sister Angela is beautiful and clever, and Jeanne, she's younger and merry. But I always seem to do and say the wrong things. My father finds it funny but my mother doesn't. She raked me across the hands once for sympathizing with the Germans in front of everyone at the dinner table!"

A swift smile came to Lianne's lips.

"So, you see, no family is perfect, and you're close to your brother aren't you?"

"David." Her smile softened. "I'd do anything for him . . . *anything*."

CHAPTER ELEVEN

Including murder? I wanted to ask. Instead, I sighed. "I wish I had a brother . . . a wicked brother like Branwell Brontë."

"Branwell Brontë," Lianne mused. "Don't think I know him. Does he live in London?"

I tried not to laugh. "You've never heard of the Brontë sisters? The *Brontës*. The famous writers?"

She shook her head and I sensed an impatience within her to change the subject. It was an interesting reaction, one indicating a negligent education or perhaps a reluctance to admit to a reading problem. She felt comfortable asking *me* questions, but when the reverse occurred, she stiffened. "Is your family rich?"

"We are . . . comfortable."

"Maybe that's why Mummy likes you. Now David's free, Mummy wants *you* to marry him."

It was all so simple and conclusive in her mind. I stared at her, mouth agape. How could she dismiss Victoria with so little remorse? Had she no finesse, no moral sense?

No wonder her mother kept her on a tight leash. "If that is your mother's reason for her interest in me, I shall not visit. It's not right to be even *thinking* . . ."

"Right or wrong," taunted Lianne as she rearranged a few pieces in her dollhouse, inviting me to help.

"This dollhouse was made in the Elizabethan era," she said, proudly giving me the "tour."

"I had a dollhouse once," I said, amazed by the particular care she took in placing everything "just so."

"Did you play with it with your sisters?"

I nodded.

"I wish I had a sister. It's so lonely here."

"You could go away to school," I suggested. "That's what I did. I loved it."

"Oh, Mummy would never agree, and I don't think I could leave the house . . ." Glancing at the walls surrounding us, she acknowledged them with a fond sigh. "I love it here. This is my home. And I've no need to go away to school, for Jenny teaches me. You'll meet Jenny soon but not today. *Today,* I'm keeping you to myself."

"I ought to be at the abbey," I said, half-laughing, "but I do so love this house, too."

"Then you must come here often. You can come not as a guest but as my *particular* friend. I've never really had a friend before. Jenny says it's because we're so isolated and Mummy doesn't want me mixing with the locals. They're not good enough for *her.* But she can't say anything about you. You're our equal."

Snobbery was an unfortunate curse. Ladies like Lady Hartley bred it as keenly as orchids.

"Oh, I'm so glad you're here!" Lianne exclaimed, embracing me before skipping back to her dollhouse. I'd seen loneliness in many a girl, but none more so than Lianne Hartley. True, she amused herself and she was a trifle odd, but her craving for love and attention was touching. I wondered which parent she was most like—her mother or her father?

"I'm here to be *your friend,*" I expressed. "We'll do things together . . . and *together,*" I added, my voice dropping to a conspiratorial whisper, "we'll solve the mystery about Victoria. It'll be our very own little adventure."

Her eyes flashed pure fear. Chewing on the edge of her sleeve, she regarded me with the timidity of a cornered animal. "What if . . . what if it leads to someone dangerous? What shall you do then?"

I noticed she said what shall *you* do then, not what shall *we* do then. Sensing something significant lurked behind these changeable moods, I saw I'd have to tread cautiously. "I guess I'll just try to protect myself whilst finding the truth."

"Truth," she echoed and, reclining upon her bed, propped her hand under her chin to view me. "You're a writer who likes to write stories and such. You should know what to do in such situations. Do your characters murder, Daphne?"

"Do my characters murder?" I pondered. "I'm writing my first saga and I suppose I'll have some kind of murder in it."

"What do you think makes people murder?"

"It's complicated and there are many answers. Ever read the papers? Even good people are driven to murder."

"Good people," Lianne echoed, "truly good people don't do bad things."

"Yes, they do. When pushed or suffering extreme trauma through various circumstances, they turn desperate. And desperation breeds trouble."

"But how do *good* people hide the bodies and get away with it? And do they ever confess?"

"Hiding bodies depends on the moment, and confession, well, confession may take years. The mind hides many secrets. You know, my family often does this sort of thing at home . . . sitting up late at night, discussing people, motivations, exploring what lies beneath the surface—"

"Oh, I'd love to do that!"

Her face turned instantly glum. "But we don't have interesting people here. And *I* have no one to talk to. They're all boring and go to bed early. I wish I had a family like yours."

"It doesn't matter where you are," I countered. "London is different from Fowey, just as Padthaway is different from the village.

67

If you came to my home at Ferryside, you might be bored. What we can't find around us, we must 'imagine.'"

"Like daydreaming? Is that how you get ideas for your stories?"

She sounded so excited. I couldn't help but humor her. "Yes, indeed. I confess I am in love with your home and often daydream about what it must be like to live here."

"Really? Do you love it enough to murder for it?"

When I grew silent, she chuckled. "I'm only vexing, I didn't mean it, Daphne, truly I didn't. It's just that . . ."

She broke off and I guessed she was thinking about Victoria.

"I understand," I said warmly, and gave her my hand.

"No explanations?" she queried, uncertain.

"No explanations."

Mine was certainly no match for Victoria Bastion's beauty.

The mirror always told the truth. My shoulder-length hair was of a rather nondescript color. But I possessed a pert nose, a well-formed chin, lips of adequate shape, smooth skin lightly tanned, and decent green-gray eyes with dark enough sweeping lashes. I supposed, in the end, from a writer's point of view, I wasn't bad-looking.

But Victoria had been beautiful even in death.

"Daphne! Are you ready yet?"

Ewe Sinclaire's irritableness outdid Lady Hartley's. I'd love to see the two at war.

An impossibility, for the Lady Hartleys of this world did not mix with those considered belowstairs and Ewe, as a former professional nurse, exuded the working tab abhorrent to her ladyship.

"Oh, she's always been willful," divulged Ewe in a confessional manner to her good friend Mrs. Penmark after Ewe had shepherded me out of the cottage for our afternoon visit to the baker's wife. "Got worse after Lord H shot himself," she declared, piling a third helping of seed cake onto Mrs. Penmark's prized china plates. "*Scandal,* I tell you, and bless me *no* money to keep up the grand parties then."

"Parties?" I repeated.

"Oh, the *grandest* parties ever were to be seen," Ewe went on, entirely swept away by the memory. "But as I said, after Lord Hartley done himself in, a great quiet descended on Padthaway. No great parties. No great visitors. Just . . . silence."

"We see Mrs. Trehearn every now and then," Mrs. Penmark said. "She likes to do a village run every Sunday and stops by the bakery."

"Oh, hmmm? And what does the great Mrs. T buy from you, Mrs. P?"

"She fancies those pastries I make. I feel sorry for her. So tied up to Padthaway and Lady Hartley . . . she's got no chance of ever escaping."

"Perhaps she doesn't want to escape," I said. "Perhaps she loves her job and her place."

Ewe's response accompanied a hefty sigh and another "yes" to a piece of Mrs. Penmark's favorite sweet pastry. "You ought to know, Cynthia, having been in service before you married your good Mr. Penmark. A woman's got to have an occupation and Daphne's right, Mrs. Trehearn *loves* her place. She queens it among us, just like her mistress, Lady H of the *hated* kind."

"The hated kind?" I asked.

"Oh, that Lady H is a scarlet woman. She carries on with men on her staff."

"Oh?" I lifted a brow.

" 'Tis true," Ewe supported. "Ridgeway Soames. I saw him just this afternoon, on his way into town again."

This comment elicited a sigh from Mrs. Penmark.

"Ridgeway Soames, the cook," Ewe put in for my benefit. "A gilded peacock if ever I saw one and hired by Lady H of Padthaway herself. Did you happen to see him when you were there?"

"No . . ." I thought over my entire acquaintance with the house up to this point. "I can't remember anyone by that name."

"Who served dinner?"

"Housemaids. A skinny one and a fat one."

"Ah." Mrs. Penmark nodded. "Betsy and Annie. They're local girls. Cousins, I think. In any case, they *serve* at Padthaway along with this Mr. Soames."

A raucous laughter rumbled from Ewe. "Her ladyship likes them young, doesn't she? I s'pose it's her money that gets them."

"She is still very comely for her age," Mrs. Penmark reminded. "If you didn't know it, you'd never think Lord David her son!"

"True, true," Ewe admitted. "That poor Vicky Bastion. Lady Muck didn't look upon the match with a friendly eye, did she?"

Mrs. Penmark seemed reluctant to comment.

"The girl's dead." Ewe loaded her fork with the last crumbs on her plate. "A lethal death, I'd say, for Vicky Bastion was one of us—a *commoner*. The Bastions are village folk, always were, and always have been, and not good enough for the likes of Lady Florence Hartley, daughter of an earl."

Ewe turned to wink at me. "I've got it on good authority Mrs. B fancied herself living up at Padthaway one day."

"Mrs. Bastion still keeps to her room, I hear," Mrs. Penmark whispered, clearly distressed over the whole situation. "One would think Lord David would have called on her by now. She was, after all, to be his mother-in-law."

CHAPTER TWELVE

It's a very odd setup at Padthaway, (I noted in my journal) *and I'm not sure if I should meddle, but I can't help myself. For I did not ask, did I, to find a body? Therefore I am innocent, an unwilling participant drawn into this whole ugly affair. From what I have gleaned thus far, everybody is absolutely certain the Hartley family is to blame and will get away with the crime.*

Crime.

But was she truly murdered?

And if so, why?

Putting my journal to the side, I found Ewe weeding in the garden.

"I'm off to the post office to mail a letter to my sisters," I said, peering over her shoulder and tapping the letter in my hand. "Ewe, I've been wondering . . . is Mr. Soames really Lady Hartley's lover?"

Ewe readjusted her apron. "I do believe so. A *secondary* occupation for a cook, if ye ask me, and he's *cooked* himself up a treat there, didn't he! Servicin' her . . . but I s'pose she pays well and he gets to drive the motorcars as young devils are wont to do."

I was struck by an acute urge to visit Padthaway in search of this

Ridgeway Soames. I didn't need an invitation to visit as Lianne's friend. I could march up there and demand to see the cook, though that was Sir Edward's job, not mine, I thought as I headed out the gate.

Wandering into the village, I overheard two women talking outside the grocer.

". . . it's a dreadful thing and Mrs. B's shut herself up."

"Curtains still drawn at the Bastion cottage," the other remarked. "Mrs. B had her hat down low yesterdee. Connan took her out to get some fresh air. He's a blessin' for her to have, that boy."

"Before Lord David throws him out of town."

"He'd not dare!"

"Oh, yes, he would. Those Hartleys don't care for any of us."

I lingered over the fruit on display, picking up and inspecting an item or two. I kept my ears poised as the women rattled on.

"Connan's not the sort to be put aside, and he just adored Victoria as we all know." A long sigh exuded out of her mouth. "It's sad when I think of them two runnin' in the woods and skippin' down the lane, hand-in-hand . . ."

"I tried to find out what Miss Osborn thinks," her companion confessed, her hand flapping up as a shield.

"Ye won't get anythin' out of her. Her mouth's stopped up like a fish!"

"Ye seem to be spendin' a long time there, miss. Can I help ye?"

I suddenly found myself staring at the grocer. "Oh, um, these apples, please. And one or two oranges."

"That's Miss Daphne du Maurier," I heard one woman say to the other as I scuttled off.

"Oh, who's she when she's home, then?"

I smiled. Someone who hadn't heard of my father's fame. What blissful anonymity!

The post office, located in the center of the village, was typical of small-town England: quaint, busy, and served by the same postmistress for years, a disgruntled cantankerous creature, all thin, wispy hair and wiry eyes.

"Yes?"

"I'd just like to post this, please, miss . . . ?"

She ignored me. Stamping the envelope, she put it in a tray and I paid her the money. I must have looked as bewildered as I felt, for as I left a young man riding a bicycle paused.

"Something wrong, miss?"

His extraordinary looks left me speechless. He was of average height and muscular, with sweeping dark hair framing an angelic face: a short, straight nose; full lips; large, thick-lashed violet eyes; and a charming grin. He'd bring any girl to her knees and I guessed at once that this must be Connan Bastion, Victoria's brother.

"Ye're new to the area, aren't ye? Visitin' or just passin' through?"

I didn't know what to say. Instead, I offered my hand for him to shake. "I'm Daphne du Maurier."

His face turned white. "Ah . . ."

"I'm sorry." I glanced down at the dirt beneath my shoes.

"So am I," he said, readying his bicycle again.

I examined his sailor's uniform, thinking he looked very fine in it, and casually inquired after the latest catch. "My family has a house in Fowey," I explained. "And my father loves to fish . . . when he has the chance of it. I'm interested in boating, too."

"Well, Miss Daphne, maybe sometime I could take you out in my boat. I have a little one I use when I'm not working."

I thanked him for the offer and I watched in appreciation as he rode off. It couldn't be denied. Good looks always set people ahead in this world and Connan possessed them, just as his sister had. They shared the same eyes, violet blue and dark-lashed. I wished I had such eyes.

"Tch, tch," Ewe beamed later that day as I dressed for another dinner at Padthaway. "You've *made an impression*. Two invitations to dine! Next, Lord David will be after the first two waltzes."

I hesitated over whether to mention my brief encounter with Connan Bastion to Ewe, and eventually decided against it. It was unlikely he'd make good on his promise to take me out on his boat, and it was unlikely he'd seek me out whilst I remained in the village.

However, I could not erase him, or the fierce spark in his eye when I mentioned my connection with his dead sister, from my mind. Did he also think David Hartley a killer?

A dashingly attired David Hartley greeted Sir Edward and me at the door—a gesture of regard for Sir Edward and myself.

Sir Edward's jittery nerves on the journey to the house led me to suspect that he had something of importance to announce this eve, and that the announcement was not altogether pleasant.

"Is Mrs. Bastion here?" were Sir Edward's first words to David.

Promptly taking out a cigarette, he answered, "No, she hasn't arrived yet. Shall we join the others in the dining room?"

After a cursory nod to me, he marched toward the dining room, and Sir Edward escorted me in his wake.

In spite of myself, I felt pity for Lord David, having to endure whatever news Sir Edward planned to deliver. As we ferried ourselves to the dining room, I wondered if Connan Bastion would escort his mother this evening, or if she would choose to arrive alone. I awaited the outcome in silence as we made our way to the Queen Anne dining room.

The room lived up to its majestic title. Large and somewhat formidable, with an oversized table fit for a castle, it bore the charm of yesteryear with its plush burgundy upholstered chairs, matching velvet wall drapes framing family portraits of long-dead ancestors, and gleaming silver tableware.

The gentlemen stood when we arrived. Sir Edward, by my side, greeted the company in his pompous manner. The Vicar Nortby, whom I'd heard so much about, was a wizened old fellow flashing grotesque yellowed teeth and an uncertain nature; Lady Hartley was bedecked in her usual splendor; and, to my infinite surprise, a dour-faced Mrs. Trehearn also graced the table. At her side sat a woman I hadn't yet met, Lianne's nurse Jenny, plumpish and merry-faced. Lastly, I was introduced to one Mr. Ridgeway Soames.

I was seated between Lady Hartley and a smugly attired Mr. Soames, his handsome face shaven to perfection. Black-haired, tall, lean, and smartly dressed, his sangfroid overwhelmed the table.

"Daphne," I grinned, and promptly shook hands with him.

"Ridgeway Soames," said he, very debonair. "I'm the chef here at Padthaway. I hope you approve of tonight's menu."

"What is tonight's menu?" I asked gaily, accepting the gracious pouring of a fine champagne into my glass.

"Oh," replied he, "I say it'll be one dinner you won't ever forget."

His curious gaze then ran over me. "You're here as witness?"

"I wish I wasn't," I confessed. "This is all rather horrid, yet I must do my duty."

"Duty? To whom?" His dark eyes seemed to bore into my soul.

"Oh, I feel a duty to the investigation, as I found the body. That's why I'm here."

"Yes, I know," said he, quickly downing his glass. "The facts of the case cannot be concealed as well as some might wish it . . ."

His voice trailed off as he glanced in the direction of David Hartley, who sat at the head of the table. His mother sat at the opposite end with Vicar Nortby. Lianne, squeezed near her brother and nurse, sent me a timid smile. I dreaded the next, and last, arrival.

Sir Edward kept glancing at the door and soon all gazes followed, until the last guest, Mrs. Bastion, arrived.

"Please sit down, Mrs. Bastion." Attempting a calming lilt, Sir Edward drew back a chair for Mrs. Bastion.

Lady Hartley rang the bell and the strangest dinner of my life commenced. Sir Edward's impending announcement filled the air with expectation, but he'd decided to leave it for after dinner.

It seemed a wise notion. The redness of Mrs. Bastion's face matched mine but hers bore no creams or colors to conceal it. She'd dressed in severe black, her graying hair raked behind her. How could this woman be Victoria's mother? I'd expected a beautiful woman, not this half-starved scarecrow boring into the eyes of everybody at the table. Why Connan had not come to support his mother I didn't understand. If he hated Lord David or suspected him of murder, why not show his stance here, now, in front of all the witnesses involved?

Victoria's mother wouldn't stop looking at me and suddenly sprang out of her chair, pointed her finger. "She'll *not* be my daughter's replacement! Not now! Not ever! I won't have it, I tell you! My Vicky were *murdered,* yes, *murdered*! Someone didn't want her bein' Lady Hartley and that's the whole truth, I swear it."

She took her seat again only at the insistent urging of Sir Edward. Poor Sir Edward had the unpleasant duty of delivering a verdict to the estimable Mrs. Bastion.

After a good half hour she waved her finger at Lord David. "Dinin' mighty fine tonight aren't we, milord! While me girl lies cold, you sit here celebratin'!" Her eyes turned into icy slivers.

"How are your medicines coming along, Mrs. Trehearn?" asked Jenny, trying to change the subject. "I do say I must confess I am fascinated."

I lifted a brow. "Oh? Did you work with medicines during the war?"

Mrs. Trehearn retained her usual icy demeanor. "Yes, I was a nurse."

"A nurse? And which Red Cross hospital did you work in?"

Mrs. Trehearn remained silent, perhaps for fear of enraging Mrs. Bastion.

I forced her response. "Torquay, perhaps, Mrs. Trehearn? I heard they trained many nurses for the war efforts."

"Yes," she acknowledged through clenched teeth. I would have found some means of extracting more out of her had not Sir Edward chosen that very moment to slide out of his chair.

"Thank you for all coming," he began, his tone dire and monotonous. "It is my solemn and unpleasant duty to formally deliver the death certificate for the late Victoria Bastion."

Laying a calming hand on Mrs. Bastion's shoulder, he cleared his throat. "Mrs. Bastion, as the deceased's closest relative, I declare it is my solemn duty to inform you that your daughter passed away by 'death accidental.' "

"Accidental!" Mrs. Bastion immediately shouted.

"Yes," Sir Edward confirmed, his tone graver than a tomb. "After extensive inquiries and two *thorough* examinations of the body, the official verdict from the chief of police is 'death by accident.' "

CHAPTER THIRTEEN

"I don't believe it."

Ewe and I stayed up very late that eve.

"She's sure to cause a storm, Mrs. B."

"She certainly stormed out of the house," I said. "After swearing the Hartleys would get 'their due.'"

"Tough mettle, showin' without her Connan." Ewe nodded. "Makes ye wonder whether he were there, peerin' through the windows."

I pointed out to Ewe that the location of the Queen Anne dining room on the second level discounted such a possibility.

"Never stopped Romeo, did it?"

When we finally retired to bed, sleep eluded me. The vision of Connan Bastion climbing up the ivy-covered walls and slipping into the house unobserved played over and over in my mind. Restless until dawn, I listened to the birds waking before getting up and dressing for an early-morning walk. It was still dark outside, Ewe's cuckoo clock striking the sixth hour. I slipped out of the cottage and stumbled my way into the woods.

A flock of birds circled above me, heading for the sea. I hurried after them. Reliable guides, they led me through the eerie woods and into the daylight that flooded the horizon.

Nothing, I vowed, could be more beautiful than the sunrise over a Cornish sea. Radiant colors collided and burst, and all the while the birds circled high, their defining squawk heralding the morning.

Turning away from the sunrise, I began my search for Victoria's missing shoes. I hunted all around the headland, returning to the place where Victoria had lain. The sand felt hard beneath my fingers and I shuddered. Death had laid here.

The formation above, the sharp jagged cliffs, produced no clues. She could have fallen, she could have been pushed, but her shoes were nowhere to be found.

I sat down for a moment, allowing the early breeze to rifle through my hair. It refreshed the mind and spirit. "Victoria, Victoria," I murmured to the wind. "What happened to you?"

"Daphne!?" A voice pierced the early-morning calm.

"Daphne!" said the incredulous voice again. "Is that you?"

I glanced up.

Lianne waved from the top of the cliff. "Wait!" she cried. "I'll come down."

She slid down a path that seemed very familiar to her. I wondered whether she came to this spot often.

"Oh, Davie and I used to come here all the time. Davie says this is the best headland in the country."

"Do you believe everything your brother says?"

She didn't take offense for I tempered my comment with a smile.

Wrinkling her nose, she rolled her eyes. "Noooo. I'm not stupid. Everyone *thinks* I'm stupid."

Immediately downcast, I tried to pacify her mood by asking for the news.

"Sir Edward," she groaned. "We had to feed him breakfast while he came to talk to Davie about . . ."

"Yes," I prompted, "he came to talk to Davie about what?"

"I shouldn't really say—it's *confidential.*"

"But if it's to do with the murder, it'll come out in the papers somehow."

She frowned, unwilling to go on.

Eager to learn more, I accepted her invitation to breakfast with the family.

"Oh, goody! We can paint and draw and do anything you like. I don't often have friends. I should like company."

We strolled across the grassland toward the house, plucking a wildflower or two on the way.

"I know!" She suddenly twisted and turned. "You like to write. When the abbey bores you, you can come to Padthaway and write. It's a huge house and quiet and perfect for that kind of thing. Mummy won't mind, nor will David."

I said I'd think over her extremely generous invitation.

"Wait and see." Lianne grimaced. "You'll come; I know you will! You can't keep away."

I allowed myself a little smile. Lianne had read my mind. How could I refuse an invitation to any grand house—and this house in particular?

"It won't be boring." Lianne tempted me, eyes hopeful. "There's a lot to explore. The old tower, for one. I found its secret room— would you like to see it?"

The mention of a secret room and old tower led me to imagine myself inside the house, exploring its inward paths, its forbidden rooms, unraveling its mysterious call. I yearned to learn everything about it and its secrets, to unravel the mystery of Victoria's death.

As we arrived the house greeted us in silence.

"You are so lucky," I whispered to Lianne, "to belong to such a place. I'm quite envious, you know."

She lifted a shoulder. "It's sad and lonely at times. When Papa was alive, it was different. But it all changed."

I wondered why things had changed. Was there some mystery attached to the death of the late Lord Hartley?

One couldn't discount the numerous misgivings on the character of Lady Florence Hartley, daughter of an earl.

It amazed me how the aristocracy often thought themselves

above crime. I'd seen it many times, in many differing cases. Sensational cases intrigued my father, too, and we'd often sit up late at night deliberating over the available facts.

I suppressed an urge to telephone my father. I'd have to call home soon enough, for Mother was bound to worry, and if I didn't allay her fears, they'd descend upon Ewe's door and cart me off back to London. That eventuality had to be delayed at all costs.

Lianne insisted on my using her boudoir to refresh myself before breakfast. I did so, making liberal use of all the powders and creams on display. The Hartley's were *very* rich, but were they capable of buying a verdict?

I put such thoughts out of my mind, for I'd arrived as a guest and Lianne's friend.

As I primped I felt as if I'd stepped into the pages of a Jane Austen novel, or a work of Mrs. Gaskell, who loved to pen the dark, gothic tales of murder, mystery, and revenge.

"Daphne? Are you all right in there?"

"Oh yes." I quickly made haste, pinching my cheeks for color. "I'm ready. Will breakfast be ready yet, do you think?"

"Yes," she said, her curious eye examining me from head to toe. "I sent a note to Mrs. Trehearn to have all ready early. Mummy's a late riser. She has breakfast in her room, mostly. Davie likes to have it early. If we go down now, we might catch him."

"Perhaps he doesn't wish to be interrupted?" I said on the way down the grand staircase.

"Let's see."

Her mischievous smile sent a wave of nerves through me. I had to confess I found David Hartley quite the romantic, forlorn hero.

"Good morning, Miss du Maurier!"

Lord David sprang out of his chair when Lianne and I entered the breakfast room.

"What a delight to have you here at our table."

"You are very kind, my lord," I replied, accepting a seat.

"There are all kinds of hot and cold dishes," he advised. "And coffee or tea? Which do you prefer?"

"Coffee, please," I smiled, and he delivered the order to a stone-faced Mrs. Trehearn.

"I met Daphne on my walk this morning." Lianne began the conversation, leading me to the bread basket.

"You rise early, Miss Daphne?"

"Please, just Daphne, my lord—"

"Then, please, just David, Daphne . . ."

We shared a look.

"Yes," I went on with a smile, "I am very fond of walking, and like your sister, I rise early as a rule."

"A rule?" he questioned.

"It's just my routine. I love to be up early with the birds . . . and the sunrise. There's something sacred about the mornings."

"I couldn't agree more with you."

His solemn, reflective response warmed me to him. It was difficult to think him a murderer. I detected pain and grief etched in the taut lines of his face, and hoped that he'd loved and adored Victoria.

David's words repeated in my head. *I couldn't agree with you more.*

"You're frowning? Coffee not good?"

"Oh." I stopped stirring the milk in my coffee. "Forgive me. I silently correct grammar in my head sometimes. I'm afraid it's a very bad habit."

He laughed. "You sound like my old English teacher at Eton, Professor Brasic. Devilishly strict on the grammar. Were your teachers the same?"

A friendly tête-à-tête on our education and experiences commenced, with Lianne listening and asking dozens of questions. Although going away to school was not for her, she wanted to hear everything her brother and I had to say on the matter.

"I met Miss Perony, your local schoolteacher," I said at the end. "She's a very interesting character."

Lord David choked on his coffee.

"Oh, she doesn't like us," Lianne scoffed. "Mummy says she's a bluestocking."

The straight and direct Miss Perony *would* seem like a bluestocking to Lady Hartley. What didn't she like? That Miss Perony had the ability to address them as an equal? That she did not fear the loss of her post, despite the Hartley influence?

"Miss Perony," David coughed, "is very knowledgeable, and her cousin, I believe, is at the abbey. Perhaps she mentioned it?"

"Yes, she did. I am to meet her tomorrow."

"But Davie is a better guide," Lianne said sweetly, smiling at her brother. She looked at me eagerly. "We can make a day of it, can't we, Davie? Take Daphne to the abbey and you can show her the records. Old Quinlain can't refuse you."

Lord David considered the idea.

"Very well," he smiled, "shall I pick you up at ten, Miss du Maurier?"

CHAPTER FOURTEEN

The official verdict was diligently peddled about the village by Ewe Sinclaire and others.

"Death *accidental*," I heard the old gossipmongers reporting. "Oh *yes*. And we all know who got away with it, don't we? *Them Hartleys*. Don't know which one of 'em did it. I'd 'ave me money on her ladyship, but ye never know. There's that odd sister, Miss Lianne, she could 'ave pushed poor Vicky over the cliffs to her death. . . ."

Ready to make the most of wagging tongues, I placed myself in a strategic position outside the bakery and sighed, "Oh, it's all too *horrid*. I shan't cope!"

I strode off and one of the village ladies pursued me, as I'd intended.

"Oh, miss, wait, would ye?"

I waited . . . with a huff, feigning reluctance.

"I heard ye. Yes, it's horrid. It's *all* horrid. And I know what ye feelin'. Dear Vicky. I knew her as a babe and I knew Lord David, too. I were his former nurse before Jenny stepped in, y'know, so I know them both. It's an *awful* tragedy. But I can't think my David guilty, not for one bit. For Vicky, well, she were a secret child. She kept lots of secrets from her parents and such. I often wonder . . ."

I stared at this creature in absolute wonderment. "What is your name?" I heard myself asking.

"Rebecca Shaw" came the reply. "*Mrs.* Rebecca Shaw. I gave up nursin' a long time ago."

"And you live here now? Windemere Lane? Cornwall?"

"Oh, miss, so many questions!"

"I'm sorry." I swallowed. "I shouldn't be so interested except . . ."

"Except ye found the body and them Hartleys want ye on their side?"

The succinct summary sent a chill through my veins.

"Well, if ye askin' my opinion, which ye not, I'd say run away from them Hartleys. They're trouble. *Big* trouble."

"What kind of trouble?"

"Ay," said Mrs. Rebecca Shaw, blushing, "I'm not one for sayin'. My head be lopped off by me husband if he heard me speak so ill of the Hartleys. He works in a mine owned by them, y'know. He's what they call a 'supervisor.' "

"Ah," I sympathized. "The job brings responsibilities . . . and loyalties."

"Oh, aye," agreed Mrs. Shaw, ever so ready. "I often say to Mick it were a pity we're stuck here with them such. I'd rather serve somewhere else, with no big dark cloud attached, y'know. I reckon—"

A passerby disrupted her final comment and I gazed at the departing figure of Mrs. Shaw in utter hopelessness.

"Ye just be careful, miss!" came the shout, and I doubted I'd ever see Mrs. Rebecca Shaw again.

Oh, yes, indeed, the Hartleys held sway over everything living in this village and yonder. Exactly as in medieval times, as Miss Perony had said.

I spent the morning with my gaze fixed on the ticking hands of the cuckoo clock, striking nine thirty, then a quarter to ten, then ten o'clock, then ten fifteen. And still no cancellation note, nor a David Hartley at the door to collect me for our abbey excursion.

"He's not comin'," Ewe stated, having observed my overly frequent and frantic clock-bound glances.

I started to pace. "Something's delayed him . . ."

"His dead bride." Ewe crooked her finger at me. "He can't be trusted. Death by accident, they say. I think they've got it wrong and a body don't lie."

A body don't lie.

I thought of those words all afternoon. Terrible grammar, mind. A body doesn't lie; it has no need to do so.

At half past two, a note arrived.

> *Dear Miss du Maurier,*
> *I apologize for neglecting to pick you up at ten this morning. An unexpected visitor is to blame.*
> *Perhaps we may postpone our excursion for another day?*
>
> *David Hartley*

"He's a very nice hand, that Davie boy."

Ewe couldn't resist reading the note a dozen times, flicking it thoughtfully across her lips. "An unexpected visitor . . . to do with the murder?"

"It's not a murder now," I reminded. "We're to believe it was an accident."

"Oh, defendin' the Hartleys already, are ye? Caution, my dear. Caution. Caution never killed anyone."

"Accidents *do* happen. You can't out-rule the fact."

"Humph!" Ewe huffed, and I asked her what she knew of Rebecca Shaw.

"Becky Shaw," Ewe mused. "Married Michael Shaw. A fine man, good worker. She were a nurse up at the house before Jenny Pollock came along."

"She warned me to be careful, and that the Hartleys were big trouble."

Ewe clicked her tongue. "Same thing I said. But you can't help yeself."

"Nor can you," I retorted. "We both want to know what really happened to her. It's natural. Well, now that this morning's mystery is solved, I'm off. I'll go to the abbey anyway, with or without David Hartley. See you later."

I departed with a mischievous grimace; Ewe's stern demeanor monitored my escape into the woods. I knew I should heed her advice. She knew this village and the Hartleys better than I and uttered warnings for my benefit. Both of us understood the dangers of becoming too involved and too close to this momentous scandal.

I paused to think about telephoning my father, but the abbey beckoned and the lost scrolls of Charlemagne won my affections.

I found it difficult to concentrate, working around Sister Agatha and Sister Sonya in their frustrated attempts to put the papers in order. Upon watching them, I offered a few suggestions, which were overheard by Abbess Dorcas Quinlain.

"Are you volunteering to help, Miss du Maurier? If so, I am sure Sister Agatha and Sister Sonya would appreciate it."

Sister Agatha, so unlike her refined cousin Perony Osborn, wiped her hand across her forehead. "Oh, yes, please! Can't make any sense of half of 'em!"

Sister Sonya responded affirmatively to the abbess, nodding, relieved to have me as their guide.

I queried the abbess about her refusal to employ a proper researcher.

"Oh, Lord David said he'd do it. He enjoys the work, like you do."

"He was supposed to give me a private tour today," I murmured, "but something unexpected came up. A visitor."

"Then you've not heard?"

To my surprise, the abbess shepherded me into her office and closed the door.

"Heard what?"

"The cause of Victoria's death. It's poison. Could change the verdict."

I noted her emphasis on "could."

"How do you know?"

She sighed. "Lord David told me himself. He telephoned to say you were coming and to assist you in his absence."

I wanted to know the depth of their relationship. "You are a friend of his?"

"I wouldn't say 'friend,' exactly. We do share a love for the abbey, the preservation of its culture and history, and Lord David has been very generous . . . far more generous than his father ever was."

"You didn't like his father?"

"Like? What curious terms you use, child. That man was a beast."

"But poison? Poison?" My inquisitive question echoed through the silence of the room. "What kind of poison, do you know?"

The abbess shrugged. "Something common called ricin."

Perhaps Victoria occasionally dabbled in some form of drugs? Perhaps she took sleeping powders, too? How did one differentiate between drugs and powders?

"Surely this will change everything—imagine how the mother will feel. Poison! Even if it was an accident."

"Unlikely," I heard myself muttering under my breath while the abbess looked at me in stony silence. "Do you believe Sir Edward will continue his investigation?"

"He'll have to. One must follow the expected protocol."

I thought I better telephone my father before he heard.

I went down to the post office to make the call.

"Hello, Papa? It's Daphne."

"My darling girl. How's the weather down there?"

I glanced outside. "Bleak, as usual."

"Found any 'Bleak Houses' down there, sweetheart?"

I hesitated.

"Daphne?"

Families and close friends have a natural aptitude for wheedling out information. "Yes."

Within minutes, he knew what I knew. I did leave out one or two little things, nothing of any importance and mostly in relation to David Hartley and his affiliation with Rothmarten Abbey.

"I'm not certain I want you down there, honey. It mightn't be safe—a murderer on the loose and when your mother finds out—"

"She rarely reads the papers, Papa."

"True, but women have a way of knowing all about the scandals. So who was this girl? You said she was about to marry the great lord of the county?"

"She was a local girl from a low-class family. Used to be a maid up at the house—that's how she met David Hartley."

"Ooohh, I see."

I heard the warning in my father's voice.

"I know what you're going to say," I sighed. "And I promise I'll take care." I told him about the abbey work. "This is just perfect. If I help them catalog, I can truly explore what I came here to find."

"For what purpose?"

I couldn't help suppressing a slight mischievous laugh. "Find some lost scroll and write a sensational piece for the papers."

My father laughed. "Nothing like a healthy competitive spirit, my girl. Whatever you find and write, though"—his voice dropped to a cautionary tone—"show it to the abbess first."

"Of course I would! I'm hoping, too, that the papers will pay handsomely and the money can go as a contribution for abbey restorations."

"You'd need to write a book for that, darling."

"Perhaps I will someday," I smiled. "There is ample inspiration here."

As I said good-bye, an unpleasant sensation trickled up my spine.

I spun around.

The door to the post office slammed, bells ringing to announce an abrupt departure.

I darted outside and glanced down the lane, left and right, but I couldn't see anyone.

However, I knew someone had been watching me.

CHAPTER FIFTEEN

A scrappy note awaited me at Ewe's cottage.

> *Daphne Dearest!*
> *Imagine! Poison! Ooh, it's getting very interesting,*
> *isn't it? I must peddle the news about.*
> *Oh, and, can you be a dear and wash the dishes?*
> > *See you soon.*
> > > *E*

Wash the dishes? I hadn't performed such a menial task in years. Raising my eyebrows, I pulled up my sleeves and imagined how it might be done. I thought of the brief moments I'd seen the servants in the kitchen at our houses. Surely it couldn't be that difficult?

Water on the boil, I stacked the dirty assortment into the sink and located the plug. Rummaging through Ewe's messy, disorganized cupboards below, I found "washing powder" of a kind, shrugged, and sprinkled it in the water. It foamed and bubbled and seemed the right thing to use. Adding a scrubbing utensil and scourer to the mix, I successfully, and I must admit, rather cheerfully, finished the job as I analyzed this latest development.

Poison! Now the verdict had to change to murder or suicide.

Although it did not seem that Victoria had reason to take her own life, what did one truly know of another's private pressures, struggles, and secrets?

"Lo!" Ewe's stormy entrance was full of her usual penchant for drama. "It's poison! Murder!"

Removing her hat, scarf, and gloves, she raised her eyes to the ceiling. "This is certain to topple her ladyship from her throne, mark my words. We all know one of them at the house killed the girl. Sly of them, mixing poison in her food—"

"*Was* it in her food?"

"They found doses of ricin in her. Comes from the castor bean, you know. Clever of them to use it. And how else do you think it got there if she didn't eat it?"

"It could be accidental poisoning," I pointed out. "It has happened before . . . remember that young mother in Devon? I forget what the plant was, just a common one, and she had it by her bed in her room and during the night, couldn't breathe, and the next morning she was found dead."

"But wait." Halting her breath, Ewe placed a hand over her heart. "You haven't heard the worst."

She paused, as was her annoying custom, and blinked. "Bet the abbess said nothin' though she would've known."

My patience had run out. "Known what, Ewe?"

"Victoria was three months pregnant."

"A baby!"

"Oh yes, a baby," Ewe said, nodding. "Want to keep it all hush-hush. More fools them. Worse, how it's now come out. I suppose they'd have the weddin' and then the baby comes along early. Ay, it's all about hushin' up a scandal, if ye ask me."

I gaped at Ewe, thunderstruck.

"Now *there's* a good reason for murder. Lord Davie thinkin' the child's his and he finds out it isn't and kills her."

I slowly digested her summary. "Wouldn't it be easier to call off the wedding if he found out the child isn't his? Why kill her?"

"Not if she threatened blackmail."

"Blackmail? What elaborate scheme are you conjuring up now?"

"No elaborate scheme," Ewe whispered. "But I can tell you, my dear girl, that those Hartleys have long been immersed in nefarious affairs."

"What kind of affairs?"

Suddenly coy, she briefly closed her eyes. "I don't like to say. But since you're practically *family,* I'll mention a few. Smuggling, for one."

A long pause ensued.

"Extortion. Fraud. Hmm, and that old Lord Hartley was a very bad fellow. And Lady Muck, humph! She's the devil's apprentice."

"Devil's apprentice," I mused to myself afterward. Would Lady Hartley, robbed of her position of power and prestige, have murdered her pregnant daughter-in-law and made the crime look like suicide?

I shuddered, thinking of Victoria, scrambling for life. It had been a full tide that evening and the tide has been known to catch even the most stalwart sailors unaware.

As I mulled over the facts of the case, the next invitation to Hartley House arrived in the childish hand of Lianne Hartley.

> *Dafne*
> *I hope thats how you spell your name?*
> *I and my brother want to invite you to high tea at our house.*
> *Please come at 3.*
>
> *Lianne Hartley*

"There you have it," Ewe remarked before I left the cottage. "You don't see the Bastion's puttin' up any visitors, do ye? Havin' high teas, and the like? Does that mean they're guilty?"

I pulled on my gloves. "Or numbed by the . . ." The what? I

couldn't even find a word to describe it. The horror? The tragedy? The . . . murder?

Plain and simple, and yet, as far as I'd heard, the verdict had not been changed and nobody had been charged with the supposed crime.

Ewe followed me to the door, down the garden path, to the cottage gate, and further down the lane. "Well, be careful, then. Folk go missin' up there and that Mrs. T, Trehearn, none of us like her or trust her. Used to be one of us. Now she thinks herself too good to associate down here."

"I will be careful," I promised, and kissed her cheek and set off on my merry way. "Lianne Hartley needs a friend and since I am involved in this affair whether I wished it or not, I shall go."

The walk to Padthaway filled me with a nervous apprehension.

The house ached to yield its secrets. It yearned for a friend, someone who understood it.

I liked to think I understood such ancient houses. I liked to think I knew a great deal about life, about people and their emotions, but really I was an innocent. I sensed this time in Windemere Lane would teach me a vast thing or two.

I smiled, enjoying the glorious Cornish coastline. I'd opted to take the walk through the woods down to the sea to breathe its fresh salty air and ripened sense of danger. The ocean had always been a changeling; no one could ever read it, not even the greatest fisherman or sailing captain. Changeable and unreadable, the sea was like Victoria Bastion, a simple country girl who'd transcended into a complex victim.

Victim. Perhaps I was wrong to call her that, for she had lived large and hard, climbing from class to class, embracing new friends and exploring new boundaries.

I turned up the road to Padthaway and wondered what kind of reception awaited me.

The great house dawned and I stepped up to its austere, imposing silence and boldly rang the bell.

"Ah, Miss du Maurier," Mrs. Trehearn greeted. "Her ladyship will see you now. Leave your coat here, if you please."

Summoned to Lady Hartley on arrival. Did the summoning entail some unpleasantness? Whatever the case, I dreaded the moment I would be left alone in Lady Hartley's presence.

"Her ladyship's rooms are in the west wing," Mrs. Trehearn informed.

I followed her along the eerily quiet and sunny paneled corridor leading toward the sea.

"This is the oldest part of the house," Mrs. Trehearn said. "The eastern wing suffered a fire during the civil war, but the fire never reached the west. It remains largely untouched, as it was in 1558."

"What of the tower?" I asked, pausing to admire the view from one of the graceful arched windows.

"The tower is a ruin." Mrs. Trehearn made the sign of the cross over her breast. "A *cursed* ruin. This way now."

We climbed up a wide stairway leading to two magnificent bronze doors. At least two times my height, they reached up to the cathedral groin vaulted ceilings above, decorated by an impressive fresco of biblical design, the doors sporting a huge pair of lion-head golden handles to finish the picture.

Mrs. Trehearn's long bony fingers sprawled across the handle of the door. "They are Moorish—"

"Thank you, Mrs. T. I'll take over from here." Lord David stood in the darkened corridor opposite, casually observing us. There was something about his approach that suggested he'd been waiting for our arrival.

I could have wept with relief.

A startled Mrs. Trehearn frowned. "My lord! But her ladyship said—"

"*I* am master here" was the cool response.

Mrs. Trehearn nodded deftly and left.

"I apologize for the intrusion, Miss du Maurier," Lord David smiled, "but I wish to speak with you."

Wish to speak with me? My heart thundered inside my chest. He had a magnetism about him that I found irresistibly charming. He knew he possessed it, too, I ascertained by the look in his eyes and the way he spoke, so cultured and refined, even in grief. I found myself studying the sleepless shadows around his eyes.

An elusive smile tempered his lips. "Will you allow me to give you a quick tour of the house, Daphne?"

"I'd be delighted," I replied, and accepted his arm.

Drawing me away from the Moorish doors, he guided me slowly down the southern passageway. His proximity, his very *alive* proximity, and the fact that he might very well be a murderer, tripled my senses and warning bells endlessly tolled inside my head.

"I wanted to show you the library," he began, his voice low and resonant in the silence.

I managed a nod.

"We can talk alone there."

Talk alone? What about? Respecting his need for privacy, I endeavored to keep my curiosity at bay. I thought of Mrs. Trehearn, rushing away to report to Lady Hartley.

Entering a large room boasting splendid paintings, Lord David grimaced. "You recognize the Gainsborough?"

"Yes," I whispered, unable to resist being besotted with the painting. "Who is she?"

"The *Beneficent Bride,* we call her. My father won her at a gaming table in Monte Carlo. She came from a wealthy Italian count . . . she must have been an ancestress."

"She's magnificent," I breathed. "See how the light holds her in the garden swing? It's a beautiful picture, my lord." I swallowed, intensely uncomfortable in his company.

"Please call me David." Stepping away from me, he gestured we head to the next room.

I held in a breath, and nodded.

"These chambers traditionally belong to the master of the house—"

"So this is your wing, my lord?"

"I hope, one day. The other parts are closed off, awaiting restoration. The library is the last room my father restored."

I understood why he was proud of his library. Like entering a secret garden, the modest double doors opened to reveal a circular room of dynamic wonder. Tall ceilings, three levels of books, a wrought-iron spiraled staircase leading to the upper rows, reading nooks by stain-glassed windows of Camelot style, medieval furnishings, and one huge stuffed tiger.

I recoiled in horror. "Is that real?"

"Another of my father's gambling wins." Indicating we should sit at the grand walnut desk stacked with books and papers, he faced me directly. "You'll be wondering why I wanted to see you before my mother. I don't know what she's planning, but she's up to something concerning you."

"Me?"

"My mother instructed Lianne to invite you today. She is never interested in people without a reason, and you are from a notable family. Will you heed my advice and be on guard?"

"Er, yes I will, my lord."

"It's David," he smiled, "and I'm glad you accepted our invitation. Lianne needs a friend."

"Is she . . . ?"

"Mad?" A faint laugh left his lips and I was captivated by the languid allure of his voice. "I don't think so. A little strange perhaps, but we all have our strange moments, don't you agree?"

I did agree.

"Please consider this house your own. You are free to go anywhere you wish, but do be careful through these parts. Accidents have occurred before."

Sensing it was time for me to go, I asked him if he wanted to talk to me about anything else, but he shook his head. However, when I stood to leave, I saw his hand move ever so slightly.

"There is another thing . . . thank you for what you did at the beach. I couldn't bear the thought of the sea claiming her. You rescued her and led her to safety. Thank you . . . Daphne."

He turned around to hide his emotion and I quickly scrambled back to Lady Hartley's room. My heart beat wildly. I loved this house . . . the mystery . . . the people, even the air of tragedy. I didn't want to leave it.

Levering open the Moorish doors, I entered perhaps the loveliest chamber I'd ever seen. Full-size windows facing west encased by cascading sheer white curtains looked over the sea. A lively breeze rustled the swirling curtains, lapping against wooden floorboards where two multicolored Turkish rugs lay. A massive canopied four-poster dominated the room, also draped in sheer white, while two decorative archways formed doorways to other rooms. Out of one of these strolled Lady Hartley.

"Ah, there you are. Come with me."

Taken through the right archway, I found myself in a cozy antechamber. Beyond the armchairs and fireplace existed yet another door.

"Do sit down" was the command issued.

Still clutching my handbag, I obeyed, observing an open fashion magazine advertising a bridal gown on the circular marble coffee table.

"Won't be needing that now." Lady Hartley shut the magazine, relaxing into one of the armchairs. "So you're Gerald's girl . . . how interesting. What is your father up to these days?"

Expecting this, I gave her a brief account of his affairs. Lord David was right. She had a plan concerning me. Or rather, she had a plan involving my father, his fame, and his connections. I'd met many people like her before and saw the speculative glimmer flashing through her eyes.

"Care for a cup of tea? Will your family, your father, join you down here, do you think?"

I declined the tea. "I couldn't say, your ladyship. My father does all things unexpectedly. It's how he lives."

"Fascinating, fascinating." Gazing about the room, a sadness reflected in her face. "We don't receive many visitors down here. And now, with this present gloom surrounding us, I fear we shall became outcasts."

"Outcasts, my lady?"

"Oh, do call me Florence, or Flo if you wish, or Lady Flo if that's more comfortable. Yes, outcasts. We are too often alone. It is sad. Money is needed, you see, for the restoration. David is adamant. But sometimes I do so long for lively company—any company, in fact." Her eyes searched mine. "My daughter has taken a shine to you. She hardly ever takes a shine to anyone. Perhaps I can ask a favor of you? Would you invite your family down for a while? Any member is welcome here and the house is large enough. . . . We used to have so many parties, perhaps they can be persuaded for a weekend affair?"

When I didn't immediately answer, she quickly chirped, "I shall leave it to your discretion, for you may wish to spend some time with my daughter first. It's been a year or so since she's invited a friend to visit. The poor girl doesn't like too many people, you know. You, Daphne, are *special.*"

"Thank you, your ladyship," I replied. "I enjoy Miss Lianne's company very much and am pleased to visit."

Lady Hartley nodded, suddenly serious. "Oh, visit all you like. You will find Lianne very odd. You mustn't think we are all like that. I fear Lianne has inherited some of her father's quirks."

"How so, my lady?"

"Oh, he forgot things. His mind wandered . . . and he was fanciful. Lianne, I fear, is the same. You mustn't take any notice of what she says."

"No?"

"No." Lady Hartley looked at me directly. "For I must warn you, Lianne is exactly like her father. A consummate liar."

CHAPTER SIXTEEN

Leaving Lady Hartley's room, I paused by the huge doors.

An unusual serenity from a bygone era occupied the area—the sound of the ocean flickering down the cloister-style corridor; the aged, musty smell of the paneling; the silent portraits and statues peering at those trespassing below . . .

History enchanted the house. Closing my eyes, I imagined previous generations, each adorned in the costumes of their period—their lives, their loves, their secrets, their tragedies. A house, I strongly believe, is never complete without a past.

Indulging in the wondrous surroundings, I returned to the parts David warned me of. He had said I was free to venture out on my own, and I figured I had a little time before Lianne or Mrs. Trehearn noticed my absence.

Soft-footed, with only the faint creak of the floors underneath, I wandered by a tiny alcove of rooms, some furnished, some empty, some locked. Noting dusty white sheets, closed boxes and planks, I entered the closed-off section, which awaited renovation and was filled with forbidden temptation.

I stood at the base of the tower. The *cursed* tower. The circular stone structure mounted high, its levels sprouting half-rotting floors while an upper wind whipped an eerie cry. I thought it a splendid place for inspiration, if somewhat dangerous, but the danger only enhanced the appeal.

Seeing a way up through an adjacent stairwell, I crossed a leg over the forbidden cord.

"What are you doing? Don't you know it's dangerous here?"

Bewildered, I stopped.

Seeing Lianne's frown, I understood the reason for her peevish mood. She'd wanted to show me the house herself.

"Come, Daphne. Let us go to my room."

As the door slammed upon said room, I collapsed upon her bed and uttered a long sigh of relief. Lianne was a lovable girl, but so exhausting. Was she mad? Who could say?

Inspired, I lay there looking blankly at the ceiling. She followed suit, and together we lay united, staring and imagining, free to think of whatever infiltrated into our brains, free to daydream, free to do whatever our mood dictated.

As Lianne suddenly left the room, my daydream began with the body on the beach . . . Victoria.

The dead girl, the beauty destined to be mistress of the house. What secrets had she carried to her death? Circling her name in my memory, I mentally scribbled a large question mark beside it. Somewhere in the deep recesses of my mind, a new thought flashed for a future novel: a timid heroine, a dead mistress of a grand house, a mystery . . .

A noise outside the door ended my indulgent fantasies and, annoyed by the unexpected interruption, I crept toward the raised voices.

Mrs. Trehearn stood outside the door, arms akimbo, arguing with a red-faced Lianne.

"Trehearn! *Do as I say.* It's all arranged. She'll stay the night at Padthaway."

Stay the night at Padthaway!

"Now, we mustn't have tantrums in front of our guests, Miss Lianne," Mrs. Trehearn soothed. "You might frighten Miss Daphne away."

Lianne paused to reflect and I saw a hardiness in Mrs. Trehearn I hadn't noticed before. Her experience in handling Lianne showed, even though she eventually lost the battle.

"Old dragon." Lianne rolled her eyes, closing her bedroom door on Trehearn, and dismissing all of my protests as to why I couldn't stay the night. "She always does this when guests come to stay— putting them downstairs or in a room to 'watch' them. She doesn't trust anyone."

I learned Mrs. Trehearn had come to the house years ago as governess for both children. From governess to housekeeper . . . it was no minor elevation, and I wondered what Mrs. Trehearn truly thought of Victoria.

Two men arrived at the door, carting in a makeshift bed to Miss Lianne's room. My refusal again went unheard and as I thought of the myriad of splendid rooms downstairs, I wished Mrs. Trehearn *had* won, even if she intended to spy on me.

The difference between the two men was startling. I hadn't meant to stare, but I couldn't seem to help it. One dressed in overalls, the gardener obviously, had wild graying hair and wild eyes, and the other, a sleekly dressed dark-haired man, sported the confidence that came with flashy good looks and an arrogant nature.

"Ben the gardener and of course you'd remember Soames the cook from dinner?" Lianne said archly, amused by my stares.

"Soames," Lianne said, and grimaced, standing to her feet and pulling me along with her, "we'd like a fresh pot of tea and some jam scones brought up."

Soames dipped his head. "Yes, Miss Lianne."

"Oh, and some cream, too."

"Of course" came the jaunty response, and he nodded to me. "Welcome, Miss du Maurier. Do you take milk in your tea?"

"Er, no," I smiled.

After they left, I said I'd never seen such a debonair-looking cook.

"Mummy found him . . . he thinks a lot of himself."

Why? Did he aspire to become lord of the castle by marrying the lady everyone in the village despised?

It was a vastly curious mix, this household. A gloomy, mistrustful atmosphere prevailed and nothing echoed right. Where else did servants rise to marry lords, and governesses to housekeepers? Why did the family keep themselves so isolated?

The word *guilt* blazoned alongside the arriving scones and fresh strawberry jam.

I shall never forget that night at Padthaway, I, a stranger, dining with a family in grief and perhaps full of guilt.

The strangeness of the circumstances, the haunting beauty of the house and the silent, dimly lit lights led me further into its labyrinth of mystique.

Upon seeing a maid dusting a vase, I had asked the way to the dining room.

"I'll show ye the way, miss."

Grateful, I followed her along the newly carpeted maze, admiring the paintings and idiosyncrasies of old decor.

The magnificence only increased as we reached a set of half-ajar doors.

Lord David opened the door.

Shown into the opulent room bustling with an overindulgence of French gilded furniture, sweeping burgundy velvet drapes, and a silver table centerpiece of ambitious height and proportion, I made my apologies.

Lady Hartley waved it aside. "Do sit down, Daphne. Here, beside me."

Submitting to her directive, I concealed a faint smile for the aristocracy's adherence to protocol. Lady Hartley and I occupied one end of the table while Lord David and Lianne sat at the far opposite. We could scarcely see each other through the sprawling floral display.

I should not have concerned myself with my appearance and

selecting the appropriate outfit for a time of mourning, for Lady Hartley shimmered in purple satin and a string of pearls, an odd choice, thought I, for a solemn occasion.

We started with soup and I longed to hear music, or anything other than the ticking clock above the marble fireplace. Having already endured countless hours of drilling from Lady Hartley over "my connections," I experienced acute relief when Lord David intervened by giving a brief account of the house's history.

Listening to his voice lulled me into a dreamy fantasy. If ever a voice seduced, David Hartley's did so without preamble, intention, or device. All I could think was how he truly bore the death of his bride and child with such control. Did he mourn her? Did he love her? Did he . . . kill her?

"The funeral," Lady Hartley began after the servants cleared away the dishes, the unexpected phrase sending my fork scuttling across the table, "is arranged for Sunday. Vicar Nortby has dug a plot for Victoria in the local—"

"No." David slammed his fist on the table. "She will go in the crypt."

Lady Hartley calmly rested her hand on the table. "The family crypt, darling? What a gloomy place. I think she'd rather be next to her folk—"

A caustic laugh escaped David's lips. "*You'd* prefer her with her folk. It's what you wanted from the beginning, isn't it, Mother? Each person put in their station . . . even if that person would now have been my wife."

Throwing his napkin on the table, he abruptly left.

The clock ticked away.

I reached for another sip of wine. I hadn't truly considered the ramifications of being a guest at Padthaway during such a catastrophic time. Instead of humoring Lianne, I should have gone back to the cottage. I could only imagine what awaited me, with Ewe wanting to know how I fared with a nest of suspected murderers.

The room suddenly grew chilly. I reached for my wrap, but I had brought none, and failed to stop the shiver creeping up my spine.

"Please excuse my son's outburst, Daphne," Lady Hartley murmured. "He'll be over it in a month, mark my words. I know my own son, and he never *really* loved her. Oh, she had her charms about her. Even beauty. But brains or breeding? No, no, no."

Breeding, brains, and beauty. I carried her words away with me that night, my first night at the mansion on the cliffs. I felt the stirrings of a new idea, a story involving a woman of breeding, brains, and beauty.

CHAPTER SEVENTEEN

I woke early the next day.

I couldn't wait to continue my explorations of the house.

Lianne watched me as I sat at her dresser. Flicking through my toilette case that Ewe had sent for my stay, she behaved like a young, curious, and impertinent sister. Picking up powder puffs, examining jewelry, perfume, and hair accessories . . . poor girl. She ached for a friend.

It seemed she made no friend in Victoria.

The complexity of the victim intrigued me. How had a local-girl-cum-kitchen-maid trapped the lord of the house? Where had she and Lord David conducted their romance? How had it started and developed into a serious engagement?

Isolation must have helped cause this grand eventuality. I knew little of Lord David's movements, but he didn't seem to be the kind of man to be driving up to London every weekend or inviting large parties of friends down to his house.

Who *were* his friends? Did the family pursue *any* social acquaintances? If they were tight for money, how much did a small dinner cost? Or a lunch on the terrace?

I drew to the window to have a better look at the gardens leading down to the sea. The gardens were a narrow strip of sublime arrangement and radiant color intermingled with a series of stone statues of fish, quaint and charming, like the Romans used in the gladiator ring to count the laps. A grouping of weathered French country chairs and tables looked on, sadly neglected. I mentioned the shame of it to Lianne.

She did not join me at the window. "They used to have the grand parties out there—in the old days. Summer, especially. Flocks of them would come down from London and there'd be music, dancing, and champagne all night. The servants would sneak down to the gardener's shed and watch them."

"Why is it not used now?"

"Simple, really. My father shot himself there."

Old Lord Hartley, the consummate liar. I recalled what Lady Hartley had said of him and his daughter.

Why did he shoot himself? I longed to ask but prudence dictated I not continue a subject presumably distasteful to Lianne. She'd lost her father; I wouldn't know what to do if I lost mine.

I had the impression the death of Lord Hartley had occurred a long time ago, so perhaps Lianne never knew her father. From Lady Hartley's cool reference to her dead husband, it was clear the marriage had its troubles. But what marriage didn't?

Had his death propelled the family fortune downhill? I tried to think of the ramifications of a scandalous suicide on a private country estate. Lord Terrence Hartley hadn't been a nobody even if he had purchased his title, and there had to be a newspaper article about his passing somewhere.

The house felt different in the morning. Light guided our feet down the carpeted stairs devoid of night's shadowy distrust. I loved the breakfast parlor, a closed-in conservatory, one side of windows facing the front drive while the opposing French doors looked over the inner courtyard. Bathed in light, surrounded by nature's soothing greens, reds, yellows, and pinks, I drank in the sweetness, unwilling to ever leave.

Lianne and I breakfasted alone—Lord David having arisen at six for his daily ride, then breakfasting alone in his study or library afterward. Lady Hartley rarely ventured out of her rooms before ten.

"And Victoria?" I asked of her morning ritual.

Lianne looked at me slyly. "She liked to have her tea and toast in the courtyard, served by Soames."

The way she said "served by Soames" caused me to raise a brow. Victoria would have worked under Soames until she became the fiancée to the lord of the house. It was an interesting plethora of events. "Where did your mother find this Soames?"

"On one of her cruises. She bribed him to come here."

"Bribed?"

"Soames likes the glamour life. Before the cruise ship, he worked for a duchess in London, and before that at a famous painter's house in Paris."

I asked which painter, thinking I might know him considering I'd spent a substantial part of my schooling in Paris.

Lianne dropped her spoon. "*You* went to school in Paris? What was it like?"

"Difficult and pleasant. The French are very strict but I soon learned their ways and became a bit Parisian." A grin lurked at the corners of my mouth. "And the French men are charming experts. I suppose this is where your Mr. Soames learned his trade?"

"Soames," Lianne sniffed. "I don't find him that handsome *or* charming. Don't know what they see in him. He's just a cook."

An *exalted* cook. I took the "they" to be Victoria, Lady Hartley, and other women of the neighborhood. "I find it odd such a man works here when it's so . . ."

"Isolated?" Lianne taunted. "Oh don't worry about him. He finds *ample* amusement for himself." A mocking undercurrent lurked in her voice.

"I'll show you the whole house today," Lianne promised, "even the *forbidden* quarters, but we'll have to time it right. There are eyes everywhere here."

"Mrs. Trehearn?"

"Among others."

Yes, I'd sensed that, too. One had a premonition of being watched every second, each movement calculated, weighed, and judged.

Mrs. Trehearn's frequent patrols of the house betrayed her obsession with it. Even when Lianne and I left the room, I half expected to see her skirts flouncing around a corner or to meet that steely gaze at a turn. "Mrs. Trehearn mentioned something about the tower being cursed?"

"Yes." Lianne skipped on ahead. "It's the best part of the house." She stopped to smile. "You think we're odd, don't you? Morbid? Unlike your fancy city friends?"

"I am prone to morbidness," I shot back. "In varying degrees, we all are fascinated by legend, superstition, and—"

"Death?" She grimaced, legging over a restrictive rope farther down the corridor. "It'll be great when this is fixed up, but somehow I prefer it how it is."

So did I. Entranced, I moved toward the base of the spiraled stairs, ready to climb this splendid ruin. I imagined I were Princess Elizabeth, a captive of the tower. . . .

"Not that way, silly."

Lianne pulled me back with such force I stumbled.

"It's dangerous."

Danger bred through this household like a disease. How exciting, for this house provided more than a lush canvas for my book. I had a real mystery to solve, a place to explore, characters to unravel, and somewhere during my sojourn here, I hoped to write something worthy of publication, something Aunt Billy, my sternest critic, would approve of.

Around the corner, Lianne searched the paneling with her fingers. Glancing about for intruders or a patrolling Mrs. Trehearn, she pressed a slight knob imbedded in the wood and the panel creaked open.

A secret door. "I love this place!"

"Shhh!" She drew me inside. "We mustn't let anyone see us. Last time a maid stumbled up here, she fell."

Squinting, I peered up at the faint light ahead. "To her death?"

"Not her, but others have."

"Others? How many others?" I must have voiced.

Lianne answered, her tone curiously ambivalent. "Oh, one or two. They're not supposed to know about it. Only the family. That's what they get for snooping about. They think my brother's not serious about the danger of the old parts. Nor do they heed the warning."

"The curse?"

"The first lord imprisoned a monk in the tower. Shut him up and left him to rot—his bones lie around here somewhere. But before he died, he damned the place and scratched into the wall: *Cavete intus serpentem est.* It's Latin and it means 'Beware within a serpent there is.' Apparently, 'twas his own cousin who threw him in here, so I guess the warning is clear."

Cavete intus serpentem est.

How profound. The serpent lurking beneath the surface, the unknown Judas, was often of one's own family or intimate connections. The Judas perhaps murdered his scholarly cousin for this house.

Yes, people murdered for money and houses. In fact, wills and inheritances always complicated matters, tearing apart families and inciting desperation and violence. Reflecting upon it, I wondered what I'd do given the temptation.

The subject intrigued me. What induced one to kill? It depended on character, emotion, a deep motivation lurking under the surface, an emotion that, if kindled, proved fatal. Had such elements driven Victoria to her death? "Did Victoria ever come here?"

"Yes." Lianne rolled her eyes. "David showed her. I followed them once, heard her giggling up the stairs."

I smiled. What a glorious idea for a romantic date, exploring an old house with its darkened corridors, endless rooms, and enchanting gardens.

Conquering the winding upward stairs, we reached the turret landing. Having seen the tower from Lianne's room, the gothic slatted windows and the open parapet, the inside did not disappoint. Now standing ready for my own exploration, I drew closer to the bright scarlet rope.

"It's all that remains of the old castle," Lianne whispered, caressing the stone with her fingers. "This is next to be demolished." Lianne peered over the edge. "It's dangerous to rebuild, but Davie is determined. He wants it as it was: a lord's solar."

A bedroom in the medieval style. I suppressed a sigh. How this man resonated with my soul!

"Come see the top level." Lianne darted ahead. "It's finished."

The top level proved another circular room, transformed into a modern-day retreat. Light from the dome-shaped slatted windows illuminated restful day lounges hugging the walls, but it was the room's centerpiece that attracted me: an exotic garden bearing herbs and rare flowers. I paused to inhale an unusually shaped pink and white orchid.

"Careful!" Lianne wrenched me back. "Some are poisonous. You might get a reaction."

Here lurked an abundance of poison. Withdrawing to a safe distance, I casually mentioned the poison they'd found in Victoria.

"Oh, the police have been here to check," she shrugged. "They didn't find anything, not even in Mrs. T's, and she has *everything*."

"Oh? Where?"

"In the greenhouse. Trehearn uses her plants for her medicines and sells them to the locals. They come to her for all kinds of complaints."

It appeared I had misjudged the wintry Mrs. Trehearn. A multifarious personality of hidden depth, a woman who prized her job above all else. "Your mother permits this, without a price?"

"Oh, they share the money," Lianne didn't seem to mind my rude question.

So I continued. "And are your mother and Mrs. Trehearn special friends?"

Inspecting a tiny green plant from a cautious distance, Lianne snorted. "Friends! Sometimes I think they hate each other, but they've got an odd relationship. Mother relies upon her. Says she can't do without her 'talents.'"

"Talents? Do such talents include murder?" I said it, half jokingly, half in deadly earnest.

"No, silly, it's Trehearn's sleeping tonic she makes up for Mummy."

Sleeping tonics. Hmm, so I had my answer and yet I wasn't satisfied. Something in the way Lianne mouthed "talents" led me to believe more lurked beneath Mrs. Trehearn's talent for plants, poisons, and the like. If she knew the police were coming, any trace of the poison would have disappeared.

And did Trehearn, like I, suspect a member of the family? Having unknowingly supplied the poison and then finding it missing, did she hide any evidence to protect her and her employers?

CHAPTER EIGHTEEN

I agreed to stay with Lianne at Padthaway until two.

"Two! But we've only done half the house and I've so much to show you. You can stay again tonight. Old Ewe Sinclaire won't mind. We can send a note around to her—"

"No," I said firmly. "I am staying at the cottage." I did not say *my parents would never permit me to stay beneath the roof of suspected murderers for an extended stay.* Saint Christopher! Any female of marriageable age being in residence here would be written about in the papers and they'd assume—

I swallowed. However unjust and without any foundation, they'd assume Lord David and I—

"Let's see Jenny."

Pulled across the foyer, I asked where she lived.

Lianne giggled. "Here, of course. I love Jenny."

Her soft smile indicated the depth of their relationship and I understood. Children of aristocratic households were often left to nannies, nurses, governesses, and boarding schools. I had been fortunate with my own family. Perhaps because they dabbled so much in the theatrical arts, the world of literature and politics, with all of its social pursuits, had been open to me.

Jenny Pollock, I learned on the way to the servant's quarters, was your typical part-of-the-furniture employee. She'd started off as a nursery maid when Lord David was born and grew to the rank of head nurse over the years. Never having married, her "babies" were everything to her, and I saw this reflected in her face when she greeted Lianne.

She was a stout woman, forty or thereabouts, pleasant-looking with rosy cheeks and a merry outlook. Abandoning her rocking chair and knitting, she drew us into her cozy parlor overlooking a part of the garden and went to switch on the kettle.

"So ye're the du Maurier lass." Jenny waddled back into her sitting room, fluffing cushions and undertaking to make a new guest comfortable and welcome. "Very nice ye've been to my Lee Lee . . . nasty business all that. Murder, they think."

Chattering on, she disappeared to pour our tea. "Poor lass. I'm glad that fuddy inspector ain't lettin' 'em off. Somebody done her in, I say. Pretty girl like that, set to marry my David. I ask ye. Who'd go and kill themselves when she had so much to live for? A baby, mind!"

Expressing shock and outrage, tinged with a large degree of sorrow, Jenny soon returned with a tea tray bearing spiced lemon biscuits that she had baked herself.

"Didn't like 'er at first when she came here. I call such pretty girls 'players.' And Vicky was cruel to my Lee Lee after catchin' my David's eye. I warned him, but he wouldn't listen. Smitten, he were. Then Vicky comes here to get me on her side. But I knew her game and she didn't like me warnin' me boy."

"I can imagine not," I said, catching Lianne's sneer across the room. I wondered how much truth lived in Jenny's assessment. Was Victoria truly cruel to Lianne? Or perhaps in exercising her new role, Victoria's firmness didn't appeal to Lianne and such firmness translated to cruelty in Jenny's eyes. The servants would know. I'd have to question those girls when I saw them again.

Frowning, Jenny Pollock resumed her rocking chair, tea in hand. "I told Lee Lee to be nice to her when I saw David were serious. Vicky kept coming here. She wanted my approval. Or David did. I soon saw she just carried on to get attention. The pretty ones often do. She knew she'd have a hard fight to get past her ladyship."

"She did it deliberately," Lianne said, munching on her biscuit. "To get at me. She was a player, like you said. She enjoyed causing trouble."

The resentful younger sister, I thought. Though I didn't have a brother, I appreciated Lianne's dilemma. A beloved older brother and a hated girlfriend who commandeered his affection and time, and *flaunted* it.

Jenny sighed. "I just want all my babies to be happy. When I knew it were serious with Vicky," she lowered her voice for emphasis, "I opened me heart to 'er. She was really a nice lass under all that and she did *try* with my Lee Lee—"

"Only because you told her to," Lianne interrupted. "She would've gone on tormenting me if David didn't love you as he does."

Twisting to me, Lianne's smile, upon mentioning her brother, softened. "Jenny's more than a nurse to us. She's a true mummy. It was she who dried our tears and stayed up with us when we were sick. My *real* mother would never do those things."

A common complaint in many aristocratic households. The children were wanted for appearances, to carry on the family name; the parents also followed a code, a code of no affection in some cases, and I pitied Lianne and David. But any warmth and security they'd missed with their parents they'd certainly gained with Jenny. "So you believe Victoria may have been murdered, Mrs. Pollock?"

Jenny blushed. "I ain't no Mrs. and Jenny's me name. Murder . . . yes, I say it's that."

"But *who*? And why?"

Jenny's lips sealed. "I don't like to say but I've got me suspicions."

"She thinks Mummy did it," Lianne blurted out.

Jenny expressed a natural, motherly concern. "All I wish is that it doesn't go bad for my Davie. He don't need the stress, poor lad."

"But how can it go bad for him unless he did it? Why would he want to kill his own bride and child?"

"There are those who hate him and will say anything. That Connan Bastion, for one, Vicky's brother. He was always after money, and when Lord David put his foot down, Connan didn't like it. Then his sister winds up dead. No, no, no, my Davie's innocent. I'd stake my life on it. It's the others I ain't so sure about."

"The others?"

"Her ladyship, Mrs. T, and Soames. I can never quite tell what Soames is doin' or thinkin', and I don't like it. Nor did I like how friendly he and Victoria were."

I smiled at the overtalkative Jenny and said how she reminded me of Ewe Sinclaire.

"Don't know Ewe but heard of her as I'm housebound these days. Oh," she said, patting my hand, "I'm so glad you've come to visit. You must come and have lots of cups of tea with me now, won't ye?"

I promised to do so.

"She's lovely," I said to Lianne on the way out. "But how can she stay here if she and your mother don't get along?"

"Oh, they put up with each other, and Jenny's been here so long, Mother'll never get rid of her. Davie wouldn't let her, anyway. I suppose you've heard Mother doesn't get on with many people, only those whom she wants to impress."

It interested me that a woman so acutely aware of her own prominence had married so far beneath her. She had been an earl's daughter married to an obscure lord in possession of only one house. Though on seeing more of the house, I understood the attraction. If the children were anything to judge by, Lord Hartley must have presented a dashing image to the young impressionable debutante now mistress of the house.

Mrs. Trehearn summoned us for luncheon. With such a cold, unreadable face, she looked the kind to mix poisons in the dark hours of the night.

We were directed to the Green Salon, a charming airy room of Lady Hartley's dominion, tastefully decorated with a Victorian oval table and drapes and furnishings in swirling cream and sage greens. A roving green ivy wallpaper covered the walls, the gentle hue matching the twin divans perched under three landscape watercolor paintings.

"I painted those," Lady Hartley beamed. "I consider it a rare accomplishment. Do you paint, Daphne?"

"No, I write."

"Oh, how *interesting*. You'll find much here to amuse the mind, won't you? David has mentioned your passion for the abbey records."

The way she said "passion" sent my face aflame, the blush deepening as her spidery eyes assessed me, her mouth poised in some kind of private amusement. I saw in that moment the hardness of a murderer, and it certainly added weight to Jenny's suspicions.

I loved the room and the circular table set out for luncheon with its pristine white cloth and sparkling silver. I noticed the table was set for four and hoped it meant David would be joining us. The likelihood aroused a quick flutter of the heart, and to silence it, I wandered across the room to examine the table of photographs.

"My father, the late earl." Lady Hartley marched to my side, pointing to the first silver frame. "David gets his height from him."

She was right. The late earl stood outside his mansion in hunting gear, his proud, strong features mirroring her own.

"And this is my mother. . . ."

I nodded politely to the line-up of her family, seeing no resemblance for Lianne and David until at last we came to the photograph I wanted to see: the late Lord Hartley. The madman who'd shot himself.

It was a wedding photograph: Lady Hartley, the beautiful, young, radiant bride, haughty and aloof; and beside her, a David.

My heart stopped.

"Yes," Lady Hartley smiled. "The likeness is amazing, isn't it?"

On closer inspection, I located a few minor differences. David's father had a sharper jawline and smaller eyes, and a faint cleft in the center of his chin. Picking up the photograph beside it, a recent one of David and Lianne, I compared the likenesses.

Lianne had inherited her father's eyes and something of his expression.

"I hope she's not boring you with the family history, Miss du Maurier," drifted a voice from behind.

Lord David's composed entrance, the grace of his poise and attire, left me feeling quite numb. I didn't know what to make of him, or what to think of him. Do I consider him an acquaintance, a friend, or a murderer? Should I even be here, conversing with any of these people? I wondered.

Shaking, I promptly set the photograph down, smoothened my skirt, suddenly conscious of my hair and how I looked in my day ensemble and nondescript mauve blouse.

"You must be famished." Lady Hartley directed us to the table by ringing the bell.

I sat down in a daze, not feeling hungry in the slightest. "I cannot believe the resemblance between you and your father, my lord," I began, attempting a normal conversation.

Glancing at the photograph, his face turned gray and his mouth tightened. I kicked myself under the table. I shouldn't have mentioned his father.

"Where's the photograph of Victoria?"

"I moved it," Lady Hartley answered, instructing the maid to fill three glasses of wine and a juice for Lianne.

Waiting until the maid left, David frowned. "You had no right to do that."

Shrugging, Lady Hartley reached for her glass. I did the same, feeling the tension between them.

"Why keep it there? Why torment yourself?"

"It ought to go back, Mother, and you know it."

"Oh." Lady Hartley swallowed her wine. "I'll put it back if you insist, but I don't see—"

"Stop it, please," Lianne pleaded. "You're making Daphne uncomfortable."

I felt uncomfortable to the extreme. To help the situation, I sipped a little more wine and Lianne asked me about my father's theater business. During the serving and consummation of lunch, I babbled on, assisted by the crisp white wine, revealing the secret of Papa's next upcoming play for I didn't know what else to say. The theater was a safe subject and it seemed to ease all the tensions.

However, an unpleasant side effect loomed. It reminded me of the one incident in my past where I'd been on holiday with Fernande, my French teacher and dearest friend, and she'd deliberately refilled my wineglass again and again so I should learn a lesson. Violently ill that night and the following day, I certainly did learn my lesson, and feeling flushed for a second time, I experienced all the familiar warning signs.

After my third glass, my stomach began to gurgle. The mix of nervousness and wine was a nefarious combination, and I glanced around, frantic for an escape route.

"I've a sudden urge to stretch my legs," David declared, leaving his seat. "Would you join me for a stroll outside, Miss du Maurier?"

"Oh, yes." I shot to my feet, catching Lady Hartley tapping Lianne's hand to let us go alone. "But I must be back at the cottage by two."

"Two o'clock, you shall be," he promised.

"Thank you," I whispered once outside the room and speeding toward fresh air. "Another moment and I . . ."

"I know," David pressed my hand. "How's the stomach and the head?"

"Fine now," I replied, smiling. "The wine was nice, though."

"Yes, it was, and I thank you. I don't know how we manage sometimes. What is there to talk about but—"

His voice snapped off and silence accompanied us the remainder of the way. I didn't mind. My spinning head demanded I just focus on walking and controlling my swirling stomach so as not to make another embarrassing scene in front of David.

Summoning a strength of will I did not feel, I made it to the little labyrinth garden at the rear of the conservatory where David promptly steered me to a seat. Watching me clinging to the edge, a faint smile on his lips, he joined me, his face full of concern.

"Would you like some water?"

I nodded, and he went. I thought how kind and considerate he was, how lucky Victoria was to have secured such a fine man, in spite of, I dared to add, the encumbrance of having a mother-in-law like Lady Hartley.

Somewhat revived by the water and fresh air, Lord David insisted on driving me home and I conceded.

He brought the car around to the front of the house, and I caught a glimpse of Mrs. Trehearn's stony face watching us.

I shivered.

"Don't be frightened of old Mrs. T," David joked as we followed the circular drive and passed through the gates. "She's part of the furniture here, as is Jenny. You met Jenny? You talked to her?"

"Yes, my lord."

He crooked his finger at me. "It's David. And we love our Jenny very much, that's why she's still here. Part Lianne's nurse, part live-in family, yet not family. You understand?"

I said I did. We had many nurses and governesses we grew close to during childhood years.

"You'll be thinking my sister's too old for a nurse, but Lianne is fragile. She's so desperate for a friend, too, sometimes she becomes a little overeager, and I wouldn't want you to end up despising her."

"I wouldn't. My sisters and I have very different personalities, yet we get along."

He smiled. "Your father sounds very interesting. I'm trying to imagine him in his *Phantom of the Opera* costume."

"Yes," I laughed. "He makes a habit of surprising us."

We started up the village lane and I cringed upon seeing Mrs. Penmark, the baker's wife, recognizing me in Lord David's car. Oh! What will they make of that now? I feared.

It didn't seem to bother Lord David. He drove me up as far as possible, wished me well, and invited me to resume our tour of Rothmarten Abbey. He asked me my intentions regarding the abbey and I replied with honesty.

He nodded gravely. "You must allow me to assist you. There are lost scrolls there, you know, somewhere hidden. I think old Dorcas knows where they are, or at least their vicinity, but she fears if they come out in the wrong hands, they'll disappear or be taken from the abbey. The abbey, you see, was entrusted with these records, brought to Cornwall by the crusaders."

I didn't want the journey to end. "Thank you, my lord."

He opened the door. "It's David, remember."

CHAPTER NINETEEN

Slipping out of bed the next morning, I washed and perused my wardrobe for something suitable to wear on our excursion to the abbey. I wanted to make an impression. Selecting a simple elegant blue dress, I added a silver locket my father had given me and pinned two sides of my hair. There was no time to apply curlers or to color my lips, and besides, I felt it was a little too early to be coloring my lips under the circumstances. I didn't want to be viewed as making a special effort for David.

Lianne came to the door to fetch me.

"Oh, hello, dear," Ewe chimed, popping her head around the corner.

Lianne, smartly dressed, acknowledged the greeting with a curt nod. I suppose she considered Ewe beneath her and followed the example set by her mother. One did not associate with lowly village folk.

It felt a little odd to make a day excursion when death and murder and suspicion occupied the whole town.

"Morning," David said. "Have to stop by the Goring farm on the way, if you don't mind?"

I shrugged obligingly.

"How is your brother, really?" I asked Lianne when he slipped out of the car.

Her eyes lowered, and her lips quibbled. "I saw him wiping his eyes this morning. They were red. Poor Davie. I never liked her, but he was going to marry her and have his baby."

"Did you ever meet Victoria's mother?"

"She came to the house once or twice." Wrinkling her nose, Lianne tried to copy the way I'd pinned the clip in my hair. "I saw her arrive in the car wearing her Sunday best with her silly little velvet hat. She came to make a point."

"Victoria asked her over?"

"Yes, it was a plan between them. Oh, I can't do this!"

Taking the lovely enameled flower-comb from her hand, I completed the task. "What kind of plan?"

"Victoria took her to the *drawing* room, the room where Mother always goes to give Soames the menu list for the day."

I failed to see the significance.

"She took her there," Lianne continued, eyes wide, "*knowing* Mummy sat there between ten and eleven. Mother prefers to take her morning callers in the drawing room. Victoria knew that, too."

It was as I had thought. Victoria had exerted her new authority and set a future precedent. "So what happened?"

"I didn't see, but I heard about it afterward."

"From Mrs. Trehearn?"

"No. From the kitchen."

The kitchen. I should have expected it. Where else does one go to learn household gossip?

David returned, and judging from the expression on his face, he was not too happy. Something had upset him inside the Goring farm. Something to do with Victoria, I wondered? The Bastions lived closest to the Goring farm, on the outskirts of the village. I saw the cottage on the way. The curtains were still drawn, no hint of life evident, the garden untended, the cottage and its grieving inhabitants shut off from the world.

As a mother, Mrs. Bastion would fight the Hartleys, but what of her son, Connan? I ached to ask Lianne about him.

The abbess expected us and invited us to her study first.

"The lost scrolls," Lord David teased. "Surely Miss du Maurier's hands are safe enough to compose and deliver its exposé?"

I could see the lost scrolls had been a contentious issue between them for some time.

"As I've said before, my lord, the scrolls are not for public consumption. And you know the reason why."

"Treasure hunters," Lord David grinned at me. "Concealed within all the philosophic drivel there's the promise of riches and maps."

"If word got out," the abbess went on, "it would ruin our peace here. The Hartley family are protectors, as am I, and despite, my lord, your mother's continuous attempts to see them 'only for a moment,' I cannot release them to any hands, safe or otherwise."

"I understand completely," I replied, "and I'd do the same thing in your position. The lure of greed breeds trouble and death."

As I uttered the words, I thought of Lady Hartley. A greedy woman.

I suddenly glanced at Lord David. Until the matter of Victoria's death was settled, he, too, was not safe. Jenny Pollock thought so and had spoken of it. "Lord Davie has his enemies . . ."

A desperate enemy might frame someone for murder.

Those who knew him swore to his innocence.

And those who hated him, had they framed him for murder?

Later, as I strolled through the village, I came upon the Bastion home. The curtains remained drawn at the tiny cottage.

I wanted to offer my condolences and marched up to the front door.

And lost the courage to knock.

Instead, I composed a note.

I said nothing of this to Ewe, as I had my own reservations. Who was I, after all, a stranger in town, to send a card of sympathy?

However, I *had* discovered the body with Lianne, I reminded myself, screwing up the fifth draft and settling upon the following:

> *September 25, 1921*
> *Dear Mrs. Bastion and Family,*
> *I wish to express my deepest sympathies on the*
> *unexpected death of your daughter, Victoria.*
>
> > *As you are aware, I am a stranger to the area and*
> > *regret to have caused you pain by my unplanned*
> > *involvement.*
> >
> > *If there is anything I can do to help, please let me*
> > *know.*
>
> > > *Yours sincerely,*
> > > *Daphne du Maurier*

I kept seeing Victoria's mother, her wizened, crowlike face, and her finger cranked at me, yelling *"You'll not be my daughter's replacement. Not now, not ever. My Vicky were murdered. Someone didn't want her bein' Lady Hartley."*

I ached to speak with Mrs. Bastion myself, purely for clues, I justified, dropping the sealed envelope into the Bastion letterbox. Mrs. Bastion hated me because she feared I'd replace her daughter. I wondered what Connan believed.

"Whatever ill-feeling exists," I said to Ewe and Mrs. Penmark over a fresh pot of tea, "David Hartley will honor his word and keep Connan in employ. So, he works on one of the Hartley boats?"

"Has done since he dropped out of school," Mrs. Penmark nodded. "A clever lad with his hands, but his brain don't work too good."

"Good-looking and dumb," Ewe seconded. "Victoria had the brains in that family. She was the only one to finish school."

"You forget the young ones," Mrs. Penmark corrected. "They miss a lot of school, but it's too early to judge yet."

I pictured Mrs. Bastion's days, inside her cottage, stranded with her children, entirely reliant upon Connan's wage. What a blessing, a dream it must have been, when her daughter announced her engagement to Lord David! Mrs. Bastion must have thought her future secure. "Is the Bastion cottage rented from the Hartleys?"

"No, a private lease. Landlord Tims." Ewe searched the vast resource of her memory. "They're related in some way. I think the cottage rent is 'reduced.'"

"Do you know if Mrs. Bastion had aspirations of moving into Padthaway?"

"No doubt she did!" Mrs. Penmark cried. "And her ladyship wouldn't 'ave a jot of that. Low-class fisher's wife and her brats runnin' through the manor. Oh, no, no, no. It's she who did it, I reckon. For if our Vicky were pregnant, she might have wanted her mother with her, to help raise the bub, the Hartley *heir,* mind, and a wife has a way of turnin' her husband's head."

"Lord David, war between mother and wife," Ewe said, and whistled. "I don't envy him. S'pose that's all ended now, now that she's dead."

Those final words sent an eerie shiver through me. How convenient it was for Lady Hartley that Victoria had died when she did, *before* the wedding. Surely she wouldn't have murdered her own grandchild?

"There's no reason to suspect Victoria carried someone else's child, is there?" I dared to pose the unthinkable to Ewe that night.

Draining water from the boiled vegetables, Ewe lifted her shoulders. "She had plenty after her, you just ask Miss Osborn. Here, and in town, from what I've heard. Used to work at some fancy club, too. And ye didn't hear it from me, but I'll bet there were something goin' on at some stage between that Mr. Soames and Vicky Bastion. How else do ye think she got the job!"

"Yes, Jenny Pollock said she didn't like how they were 'very close.'"

"Well, one thing is certain. He wouldn't like her throwin' him over for Lord David."

No, I agreed silently, recalling Sir Edward's asking me if I thought Victoria a girl of "relaxed morals."

I reflected that Victoria and I, two girls of similar age, from differing stations in life and times had changed since the Great War. We no longer lived in the Victorian age of strictures, and engaged couples often enjoyed a sexual relationship before marriage. To the world it appeared to not be the case, yet I'd known of at least two couples who met discreetly in town prior to the wedding day.

"Victoria's room at the house . . ." I murmured under my breath. "Close to Lord David's? Did she sneak into his room at night?"

"What are you muttering about?" Ewe burst out of her bedroom, hunting for her reading spectacles. Helping her search the room, I soon found them precariously lingering under a cushion. "Good thing someone didn't sit on it," I smiled, and asked if she had any visitors today.

"Not today," she replied mysteriously. "But on Sunday, we will. A *special* visitor."

"Oh? Who?"

"You'll have to wait and see, won't ye?" Ewe smarted. "I did have Saturdee in mind first but that's the funeral, so I changed it."

"And our visitor is aware of this change?"

"Indeed, he is. And a visitor ye father would approve of."

"Oh no." I rolled my eyes. "Don't tell me you've invited Timothy Carathers! I can't abide him. I won't be here. I shall go to Padthaway."

"Not him," Ewe gave me her deepest frown of disapproval. "Tho' he'd be a good match for ye. Richest in the county but for . . ."

Her words trailed off. "Richest in the county but for Lord David Hartley," I finished for her. "The Lord David Hartley suspected of murdering his bride."

"The very one." Ewe nodded. "And don't ye be forgettin' it."

Easier said than done.

I had no compunction on using the term in my journal.

I tried to imagine myself in Sir Edward's shoes, as a police inspector. Would I blanch at horrific sights of bodies? What kind of methods did he employ to catch a killer?

"Oh, he is very capable."

I bumped into Miss Perony on her way to start morning class at the school.

"*More* than capable," she reiterated, "and I now have utmost confidence that he will solve this dreadful, dreadful affair. He has to, for we are all watching and waiting for the right turnout."

I noted she did not use the words *murder* or *mystery*.

"I'm glad we've run into each other like this, Daphne. It saves me a visit as I have a message for you from Mrs. Bastion."

"Oh? I didn't expect—"

"Nor did I, when she told me," Miss Perony confessed. "She wishes you to visit her tomorrow afternoon."

Tomorrow was the day before the funeral.

"Yes . . . it's the day before the funeral. Perhaps you could offer some assistance?"

Yes, I blushed. Perhaps I could. But what?

"Good-day, Daphne."

"Good-day, Miss Perony."

I had to add the "miss," for a schoolteacher demanded it, out of habit, I assumed. "Every person has a habit," I said to myself on my morning walk. "Victims and killers."

I wandered far into the village hills, past the old church where the funeral would take place on Saturday. I envisaged a frazzled Vicar Nortby preparing the service. Did he secretly object to giving a service to an unwed mother? Was he nervous as to the publicity the event would attract? Cameramen, newspapermen, and policemen were sure to swarm the town.

The early-morning light flickered on the horizon, across a dazzling sea, and within minutes, my feet entered the grounds of Padthaway. I intended to slip into the gardens by the house—

undetected, if possible. Abandoning the path, I opted for the opposite route, a southern one of unchartered territory. I enjoyed nothing more than my early-morning or late-evening walks, alone, where I could indulge the senses and dream away to my heart's content.

Passing the gateway to the established Padthaway gardens, I saw a dog sniffing in the bushes, a great hairy beast of a dog, and delighted, I went to play with him.

"What's your name then? Fred? Rufus?"

"It's Jasper."

A large head loomed up out of the bushes and I recognized Ben, the gardener, who'd carried my makeshift bed into Lianne's room with Soames.

His eyes bored into mine, blank, motionless. "It's Jasper," he repeated.

"Ah, Jasper." I bent down to pat the dog, giving him a good rub on his tummy before toying with his ears. "I had a dog named Jock once. Jasper looks as if he needs a bath, though."

Ben stared at me, his crazed eyes trying to place me. "I've seen ye before . . ."

"In Miss Lianne's room," I reminded him. "You brought the bed up. My name's Daphne. What's yours?"

He didn't seem to register any of my words and even when I waved good-bye, he still stared after me, wooden, lifeless.

"What an odd fellow," I remarked to the wind, thinking it kind of Lord David to keep him on. Mad old Ben looked as if he'd lived his whole life at Padthaway and the gardens were his life, his domain.

Since I'd encountered Ben, I slipped out through the back gate to embrace the enchantment of Cornwall: its coastline, wildflowers burgeoning across its jagged proportions.

"Whoa! Steady, boy!"

Dazed, I confronted the sudden galloping intruder.

Man and horse, Lord David steadying his snorting, muscular black beast, reining him in hard. "Hallo there. Sorry, we didn't see you."

"Nor did I," I managed, gulping at the fear of a near-death collision. I might have been trampled under by those powerful legs.

"Do you ride, Daphne?"

I said that I did.

"So you're not afraid of horses?"

"Certainly not."

To prove it, I calmed the rapid-breathing beast with a few words of my own.

He smiled. "You're privileged. He likes you. Do you prefer walking to riding?"

"Yes," I replied, "it requires less effort."

He dismounted. "Then may I walk with you for a while?"

I nodded. I couldn't seem to do anything else.

"I'm so glad we've met like this," he murmured. "Out here . . . on the coast . . . nothing matters. That's the most important lesson we can learn in life: nothing matters."

Not even murder? "What about Victoria?"

I didn't mean to, but the question just spilled out of my mouth.

"I'm sorry," I whispered, keeping my gaze focused on the ground. "That was thoughtless of me, but I do care about you and Lianne. I can only imagine how terrible it must be."

The wind whipped through his hair and he nodded, his face taut and unreadable.

I kicked myself for my tactless comment.

We walked on in companionable silence, inhaling the fresh air, savoring the wayward landscape, acknowledging the cry of the seagulls above and the echo of the wind raging over the grassy headland. There was no place on earth quite like here, I thought, and I sensed my future lay here, somewhere within this wild, primitive countryside.

"Miss du Maurier, Daphne, I need to ask a favor of you."

We paused a few feet away from the edge of the cliff. I shuddered, looking over, seeing the image of Victoria hurtling to her death. Had she been pushed or had she jumped? Or neither? Had someone laid her below on the beach to confuse the cause of death?

"Daphne?"

Lord David's low voice sent further chills up my spine.

"Daphne . . . Miss du Maurier. If anything should ever happen to me, I'd like you to be a friend to Lianne, someone she can turn to in times of trouble. I know this is a large favor to ask and one you may find odd considering our brief acquaintance, but I trust you."

"O-Oh," I stammered, "yes, of course, I shall do as you ask, but it is no favor."

"That's nice of you to say so. She's a difficult girl, but she's my sister and Mother cannot always be counted upon to look after her best interests."

"She's not alone. She has Jenny . . . and me as a friend, if she wants. I give you my word."

He thanked me and I thought I glimpsed an acute sense of relief flicker across his face. Did he fear tomorrow? Did he fear he'd be charged with the murder and taken away after the funeral?

I watched him mount his horse and ride away.

CHAPTER TWENTY

"What does one really know of ricin?"

"Whoever examined the body is sure to know a thing or two." Ewe shrugged. Her sarcasm had heightened throughout the day.

"You're not nervous about this important visitor you're having on Sunday?"

Offended, she snapped down the special napkins she'd washed and pressed and was now in the process of folding just so. "Do I *look* nervous?"

"Yes!" I laughed, taking the napkins from her. "Let me show you. This is something worthwhile I learned in my girlhood. Not that I had a *choice,* since Mother forced us. She has great aspirations of us becoming grand hostesses one day."

While I folded the napkins and set them out on the table already prepared for Sunday, I relayed how I'd chanced upon David Hartley upon my walk.

"Oh, dearie! This doesn't bode well."

I studied Ewe's crestfallen face. She'd taken the place of parent in the absence of my parents and didn't think it wise for me to associate too closely with the Hartley family. Nor did I, if I were to judge objectively.

"Well? What did he say? What did he do?"

"He didn't *do* anything. He walked with me a little . . . and asked that if something should happen to him, would I treat Lianne kindly, as a friend."

Ewe deliberated. "Humph. So he thinks he's going to hang for it."

"Hang for what? He *didn't* do it. I think he's been framed. Framed by an enemy, someone who wanted to even up the score, so to speak."

"I'd wager he didn't do it either." Sinking into her most cozy armchair in the parlor, Ewe pondered Lord David's dire situation. "I mean, he's the obvious suspect. Everyone will think it must be him. I've lived in this village my whole life; I know the Hartleys through and through, and David Hartley is no killer. No, no, no, there is foul play here. Someone is out to 'get even.' And I think . . ."

I remained perched on the edge of my seat. "You think?"

"I think . . ." she said again, thinking. "I think . . ." She turned to me suddenly. "I think you shouldn't be mixed up in all of this. I worry for you. I am supposed to care for you while you are here, under my roof. I *worry*."

"I know you worry." I kissed her cheek. "But please have a little faith in me. I intend to solve this mystery, *with* or without your help."

Ewe faced me with a cranked finger. "Think you'll get to the bottom of this before Sir Edward, do you? Think you've got something he doesn't have?"

"Yes, I do," I retorted. "I have 'character insight.'"

"Character insight!" she huffed.

"It's nothing and yet it's everything," I defended. "I don't profess to know a great deal about the world and its workings, but I do know people. I study them. I want to be a writer of novels. How else do you think I can do that without studying people and their motivations? Don't you see, dear Ewe? I would make the best inspector!"

I proclaimed it without thinking, and without regret. I spoke the truth.

And Ewe knew it.

"Well," she conceded, "you just be careful with the Hartleys. If you're right, and if *someone* wants to harm them and Lord David, that puts you in danger. *Grave* danger," she pointed out, "particularly if you continue on and discover things you oughtn't."

"Ought not," I echoed. "And if I didn't, who else should?"

Ewe pondered over this and I restrained myself. I didn't tell her about my appointment with Mrs. Bastion. I so wanted to, but reminded myself that if I truly wanted to investigate, I could not relay the full details to friends. I found the whole subject of bodies, mystery, and murder a fascinating study of motivation. It was pure fodder for my future novels.

I thus presented myself at Mrs. Bastion's door, as witness and spectator.

"Hallo." The door was answered by a little boy no more than four years of age.

"I'm Daphne," I said, shaking his hand.

"I'm Petroc," he said proudly, shaking mine back. "And Mum says to bring you to the courtyard, so I'll do that."

The courtyard, thought I, *that's unusual.* Shrugging my shoulders, I followed this little dark-haired boy to the courtyard, a tiny enclosed garden enjoyed by those who owned cottages and intended to make the best of a garden.

She was already seated in one of the cane rocking chairs, a glass of beer cider on her right, studying me intensely as I entered. "You found my girl."

"Yes," I whispered, dusting a seat.

"How did you find her? I want to know!"

I saw the anguish in her face so I described exactly how I'd stumbled upon Victoria that fateful morning. I said how beautiful I thought Victoria was and how unfair it was that she, so young, should perish in such dire circumstances.

"Unfair, aye," said the mother. "It weren't no accident. She's dead! *Dead!*" Shoulders heaving, Mrs. Bastion spun her accusing gaze over the innocent courtyard plants. "Don't know which one of ye did it, but I won't rest until somebody pays. Somebody's *got* to pay."

She sat there, lifeless, drained of any moral fiber while her beautiful daughter languished below, not even in a grave.

"Oh, this is too much to bear!" she cried. "*You* found her, yet I *bore* her. There is a difference. I am her mother, the one who gave her life. You understand?"

"I understand completely," I said with authoritative confidence.

It was just the thing to do, even though I had no experience. I had never borne a child, seen it reared, only to hear of its death, well before its years.

"You"—she pointed at me—"You! Bring her to justice."

Unsettled by such unbridled emotion, I nodded. "I will," I promised. "Whatever it takes, I'll do my best. You understand?"

She nodded, rocking in her chair.

"My poor girl was murdered, I tell you. I don't know by whom or what for, but I just know. As life breeds from me to her, I just know."

I shook her hand. "I vow I will bring the killer to justice."

She smiled, her scrawny face bleak. "You do that, Miss du Maurier."

Upon leaving the Bastion cottage, I spied Connan Bastion whistling up ahead. He was home early from fishing, it appeared, his cap bent down low across his face. Turning into the pathway to his house, he didn't see me.

"Connan," I said.

"What, er?" The bag slung over his right shoulder slipped to the ground as he quickly turned toward me.

"Sorry to startle you. I came to visit your mother."

He frowned at this news, his violet eyes accusing and cautious. "Why?"

I colored. "To . . . offer my condolences and my help, if you need it."

"Need it? You're one of them. Worse, a *friend* of them."

He'd heard, then, of my visiting Padthaway and that I'd been seen driving in the motorcar with David and Lianne Hartley. "I'm everyone's friend. I don't like to have enemies, do you?"

The question caught him off guard.

"Especially ones who own land and shipping companies," I added.

Kicking the dirt beneath his shoes, he crossed his arms. "Ye've just come here. You don't know nothin' about the Hartleys. They killed my sister." His fingers curled into a shaking fist. "Had to do it like cowards, too. Poisonin' her like she were some animal to be put down."

"Did you know your sister was pregnant?"

His face darkened.

I took the answer for a "no."

"We shared so much but she never told me. She should've done. I'd have saved her."

"How?" I dared to ask.

He laughed, but it was not a pleasant sound. The sound of anguish and grief and hysterical irony.

"Lady Hartley. She were hopin' the weddin' would be called off right up to the day. Vicky said she was scared of her. *Scared* of the mother."

I conveyed my sympathies by shifting my foot, one on top of the other, deep in thought. I deliberated whether to share something with him in return and decided I would. "Sir Edward—"

"Him! The Hartleys *own* him, too. They own everything!"

"Lives and souls," I echoed. "Sir Edward asked me if Lady Hartley scared me, too. I've only met her once or twice but I can see she is a very forceful lady."

"Forceful! She's a . . ."

I closed my eyes at the expletives rushing out of his mouth.

"Sorry," he mumbled. "I'm a sailor and I've got a sailor's tongue."

"Don't apologize. I'd do the same if I were you. I can't even begin to think if one of my sisters was found like that, just before her wedding. Do you really think Lady Hartley is truly capable of committing such a crime? So publicly? So openly?"

Connan lifted one wiry eyebrow. "She's gotten away with it before. Who's to stop her now?"

"'She's gotten away with it before' were his words. What does he mean? Who has died suspiciously in the last twenty years or so? Can you think of anyone?"

"Her husband," Ewe blurted.

"Lord Hartley! The father . . ."

"Gunshot to the head. Suicide. I didn't believe it at the time and I still don't."

"Anyone else?"

"Humph! Madame Muck's always had her fingers into things she oughtn't."

"Perhaps she's formed associates over the years while being involved in these forbidden things? Perhaps that's where she purchased the poison."

"Mrs. T. She's no innocent. But whatever or *how*ever they did it, they've hidden it good and proper."

"Sir Edward needs evidence to convict," I spoke aloud. "Finding poison in her body isn't enough to convict."

"A receipt for poison would be. But ye'll not find that lying around. It'd take an army to search that house."

Search the house. I wondered if Sir Edward and his people had managed to do so yet. He probably wanted to conduct a full search after the funeral. Victoria's room would have been searched already, though. I ached to go there, to Padthaway, to see her room. There *had* to be clues. Clues maybe only a woman could find, like letters hidden inside dolls. I doubted Sir Edward and his men possessed the insight to look in such places.

I'd only seen a little of the house. I had to finish the tour, and it was a good enough excuse as any to make a late-afternoon visit. As I made my way toward the house, I kept my eye on the time, conscious of the pale sun speeding down to the horizon. Lapping, white-tinged waves reared, bucking against the oncoming night. I walked faster, determined to get there at a respectable time.

To my surprise, no one answered the door when I rang.

Huffing, for I'd walked all this way for nothing, I turned to go, but then tried the door latch.

It opened with a slight creak.

Taken aback, I tiptoed inside. Crossing the parlor, I crept up the stairs, cringing at the slightest noise. "Lianne? Mrs. Trehearn? Is anyone home?"

The silence of the house greeted me. Relieved, I climbed to the second floor and waltzed halfway down when a pair of maids gossiping outside a room caught my attention.

"The secret's out now. Don't need to worry no more."

They lowered their voices to whisper more and I leaned forward, straining to hear.

"Did ye hear somethin'? I think someone's here."

Heart racing, I dashed down the stairs, spun around, and pretended to walk up again.

"Oh." The older maid blushed. "Sorry, miss. We didn't see ye. If ye lookin' for Miss Lianne, she's out."

"I shouldn't have walked in," I replied, "but the door was opened a crack . . . it's Betsy, isn't it?"

"Betsy and Annie, miss. We're cousins."

Annie smiled her welcome at me.

"Forgive me," I whispered, "but I heard you talking about Lord David. How is he managing, really?"

"Poor Lord Davie," Annie sighed. "Don't know how he'll go on now . . . after all this."

"He'll manage all right. They always do."

I joined the two of them as they dusted. "So, nobody had any idea Victoria was pregnant?"

Lowering her eyes, Annie colored. "I did but—"

"Shh!" Betsy scolded. "What did I tell ye?"

Annie looked suitably chastened.

"Annie, Miss Daphne, has a way of lettin' her mouth run off with her. I've warned her about it. Best keep silent unless ye're sure, and now the secret's out, it don't matter no more."

"What doesn't matter any more? Did you see or hear something, Annie, about Victoria?"

Frowning at me, Betsy shook her head at her cousin.

Annie looked down.

"Oh, please." I laid my hand on Betsy's arm. "You can trust me. I won't say anything. Since I've just arrived, I know nothing and find all of this quite . . . overwhelming."

"Ain't it that," Betsy huffed. "Knew she were trouble from the day she came . . . had her eye for Lord Davie and nobody else. Got herself pregnant, but I ain't so sure Lord Davie is the father."

"Why do you say that?"

Betsy hesitated but I insisted, assuring them of my complete silence.

"It's something Annie heard the night before she died. There was a big row. Go on, Annie, you tell her what ye heard."

Abandoning her feather duster, Annie leaned across the balustrade to whisper in my ear.

"She asked for a cup of tea so I went up to her room and I heard her and Lord David yellin' at each other. I didn't know what to do so I put the cup of tea on the floor. Oh, the row was so terrible the floors shook."

"We don't need the labor pains, Annie." Betsy rolled her eyes. "What did you hear Victoria say to Lord David?"

Gulping, petrified of being caught by Mrs. Trehearn, Annie clutched my hand. "I heard her . . . that Victoria . . . say to Lord David: 'How do you know you're not the father of my child?'"

CHAPTER TWENTY-ONE

The funeral approached.

Ewe and I stood outside the bakery to watch the motorcars roll in to disturb the peace.

"Reminds me of the war," an old man nearby said.

I asked him if he served during the war.

"Aye." He shook his head. "And I don't like to see it. Fancy black cars. They're evil."

"They're all stayin' at the inn." Mrs. Penmark spoke from the shop window. "Might be good for business." She meant the sensation of the murder would bring curious visitors to town.

Ewe and I talked about it on the way home.

"We don't want to go on the map for murder!"

"You can't help it, Ewe. You already are. Look ahead."

A journalist stood in the woodland grove, setting up his camera.

"Beastly things. They'll snap, too, if ye don't look out."

Yes, I dreaded it. I dreaded my photograph being taken and recognized by my mother. My father sanctioned my stay here, though with a large degree of caution. However, if my mother knew the truth, there would be hell to pay.

I despaired over what to wear. I had nothing appropriate for a funeral, since I'd not planned on attending one, coming on a quiet holiday. A quiet holiday. I laughed, for this affair at Padthaway proved the least quiet holiday of my existence, one I never would have expected in sleepy old Cornwall.

"I've a black skirt," I informed Ewe, helping her arrange the table for her lunch party tomorrow. "Do you have a black coat I can borrow? Mine is too much a shade of gray."

"Lots of gray shades round here, ain't there." Her eyes squinted at me. "And I heard you went up to the Bastion cottage. Ye were seen talkin' to Connan Bastion."

She looked hurt that I'd kept it secret from her. I repaired the damage by relaying the conversation I'd had with Annie and Betsy, the maids.

Ewe had to sit down to contemplate the latest news. "She probably said it to vex him. I still can't believe it . . . about the baby." She paused over a spoonful of hot porridge. "And what does Connan Bastion have to say for himself, hmm?"

"Not a great deal," I said truthfully.

Ewe studied me through those shrewd eyes of hers. "He's a good-looking lad, dearie. Wild, like his sister. Not your class."

Not my class. I chanted the phrase as I dressed for the funeral, in the smartest black attire I could manage. Pinning up half my hair, I opted for the merest touch of gloss on my lips and pinched my cheeks for color.

"Modest," Ewe chirped her approval. "Ye'll disappear in the crowd."

"Which is exactly my intention. I wish to observe all the faces and emotions, don't you?"

I could see the thought had occurred to her.

"Wonder what'll happen."

It looked like the whole village thrived on the suspense. Wondering, waiting, every face bearing question marks of its own.

This became more evident upon our walk to the old church. I'd walked by the church many times before, curious to go inside, and it felt odd that I should enter it now, for a funeral.

"Vicar'll be out of sorts. He'll have a heart attack at all these people."

I pitied Vicar Nortby. To be on such display, amid a plethora of shiny motorcars lined up across the field, cameramen and reporters scrambling with their equipment while village children ogled the spectacle, was not an enviable position.

I don't think anyone expected such an enormous turnout, and I kept my head lowered, fearful someone might recognize me. From the crème de la crème of society to the village folk wearing their Sunday bests, a large group supported the Bastion family. "Commoner versus nobleman," I whispered to Ewe, as she shoved us toward the tiny church.

Could it hold such a group? I spared a moment to admire the dark weathered stone, the sleek steeple, and the gothic architecture while being pushed through a hail of snapping photographers.

"Miss du Maurier!"

I cringed.

"Miss du Maurier!"

I had no choice but to turn and smile at the reporter's greedy scanning eyes.

"What do you say about the murder?"

His companion photographer snapped away.

I groaned. Just what I needed. My picture in the paper, and holding my hand halfway up to my face hadn't dissuaded them.

"The *murder,*" the reporter prompted. "It *is* a murder, says Mrs. Bastion."

My father taught me avoidance with the media was the best defense. Biting my tongue (though I was sorely tempted to point out the "open investigation" status), I tagged on the heels of Ewe to the nearest side pew.

Vicar Nortby perspired on the pulpit. He, like everyone else, awaited the Hartley family, the front pew left vacant as was the custom.

The atmosphere inside the church matched the gloomy nature of the occasion. Stilted whispers, grave faces, lifting eyebrows, and rounded eyes filled the room. It was a community divided, those of the lower class sitting on one side and those of the upper on the other.

Mrs. Bastion remained stony-faced, second row from the front, her son Connan's arm around her for support. The next eldest Bastion, a girl of ten or so, looked after the little children.

Victoria's little sister, I thought. I wondered how much she knew of her sister's life. Probably nothing. I said little of my inner thoughts to my elder sister Angela, and certainly nothing to my younger sister Jeanne. It made me wonder why females prefer to conceal so much. Pride? Fear of reproach? Fear of interference?

Vicar Nortby took the stand.

All eyes turned to the front door where Lady Hartley, David, and Lianne, made a sweeping entrance. Lady Hartley, her arm interloped with that of her son, guiding him to the front pew, was *far* removed from Mrs. Bastion and her ilk.

I watched Mrs. Bastion's face. It showed a stony silence. Connan's jaw, however, twitched in anger.

Throughout the service that followed, with the good vicar mopping his brow at regular intervals, I kept my gaze fixed on the radiant Victoria. Lying there in her casket, half hidden from the world and half on display, adorned all in white, she was radiant, ghostly, and beautiful.

The service ended.

David led the mourners to the grave site where Victoria was placed in the family crypt. Lady Hartley's disapproval was still evident by the taut line of her mouth.

The ritualistic closing of the crypt unleashed the emotional mother. Tearing across the manicured lawn, Mrs. Bastion spluttered the anguished cry of the grief-stricken. "It's murder! Murder, I tell you! *You* killed her!"

She was looking at David.

He visibly paled, hesitant sympathy flooding his tense face. Extending an arm to her, he tried to console her in a humane fashion.

She shook him off, having none of it. "No, it was *no* accident. One of you did it! One of you killed my baby! *You!*"

She accused the mother, Lady Hartley.

"Yes, *you!* You killed my girl."

Lady Hartley snorted her indignation, her defiance. "Don't be absurd, woman. I did not kill your daughter."

Mrs. Bastion sobbed away, comforted by the protective gleam in her son's eye, still looking back at Lord David, and Lianne, and especially Lady Hartley.

The excitable reporters danced to this graphic tune, snapping, scribbling, recording every nuance of the sensational outburst.

Mrs. Bastion's crowd of supporters, after some persuasion, guided her away from the grave site and into her home. Staring after the sad, bewildered family and friends, I knew, beyond a doubt, they suspected murder, too.

Sighing, Lianne came up to nudge me. "Thank goodness that's over."

"Come with me," Lianne chimed, pulling me from the grave site to the open lavender field.

"Whatever for?" I stopped her.

She shrugged. "Just because I want to and we've little time."

Little time for what? I wanted to ask, but allowed her to lead me to a seat amongst the swaying grass.

"Phew!" She fanned herself. "How *stressful*. And poor Davie! And Mama! I felt sorry for them."

I noticed she used "mama" on this occasion instead of "mother."

"Mummy didn't do it. Davie didn't do it. Victoria did it herself. She wanted to die. She was so scared of David finding out."

"Finding out what?" I queried, trying to appear casual and squashing the urge to shake the girl's shoulders.

"Oh," she giggled. "About," she paused, blushing, lowering her long, dark-lashed eyes to a piece of swaying grass, "her secret life."

"Victoria's secret life?"

She nodded.

So did I. "I thought she might have had one. She was so beautiful."

Lianne's face instantly hardened. "She was a whore! She *deserved* to die!"

She ran away, and I stood witness to a child's emotions, but was she truly a child? Was she, I hated to ponder, capable of murder?

"Absolutely."

"Absolutely?"

"Absolutely that Miss Lianne could do anything and her mother, her brother, or Jenny Pollock would cover for her. She's born *mad,* she's been indulged since day one of breathing. Do you think murder could be far from her? They lock her up all day in that big house with only softy Jenny Pollock to keep her in check. Oh, aye, Miss Lianne is capable of murder."

"I can't believe it," I echoed, yet I challenged my own words. For what I'd seen that day in that child's face confirmed my worst suspicions. Yes, a child could and would commit such a crime. Of course, such a crime must be proven.

Mounting suspicion generated two separate wakes, one held at Padthaway and one at the Bastion cottage in the village. Knowing I'd hear all the news of the village gathering from Ewe in the morning, I chose to promenade amongst the society romp, a masterful affair filling the graceful inner courtyard at the splendid, dignified mansion.

Mrs. Trehearn and Mr. Soames had outdone themselves, their prowess evident by the smooth running of the function, the correct choice of refreshment, and the singular attentiveness shown to guests.

Fortunately, I knew none of this London set. The Hartleys must have mixed in different circles for I did not recognize one face. A good thing, for it suited my purpose. I wanted to observe and monitor the event.

With Lianne disposed of chatting to two girls her own age, I pursed my lips and became the huntress. Scanning for adequate prey, I found an unassuming freckled male of thirty or so who grinned at my meandering approach.

"Dreadful business, all this," he said, shaking his auburn head. "Thought old Davie would've wed that American heiress, not a simple country lass. Family needs the money, y'know. Things haven't traveled well since the old mad fellow shot himself. Some say family's cursed."

I hadn't expected such an easy victory. "Were you here when it happened, Mr. . . . ?"

"Cameron. Bruce Cameron." He bowed, taking my hand. "And you are?"

I gave him my name.

A flicker of recognition danced in his eyes. "Ah, I know your father, I believe."

"Yes, most do," I smiled, turning back to the subject at hand. "You've known the family long, Mr. Cameron?"

"For years," he enthused, pausing to pick a pastry from a passing plate. "Davie and I were at Oxford together. I often came down here to spend the holidays. Grand, fun old days, they were."

"When the family had money," I reminded, lowering my voice. "How did they lose it, if you don't mind me asking? Lord David did mention something about his father's gambling habits?"

"Yes," he flushed, "lost quite a bit. Eventually they had to sell off the town houses. It was either those or this house, the family home, and David would never give up Padthaway. Anyway, afterward, the family buried themselves down here, living quiet as monks. I suppose they had no choice."

"When did this happen?"

Mr. Cameron hesitated and I realized I'd reached the point where one must share a little of themselves to garner assurance.

Choosing honesty, I told him how I'd come down here for a quiet holiday and stumbled into this catastrophic event.

He seemed to know about that. "The papers," he grinned. "They mentioned a Miss Daphne du Maurier and a Miss Lianne Hartley had found the body. Tell me," he said, and lowered his voice, "it must have been gruesome."

"It was," I confirmed, shivering at the memory.

Mr. Cameron now thought back, his former mistrust banished. "It was straight after the old fellow shot himself. Poor Davie. Had to deal with that and then take on the helm of the family responsibilities. Awfully tough for a sixteen-year-old. He's done well, though I wonder—"

"If he's happy?"

A shadow passed Mr. Cameron's face, the expression of his eyes hidden behind his spectacles. "Hmm. He's cut himself off, y'know. I worry about him. Good that you're about in the neighborhood, Miss du Maurier, might liven things up a little. I hear Miss Lianne and Lady Hartley have taken a shine to you."

I colored deeply.

"Oh, don't let it unsettle you," came the friendly advice. "Miss Lianne needs a friend and Lady Hartley, well, forgive me for saying so, Miss du Maurier, but you'd be a better candidate for mistress of this house than Victoria Bastion."

Something about the curl of his mouth suggested a negative reading of Victoria. I decided to test it. "You didn't think she was the right girl for him?"

"No, I didn't."

Playing the innocent, I examined his face carefully. "Whatever do you mean?"

Fighting the instinct not to divulge but losing the battle, he leaned down to whisper in my ear. "Between you and I, Miss du Maurier, I saw his *intended* in London at a place I cannot call respectable. I never forget a face, especially one as beautiful as hers and . . ." Mr. Cameron then added significantly, "she wasn't alone."

CHAPTER TWENTY-TWO

Ewe had never heard of a Mr. Cameron.

"London folk," she snorted. "Not good enough for the likes of us, and Missy Victoria mixed with that lot a good deal. Once she'd caught Lord David's eye, she had to keep him, if you read me."

"I cannot read you all the time, Ewe. You are a lady of secrets."

Her plump cheeks brightened. "The Hartleys run with the London crowd. Not Lord David so much, mind. He's a man of the land, the best landlord."

"Sir Edward's landlord, too," I pointed out. "Where is this Castle Mor? I am eager to see it."

"You won't be seein' it till after my lunch party. Oh, dear! How's everything look, then?"

I turned around to survey the organized lunch party paraphernalia. The napkins were folded, the cutlery and table setting dusted and placed, and the chairs arranged; Ewe's tiny cottage gleamed from head to toe and I told her so. "You know my father never stopped talking about your pasties. He used to say: 'Old Ewe Sinclaire makes the *best* Cornish pasty. If you ever meet her, Daph, you'll love her. She's a people watcher, too.'"

"People watcher!" Huffing, Ewe steered me to the kitchen to show off her famous batch of newly baked pasties.

"Everything looks perfect," I assured her. "Do you wish me to check the table once more? And that the curtains are dusted?"

"Yes, yes," she nodded.

I went to the window instead, making one cursory glance over table and curtains. "The prevailing question," I muttered aloud, "is who killed Victoria and why?"

I'd not forget my oath to Mrs. Bastion. I'd do my best to find her killer. I didn't understand what stroke of fate had sent me to Cornwall at this time, to stumble upon a beautiful dead bride, to yearn to discover her secret life, but eventually, I would learn the cause of her death.

Men like Sir Edward and his London associates looked upon solving murder as a business, and a business it was, to a certain extent. But then there was the human part of it; a life lost, a grieving family, a murderer on the loose.

I reminded myself she may have taken her own life. "The business of death," I whispered, slipping my fingers through Ewe's fine lace curtains.

"What did you say?" Ewe yelled from the other room. "Has anyone arrived yet?"

"Not yet. Who makes you so nervous?"

Tugging off her apron, she pressed down the rolled sides of her hair. "We've got new folk drivin' down today." Winking at me, she whipped up some kind of cream concoction. "Fancy ones to rival yesterday's offerings."

I loved Ewe's translation for the London crowd. *Yesterday's offerings.* How charming.

"Did you ever see such snobs! Pegasus noses, poked higher in the air than a kite. Poor Mrs. B had a hard time of it. She ain't finished with 'em either. Plannin' something. Maybe," Ewe said, her eyes rounded to saucers, "a *revenge* killin'."

She was talking of the village "wake," the one held at Mrs. Bastion's cottage. I wished I could have gone to both. "And are you sure nothing else happened? Did Mrs. Bastion mention David or his mother?"

Emerging from behind the kitchen stove, Ewe sported her new starched white-collared blue dress. "Do I look as I should?"

I assured her she did.

Appeased, she marched to the window. "Can you see to the flowers for me, Miss Snoopy Socks? Thanks, there's a good girl. No, Mrs. B said no names. Connan held his tongue, too. Clip-lipped he was, but he was angry. Boilin' beneath the skin."

"They do not lease the cottage through the Hartleys. They are independent, apart from Connan's working for the shipping company. I am certain that Connan knows something if he was close to Victoria like Miss Perony said."

"Pregnant! Not that I'm surprised. She always had that look about 'er. Goin' up to London so often. Probably snagged Lord Davie that way. Simple country lass can't learn the tricks here. Had to go to town to do it. Oh yes, saw her drive back with Lord D one day. Grinning like a cat, she was, wearin' that pink smock her mother made for Christmas. Can't get past old Ewe. I says to myself that day: that girl's trouble."

Trouble, yes, but deserving of death?

"And now, pregnant! That explains the 'quickie' wedding. Did Lady Muck know about it?"

"I don't think so," I said. "Lady Hartley seems as shocked as the others, as far as I can find out. Obviously, Victoria's mother didn't know either?"

Ewe shook her head. "Mrs. B didn't know."

"Connan knew. I wonder if he's told the police." Seeing the dread on Ewe's face, I followed her gaze. "What? What is it?"

"They're here. Our first guests."

"Oh. I'll see to the door."

She nodded and fled to the kitchen, leaving me to watch the door. I loved watching the arrivals. I used to hide behind the curtain as a child when company arrived and never appeared to have grown out of the habit.

This time, however, I was caught peeking behind the lace

curtain by a pair of curious, darkly amused eyes, and I scuttled away.

The eyes belonged to a man, a little older than me, of standard height and bearing wearing casual beige pants and a cream sweater roped around his neck. He looked as if he'd just come from his tennis club and I thought it very bad taste considering Ewe Sinclaire's *formal* invitation.

"Daphne!" Ewe summoned. "*Do* get the door."

Oh no, dread of dreads. It was bad enough to have been caught watching from the window, worse to have to answer the door and face the consequences.

Adopting a nonchalant approach, I opened the door, prepared to dismiss the incident.

A knowing smirk greeted me. "Brown. Thomas Brown. And you must be the lady at the curtain? Does the lady at the curtain have a name?"

I realized I'd unconsciously barred him from entering, standing there in the middle of the doorway. Something about his manner irked me as I replied, "Mr. Brown. Welcome. Have you just come from work?"

"Work?"

"At the tennis club."

"Ah," he smiled, removing the sweater around his neck. "Miss Sinclaire is fortunate to have such an insightful housekeeper."

"Housekeeper!" I stood back, incensed. "I am no housekeeper."

"And I am no tennis caddy. Shall we call a truce, then?"

Without waiting for a response, he cruised past me and I hoped Ewe hadn't heard a word of this conversation. She'd be furious with my behavior, for I suspected he was one of her special guests and I hadn't fulfilled my obligation as the welcomer. Trotting after Mr. Brown, I felt I ought to give him an apology and started to form the words when he laid his sweater over my arm.

"Can you see to this, Miss . . . ?"

"Du Maurier," I seethed, seeking to fling his sweater somewhere on Ewe's dusted and gleaming coat stand. I couldn't say why he annoyed me; I'd only just met him. Perhaps the manner of his entry, yes, that was it. He was not conceited, but a peculiar blend of self-assurance enshrouded him.

The doorbell rang again, and happy to ignore the amiable Mr. Brown trying his charm on Ewe, I let in the remaining guests.

All in all there were three gentleman, although I hesitate to call Mr. Brown a gentleman considering his casual attire, and five ladies not counting myself and Ewe. I was delighted to see Miss Perony among the other ladies, two local unmarried girls in their late twenties who came accompanied by their parents. Thus Ewe had her perfect table of ten and since she'd gone to a great deal of effort, I put the smug Mr. Brown out of my mind to play a gracious guest.

Over luncheon, we spoke of little else but the death. "Mystery death" is what the papers were calling it, and for this sleepy Cornish town, the interest outdid the Germanic threat one to ten.

"It's in every paper," one of the girls gushed, fluttering her eye-lashes again at Mr. Brown. "Can it be true what they say? *Can* it be murder?"

"Of course it can," Ewe chimed, loving any kind of gossip, "the whole village is convinced of it. I know you folk are new here, so please feel free to ask any manner of questions. We're not the sort to hide things, are we, my dear Daphne?"

"Certainly not," I chorused, conscious of Mr. Brown's intent gaze upon me.

Mr. Brown asked me to pass the salt. I did so grudgingly, since this was the third time he'd asked me to pass something to him. First, it was the potato dish; second, the meat tray; third, the salt. What was next?

"And the pepper, too, please."

Groaning inside, I considered throwing the pepper at him, but I restrained myself, feeling Ewe's sharp eye monitoring me serving her special guest. Like Mrs. Trehearn, she didn't miss much, but whereas the former concealed, Ewe did the complete opposite.

Perhaps sensing the tension between us and determined to redirect it, one of the ladies attached herself to Mr. Brown.

"Oh, Mr. Brown, what are your thoughts on the whole affair?"

"A mother's accusation is no proof."

"But the secret baby! Mrs. Bastion is right to suspect the Hartleys. If they didn't think her daughter good enough . . ."

"Social disparities are not motivation for murder," Mr. Brown replied matter-of-factly. "Wouldn't you agree, Miss du Maurier?"

Having run out of table items for me to pass to him, he now roped me into the debate. "Oh, I don't know," I accepted the challenge. "If one felt strongly about an issue, one might murder because of it."

"Lord David or Lady Hartley?"

His dark-green eyes arrested mine.

Blazing at his deliberate baiting to try and make me look a fool, I simply shrugged my shoulders. "The verdict is the verdict."

"What do you think, Miss du Maurier? You should have *some* idea, since you're a regular guest at Padthaway."

"You're invited to go there?" cried the girl beside Mr. Brown.

"Yes, at *Padthaway*," Ewe name-dropped, "as a *guest*. She even stayed the night."

"That's right," the mother of the girls nodded. "They mentioned you in the paper. A Miss du Maurier found the body along with Miss Hartley."

Now, he'd really goaded me. I had wanted to remain somewhat incognito at this luncheon, to gauge everybody's thoughts and reactions, not to have to deliver my own. "The death is an odd one. I believe something or someone drove her from the house and out to the cliffs that night."

"A man in a car could be some*thing* and some*one*," Mr. Brown suggested.

Sending him a scathing look, I added, "*If* she was *driven* there, by vehicle or feet, where are her shoes?"

A short silence occupied the table.

"Excellent notion," the fathers of the girls saluted.

"That's me clever girl," Ewe said proudly, letting herself ramble on about my accomplishments.

"Please," I pleaded, "you embarrass me."

The family, having learned of my father, now regarded me differently. Mr. Brown, I failed to read. Nothing showed in his face whilst listening to Ewe extolling the virtues of my existence. At the end of it, however, he exhibited a little yawn, which prompted Ewe to clear the table for coffee and cake.

The interim provided the perfect excuse to escape so I waved Ewe down, offering to do all the work.

"I shall help you," Mr. Brown said, and having risen with plate in hand, gave me no opportunity to refuse.

At the kitchen sink, I took the serving dish from him. "There's no need, Mr. Brown. *Do* sit down."

"I have the distinct impression I'm not wanted around here," Mr. Brown winked to Ewe. "Do you know what I think?"

"I am not interested in your observations, Mr. Brown."

A mild smile assailed his lips. "I was actually speaking to Mrs. . . ."

"Mrs. Can't Remember? Oh."

I hurried away to save my pride as much as to collect the last of the plates.

"I *think*," Mr. Brown said loudly enough for me to overhear, "our sleuth likes her shell."

"I have no reason to hide," I countered on my return.

"I inferred no reason. You did, Miss du Maurier."

So I had and it appeared I had misjudged Mr. Brown. His level of intelligence rose far above my first assumption of him.

"Daphne likes to play tennis, too," Ewe, wickedly enjoying the battle between us, said whilst strolling by with cake in hand. "Mr. Brown, please bring the cream. Daphne, the knife."

With our assigned jobs, we returned to the table, where I met the hostile glare of the girl beside Mr. Brown. Understanding her frustration, for I'd distracted Mr. Brown even though I had no interest in him, I sent her a reassuring smile. I was tempted, however, to gush, "Oh, what a lovely couple you make" and see how Mr. Brown handled the situation.

"Speaking of shocks," Ewe said, her eyes glittering at the cake in front of her, "did anyone see Soames at the funeral? He had no word for the papers and for an eagle like Soames, that's curious."

"Perhaps Lord David asked him not to speak to the papers?" Mr. Brown resumed his seat. "He has a right to, as his boss."

"Lord David would never restrain his employees," I said, meeting Mr. Brown's gaze across the table.

"Well, Victoria was a gadabout," Ewe declared. "Often saw her drivin' about and hardly ever alone. She had many a male friend, that one."

How do you know you're not the father of my child? The phrase leapt before me, followed by Mr. Cameron's slow murmur *I saw her at a place I cannot call respectable.*

"She's certainly a mystery, this Victoria," Mr. Brown surmised, echoing my own silent thoughts.

Tea and cake ended Ewe's fine luncheon in triumph, and eventually, we all collected our bags and coats and filed out the door. Mr. Brown lingered behind, much to the distress of the girl who promptly invited him for dinner. He politely declined, saying he had another important engagement.

"Another engagement?" I dared to ask, waving them off alongside a devilishly proud Ewe.

"Yes," Mr. Brown smiled, taking his sweater and kissing Ewe's hand in farewell, "an important fishing trip with my uncle."

CHAPTER TWENTY-THREE

He kept walking and did not look back. "Who is he?" I felt myself say aloud. "What does he do?"

"Don't know much about him," Ewe confessed. "Out-of-towner, obviously. His uncle lives around here but was too sick to come, so Mr. Brown came in his place."

"He just showed up then? How rude of him."

"Oh, no," Ewe corrected me, "he called by after the funeral."

"He was at the funeral?"

"Yes, that's where I met him."

"He seemed to know all about me; like he knew I was staying here, with you?"

Ewe shrugged. "Well, I never mentioned you."

I wondered about Mr. Brown on my way back to the house. He had an uncle here, he went to the funeral, but what was his business? I was not entirely sure of this Mr. Brown.

Tired from the day's affairs, I thought I'd visit Padthaway instead of Castle Mor, to visit Miss Lianne and be a friend to her. Hadn't Lord David himself asked this favor of me? And it was no chore. I was fond of the girl even if she proved a little spoiled, which was not entirely her fault. If she proved a little misplaced in the mind, one could put it down to the bad blood running through her veins.

I found Lianne alone at her Sunday afternoon siesta in the drawing room.

Mrs. Trehearn hovered in the background, asking if I wished a fresh pot of coffee.

"Yes, please," I smiled. "That would be lovely."

She departed, her blank expression disconcerting me. I yearned to learn of her experiences with Victoria, the kitchen maid who'd risen from the ranks to future mistress of the house, a woman with the power to fire Mrs. Trehearn if she so pleased.

Sensing Lianne in a good mood, I settled on asking her about Victoria's last days at the house.

"She was snappy that last week. I should have pieced it together but I thought she was just being her usual self. Now some things begin to make sense."

"What kind of things?" I asked.

"Oh, just little things like picking at the servants and ranting at poor Annie and Betsy when they accidentally dropped her dress box from London. She accused them of doing it deliberately."

That sparked my interest. Victoria seemed convinced everybody was against her. "Was the wedding dress damaged?"

"No! It's still hanging in her room. I'll take you there when I can steal the key off Mrs. T. She only got it back this morning from Sir Edward."

So there was only one key to Victoria's room and Sir Edward had finished his investigation.

"That night, she was drinking more than usual. I remember David kept trying to take the bottle off her but she kept drinking."

"Why? Was she upset?"

There was no time to answer.

Lady Hartley swept down the stairs on David's arm and past where we were sitting. Both immaculately cloaked in austere black, they slid into the first humming polished Bentley waiting in the drive.

"Where are they going?" I whispered.

Lianne seemed as surprised as I. "I don't know. They always shut me out. I'm just the 'child.'"

"You're not just a child," I said in her defense. "You're my friend. And I like having you as friend."

Happiness gleamed in her face. "Thank you, Daphne. I really like you, too."

"I love your dress," I gushed.

She wore a pink lace dress, tied with a neat bow at the back.

"Jenny did it." She glowed when I said how pretty she looked. "Jenny's good with bows."

"Is it a new dress? Did you ask your mother?"

Finding a spot for her little pink bag and gloves, Lianne faced me coyly. "I don't need Mother's permission. I'm a grown-up.

"It's so awful," Lianne whispered as we went outside to enjoy a spot of sunshine. "I knew she'd been sick one morning but I just thought she drank too much wine. Victoria liked her wine."

"Not champagne?"

Lianne shook her head. "Mother prefers champagne. Victoria liked red wine. She drank lots of it. She said it 'relaxed' her."

"Oh? Did she become merry and slur her words?"

Lianne reflected. "She got silly at times, but that's odd. And yet, on the night she disappeared, she drank."

"She drank what?" I insisted. "What?"

"Oh, I don't know. Lots, I suppose. Lots of what she shouldn't have . . . if she was carrying a child."

"Did her drinking affect your brother? What was his reaction?"

My question raised a serious brow of concern. Maybe I shouldn't have asked such a question.

Mrs. Trehearn chose that moment to make her entry and inquire whether I required more coffee. I said "no" in a cool manner and Lianne quivered behind the chair. When she'd gone, I lifted a brow. "So, you're scared of her, aren't you?"

"No, I'm not!" came the defensive answer.

"You aren't but you are," I revised, and nodded. "It's understandable. I was scared of *three* of our housekeepers. They're scary creatures, wouldn't you agree?"

Lianne laughed. "*You* scared, Daphne? But I thought nothing frightened you."

"Oh, death without natural causes frightens me. Doesn't it you?"

"What's that?"

"It's death with a murderous intent," I explained. "It's very unpleasant. And very cowardly."

"Cowardly," she mused, thoughtful. "Murder makes one strong, doesn't it?"

Her question disturbed me. I stared unseeing at her for a time. Could she really have murdered Victoria? I wondered.

I walked to Rothmarten Abbey in the rain. It was foolish of me, considering it blew sideways, and by the time I reached the abbey grounds, my soaking skirt clung to my legs in a most unpleasant fashion. Windswept, I entered the abbey through a gust of rain. Not precisely the graceful entrance I wished in the shocking presence of David, Sir Edward, and the abbess.

The three of them gaped, eyebrows lifted in unison.

"You walked all that way in the rain, Miss du Maurier?" Lord David asked, concerned.

"Come in here," the abbess cried. "You'll catch a chill."

I submitted, conscious that I'd interrupted a private meeting between the three of them. "I hope I didn't disturb you," I began, accepting a spare habit the abbess handed to me. Taking off my wet clothes, she helped me into it.

"We were only discussing abbey security."

I suspected a very different subject occupied the three of them. "Did Victoria ever come here?"

"Once," the abbess replied, guarded. "She came with Lord David."

She turned and left, leaving me to finish dressing and emerge in my new attire. Sir Edward had gone, but I spied Lord David in a corner with Sister Agatha and his lips curled into a smile when he saw me.

"Is that comfortable?"

"Better than wet clothes," I said, noting his pale, drawn face, no doubt suffering from many sleepless nights.

Returning to the section where I'd worked under Sister Agatha's supervision, I commenced where I'd left off, not sure whether I should say something to Lord David or not. What did one say two days after the funeral?

The papers had not been kind, my father said, casting further doubt as to Sir Edward's ability to investigate his own landlord. Sir Edward had looked grim and I wondered if he'd be replaced.

Lord David said nothing, keeping focused on the job at hand and this in itself helped with the grieving process. I saw one or two nuns pause and shake their heads sympathetically. None of them showed the slightest doubt in his innocence.

Victoria, I petitioned the dusty pigeonholes. *What secrets are you hiding?*

"Poor laddie," Sister Sonya crowed beside me. "Not fair if he should hang for that strumpet's sake."

The words had tumbled out and Sister Sonya, recognizing her mistake, covered her hand over her mouth. "Forgive me. I shall do penance, speaking ill of the dead."

She tried to scuttle away but I pulled her back. "Why do you call her a strumpet?"

Her face reddened.

I pleaded with her again.

"Very well," sighed she. "If ye must know, she's the spawn of a strumpet. Mrs. Bastion were no Mrs. Bastion when she had her eldest two. Oh no, no. They are the spawn of her rich cousin; that's why she leases the cottage from him. Mr. Bastion, he came along later. Just a plain old sailor and father of the little ones. But the eldest two . . ." She leaned over to whisper haltingly in my ear, "they are changelings . . . and dangerous ones. Oh, Saint Mary and Joseph!"

The abbess headed straight for us.

"I shouldn't have said anything."

"I *pray* Sister Sonya is not regaling you with any untrue tales, Miss Daphne," the abbess addressed me, casting one mortifying glance in poor Sister Sonya's direction.

"Oh, no, indeed," I strived to dispel some of Sister Sonya's dread. "Her concern was that I should leave Windemere Lane earlier than expected."

My ploy worked. Lifting a brow, the abbess questioned my plans.

"My plans," I echoed, loud enough for Lord David to hear in the far distance, "are yet unfixed."

"Until I give permission for you to release details of our treasure?" the abbess teased.

"Whether you do or not," I replied, "it is of little significance. I came to Windemere Lane to visit my mother's old nurse . . . and to enjoy a holiday. Anything else I do here is a bonus."

"A bonus. Would you come with me, Miss du Maurier?"

Commanded by the abbess, I had no choice but to agree, leaving a stupefied Sister Sonya in my wake.

"I didn't want to say anything out there," she said upon closing the doors to her private study. "But you are in a unique position, Miss du Maurier."

"Oh? How so?"

"*You* are instrumental in this case now, since you found the body. Lord David is innocent, I tell you. I *know* him. I don't know what happened to Victoria. Lady Hartley is not to be ruled out as suspect and suspect she ought to be more than Lord David! I've known the boy since a child and he doesn't have the heart to murder . . ."

"But Lady Hartley does?"

She didn't answer. She didn't want to, but her silence answered for her. I nodded, asking, "Will they replace Sir Edward?"

"I don't know" came the shrill whisper. "Someone in London doesn't want this to be wrapped up quietly. *Someone* is out to get

Lord David. If you gave me the Bible now, I'd swear on it. I'd swear someone wants Lord David dead and buried alongside his bride."

Her words left a marked shiver down my spine. "You said I was in a unique position. How do you think I can help?"

"Stay close to Padthaway," she mouthed as if in a trance. "To Lady Hartley and Miss Lianne, especially. Neither can be trusted."

"Miss Lianne!" I cried. "But she's just a child!"

"A child she may be," came the definitive answer, "but she's the daughter of a madman and bad blood doesn't lay silent."

CHAPTER TWENTY-FOUR

Stay close to Padthaway.

I didn't mind, in truth. I loved the old house and any excuse to visit was a pleasure. I was commissioned now by two ladies to solve the mystery, Mrs. Bastion and the abbess of Rothmarten Abbey.

I understood their desperation. Abbess Quinlain for the preservation of her abbey and the sacred records guarded by David; Mrs. Bastion for the honor of her dead daughter, the injustice done, and for robbing her and her young children of a secure, comfortable future.

So I went to Padthaway once again, only to be informed by a cool Mrs. Trehearn that the family was out for the day and did I wish to leave a card? I said I had no printed card to leave and certainly would not write one. While we were standing there during the whole debacle, Jenny Pollock happened by and braved Mrs. Trehearn's displeasure by inviting me in to take tea with her.

Mrs. Trehearn could scarce say no since Jenny Pollock enjoyed the same privileged status she did.

So inside Jenny Pollock's parlor I found myself, enjoying a fresh pot of tea and gossiping about the funeral.

"How dreadful for Davie . . . my heart *bled* for him, having to sit there, listen to all the accusations, and he bore it like a saint!"

I never venture into town, never ever, but I went to the church for him. I sat up the back, my head covered in a veil. You probably didn't see me?"

"No, I didn't. It must be a relief to you all that it's now over."

"Well, it's not over, not until they get the murderess." Her eyes narrowing, Jenny hoped I'd not heard what she'd just said but I most certainly had.

"Oh, take no notice of me, Miss Daphne. My mouth runs away from me—it always did and it's got me into trouble."

"So you're afraid of trouble now? If you speak out with what you know?"

She stared at me dumbly. "What I know?"

"About Victoria's death? Her secret life?"

Jenny looked scared. "I know *nothing,* nothing really. She came here to work in the kitchen, under Soames. Now, if you're a cluey miss and you're after diggin' up what happened to her, Soames is the one to question. Go and try your luck with him. Go on."

She goaded me to it and after finishing my cup of tea, I agreed. I'd go to the kitchen on a pretext of fetching more tea and see what transpired.

To my luck, I found Mr. Soames alone in the kitchen, tidying up what appeared to have been a large effort.

"A big lunch?" I asked.

Keeping his head down, he nodded. He didn't want to talk and his expression remained taut and closed. I should have just left it there, ordered my tea and left, but something within impelled me to say, "I heard you worked in Paris. I attended a finishing school there. Who'd you work for? Lianne said it was for a famous painter?"

Endeavoring to be as casual as possible, I noticed his lips tightening at the questions. He was not the polished Soames today. Something was bothering him and I suspected it had to do with Victoria.

Setting down his fry pan, he retreated into busy mode. "Ah, Paris! Isn't it wonderful?"

I watched him bustle about while he made my tea, his edginess increasing by the minute.

Handing me my tea, he saw he'd forgotten the milk.

"Forgive me, Miss du Maurier, my thoughts were elsewhere."

"I believe I understand," I murmured, accepting the little pot of milk from his hand. "Victoria worked in your kitchen, didn't she? Of course you are upset. The whole house is."

Surprisingly, he guffawed at that and I lifted a mild, probing brow. Hating to use these tactics, I pressed my hand gently on his arm. "How long did she work for you?"

"Not long. A year at most."

"She wanted to be a cook?"

"She a cook!? No, she came here to . . ."

"To?"

Silence.

"To strive for a better life?"

Immeasurably uncomfortable, Mr. Soames abandoned my hand, taking refuge among his pots and pans. Remembering his face when Sir Edward delivered the verdict and accompanying news, I nodded my sympathy. "Did you know her mother?"

"No. I knew none of her family."

The abrupt denial, followed by a speedy demonstration of rearranging wine glasses and calling for assistance forced me out of my chair. It did not seem wise to press Mr. Soames.

Leaving him to mull over the encounter, I carried the remainder of my tea to the parlor. As I expected, I drank my tea in silence and curled up on one of the settees to await Miss Lianne.

And Miss Lianne, in her heavy-footed mode, soon bowled in to see me.

"Oh, the most *annoying* tea party! Mother was somewhere else. Mrs. Beechley had to ask her the same thing *three* times."

It seemed everyone's mind existed somewhere else. "Do you think she's worried about Mrs. Bastion's threat? At the funeral, I mean."

Lianne's mordant look said "I don't think so." "She did have a row with Davie just after the funeral. . . . I heard them in the garden. It's the money thing. They're always fighting about money."

Yes, money was the cause of many family disruptions, but I sensed a significance to this particular row, so soon after the funeral. Surely, one could leave such affairs to a later date? "Did you hear anything else?"

Wriggling her nose, she reflected. "David said something like '*I won't have her name besmirched any more than it has.*'"

Did David suspect his mother's involvement in the blackening of his beloved's good name?

"So what do you want to do now?" Eager, Lianne presented me with several possibilities.

I listened to them all. "I think I should like to stay here, in the house. Perhaps we can spend the day with Jenny?"

"Jenny?" Her nose screwed up. "We can see her another day."

"But you like spending time with her," I reminded, "and it's a kind thing to do to visit someone who is lonely. Why does she never venture into the village? Has she no friends? Is she scared of seeing someone there?"

I could see the thought had never occurred to Lianne. "Scared of someone? I don't think Jenny's afraid of anyone or anything."

While escorting me through the house to Jenny's parlor, I tried to steer Lianne toward the murder case. I longed to explore Mrs. Trehearn's famous greenhouse and Victoria's room. I felt confident I'd find something the police had missed. I remembered in my reading of mystery books that a tiny clue, of the smallest significance, could lead to the answer.

I had one or two clues already. The absence of Victoria's shoes remained my primary focus. Were they hiding somewhere or had the murderer thrown them out? Or did they rest neatly in her closet wardrobe? Had she fallen, or was she pushed or placed on the cliffs, in her nightgown, poisoned by a fatal dose of ricin?

Jenny's place in the house bloomed like a summery haven for the second time that day. Lianne and I listened to her account of the wake at the Bastion cottage.

"Soames took me. Got to see Mrs. Bastion. Sad, that were. Lots of screamin', cryin', papermen and the like. It's been years since I seen townfolk, I s'pose, and my life's here now. They thought me a big snob when I stopped goin' into the village. My friends back then, they were all jealous I'd such a great post at Padthaway. It's a big house, you see, and they could've got a fancy nanny from London when Becky Shaw got married."

"I met Rebecca Shaw . . ."

"Oh? What did you think of her?"

"A trifle edgy. Did something happen here at Padthaway to frighten her? She didn't want to talk about it." I did not mention, of course, that Rebecca Shaw had warned me against the Hartleys.

"Can't say." Jenny lifted her hands in the air. "But gettin' back to the funeral, Mrs. B ain't good, is she? She's got it stuck in her head her girl was murdered, but I think it's more to do with the baby. The baby, the baby," she echoed, "I had no idea . . ."

Nor did anyone else but Lord David and perhaps Victoria's brother, or so it seemed.

"Vicar Nortby struggled with that one, didn't he? Them priests don't know much about life. How did Ewe's lunch go yesterdee, by and by? Meet anyone new?"

I told them about Mr. Brown.

"Don't know of him," Jenny sniffed, "but I did hear of the others movin' in. Betsy . . . she keeps me up with all the gossip. Can't live without me gossip."

"You should come next time," I said. "I think you and Ewe would get on famously."

"Lots of mischief," Jenny laughed, her face suddenly somber. "Saw me boy this morning, my Davie. He ain't good. It worries me."

"Maybe it's just the shock?"

"Yes, the shock," Jenny agreed. "Losin' his baby and all."

We shared a simple meal with Jenny and I felt far more comfortable with her than I did sitting at the Hartley table. I almost dreaded the next invitation to dinner and confided as much to Jenny.

"Yes, Madame Muck's got her eye on you. Whoops." She broke off, casting a quick look at Lianne.

"You've called her that before," Lianne smiled from her perch at the corner window as she worked on a puzzle, "so there's no point whispering. I don't care anyhow."

I shifted off my chair to view her progress but Jenny waved me down.

"Let her do her puzzle," she murmured, "it's good for her mind."

"It's a pity she doesn't have more friends," I said.

"It's because of the *sickness,*" Jenny said in a low tone. "They think she's safer here with me, and I confess I've pushed it that way. Don't want me girl goin' out to the world and gettin' hurt. At least here I can keep an eye on her."

"But she's not really mad, is she?"

Jenny paused to reflect. "I don't think so. I think she's got other problems, learnin' problems." Lowering her voice even further she added, "Her readin' and writin' is very bad, but she's still tryin' and that matters."

"Perhaps I could help," I offered. "While I'm here in the area . . ."

"Well." Jenny pressed my hand. "You're just a blessing in disguise, aren't ye? And all pretty and smart, too. No wonder her ladyship fancies ye."

CHAPTER TWENTY-FIVE

I left Padthaway at three o'clock, giving myself a full two hours to scale the cliffs and search for clues since Ewe did not expect me until five.

A late-afternoon breeze whipped across the headland. I pulled my cardigan closer, examining the gray sky. It would rain soon, the heavy clouds expanding and gathering in an ominous formation. A churning sea lapped against the shoreline and I walked the route along the top of the cliffs to the point where Victoria had fallen.

As I reached the place, looking for any discarded shoes or clues missed by the police, I saw him. Standing alone on the jutted rock, the collar of his great coat high, his face hidden beneath the brim of his hat. He was peering over the edge, precariously close to the edge, and I called out, "Be careful!"

Startled, Connan Bastion spun around, steadying himself just before I arrived.

"Oh, it's you."

The wind loosened his hat and, catching it, he flung it out to sea.

"Miss Daphne, I'm not about to kill myself."

"I certainly hope not," I said, stepping closer. "You have so much to live for."

"To live for." Throwing back his head, he laughed, his dark curls hugging the splendid contours of his face. "What do ye think I have to live for?"

"Your family."

"My family," he laughed. "Ha! What do ye know about my family?"

"That you're close," I ventured. "I know you'd do anything to support your mother and I know that you were close to your sister, Victoria."

"She were my only *true* sister," he spat. "Only we had the same father. The fancy cousin in town, my mother tells me. That's why we lease the cottage, through *him*."

"Have you met him?"

"Met him," he spat again. "Sure I have! He's my father, ain't he? Even though he's a wife of his own and five children to boot. Don't really care about any of us, just payin' us off, as it were, leavin' Mum and us two."

"Then your stepfather came along, Mr. Bastion."

"Bastion." He rolled his eyes. "That ain't my true name. Don't really have a true name, do I? Since me own father won't acknowledge me. I *should* be Connan Wright. Yes, Mr. Wright, if ye please."

"Was your stepfather kind to you, Connan?"

Like a wild animal, he stared out at the sea. "Yeah, he were a decent fellow. Taught me how to get into the fishin' business. *Landed* me with a job workin' for a company owned by the Hartleys!"

"Did it bother you before Victoria met Lord David?"

"Bother me?" he repeated. "I s'pose not. Then Vicky gets a job up *there*. I warned her. I warned her from the beginnin'. But do ye think she listens to me? No."

I nodded my head in sympathy. "Girls don't often listen to the wise advice of brothers and fathers. I know, because I should have listened to my father once—it was about a boy—but I didn't listen and now I would, though. I realize now that what they say is often for our own good."

He nodded deeply and I suspected he'd been drinking at the

local pub since lunchtime. "You do think your sister was murdered, don't you? But you worry you can't prove it?"

He lifted his hand up. "How can I? How can I go against the
man who pays me? Tell me that!"

"But you already have, haven't you? You've told the police what
you think, your suspicions? Connan, did Victoria tell *you* she was
pregnant?"

"Aye, she told me. Me and him, she said."

"No other? Did she name the father of the child? It must be
Lord David's!"

"Maybe," he shrugged. "And knowin' Vicky, she'd not risk her
chance of gettin' to be a lady, if ye know what I mean. So Hartley's
it must be, tho' she had plenty after her. Always had, from school. I
had to punch out quite a few in my time, I can tell ye."

"You never tried to punch out Lord David?"

He sent me a woebegone look.

"I suppose not. Yet you must have wanted to. I mean, what did
you think when she said she was seeing him?"

"I warned her," he said after a long pause, not sure whether to
trust me or not.

"You can trust me," I assured him.

"I warned her not to be with the likes of them. They'd use her
and spit her out dry. She don't listen to me, though. Then, she tells
me she's with child, she's engaged! Engaged to Hartley! I laughed
and she slapped my face. Then I realize she's not joking. She really
is going to marry him."

"What convinced you?"

"She showed me the ring. The *diamond* ring." His face paled.
"You would have seen it on her finger."

I nodded, still uncertain of his present mood and intentions.
Examining his profile, the heavy-lidded, red-rimmed eyes bespoke
a hard night or two on the liquor. The pinched cheeks and steely
jawline suggested anger and a frustration bordering on desperation.

"You found the body, didn't you? How'd she look?"

Overcome by a profound sadness and stepping closer to the edge of the cliff, I searched for the sandy spot below, shivering at the memory of the young bride lying there. "She looked beautiful . . . almost peaceful."

"She were pretty, Vicky. The prettiest girl around."

A deep resonating pain echoed in his voice and I pictured the two of them as children, running hand in hand across the open fields. Two fatherless children, finding solace and comfort in each other. "Connan," I said softly, "I met a Mr. Cameron at the funeral. Was he a friend of Victoria's?"

His mouth hardened at the name.

"A tall auburn-haired fellow? He rents a flat in London?"

"Friend!" Connan spat. "He just used her like the others. I warned her not to get that job in London. I warned her not to go to the club, but does she listen to me?"

"Why do you think she did it? She never fit into the village life, did she?"

He shook his head.

"She wanted to rise above; she wanted to join that class." He snapped a look at me. "*Your* class."

"Yes, my class, and maybe it's a good thing my coming here at such a time." I leaned over to whisper in his ear. "I can get inside Padthaway. I can find your sister's murderer and bring him, her, or them to justice."

He liked the sound of it, and I questioned the wisdom of my rash words. Connan didn't sneer at the suggestion, for he knew, as I did, that those of the upper class eluded justice too often.

"What did you think of Mr. Brown? Dashing, ain't he!"

I did not share Ewe's enthusiasm. "I found him arrogant."

"Well, he found you quite charming, for I saw him this very morning. He comes down to visit his uncle, another *charming* man though a bit of a recluse. I invite him *all* the time to my luncheons and one day, he'll accept."

We sat down to our simple evening meal, a meat and vegetable stew Ewe had been brewing all day.

"Didn't know if ye'd be stayin' up at the big house. Have the Londoners gone yet?"

"Nearly all of them. Lianne and I spent the day with Jenny Pollock. She's lovely. Do you remember much about her?"

Ewe stretched back her memory. "Saw her once or twice. Pretty thing, she were, Jenny. Did you see Lady Hartley? Or Lord David?"

"No, but I suspect I may see them on Wednesday. I've been invited for lunch."

"Oh, have you?"

I blushed at the inference in Ewe's tone, and quickly changed the subject.

"You know Bastion is not Connan and Victoria's real name. It is not kind to be deprived of your own identity."

"And now the funeral is over, real life can start again," Ewe finished.

But what kind of life, I wondered. Despite the ongoing investigation, Lord David had planned to marry, to become a husband and a father. Victoria was soon to become mistress of the house, much to Lady Hartley's chagrin.

Thinking on the latter, I observed Lady Hartley closely at the Wednesday luncheon in the Green Salon. She'd since put back the photograph of David and Victoria together, the happily engaged couple, and I couldn't resist viewing it before Lord David arrived.

It had been taken in the conservatory, Victoria poised in a chair with David standing behind her, his hand resting on her shoulder. She wore a slim-fitting white dress, a string of lavender beads at her neck, her beauty emphasized by the simplicity of her attire. Her fingers touched David's hand where it rested on her shoulder, her engagement ring large and sparkling. I shuddered, remembering where I'd last seen the ring—on her dead finger.

"It's so nice to have one's house back to oneself," Lady Hartley announced, dripping with jewelry, and certainly not fitting the image of a grieving mother-in-law and grandmother-to-be. As she relaxed there, proudly viewing her paintings, Lady Hartley's eerie calm behind her mask of royal hauteur chilled me. She looked like an adoring mother when David walked in, his cursory glance locating the returned photograph.

Lunch commenced and passed tolerably well, Lianne pleased to have me in attendance. Avoiding anything related to the funeral or the investigation, we spoke of trivialities, holidays we'd been on, plays and shows we'd seen, ordinary obligatory comments that were safe under the circumstances. By the end of it, I felt exhausted and dreaded that Lady Hartley would ask me to take tea.

Instead, Lianne suggested we go to the library. I loved nothing more than dwelling amongst books and couldn't wait to indulge myself with the splendid collection.

An hour passed easily before Lianne became bored and demanded we do something else. I said I had no wish to do anything else and would stay with the books unless she wished me to leave. Cautious not to trouble our friendship, she shrugged good-naturedly, leaving me alone to explore at my leisure.

I started with one section of the library, slowly progressing to the next section when I noticed that Lord David had entered the room.

I admired his obvious ritual, poised halfway up the ladder, immersed in a book and completely unaware that anyone else occupied the room.

"Hello."

Startled by my interruption, the book went flying and so did Lord David. Retrieving his balance, he made a rapid descent, displaying a graceful, athletic prowess.

"Forgive me," I grinned, "you probably had the same idea as me and here I am blundering into your private retreat."

I turned on my heel.

"Don't go."

My hand was resting on the door, but I had no intention of leaving. "Yes?"

"Please stay."

Brushing down his jacket, he collected the book from the floor. "I give you special license to blunder, Daphne du Maurier."

An almost remorseful smile accompanied this comment and a heated gulp dislodged its way down my throat. Steeling myself against the encased masterful masculinity adorning one of my favorite backdrops, a room full of books, I gestured to the book hidden behind his back.

"Oh, it's nothing," he said, hastily shoving it under papers on his desk.

Did I imagine it or did a flush of color show in the planes of his face? What kind of flush, one of embarrassment perhaps, or guilt? Why hide a book?

Immediately curious, I meandered about the room, inspecting the odd title here and there, loving the wealth and breadth of choice. "It's a fine selection . . ."

He nodded, lifting a curious brow of his own. "I thought you ladies like to take a nap before dinner?"

"I rarely nap before dinner," I replied, "but I have been known to daydream a great deal. I am often guilty of the crime, especially at inconvenient times, or so my mother tells me."

An amused chuckle left his lips and he relaxed, smiling. "Then you're not alone, for I am guilty of the same crime. Daydreaming is a remarkable escape, is it not?"

The book I'd selected slipped through my fingers. I bent down to retrieve it as did Lord David, our hands colliding over the spine.

His hand failed to move from mine. Breathless, I raised my eyes up to his smiling face.

"It's a good book . . ."

"Is it?"

I didn't even recognize the sound of my own voice. He was so very near, too near, his hand poised there across the tips of my fingers, firming its hold as he swept me to my feet.

The book dropped between us. Laughing, we both ducked again to pick it up, and this time, to my intense mortification, our foreheads touched. David's arms reached out to steady me and I swallowed, unsettled and yet excited by our proximity.

Neither of us bothered about the book. I found myself slowly drawn into the circle of his arms, half-afraid and half-elated, and totally unable to stop the pressure of his lips on mine, gentle at first, then deepening, proving he was a man of great passion and strength.

Warning myself I must be wary of this man, I slowly pulled back, my heated face silent confirmation of the success of his kiss.

To put space between us, I stepped away to find a book, any book.

"Forgive me," he said. "A momentary lapse."

"No, it's nothing," I whispered, desperately looking for a book.

Sensing the sudden awkwardness between us, he gestured to the back wall. "You might find something of interest there."

He had guessed correctly. Selecting one on the Viking age from the historical section, I flicked through it, willing the beating of my heart to slow. My relationships with men had been few, some stolen kisses with my cousin Geoffrey among others, but this kiss alarmed me with its intensity.

"You might like to flick through these, too."

Collecting a few titles about the room, he handed me the stack, his eyes searching mine.

I failed to even glance at the titles. "Thank you," I whispered. "You are very kind."

"Kind," he echoed, glancing away. "I've been called many things of late, but not kind. Thank *you,* Daphne. You make me believe in life."

I gazed up at him, the tortured, lost hero, unsure of how to cope with life in the aftermath of this tragedy.

Escaping to my own corner of the room, I tried to concentrate on the history book, the Viking men in their helmets blurring before my eyes. Why, *why* had he kissed me? Why was he trying to hide the book he'd shoved under the papers earlier? Is that why he'd kissed me, hoping to divert my attention?

I refused to leave the room until I discovered his secret. I kept my focus on the Vikings until my grand opportunity presented itself in the form of Mrs. Trehearn.

"My lord." She stepped back in astonishment when she saw me. "Your lady mother wishes a word."

"She usually does" was the irritated reply.

Lord David left directly, reluctantly, but since Mrs. Trehearn stood there holding the door open, he walked through without a backward glance. After sending me one pointed look that said "What are you doing here?" Mrs. Trehearn shut the door.

Acute relief washed over me. Now alone, I quickly hunted through Lord David's desk, looking for that book he'd hidden, sifting through his papers, suppressing any shame for going through his personal items.

And then I found it.

A letter . . . hidden inside a book on poetry and the letter began with:

My darling David . . .

CHAPTER TWENTY-SIX

My darling David,
How can you say those beastly things to me? I will
always be yours. I know what they say about me . . .
please don't believe it. It's not true, I tell you. I love
you.
   It's curious how one's past catches up with one.
We all have secrets, and I'm no exception. Someday,
I'll confess all, but know now that my heart belongs
only to you and you alone are the father of my child.
   I know we had a terrible row earlier but I can't
wait for Saturday. I shall walk proud on your arm,
the new Mrs. David Hartley.

Your devoted,
Victoria

Like a naughty child, I glanced up furtively; frantic Mrs. Trehearn
might have bowled through the door and caught me in the act. I
felt like a criminal, stealing someone's private letter, but why should
Lord David hide it there? Did he think the servants searched his
desk? Worse, did he suspect Lianne or his own mother would
search through his private affairs? From what I knew of the both of

them, I, too, would have hidden the private letter inside a book and placed it high on the shelves.

Rereading the words, I wondered if David had kept the letter because he loved her or because he felt guilty for murdering her. I saw nothing in the letter but a protestation of Victoria's love for her man, and the assurance that he was the father of her child. She said she couldn't wait to walk proud on his arm, the new Mrs. David Hartley. Her words definitely ruled out suicide, for they were the words of a woman who intended to live, to marry, and to have her child, regardless of rumors, prejudice, and even family opposition.

"Not suicide, then," I murmured aloud. "Unless something occurred between the writing of this letter and the night she died."

Returning the letter to its safe home, I went in search of Lianne. She'd be angry with me for spending too long reading after inviting me here as her particular friend.

Looking around for Betsy or Annie to guide me, for I refused to seek out Mrs. Trehearn and ask her, I wandered around the house wondering where Victoria's room was located. I began down the corridor leading to the sea and was heading toward the forbidden west wing when Lianne found me.

She wasn't alone. Her brother stood by her and both of them eyed me with an intense curiosity I found disturbing.

"We thought we'd lost you, didn't we, Davie?"

Lord David's quizzing eyes remained focused upon me.

"What time do you have to be back?" Lianne skipped to me.

I consulted my wristwatch. "In time for dinner."

"Then there is time for a tour of the dungeons, if you so wish," Lord David smiled. "Unless you've further important reading to do?"

I cringed. He not only suspected, he *knew* I'd read the letter. "A tour of the dungeons would be lovely," I said.

"Excellent."

A faint grin drifted on his lips. Removing a flashlight from his inner pocket, his smile deepened and I looked away.

"They were *working* dungeons once," Lianne rambled excitedly, skipping on ahead, "and used for *torture.* I wonder if any were used on the monk in the tower. There're still chains down there, you know, and more than likely *skeletons,* though I haven't found any yet."

"You sound annoyed," I said, wondering about her fascination with death. She had a peculiar penchant for torturous instruments and death. Had this something to do with her father shooting himself? Had the child witnessed the event?

I felt innately sorry for David and Lianne. On the night of their father's suicide, their lives were irrevocably changed. David, a sixteen-year-old boy, was thrust into a man's position earlier than anticipated, while Lianne, a six-year-old child, was abandoned to the care of her nanny.

As we entered the west wing, the breezy sea air rustled the hairs on my skin and I experienced a queer nervous sensation. Who but this house knew what secrets lay within its ancient folds? Pausing outside the Moorish doors, David knocked, opening the door for us. "The way to the dungeons is through here."

"Will your mother mind the intrusion?"

"At this time of day, my mother usually takes her tea in the courtyard."

I noted the clipped tone he used when referring to his mother. Lianne also used it and I thought what a strained, odd kind of relationship existed between the three of them. Had there ever been gaiety and happiness in this household?

The magnificent room caught at me once more, its haunting beauty stoking the fires of my imagination. Such a room demanded a beautiful heroine, a brooding hero, and a dark, rich mystery.

The door to the dungeons loomed at the end of the antechamber. As we explored the labyrinth of cobwebs and dust, a dark, eerie passage gleamed ahead, just visible by David's flashlight.

"In the old days, the smugglers dodged the coast guard by using the caves," David said. "But one captain refused to give up. Tracking the criminals, he speared the crew before going after the organizer, my great-great-great-grandfather, Lord Aiden. However, Lord Aiden employed his aristocratic privilege and thus evaded punishment, which in those days was hanging."

As he spoke, I realized that like the previous owner, Lord David might escape punishment, too, using "aristocratic privilege."

"It doesn't end there." Lianne's grin looked eerie in the darkness.

"No," David continued, "for Captain Saunders refused to give up. His reputation insulted, he infiltrated the house one night and speared Lord Aiden in his sleep. Nobody ever saw Saunders again, but he left his saber as a grim reminder. The saber now graces the gallery beside the portrait of its victim."

I nodded, and cautiously rounded the rocks forming the road out to sea. Lianne marched ahead out toward the sea, fearless. "She's never afraid, your sister."

"Are you afraid, Daphne?"

The elusive murmur drifted by my ears. "Afraid of what?" I gulped.

"I know you read the letter."

I didn't know where to look. Lianne was waving at me so I dumbly waved back at her. "I don't know what you mean."

"But you do. You're curious, which is natural. I also know you went to the Bastion cottage. That was kind of you. To offer your services."

Now I felt truly afraid.

"I don't mind," he laughed, and turned me to face him. "I'm only jesting with you, and if you read that letter, that letter I'm keeping from everyone else . . ."

"But why? Do the police know?"

"No," he said softly. "Perhaps I should have shown it to them, but you must understand, I wanted something of ours to remain *private.* Can you imagine what it's done to me, *as a man,* as her future *husband,* to know that I couldn't protect her when it counted? Can you realize, just for a moment, how this tortures me day after day?"

Examining every line of his face, I read the trueness of his declaration. "I can't imagine how I'd feel in the same situation," I whispered. "I think it would drive me mad."

"As it does *me*." Raking a hand through his hair, he stepped out to help Lianne across the rocks.

I gazed out to the sea, loving the roar of it in our ears and following Lianne's steps out to the treacherous rocky view. "How splendid. I shall never forget this place."

"Beware the tides of a moonless night," Lianne shouted. "Where death awaits those deserving it."

"Captain Saunder's cryptic message," David interpreted, directing us both back to safety. "He left it on a note speared to Lord Aiden's chest."

"Lovely," I smiled, shivering inside. Something about this place gave one the chills. Death and danger somehow cloaked the house, its past, present, and future inescapably linked.

Would I, too, suffer its dismal fate?

David offered to drive me home.

I accepted to as far as the village, as I wanted to make a late-afternoon telephone call to my father. The call also served as my excuse, for after the dungeon visit, I wanted to get away as soon as possible to think.

David, a man suspected of killing his own bride, had kissed me.

"Yes, poison," I said to my father. "Ricin, have you heard of it?"

"I have, and Daphne, darling, I do think it's time for you to come home. Your mother's frantic. She's read the papers."

"Oh, please. Not yet, not when I'm so close."

"Close to what? Your part is over. You discovered the body and reported it. I don't want you mixed up in any more of this case. It's dangerous. I'm not sure of this Lord David fellow. He might be innocent as you say, but who's to know? How's the investigation going?"

How like my father to get straight to the facts. "Still ongoing.

Since they found this poison, it's overturned 'accidental death.' Sir Edward," I coughed, "appears to be handling it."

"Daphne," rang my father's voice. "You're like me, so there's no use pretending. You want to solve this case on your own, don't you?"

"Yes," I confessed, dreading what he'd next say.

"I don't like it. I don't like it one bit."

"I know you don't like it, but you're going to have to put up with it because I'm not coming back until it's over. I just can't. The sea, the air, the mystery, it's all part of me now . . . and I love Ewe dearly. She amuses me. She's worse than we are. You should hear her. She talks of nothing else but the 'murder case.'"

"What of these visits to Padthaway, though? The Hartleys are rich and dangerous, or so I've read. It's not beyond them to murder."

"I know that." And I shared a few of my private thoughts on Lady Hartley. "She's just inhuman. There's something odd there. Out of anyone, I'd say *she* murdered Victoria. Think, Dad. If she's an earl's daughter, accustomed to being mistress of the house, and a mere *commoner,* oh no, a village *strumpet* almost, one who served as kitchen maid in her house, aspired to the affections of her only son . . . and that son *agreed* to marry her—"

"Agreed," my father echoed, "you make an interesting point. He *agreed* to marry her because she was pregnant. Do you think he'd marry her if she wasn't?"

What my father said made sense. I thought about it as I strolled home, still in a daze from the eventful visit to Padthaway. Oh, how the imagination soared! I couldn't wait to get to my journal, to jot down notes for a novel. Oh, yes, I had in mind a novel of graphic proportions, and every page filled with these events.

"Thank you, Padthaway," I said, late into the evening, lying on my bed. "I know I can truly write a novel now, with your help. A story worth publishing. A story fit for the world."

And I began to scribble in earnest, jotting down character ideas, motivations, a setting, a grand old house set by the sea, a mystery, and a dead love.

Excited, I had trouble sleeping at first. I kept dreaming of this future book. I knew it would be special. I knew it would sell, if anyone would publish it.

I dreamed of it . . .

I dreamed of an opening line.

I dreamed of Manderley . . .

CHAPTER TWENTY-SEVEN

Intensely inspired the next day, I journeyed up to Castle Mor, to the home of Sir Edward.

The castle looked splendid perched up on the hill, overlooking a lush green valley. It was the perfect place to sit and write, and dream.

"Reporting to the sleuth society?"

So lost within my pencil-chewing deliberations, I had not seen Mr. Brown approach the green. "You should know better," I said, "than to sneak up on ladies."

"I did wave to you from the other side."

Oblivious to my cool glare, he had the further audacity to peer over my shoulder. "Nice handwriting."

Shutting my journal, I tucked it under my leg and smiled my best socialite smile. "Good day, Mr. Brown. I see you're not dressed for tennis today?"

"I'm going fishing," he grinned, dropping his rod and tackle box and finding a spot on the grass beside me. "Much like you, really. What are you fishing? Let me guess . . . is this an *exclusive* abbey piece or a private unauthorized investigation report?"

I glared at him again. The man was far too arrogant for his own good. Who did he think he was, a duke? "I don't know what you mean, Mr. Brown," I returned sweetly. "I have no need to fish in *any* waters."

"Then what holds you, the glamorous socialite, in the modest hills of Cornwall?"

"Glamorous socialite," I echoed, never having heard myself described that way. Usually, such descriptions were lavished upon my sister Angela.

"Am I wrong? Shall you correct me? Do you not delight in murder for your stories?"

I couldn't believe his audacity. How dare he, a stranger, *question* my motive for staying in Cornwall! Giving him my best evil eye, I said I resented his comments and thought it inappropriate in the circumstances to trivialize a local death. He listened to everything with somber sobriety, nodding here and there, and I realized he must have learned of my writing aspirations from Ewe.

His eyes sparkled like a newly kindled fire. "You don't like me, do you, Miss du Maurier."

It was a statement, not a question. At least, I thought, a perceptive intelligence favored Mr. Brown, and if he had not so annoyed me by what he'd said, I might have mentioned the letter I'd found at Padthaway, or asked his opinion of Mrs. Trehearn. I wanted to know if he knew of her job during the war and her penchant for brewing tonics in the Padthaway greenhouse. "What do you actually *do,* Mr. Brown, other than attack ladies out in the hills?"

"The wild *isolated* hills," he replied, "are perfect for secret rendezvous."

"Then I shan't keep you a moment longer," I smiled, and getting up, prepared to leave.

His arm shot out to stop me, an amused expression lingering on what Ewe Sinclair thought his "very fine cheekbones."

"But aren't you forgetting something?"

I lifted a weary brow.

"Your journal?"

Tapping the book over his knee, he strove to look inside it. Furious, I managed to snatch it back off him. "How dare you! You are very ill-mannered. Good-day, sir!"

"Where are you off to now?" he called out after me. "Rothmarten Abbey? To shake up its secrets?"

Pausing, I spun around to see him tilt his hat and stroll off, whistling, his rod bouncing on his shoulder. Unbidden, I couldn't resist watching him swagger away. The man behaved like an overbearing ship captain. Truth be known, he was probably little more than a tennis club caddy, living in a hovel somewhere, and I felt intensely irritable that he'd walked away without my discovering anything about him. I'd learned nothing about him, whereas he seemed to know everything about me.

How can you say those beastly things to me? I will always be yours. I know what they say about me . . . please don't believe it. It's not true, I tell you. I love you.

I wrote the words down in my journal as I remembered them.

"Two callers for you this morning," Ewe said on my return. "Sir Edward and Miss Lianne Hartley. She seemed quite put out to hear you weren't here."

"Yes, she would be." The cloying attentions of a teenager were tiresome.

"And ye invited out tomorrow," Ewe chirped, "on a *country* drive with the Hartleys."

"Oh. What did Sir Edward want? Did he leave a note?"

"No. Askin' more questions, I think. Don't know what it's got to do with you. Your part is over, just as ye father said. And if you listen to ol' Ewe, ye shouldn't be seen too much with Lord David."

The warning, though friendly and delivered with a good purpose, annoyed me. "Why shouldn't I spend time up at Padthaway? He hasn't been arrested."

"But the case ain't closed yet," Ewe reminded. "And I've a care and *duty* for ye reputation while ye're under my roof."

I sighed. "What do you think I should do then? Decline tomorrow's invitation?" I looked at her suspiciously. "Has Mr. Brown been here at all?" "

Color stained Ewe's cheeks. "He bought me flowers. Thanked me for the luncheon—"

"And no doubt shared his reservations concerning my association with the Hartleys?"

Ewe couldn't deny it. She hadn't the face to lie.

"Well, I'm going," I announced, going to my room, "and I don't care what anyone says."

"Ye will care very much so if ye picture's taken with 'em," Ewe called out.

Perhaps I should have taken more care, but the fine day, and the allure of driving in a plush motorcar down the Cornish coast, were too much to resist. After my conversations with Connan Bastion and Mrs. Bastion, I no longer feared being seen in town with the Hartleys. I intended to keep my promise to them both, to discover the truth, no matter where it might lead.

They picked me up in front of the post office. From the corner of my eye, I gleaned Mrs. Penmark's head poke outside the bakery window, watching, lifting her eyebrows as I climbed into the car.

Lord David drove, Lady Hartley beside him in the front. I said hello to them all as I took a seat by Lianne, and in record time we were nosing out of the village, passing several curious villagers on the way.

"We're going to St. Mawes for lunch," Lady Hartley informed, adjusting her driving gloves. "At a place called Stall's. Have you ever been there, Daphne?"

"No," I said. "What is it?"

"A resort hotel by the sea," Lord David answered, his gaze perusing me in the rearview mirror. "I daresay you'll approve. It was once the home of a Russian countess. Late Georgian with a few

Victorian gothic touches. Your favorite form of architecture, I believe?"

I nodded, marveling at his ability to act so naturally after our kiss in the library. Then I remembered all the stolen kisses I'd shared with Geoffrey. He, too, had acted in a similar cavalier manner and I wondered if all males followed the same code.

Mercifully, the scenery usurped my troublesome reflections. It was a Cornish summer's day, still and perfect, the blue sky looming above open grasslands ablaze with red and yellow poppies, pink mallows, white clovers and yarrows, a lovely harmony of color.

"Stall's has the best shops and ice cream." Latching on to me, Lianne tugged my sleeve with childish joy.

I had decided to wear a dress, a wise choice considering the warm day. I had little time to do my hair but then, one could never keep hair in order on an open drive. Lady Hartley's hat, I noticed, preserved her manicured image. David wore no hat, his sunglasses shielding his eyes and emotions from view.

Inhaling the fresh, sweet air, I closed my eyes and let the wind assail my hair. It had been so long since I'd driven down this part of the coastland, the Roseland peninsula, and I was determined to enjoy every minute of it.

Weaving our way up to the quaint cliff top village of Portloe, where we stopped for fresh tea and scones, I immersed myself in the beauty and history of the place. Each village had something different to offer, like Veryan, with its circular thatched cottages and wide-eyed locals.

"The round shape is supposed to guard the village from evil." David happened upon me at one point while we waited for Lady Hartley and Lianne. "I hope you don't think I'm evil, Miss du Maurier."

He'd used my surname, I believed, to establish distance and formality between us. Wanting to support this wisdom, yet mildly disappointed by it, I shook my head. "No person is truly evil."

"Then you do forgive me. . . ."

"Forgive you?" I echoed.

"Do you forgive me," he murmured, "for upbraiding you the other day?"

He asked nothing about the kiss. "It is purely my fault. I shouldn't read other people's private letters."

"May I ask," he began, losing confidence halfway.

"Yes?" I prompted.

"May I ask . . . your opinion. Need I turn it in to Sir Edward?"

I didn't know what to say. It didn't incriminate him in any way but she did speak of an argument, she did speak of doubts, doubts concerning the parentage of the baby. Was it possible grounds for murder? "You should at least *show* it to Sir Edward," I advised. "For if it is somehow discovered later, it mightn't be . . ."

"Good for me?" he finished, smiling. "And what of the kiss? Do you forgive me for that, too, Daphne?"

I felt the heat rise to my face, especially as Lady Hartley and Lianne were only yards away. "It doesn't matter. Let's forget it and be friends." I held out my hand.

He shook it, a tiny smirk playing at the corners of his mouth.

I think we both embraced the drive to Stall's, a chance to dispel the awkwardness of our tête-à-tête, and the tour of St. Mawes Castle proved an excellent diversion.

The mansion of Stall's lurked on the other side of town with a view of the little boat-filled harbor. Once a private home, now an elite hotel and club, it breathed a history all of its own, the lineup of fancy cars outside the front merely a foregleam of its popularity.

I dreaded I might see someone I know. However, luck prevailed and after a sumptuous lunch surrounded by an intriguing array of dazzling hotel guests, we spent a leisurely afternoon on the terrace, sipping pink lemonade and devouring homemade ice cream. The tranquillity of the splendid seaside view with all its little boats seemed a perfect end to a perfect day.

"I don't think I've had such a lovely day in a long time," I said to Lord David when Lady Hartley and Lianne disappeared to greet old family friends.

"Nor have I," he murmured.

By the line of his mouth, I sensed something troubled him.

"Daphne, you don't think I did it, do you?"

"Did what?" I whispered, my throaty voice betraying a reluctance to allow anything to ruin this day.

"Murdered her."

I shivered, seeing the face of Victoria floating between us. "I . . . I wouldn't know," I stammered, alarmed by his deadly serious face. "Are you a murderous type, my lord?"

A half-laugh assailed his lips. "I don't know. Am I?"

I think he posed the question to test me. "Why do you ask?"

The corners of his lips lifted slightly. "Everybody else seems to think so. Just read the papers."

His mocking coldness concealed a deep and tortured soul. I noticed it and sought to sympathize using a heartening smile. "Yes, but one must realize the papers always sensationalize, and you're not exactly a nobody, are you? Don't worry. I'm sure it'll be forgotten in a month."

Forgotten in a month. What stupidity had possessed me to utter such a thoughtless thing? The breeze suddenly turned chilly.

"Lord David!"

Startled, we both turned to the gleaming eye of a photographer as he snapped us there, standing side by side on the terrace.

"Thank you, my lord." The greedy photographer bowed, racing away with his latest kill.

"Hell!"

Uttering another swear under his breath, David guided us back to the others.

"You'd think they'd have had their fill, wouldn't you?"

"Something has to sell papers," I said. "And I suppose they have to earn a living."

"Yes," he agreed. "I suppose they do."

CHAPTER TWENTY-EIGHT

"He was *given* the car by her ladyship. Oh, yes, oh, yes."

I blinked at Ewe Sinclaire's saucer eyes. "I trust you had a nice day, too?"

"Don't ye give me your smart lip, miss. I've a mind, and I nearly did trot to the post office to call ye father today."

Dropping my things in my room, I faced her with a weary turn. "And what stopped you?"

"I found out our Soames was *given* that fancy car he drives by Lady Hartley—a bonus. For what service, one can only imagine, for Lady H, I hear, gives him *private* menu instructions every morning in the drawing room. Have ye seen anything while ye've been up there? That Soames is worth investigatin', if ye ask me. *He* hired Victoria, remember. *He,* Lady H's lover, the cook!"

Something in her rambled speech made perfect sense. "Of course," I mouthed. "Of course!"

"Of course what?"

Stirring whatever concoction she was making on the stove, Ewe waited for the revelation, one arm poised on her generous hip. "What's the plan next, then?"

"I'll go to Padthaway. I'll find *some* reason to go to the kitchen, to talk to Soames. Ridgeway Soames," I mused, "such an *odd* name for a Cornishman. Who is his family?"

"No idea." Ewe shrugged. "A cagey one, that Soames. Wouldn't surprise me a bit if he and Victoria were, ye know . . ."

"Having an affair?" I pondered aloud. "Ewe." I rang up to kiss her on the cheek. "You're amazing! Of course, yes, of course, there was something between him and Victoria. Why else would he hire her?"

"Hmm." Ewe rolled her eyes. "A pretty face didn't strike ye smarty mind, did it?"

"I'm not clever in the least," I defended myself. "But you're right, Ewe. A pretty face is not the only answer. And if it began as the only answer, it ended up quite differently. I need to speak to Connan."

"Connan Bastion?"

I nodded, still deep in thought. "Where does he work? Do you know, Ewe?"

She confessed she knew the name and location of the shipping company Connan Bastion worked for, and owned by the Hartleys.

"It's a fair distance, though," she warned. "Can't get there by foot."

I was grabbing my coat and bag.

"Neither by train," Ewe's shout assailed me, "for there is none. The boys go there by company boat."

Defeated, I collapsed on my bed with a sigh. Trust the lack of local transport to thwart my investigative efforts!

"Any ideas on how to get there?" I called out.

"Well." Ewe rounded the corner, wide-eyed, and saucy wooden spoon in hand. "Ye could ask Mr. Brown. He has a car, y'know. And he's only a telephone call away."

"I'll not ask him," I said proudly. "What is he, anyway? Has he any profession?"

"I think he's a gentleman," Ewe sighed romantically, "or in the army. I don't know which, but he don't *work* for a living. He has means. I know that much. And a much better catch, I might add, than your fancy Lord David.

"I mean," Ewe continued, "if ye really serious about this murder and all that, a little phone call ain't goin' to do any harm, is it?"

So I called Mr. Brown, against my better judgment.

And he came, right on cue.

"Are you certain," he asked, driving his little nondescript motorcar, so unlike the polished numbers belonging to the Hartleys, "someone isn't paying you to investigate this sordid affair?"

"Sordid affair? Mr. Brown, the only sordid part in this whole affair is the lack of an answer."

"An answer?"

"An answer to the eternal question: Who killed Victoria and why?"

"So you believe she was murdered?"

"I don't know. She was a girl of many secrets."

"Yes, I know," he murmured. "Your Mr. Cameron, who said he spoke to you at the funeral, inferred he'd seen her at a few clubs in London. Not the kind of clubs respected ladies frequent."

"Was she hunting Lord David, do you think?" I couldn't believe I was asking this arrogant stranger a question so close to my heart.

"Possibly" came the expected reply. "She must have had a job there at one point."

"In London, do you mean?"

He nodded, nosing his noisy little motorcar into the docks where Connan Bastion worked.

"What do you intend on asking Victoria's brother? Do you want me to wait?"

"Yes, please," I said, sending him a grateful smile. "Connan is comfortable with me."

"Of course he is," Mr. Brown said under his breath. "You're a beautiful girl, or don't you realize?"

Blushing, I left the car in search of Connan. Despite the favor of a drive, I still disliked Mr. Brown and hated to have no choice but to rely upon him. And I did not appreciate the implication of his tone.

A series of whistles led me to the waiting ship. Aboard, Connan detected me and promptly deserted his position.

"What are ye doin' here?"

A good question and I had no intention of wasting his time. "I was up all night thinking. Please, Connan, tell me, did Victoria often go to London? Did she work there? Did she know any gentleman fellow? A Mr. Cameron or another? Did she speak of any?"

And then in a hushed tone I told him about the letter.

"You see, for her to write about such doubts that could break up a wedding, there must have been another suitor around. A friend of Victoria's, mayhap? Why would Lord David be concerned he might not be the father of her child?"

Biting his lips, Connan shifted his feet from one side to the other.

"You *do* know of someone, some other man," I persisted.

He still shifted his feet. "I knew she was going to town, but she never told me anything."

"This other man might have killed her, Connan. Out of spite or revenge."

Hugging his head between his hands, he cried angry tears, the tears glistening on the edges of his magnificent violet eyes that were so much like Victoria's.

"She were worried someone wanted to kill her. She told me so, the day before, a week before."

"Who she was scared of? Lady Hartley? Lord David? Some other man?"

"She said: 'Someone doesn't want me to be mistress of Padthaway and I'm not sure I want to be either. It's too dangerous.'"

"She said that? It's too dangerous?" I paused to think. "Dangerous because she could be bribed? As a rich man's wife?"

Connan colored. "It weren't me! I did ask for a bit here and there, but nothin' but pocket change to a man like Lord David."

"And then he refused you, didn't he? Did Victoria know?"

"I told her."

"What was her reaction?"

"Angry. She said she'd speak to him, and that he was only trying to protect her. Protect her! Protect her from her own *brother,* I say! Well, in the end, he couldn't do that, could he? Protect her. She's dead and she won't come back no more."

Something about that last phrase caught at me. *She won't come back no more.* I was reminded of mad old Ben, the gardener at Padthaway, with those strange rounded, vacant eyes.

A horn sounded from the dock.

"That's me foreman. I've got to get back to work."

I joined him a little of the way.

"How'd ye get here then?"

I read the suspicion in his eyes. "A Mr. Brown drove me. Do you know him? He comes to Windemere to visit his uncle."

"Yeah, I know him. I don't want him knowin' my business tho'. Already got me in enough trouble with work."

"I assure you I won't say a word. *Our* talks remain private, and if you think of anyone Victoria may have been afraid of, even if it's the *smallest* thing that comes to mind, a clue perhaps, you will come and see me, won't you?"

"Yeah, all right, Miss Daphne."

"How did you find him? Helpful?"

I avoided the question.

Mr. Brown stopped the car.

"We had an agreement, Mr. Brown," I said. "You agreed to drive me. No questions asked."

I watched the muscle in his lower jaw contract. "I promised Connan and if I can't keep to my word, I fear he might run away and never tell a soul."

We spent the remainder of the drive home discussing the prize if one of us should prove to be right about our suspicions. I regretted the loss of my independence, but I thanked Mr. Brown, trusting my cordial tone sounded genuine.

"If you ever need me again," he grinned, "on Sir Edward's case or at the abbey, let me know."

He drove off and I wondered if he was one of those treasure hunters the abbess warned me of. I worried he stalked the abbey at night, looking for a way inside, intending to steal the scrolls and sell them to one of the museums who wanted them so desperately. Since the abbey and the Hartley family only fulfilled the role as "keepers" and not owners, they could do nothing once the scrolls passed out of their hands.

I thought I had better warn Lord David of Mr. Brown. If I experienced the slightest tinge of guilt in doing so, I suppressed it. Mr. Brown had merely done me a favor. I owed him nothing, and the Hartleys came first.

Betsy answered the door. "Oh, miss! I don't know where Miss Lianne is, or Lord David. I *do* know Lady H is headin' to the greenhouse. I saw her, and if you go through there, ye'll catch her in time."

I hurried in the direction she pointed. I couldn't have planned it better myself. I was finally going to see the greenhouse where Mrs. Trehearn made her infamous tonics.

"Lady Florence," I called out, and her ladyship paused.

"Daphne, *darling*. How nice of you to visit."

I gestured to the small plant tucked under her arm. "May I join you? I'd love to see the greenhouse."

"It'd be a pleasure, Daphne."

We meandered through the lush maze of the hothouse, the entrance lurking under a wisteria-laden porch at the rear of the house. Partially attached to the southern end of the conservatory and surrounded by green wilderness, I loved the feeling inside, the light, the spasms of color, the reflection from the clean white glass windows and the aromas, sweet, pungent, and deadly.

Ricin came from the castor bean, and I glimpsed no evidence of anything remotely connected to the poison that killed Victoria as I sniffed around, following Lady Hartley through the labyrinth.

"I'm very happy you decided to visit Windemere Lane, Daphne. It is so nice to have someone of quality, someone who *understands* our ways."

Our ways or your ways, Lady Hartley? I said silently.

Reflecting on her own words, she smirked, her spidery eyes whimsical. "I suppose you think me heartless . . . like the wicked witch, I daresay, but I don't hide what I am. I never thought Victoria right for my son and time will prove it."

"Prove what, my lady?"

She stopped by a willowy orchid. "Prove I was right about that girl. She set out to entrap David—to elevate herself above her wretched beginnings. Probably planned it with her mother—despite what they say, all these commoners just desire one thing."

"And what is that?"

She looked surprised. "Why, to be one of us, of course. I have it in mind to ask you a great favor, Daphne. It is a small trifle, perhaps, but one that will satisfy my little problem."

I lifted a caustic brow.

"You see, I'm afraid Lianne's education has been somewhat neglected and Jenny said you offered to teach her a thing or two while you're here on holiday. She would benefit greatly from someone of your *caliber* and I would be eternally grateful."

"I should love to do so, Lady Florence."

"Good." She rubbed her hands as though rid of an irritant. "I know the done thing is to send the child away to school, as you were, but Lianne has that little problem."

I might have seized the opportunity to ask more of Lianne's problems inherited from her ill-fated father and Lady Hartley's dead husband had not Mrs. Trehearn chosen then to invade the peace.

I shivered. The woman put one immediately on guard, and I thought she'd make a splendid sinister character for a book one day. A creepy housekeeper, unsmiling, her black gown tracing the darkened corridors of the house.

I made an effort to be civil to Mrs. Trehearn. Her wintry face looked frightening as she snipped away at her plant, her black eyes intense on the unsuspecting floral victim.

"The sleeping tonic you make for me," Lady Hartley prompted, "I wish you to make for dear Daphne's father. Such a busy man—I am sure he will appreciate it."

Dear Daphne. Another elevation for me. Dare I concede to vanity and revel in it?

Lady Hartley was still prattling on about me. "I *do* so want Daphne to invite her family down . . . do you know her father *dines* with the prime minister? Yes, *dines,* Trehearn. Incredible, isn't it?"

Not required to answer, Mrs. Trehearn continued to snip her little plant while I took another turn about the room, sneezing at the odd plant.

"Hothouses are dangerous to some," Mrs. Trehearn said, handing me a handkerchief. "You ought to be careful, Miss du Maurier."

Her black eyes intensified.

Did she mean to warn me, I wondered?

CHAPTER TWENTY-NINE

For my first lesson with Lianne, I suggested a picnic and invited Jenny Pollock to come along with us.

Jenny was overjoyed.

"Ye want an old thing like me hangin' about?" Her plump cheeks blossomed. "I ain't done a picnic in years!"

I liked Jenny and I had a double motive for inviting her. I wanted to learn more about David and Lianne's father.

We went down to see Soames about the food. While Lianne chattered on excitedly, he followed my instructions and I thought this natural, relaxed environment the ideal time to ask how he became cook at Padthaway.

His smug expression told me more than I wanted to know. "Lady Hartley purloined me from Sir Edmund Hillary."

I cringed at the emphasis on "purloin."

"Is there anything else you wanted to ask me, Miss Daphne?"

I didn't like the way his eyes challenged mine, judging my motive for coming to Padthaway.

"Do you want to ask me about Victoria?"

My sideways glance went to Lianne but she'd already left, carrying our basket of goods and calling for me to hurry.

"This case is in no hurry, is it? We all know Sir Edward won't arrest Lord David. He hasn't the gumption."

Another spur on Sir Edward's reputation. "Did you know any of her family? Victoria's? Is that how she came to work here?"

Crossing his arms, Soames grinned. "You're a plucky one, aren't you? Do you think finding the body gives you special license to conduct your own investigation?"

"Well, yes," I said simply. "I believe it does." And repeated my question.

"No, I knew none of her family," he quickly replied, and turning his back on me, resumed stacking plates in the kitchen.

"Good-day then, Mr. Soames." I walked out, raising an eyebrow for his rapid reaction, indicating that maybe he did know her family, for how else had she gone to work at Padthaway? I wondered if Sir Edward had had any more success with Soames. He was a cagey fellow, Lady Hartley's Friday man, her personal driver, chef, and lover. The description gave him power here at Padthaway, but did he have the power to murder? He might have been a jealous ex-lover of Victoria's or just a man interested in her and spurned for the rich Lord David.

It was difficult to concentrate on the lesson I'd planned for Lianne. Outdoors, when the precious sunshine beckoned, I almost wished that I'd come out here alone to lay on my blanket on the grass and curl up with a good book.

A good book I did have, and settling on a grassy pasture overlooking the sea, I drew out the book while Jenny spread the blanket. "As your newly ordained governess," I teased Lianne in my best schoolmistress tone, "I wish you to read the first chapter, please."

She stared at me in horror. "I . . . I can't."

"What do you mean you can't?"

Her frightful glance went to Jenny before she stormed off, once again the moody teenager.

Jenny stopped twirling the wildflower in her hand. "She ain't no reader, my Lee Lee. Trehearn tried to force her once, so did Miss

Perony, but the words get muddled in her brain. Didn't Lady Muck mention the readin' problem to ye?"

"No, but I suppose she alluded to it, now that I think of it."

Jenny nodded, resuming her seat on the blanket. I followed suit, dismayed by this revelation. "Does she need glasses?"

"They tried that. She stomped on the three pairs, sayin' it weren't her eyesight." Jenny sighed. "I really don't know. The poor child's been through so much . . ."

I asked about Lianne's father.

"Lady Hartley had a fancy doctor down from London once—it were after his lordship shot himself. The silly doc said the child were mentally ill like her father because she lied about seein' him puttin' the gun to his head. Lady H washed her hands of it and Lee Lee became what they branded her."

A consummate liar, like her father. Sensing Jenny's strong disapproval of Lady Hartley's lack of maternal instinct, I smiled. "Poor Lianne. She's lucky to have you."

A softness shaded Jenny's eyes. "I'm just a hanger-on, as they say. But I couldn't bear to leave this place . . . or my two kittens."

The hanger-on nurse. She lived for her "children" and received board as payment, forever guaranteed a place because she could handle Lianne. "So was Lianne's father mad?"

Jenny fiercely shook her head. "He weren't mad, or if he were, it was *she* that sent him that way. As if *that* woman ever cared for anyone but herself."

That woman. Lady Hartley had used a similar term to describe Victoria. I mulled over the women of the house. Lady Hartley and Victoria. Jenny and Lady Hartley. Lady Hartley and Mrs. Trehearn. They all seemed to dislike one another and yet they cohabited. Jenny because of Lianne, Mrs. Trehearn because she served a function other than housekeeping, and Victoria . . . Victoria . . .

Lianne returned, breathless. "I went to the cove."

Her eyes were unusually bright and I shivered while Jenny starting arranging the lunch.

"Are you cold, Daph?"

She gazed at me like a little girl now, innocent incredulity. "I have a wrap. Do you want it?"

"No, I'm fine," I smiled. "You didn't happen to see any shoes down there, did you?"

"Shoes?" A scowl deepened her brow. "Whose shoes?"

"Victoria's." I glanced out at the sea, thoughtful. "It makes some sense that if she went midnight walking, even in her nightgown, she must have had shoes. Or at least taken them with her."

I had opened the subject and ignored Jenny's disapproving eye.

I saw Lianne's contemplating the thought. "You're clever to think of shoes, Daphne. Sir Edward hadn't thought of them, I'm sure. Isn't Daphne clever, Jenny?"

Jenny stiffened. "We'll not be discussin' this. It bodes no good."

Who for? I wanted to argue. Why not discuss the mystery openly like everyone else? What did these people at Padthaway have to hide? Who were they trying to protect?

I don't think I really wanted the answers to my own questions.

After lunch, which passed pleasantly for the sun held and the wind kept at bay, Lianne agreed to try the book.

"I'll *try* reading with you, Daphne. It's just Mrs. T I can't stand. I *hate* her."

"Lee Lee!" Jenny cried.

An unrepentant Lianne shrugged. "Why should I hide the truth? I've always hated her."

"Miss Daphne," Jenny prodded me, "don't let her speak that way."

"I understand it though, for we've had our share of bad governesses. My sister Angela and I made up names for them. We had Cross Nurse Rush; Grumpy H'm H'm, who hummed everywhere she went; Nurse Bun, who was fat and loved food; and Miss Torrance, who wasn't a bad governess on reflection but restricted our freedom."

"You see, Jenny!" Lianne cheered. "At last, *someone* understands me! But I'm afraid Daph is far too clever for me . . ."

I shook my head. "Do you know, when I arrived at the finishing school in France, they had the audacity to place me in the *lower* class. Yes, it's true. They had four classes. The *première* for the elitist, bright Frenchies, as I used to call them; the *deuxième A*, who were able but not brilliant; *deuxième B*, who were somewhat inferior; and lastly, the *troisième*, the dud class. And," I went on dramatically, "after a test, my friend Dodie and I were put in *deuxième B*. I took some comfort I wasn't with the duds, or toads as Dodie and I called them, but it was *extremely* mortifying."

Listening, Lianne still looked doubtful. "I'd be with the toads."

"No, you wouldn't," I said firmly. "Now, here is your first lesson, Miss Lianne Hartley, and remember it well for I shan't give it again."

She braced herself, a whimsical smile playing on her lips.

"Classes don't matter. What matters is *choice*. You have the choice to progress or to give up. Those who give up are the toads."

Thin brows breeding defiance lifted.

"*Cowards*," I emphasized.

The defiance sharpened and she caught the book I threw at her. "Now start practicing. Concentrate on the story, not the words, and put yourself in Robinson Crusoe's shoes. I know I do."

The novelty of being a male embarking on a great adventure swept away all of Lianne's inhibitions and we settled down to an entertaining afternoon.

However, my feet remained not with Robinson Crusoe but with Victoria and her missing shoes.

The desire to see Victoria's room grew within me to a wild urge, beckoning, unrelenting, drawing me to that part of the house time and time again.

"The trouble is," Lianne whispered to me on the way back from our picnic, "Trehearn's got the key with her all the time. She doesn't carry other keys around with her. Interesting, isn't it?"

Very much so. Why cordon off the room? Why carry *that* key and not the others? Had Lady Hartley or David ordered it locked?

I could understand the emotional aspect from David's point of view. If he truly loved her it would be terribly romantic to keep a room exactly the way it was the day she left it. However, from a murderer's point of view, how clever to keep it shut from prying eyes.

Sir Edward had finished with the room, supposedly not finding anything of interest there. Perhaps he'd overlooked something.

"Come on," Lianne nudged me, her whisper conspiratorial and full of mischief, "I'll take you to the *forbidden* room."

"Did Victoria choose this room or did your mother choose it for her?"

"Mother suggested it," Lianne grinned. "I think Victoria wanted Mother's room and asked David. Davie sorted it out."

I imagined the scene: a man caught between two women, both wanting the best room in the house. From Victoria's standpoint, she thought herself entitled to it as David's bride, while the room had belonged to Lady Hartley for years.

Heading along the breezy corridor, I put myself in Victoria's place. If I were a young bride I'd want Lady Hartley's room, too. I felt sure Victoria felt the same way, her purpose in moving here a step toward the end goal as mistress of the house. How this must have enraged Lady Hartley.

"Davie said Victoria could have this room instead. The King's Chamber. It's the best room after Mummy's."

I stared at the old oak door, alive with a history of its own. Elusively locked, I suspected the key matched those of the era, heavy and ornate. I wanted it. I wanted to see *her* room.

Mrs. Trehearn proved a cagey guardian, catching us standing there, her black eyes taunting me. *You want to see the room, don't you, Miss Daphne? You've always wanted to see it.* They were never voiced, but I saw the words there as she pointed her little chin downward and rattled the key before me.

"Well, then, do you want to see it?"

"Are we allowed to? Will Sir Edward mind?" I asked, shocked.

Mrs. Trehearn's answer was to open the door.

My heart beat faster and faster. There had to be some clue inside here, some clue the police had missed, some clue as to what had happened that tragic night.

Lianne pushed in ahead. "Come on, Daphne. Come and see."

The King's Chamber was a masculine room, owing to its name, with a heavy canopied four-poster bed dominating the expanse, cavalier tapestries and paintings adorning the walls, the thick Turkish rugs below one's feet, and a Georgian lady's dresser gracing the back wall, bearing eerie remnants of its dead owner.

Other remnants of Victoria's presence remained, including a wardrobe full of clothes and accessories, shoes, and a coat slung over the coat stand. Innately curious, I touched each item as I explored, caressing the fine silk sheets of her bed, her underclothes; the satins, the laces; admiring the subtle elegance reflected everywhere.

Victoria had a keen sense of taste and style, most of it neat and orderly; however, there was an impression of haste that disturbed the peace of the room.

Returning to the front door where Mrs. Trehearn still stood guard, her blank face squashing any attempt at conversation I may have made, I envisaged Victoria on the night of her death. What had happened? The row with Lord David, heard by Betsy and Annie, the disturbance at the dinner table, her drinking . . . then she runs back to her room in an emotional state, flings off her coat and shoes, dumps her purse on the dresser before storming to her wardrobe. Tearing off her evening dress, she changes into her nightgown.

Her nightgown. If she was upset and angry and planned to go for a walk, why get into her nightgown?

Even in an enraged, erratic moment, surely one could manage to take a pair of shoes? I thought of the rocky part on the cliffs, not exactly pleasant for bare feet.

"Has your brother ever been back here, Lianne?" I whispered out of Mrs. Trehearn's earshot.

Flicking through a magazine left by the sleek bedside table, Lianne didn't hear me.

It was a bridal magazine and I drew closer, observing the queer look on her face. Did I imagine it or did Lianne smile?

"Here it is," she found the page she was looking for. "Victoria wanted this wedding gown but some Italian opera singer snapped it up. She got into an awful rage about it. I don't know why. The wedding dress she ordered as second best is beautiful. Did you see it?"

I stared at her, dismayed. She spoke so heartlessly of the woman who had carried her brother's child and was to become his wife. "You hated her, didn't you?"

Shrugging, Lianne led me to the wardrobe to see the wedding dress. "She didn't love Davie. She trapped him with the baby just like Mummy says. And she wanted his money. His money and his title."

"Did she ever try to talk to you about her love for David?"

Lianne shook her head, hunting through the very back of the closet to find the dress, hanging there eerily white and shining with a myriad of pearls and beads and crystals, a lovely dress fit for a princess.

"It's pretty, isn't it?" Lianne sniffed. "They had to alter it and there was something wrong with it, that's why she went up to London on the Wednesday. Or so she said."

Wednesday was the day before she died. "Do you think she went up there for some other reason?"

"I don't know."

Perhaps realizing she'd said too much, Lianne left me staring at the dress. By now, I expected a whistle or something from Mrs. Trehearn to signal the end of our tour of the forbidden room, but no intrusion appeared, and that fact made me feel positively uncomfortable. Certainly, strange behavior went on in this household.

Staring at the dress one last time, the irrefutable truth occurred to me. When a dress such as this awaited, its owner did not intend to die, no matter the circumstances or inducement. She had been murdered, but how and, more importantly, why.

I began with the why, searching for a clue, a motive, hunting through her dresser, searching the perfume bottles, wondering which one Lord David favored, rose, lavender, vanilla, sweet jasmine, or lotus?

Sitting down in the dressing chair where Victoria must have sat, a queer coldness overcame me. The brushes and combs, the jewelry box, and other items of Victoria's personal life surrounded me, and I found myself reluctant to touch her things, as though it were Victoria watching me and not Mrs. Trehearn.

Victoria's cache of jewelry revealed little, a collection of beads, brooches, hat pins, bangles, and pearl necklaces, the drawers crammed full of such accessories. Remembering where I'd hidden a letter as a child, I felt underneath the dressing table, my foot feeling for anything that may have fallen in those last hurried minutes before her death. Nothing.

No, but wait . . . a perfume puffer had rolled its way to the back leg near the wall. Bending down to pick it up, I almost cut my finger on the jagged amber glass.

"What'd you find?"

"Ouch!" Checking my finger, I reinserted the stopper. "It's only a perfume puffer and the top's broken."

"Mother bought her that one. I remember when she gave it to her. It's supposed to be exotic Persian."

I sniffed the remaining liquid, instantly repelled. "It must have gone off—it's dreadful."

Mrs. Trehearn's fixed eyes detected us in the corner. "Did you find something?"

"Nothing," I lied.

Lianne thought it was amusing to see me do it, to lie about something so stupid. Maybe it wasn't so stupid, I thought. It could be a clue to piece together what had happened that night . . . had she thrown the puffer at David, or if she was in a hurry, had she knocked it under her dresser? After a furtive glance at Lianne, I put the puffer in my pocket. Since it'd rolled under the dresser, I didn't think anybody would notice it was missing.

"Two minutes," Mrs. Trehearn dictated.

"Yes, yes," Lianne rolled her eyes while I searched through Victoria's jewelry again, picking up a string of lavender beads. I'd seen those beads before . . .

"She always wore those."

Lianne stood behind me.

"Oh, yes, the photograph."

"They're not worth anything. Come, we'd better go."

Examining the beads closer, I fancied I heard a faint, mocking laugh. Glancing into the mirror, I imagined Victoria's face there, watching me with her beads.

I put down the beads and prepared to go when the clasp caught my attention. Oval, of unusual shape, with a little star-cut ruby stone at either end, it sprang open at my touch to reveal its carefully guarded secret.

To V . . . love MSR.

CHAPTER THIRTY

"And she let ye see it, just like that?"

Pulling the kettle off the stove, Ewe poured the tea, asking me a thousand questions all at once.

"Nice to have ye here for a change," she scoffed. "How did ye drive with Mr. Brown go? He's a handsome fellow! Such fine manners."

"You don't have to sell Mr. Brown to me."

"Oh?" She grew excited.

"Yes," I smiled, "for I am not interested."

Her crestfallen face adopted an ominous hue. "It's that Lord David, ain't it?"

"Getting back to Mrs. Trehearn, for it's the *mystery* that interests me more than *men,* why do you think she let Lianne and me inside the room?"

"Because ye were both standin' there like two little puppies?"

The simple explanation failed to satisfy me. "I think she knows something about Lianne. She was watching both of us like hawks, but Lianne more so."

"The child is strange. And despite what Jenny Pollock says, the father was as mad as a hatter! Shot himself, y'know."

I described the rest of the picnic to Ewe, and the mystery of Victoria's missing shoes.

"Easy. The murderer has them, or hid them."

"Or maybe she wore none, but I don't believe that. It's a rocky stretch . . . No, I'd leave behind a purse, but not shoes."

"The beads are better," Ewe nodded. "Tho' don't know if ye should be stealin' things from her room. That hawk Mrs. T will know what's missin'."

"The beads, maybe, but certainly not the puffer. It had rolled all the way under her dresser."

"I heard Mrs. B wants her daughter's things back."

This was news to me. "What would she do with all those glorious clothes? She has no occasion to wear them."

"*Sell* them." Ewe rolled her eyes. "My, my, for a smart girl, ye don't think of *everything*, do ye?"

Ewe was right. Small, little things, things a fresh mind or a stranger might see at an instant, often escaped my notice. *Had I become too close to the case? Should I even be here, embroiling myself in it? Should I remain silent?* One thing was certain. Victoria's murderer lurked out there somewhere, and they'd not take kindly to my meddling, particularly if I stumbled upon something of import.

"Ye should stop huntin'." Ewe read my thoughts.

"So should you," I retorted. "Oh, I *know* you've been to Miss Perony's a few times. . . . I've seen your basket out front."

"She's well bred and too tight-lipped for my likin'," came Ewe's report. "And she knew a lot more about Vicky Bastion than she'll tell. Even when Vicky got engaged, she still waved to Miss Perony and the like. Miss Perony said she went to tea at Padthaway once."

Could Miss Perony, the schoolteacher, know the reason for Victoria's London visits? Probably not, if it was at a *place not respectable*. "I'll try with Miss Perony."

I doubted I'd have more success than Ewe, me, a mere stranger asking questions about a local girl, when Ewe had been in the village for many years.

"The best time to see her is after school on a Tuesday or a Thursday, for Wednesdays she's off at some knittin' class and Mondays and Fridays she tutors privately."

I nodded and went as instructed, on some pretext of lending a book to Miss Perony and talking of the progress I'd made at the abbey with her cousin Agatha.

Miss Perony seemed delighted to see me.

"You're almost one of us now, Daphne. Have you extended your stay in Windemere?"

"Yes. I'll expect a letter from home soon, speeding my return."

"Your sisters must miss you terribly."

"My father more, I think. I'm very close to my father. Speaking of which, Connan Bastion said his real father couldn't acknowledge him. That father lives in London, doesn't he?"

Miss Perony removed her spectacles. "Daphne, I do advise against you associating with Connan Bastion. He's a good lad, at heart, but he's wild, like his sister. They can't be tamed."

I thought this was interesting. "I didn't know Victoria, but I imagine her being so beautiful, with a personality to go along with it. What do you mean by wild, if I may ask?"

Expressing a deep reluctance to say more, Miss Perony consented. "I know you are trustworthy, Daphne, even though I disapprove of your involvement with the Hartleys."

"Whom do you suspect? Lord David? Miss Lianne? Lady Hartley?"

Her lip trembled at the latter. "Lady Hartley is capable of anything."

"And Victoria didn't take her own life, in your opinion?"

"No."

"What makes you so sure?"

Her eyes lowered.

"It can't be breaking a confidence when she's dead, can it?" Daphne asked.

"I suppose not."

"Then?"

"She came and saw me a day or so before she died. She said she knew she was going to die. She sat there shaking, prewedding jitters apparent in every line of her body. I said it's only natural to feel nervous before the big day, and then she did the strangest thing."

"What was that?"

"She laughed. It was a hysterical laugh through which she mentioned her future mother-in-law."

"Lady Hartley?"

"Yes. Victoria and she had never seen eye to eye, and from when Lord David proposed, Victoria always feared his mother would break them apart. This time, however, she said Lady Hartley had been acting differently, so *attentive,* even to the point of buying her bride gifts and so forth."

"What was your reply?"

"I said I thought it a little odd, but naturally Lady Hartley has no choice but to accept her this close to the wedding."

"Poison," I whispered. "Lady Hartley poisoned her through the bride gifts?!"

"The Judas kiss," Miss Perony shrugged, "but they've found no evidence to link Lady Hartley to anything."

"Did Victoria talk of David?"

"Yes. She said she and David were having arguments over Connan, and money again. Connan wanted his future brother-in-law to pay his gambling debts; he'd done so before but now he'd refused."

"What of the father in London?"

A shadow came over Miss Perony's face. "I could be wrong, but I don't believe Connan and Victoria ever met their father. He disappeared . . . years ago."

"But he spoke of a father, one who refused to acknowledge them because he had a wife and children of his own."

Miss Perony nodded. "He is not their father. I think Connan and Victoria liked to fantasize about having a rich father. Their real father was just a sea lord who died out at sea, leaving his pregnant woman behind."

"So Connan and Victoria are twins?"

Miss Perony stared at me in astonishment. "Of course they were twins. Didn't anyone tell you?"

"No, but I should have guessed. The resemblance of the eyes . . ."

"Yes," Miss Perony murmured. "Beauty is dangerous. It did no favors for Victoria."

We sat there in silence for a moment. I understood Miss Perony and why she'd allowed me to speak to her. From our very first conversation, we shared a love of literature and history, and a common interest in Rothmarten Abbey and its treasure. She knew she could trust me, and she rarely trusted anyone. A lonely schoolteacher, learned and intelligent, she struggled to fit in with the village folk. She glowed in the company of Mr. Brown, if I remembered correctly, and I faintly teased her about her affection for him to see if I was right.

I was right. She blushed.

"Oh, I am nothing to him. I'm not even pretty. I think he's interested in you, Daphne."

"If you saw us driving together, it was only a favor. I hardly know Mr. Brown and find he doesn't agree with me at all. *You* he'd find enchanting, and you have it in your power to capture him."

Long-lost hope flared in her nondescript eyes. "He'd never see me in the romantic sense. In any case, I am a few years older than him."

"He prides *intelligence*," I said. "You only have to exhibit yourself a little more. Terrible to have to resort to such devices, isn't it? Since we can't all be as beautiful as Victoria and have a lineup of suitors. Speaking of which, she often went to London, didn't she? What did she do there?"

"She waited tables at a club. That's where she met Lord David. He'd never notice her driving through the village."

I nodded, thinking of the beads. "Was there another man before Lord David? Someone with the initials MSR?"

"MSR," Miss Perony echoed, and I had to explain myself. Without going into too much detail, I said Lianne and I had found a string of beads in her room and those initials were engraved inside the clasp.

"Yes, yes, I remember those beads. They were her favorite and she had them when I first came to Windemere seven years ago. She was sixteen then, and every boy in the village ogled Victoria. But she wasn't going to settle for anything less than a man with a title, and stuck to it. She went to London to catch a husband. She told me so herself, but I know of no MSR."

"Why did she confide in you?"

"She enjoyed teasing me, but she never truly confided in me; I wish now she'd done so. If she had, maybe her death could have been prevented. I knew something was troubling her deeply, but I rarely saw her, so there was nothing I could do. If I pressed her, she probably would have said nothing. Even Connan knows little."

Lady Hartley and the poisonous bride gifts.

Returning to my room in Ewe's cottage, I placed the two items I'd purloined on the tiny table serving me as a dresser.

Two clues. The beads and the broken perfume puffer. The beads.

To V, love MSR.

Who was MSR? A lover, or a secret father? Or perhaps the initials meant nothing at all. Perhaps she'd simply bought the beads in a shop selling secondhand wares and the initial V was merely a coincidence?

Hiding the two items in my underclothes, I went out for a late-afternoon walk. My favorite walk in Windemere was the one down to the sea.

I pretended I was Victoria, and unbidden, like a jolting flash, Lord David's face drifted before me, the memory of his lips on mine. We both knew what had driven him to kiss me that day in the library, yet I had to admit I enjoyed the kiss and so did he, I believed.

"Looking for a new mystery? Or still working on the old one?"

It was Mr. Brown, the one person I did not want to see today. Miserable over my foul luck, guilt, and unruly salt-splattered hair, I smiled through my teeth.

"You catch me fishing in forbidden waters." Grinning, he put down his sea rod and tackle box.

"Were you successful?" I thought I should ask.

"I am always successful." Lifting the lid of his box, he showed me the still flipping fish. "He'll steady in a minute. Hmm, a snack before dinner."

"You're cruel."

Shutting the box, he pushed up his rolled-up sleeves. "Cruelty comes in many forms. One could call driving with a man in mourning cruel. In fact, cruel is the wrong word. *Inappropriate.*"

I opened my mouth in astonishment. "You have your information wrong, Mr. Brown. I was not alone with Lord David. There was—"

"On that occasion," he tempered, his green eyes challenging me. "Why do you insist on associating with a potential murderer? Is it your intention to follow the ill-fated Victoria, for that, my dear Miss du Maurier, is where it will lead."

"I'm afraid you are entirely wrong in your assumptions," I retorted.

"Oh," he goaded, "so you *have* made progress since our last date. Was Connan—"

"Date, Mr. Brown? Our drive was no date."

"A pity. I like to think it was."

He stood there, grinning, intensely amused. "I can recommend a lady to you, Mr. Brown, if you are in want of female company. A Miss Perony Osborn."

His lip quivered. "You are unkind. How could I look at another woman now that you have waltzed into my life?"

I raised my eyes.

"Or is Lord David your primary concern now? Poor fellow. Lost one bride, he's in need of another—"

I felt my face grow hot. "How can you say that!" I stepped back, furious. "You're jealous. That's your problem. You're jealous of him because . . ."

He lifted a brow. "Because?"

"Because he has a fine house and women are attracted to him. Because he *is* a good man, despite local suspicion."

I wished he'd go away. I wished he'd not stand there and utter such unfair and completely erroneous assumptions. I had a mind to leave him without saying a word. However I'd be in a worse mood if I didn't discover his identity, and to be truthful, I was intrigued.

"Let's sit over here for a minute," Mr. Brown directed. "Out of the wind."

Locating a grassy patch on a side of a jutted rock, we sat there, overlooking the gorge below. Still breezy, I roped my hair behind my ears, pulling the odd strand out of my mouth.

"Don't you just *love* our wild Cornwall." Mr. Brown, to my horror, began gutting his fish, whistling and smiling. "You don't mind, do you? It'll save me time."

I think he wanted to shock me. It amused him to do so, so I employed the opposite reaction and swapping disgust for casual indifference, I rolled my shoulders and lulled back into the rock. "You called Cornwall 'our' Cornwall, but you don't live here."

"I'm a homeless wanderer," he laughed, "moving from one hovel to another."

"Does this hovel owner have a profession?" I smiled.

"Ah, the old profession. Why don't you hazard a guess, Miss Sleuth?"

He dressed casually, that faux pas at Ewe's an act of social disregard more than ignorance, for he spoke well, indicating a good education, and he retained a certain athletic poise, if somewhat self-confident and overdisciplined. "Military . . . and you're on holiday."

"Very good," he smiled. "I expected no less."

"Aren't you going to properly introduce yourself?"

He swept up his newly gutted fish and bowed. "Major Frederick Arthur Montague Browning the Second at your service, Miss du Maurier," he said, pausing to add with a wink, "but always Mr. Brown on holiday."

In spite of myself, I laughed. He reminded me of Rudolf Rassendyll in *The Prisoner of Zenda*. "Sometimes it's wise to go incognito on holidays," I said, "unfortunately, I can never do so."

"It's part of the package, coming from a famous family. I daresay Lady Hartley has singled you out as her future daughter-in-law. Am I correct in that assumption, Miss du Maurier?"

"I suppose you are, Major Browning."

"Does it caution you to heed a little friendly advice?"

I had prepared to listen so I waited, folding my hands together in my lap.

"There's not enough evidence to convict any of them for murder . . . unless something shows up. My reason for believing ill of Lord David is not based on idle assumptions but rather knowledge, knowledge of the madness in the family and its colorful history."

He sounded reasonable, too, darn him. "Do you suspect all of them, then?"

"Every member of the Hartley family and its associates."

"You mean Mrs. Trehearn and Mr. Soames by associates? You *know* something about Soames, don't you?"

He shrugged. "I cannot reveal *all* of my secrets, just like you. You've said nothing, yet your face betrays you. You have your doubts about the family, too, don't you?"

I deliberated over what to say. Wishing to remain loyal to my new friends, yet understanding I needed to share something with him if I wanted to learn more of his knowledge of the family, I mentioned Victoria's room.

The corners of his mouth twitched. "You *are* a sleuth, aren't you?"

"We found a broken perfume puffer in her room." I ignored his cynicism. "It might be nothing but it smells awful."

"Who's we?"

"Lianne and I."

"Lianne and you . . ." he murmured thoughtfully. "How did you get inside?"

"Mrs. Trehearn let us, just for a moment."

"Did she stay the whole time watching you? Or watching Lianne Hartley?"

I said yes, confused. "Why do you ask?"

"I told you. Any member of the Hartley family cannot be ruled out and that includes Miss Lianne—"

"But she's just a child."

"Age bears no hold on madness."

"You think she's insane, don't you?"

"I have good reason to believe so. Why else do you think Lady Hartley keeps her there under Jenny's tight rein?"

I recalled the conversation with Lady Hartley and everything said about Lianne, *a consummate liar*. Did the madness induce her to jealously poison her brother's bride and then forget she'd done it?

I felt suddenly ill. The odd comment here and there from Lianne, the intense look in her eyes, a fixated intensity, all perhaps out of her control, suddenly came to mind.

"Did you find anything else in the room?"

I thought of the smooth lavender beads, the beads she always wore, the beads now hidden in my stocking drawer, but I decided to keep that find to myself. "I must be getting back," I said, glancing at my watch. "It's late and I promised Ewe I'd help with dinner."

"Why don't you test your stolen perfume puffer then? Or are you afraid?"

"You probably just happen to know someone who works in a poison lab . . ."

"I do, actually." He cheerfully brushed aside my sarcasm. "All you have to do is hand the goods over to me. That is, if you trust me."

He was baiting me. "You're the kind of man who always knows somebody," I mocked. "May I ask what you're really doing here? I may be fishing a murder but I wager you're hunting abbey treasure."

He grimaced. "Do I look like a hunter?"

He posed for a moment, giving me his best smile.

"Good-day, Mr. Brown."

"Good-day, Miss Daphne. Mindful meddling now."

And without further ado, he collected his box and rod and disappeared.

Mindful meddling.

He didn't think I would solve the mysteries. Well, I'd prove him wrong. Yes, and I'd start by giving him the puffer, after making him wait a certain while to dismantle his arrogance.

CHAPTER THIRTY-ONE

A letter arrived from home. Ewe waved it at me while pruning her roses. The roses reminded me of Ben the gardener.

"The mad one? Been here forever. Likes to watch life, does Ben."

Likes to watch life. A vision of the blank, starry-eyed Ben stalking the gardens at night sprang to mind. Had he witnessed the death of Lord Hartley? More important, had he seen Victoria on the night of her death?

Tapping the letter between my fingers, I imagined its likely contents. A directive from home advising me to leave Windemere Lane and return to dreary old London. I was correct.

The envelope contained two letters, one from father and one from my sister Angela.

I read father's first. In true style, he'd written it on the scrappy back of his latest play flyer:

> *My dear girl,*
> *Your mother is outraged. She demands you come*
> *home. She saw your picture in the paper.*
> *Made some inquiries about the Hartley lot.*
> *Father, nutty, shot himself. Son, distant. Lady*
> *Hartley linked to more scandals than one can count.*

> *Sounds interesting, though. I can understand why*
> *you've swapped us for your Cornish mansion by the*
> *sea . . .*
>
> > *Your loving D,*
> > *Sir Gerald du Maurier*

I laughed. He always made me laugh.

Angela, my elder sister, and quite the polished beauty, composed her ensemble on crisp white writing paper scented with rose.

> *Dear Daphne,*
> *A quiet country holiday is it? D and I know it's*
> *not (see photo attached). M is out of her mind with*
> *worry. She thinks you'll be next to fall over those*
> *perilous cliffs . . .*
>
> > *Is it murder, do you think? I'm quite jealous, you*
> *know. You ought to invite me down. This Lord*
> *David creature . . . hmm, I wouldn't mind investi-*
> *gating him.*
>
> > *Love, A*
> > *P.S.: Jeanne sends her love. She's staying at*
> > *Aunt May's. Wonder if she's seen the picture?*

Trust Angela to include it. Smiling at her diligence, and for knowing me so well to want to see one's picture in the city paper, I perused the verdict. How did I look? Not bad, a trifle flash-stricken, but oh dear, was that a smut on my nose?

I shoved the paper aside, not wanting to see it, yet I felt I must.

The photographer had captured the mood of the funeral day perfectly. The old gothic church, the lineup of spectators, the grieving family, the—

I peered closer. No, it couldn't be . . .

Mr. Soames was standing beside the younger Bastion boy and they looked alarmingly alike—the broad jawline, the heavy brow.

Was it a coincidence? I recalled Soames's blatant denial . . . *No, I knew none of her family.*

"Mmmm, let me see." Putting on her strongest spectacles, Ewe perused the photograph at great length. "Mmmm, they do look alike, but it might just be ol' Cornish blood. We're all related, if ye go back far enough."

Disappointed, I sighed. "I saw your favorite person yesterday, Ewe. *Mr. Brown.* Who is *not* Mr. Brown."

"No," Ewe smiled elusively. "He is someone much more important. Why else do ye think I was so excited about his attendance at my dinner. Not for Miss Perony!"

"Poor Miss Perony," I sympathized. "I recommended her to your *Major Browning.* I told him what I'd found in Victoria's room. He had some interesting things to say about Lianne Hartley."

"Does he think *she* did it?"

Ewe's mouth remained open as I relayed his words.

"She might 'ave got jealous," Ewe considered aloud. "Lord David's looked after her like a baby. She hates her mother so he's her only friend, ain't he? And then he brings his bride into the picture and forgets about his sister, or don't pay her enough attention—"

The doorbell rang.

I jumped. "I'll go and take a look."

"Hello," Lianne smiled. "I am like you and walked here. I wanted to show you my paintings."

"Who is it?" Ewe called from inside the cottage.

"Come," I said, trying to calm the beating of my heart at being caught talking about someone just before they show up at the door, and led Lianne into the sitting parlor where Ewe nearly spilled her tea all over her skirt at the sight of us. "Meet Ewe Sinclair. Ewe Sinclaire, Miss Lianne Hartley."

"You were Daphne's mother's nurse, weren't you?"

"Aye, I were."

Getting to her feet, Ewe seemed suddenly out of place in her very own cottage. High spots of color appeared on her apple cheeks at the "unexpected" intrusion.

Gazing around, Lianne nodded. "I'm very fond of my nurse Jenny. Do you know Jenny? We should have a nurse day one day. I like your cottage, Ewe! Do I call you Ewe or Mrs. Sinclaire?"

Ewe and I shared a glance. We both felt guilty when she'd come to make such an effort with her manners and to impress my host.

"We'll have tea, jam, and scones in the garden." Bustling away, Ewe disappeared to the kitchen while I showed Lianne around the cottage and my room before taking her outside.

"Was that the funeral, the paper on your bed, Daphne?"

She had a keen eye. I hadn't expected she'd notice it. "Yes . . ."

"Why have you got it still? That's old news now."

Old news. Yes, indeed, and Miss Perony's warning shot to my mind, *the Hartleys reign supreme here.* None of them appeared the slightest dismayed over the possibility of suffering ramifications for Victoria's death.

"Here's my painting," Lianne handed to me proudly. "What do you think of it?"

Examining the four charcoal sketches of Padthaway, I breathed out a sigh of surprised admiration. "*You* did this? It's beautiful . . ."

"Do you really think so?"

She so desperately craved attention and compliments for her achievements, considering her mother's continuous and harmful lack of interest. "You're very talented, you know. I'll speak to your mother about it. This talent should be nurtured."

Her face darkened. "You mean lessons?"

"Or a respite in Switzerland . . . a week or two . . . lapping up the scenery and drawing to your heart's content. Does that sound nice?"

She looked almost wistful. "Mother'll never agree. She doesn't let me go anywhere."

I patted her hand when she slumped beside me. "Let's work on it, shall we? Who else has seen these pictures?"

"Davie . . . and Jenny, of course. Davie started me on them but Mummy says I don't have the right eye. You saw her watercolors. They're perfect."

I thought of the watercolors in the Green Salon. "I can see why your mother's proud of them, but beauty is in the eye of the beholder. I much prefer yours to hers. If this picture is any indication, your work has feeling. Did Victoria ever see any of your sketches?"

She frowned and I wondered if she received a similar response from Victoria, dismissal, or worse, a mocking admiration.

"Once. I was on my way to show Davie and *she* was there. She barely looked at it."

"Perhaps her mind was on other things?"

"Perhaps."

It wasn't much but it was an indication of her dislike for Victoria. I decided to journey a little further. "What happened on that day . . . the day before she died? I promise whatever you say stays with me. *You're* my friend, remember."

Twitching her nose, she shrugged. "She went to London to pick up her dress. Soames drove her to the station. He picked her up, too."

So she'd taken the train to pick up her wedding dress. "Did you think this was strange? Why didn't she use the car?"

"She always went on the train. Davie used to tell her to use the car but she said she liked the train ride."

Perhaps it was *Soames* she didn't like and not the car? "Did she go alone?"

Lianne nodded. "And came back later that afternoon. I caught her yelling at Annie and Betsy for dropping her wedding dress box."

Something didn't sound right to me. Why go alone to London to pick up one's wedding dress? Wouldn't you take your mother or a friend or your fiancé? "Where was David? Why didn't he go with her?"

"She wanted to go alone. I heard her say it at breakfast."

"Did your brother think this was odd?"

"No."

Well, if he didn't, I certainly did. "Maybe she planned to go alone to meet someone, someone secret?"

She shrugged again, looking for Ewe to come.

"She's probably doing the cream," I said. "She's very proud of her scones."

Lianne nodded and crossed her arms. I could see she found my questions and this subject distasteful. "What was Victoria like when she came back? Tired? Irritable? Happy?"

"Definitely not happy." A light laugh left Lianne's lips. "I suppose she was in a mood."

"Did you speak to her?"

"No, but I gave her a look when she yelled at Annie and Betsy. Victoria glared at me and said, 'Don't judge me, *child*.' "

"What did you say?"

"Nothing. I turned and left."

I didn't believe her. The scene spanned before me: the despised sister-in-law returning to the house, her nerves raw, her mood worsening from the look of censure from Lianne. "Do you think she went to meet someone in London? A man? A *lover*?"

"We have another visitor!"

The announcement arrived with Ewe, carrying napkins and cutlery, and Mr. Brown behind her, bearing the tea and scone tray, a wicked glimmer in his eyes. "Morning, ladies."

He breezed over to us and, unused to this version of a smartly dressed Mr. Brown, reminiscent of the gentlemen who came for lunch or dinner at Cumberland Terrace or Cannon Hall, I gaped.

"Miss Daphne, what a fortunate thing to find you home."

The wicked glimmer continued to spark, silently reminding me of my intention to give him the perfume puffer. *What is your interest in the investigation?* I wanted to ask, then retracted the thought. "How . . ." Words failed me.

"How what? How does a modest major like me own such attire,

or how did I happen to catch you at home? The answer to the latter is a lucky guess, and what an ideal time for tea, too."

"Ideal," I echoed, hearing Ewe's noisy chatter in my ear. "Have you met Miss Lianne? Miss Lianne of *Padthaway*?"

"No, I haven't yet had that pleasure," the major grinned, stepping past me to do so.

Sweeping a bow, he adopted the formal code of introduction.

"How nice to meet you, *Major* Browning," Lianne murmured, her smitten gaze sending a lovely flush to her face.

I suppressed an inward groan. It appeared the major had made another conquest. He made them too easily for my liking, and perturbed, I resumed my seat, leaving Lianne to his care.

As I anticipated, the major charmed his way across the table while I poured the tea. Lianne talked more than I'd seen her talk to anyone, and I noticed a few attempts of the major here and there to gently pry into the current mood at Padthaway.

"Lianne says you often go for early-morning walks," the major said, making a pretense of following me out to help wash the dishes. "Have you considered my advice for testing unknown substances?"

"I have," I whipped under my breath. "You'll have it soon."

"*Now* is a good time. Do you still have it?"

"Of course I still have it." And flinging an apron to him, went to my room to fetch it.

He slid it into the pocket of his coat hanging by the door. "Excellent."

"What *is* your interest in the murder, anyhow? Were you one of her secret lovers?"

His silent smirk did little for my good humor.

"Oh, you were a *failing* hopeful suitor. How unpleasant for you."

"How mistaken you are, Miss du Maurier."

"You didn't know her then?"

His eyes remained guarded. "As it happens, I'd seen her around town. A mysterious, beautiful woman . . . one could never tell what she was thinking."

Of course he admired her. Who wouldn't?

Lianne came into the kitchen then, trailing her fingers adoringly across the bench. "Oh, I do so love this place! We have a secret garden at Padthaway."

We agreed we should take tea in the garden next time, but her chin suddenly drooped.

"It's my brother's project. It's not finished yet."

"I'd still love to see it," I said after the major had left and I accompanied Lianne home.

Lianne paused to gaze back at the village. "The major's *so* handsome, isn't he? Do you think he'd ever look at a girl like me?"

Oh dear. If I had the beginnings of a niggling headache before, I certainly had one now.

"There's something about him. He's very charming and he's a *major*. Even Mummy couldn't say no to a major."

I tried to give her a reassuring smile.

All of a sudden, she turned her attention to me and leaned in conspiratorially. "I've got a surprise for you but it's a *secret* surprise, just for us."

She refused to say more, her elusive smile persisting until we reached the drive. "You will come inside for a lemonade, won't you? We can have *pink* lemonade in the secret garden."

How could I refuse? Giddy as two little girls, we strode into the entry hall hand-in-hand, both shocked to hear the raised voice of Lady Hartley as we passed the drawing room.

"What is the meaning of this unearthly summons?"

Raising our eyebrows, we reached the door in time to see it close on the hem of Lady Hartley's morning robe.

Lianne propelled me closer to listen. I wanted to pull her back, but curiosity overcame me and we both put our ears to the door.

"It's time you start taking responsibility for your actions, Mother. I've been patient with you long enough," Lord David said, his voice steady, low, but firm.

"My actions." Lady Hartley's chuckling scoff. "Which one in particular offends you?"

"Why did you not mention Mrs. Bastion's call?"

"It just slipped my mind . . ."

"The devil it did."

Silence, then a long sigh from David. "I spoke to her yesterday. She says you *paid* her off for the clothes."

"Miserable creature. I suppose she wants them back now. Did she return the money? Kept it, no doubt. I wanted to keep the clothes for Lianne—"

"Send the clothes away," David coolly directed.

Lianne and I stared at each other agog. Grabbing my hand, she pulled me away from the door to run into the gardens.

"It's in here."

"What's in here?" I stopped to catch my breath, still thinking of the anger in Lord David's voice regarding Victoria's clothes. Why would she be so callous? "What is this, anyhow?" I peered at the small A-framed hut.

"It's Jasper's kennel." Ducking inside, Lianne retrieved a small navy bag. "This is it. The diary. Victoria's diary. I took it from her room . . . before the police found it. It was under her pillow."

"Victoria's diary," I whispered, reluctant to receive it from Lianne's hand. "Did you tell anybody about it?"

She shook her head. "You're the first and you'll see why we have to keep it a secret when you read it. I don't want David to get in any trouble."

"Trouble?" I echoed. "Why would he get into trouble?"

Lianne's hands gripped my shoulders. "You must give me your promise. Even David doesn't know about this. If they found it . . ." She shuddered.

"I'll meet you back here in an hour," Lianne whispered, looking around her.

Giving her my promise, I went out to the cliffs to read it. It seemed the most appropriate place, under the circumstances, to do so.

Finding the windless rock I had shared with *Major* Browning, I settled down to read, wishing I'd brought a hat to shield out the fierce sun.

Being the owner of countless diaries over the years, I was surprised at the feel of the quaint slim blue book, unadorned but for a tiny flower, a modest Scarlet Pimpernel, gracing the front cover. It was the kind of diary one expected a young girl to have, not a grown woman.

The first entry, ten years ago, revealed the diary's age:

Dear Diary,
I found out today I have a different father . . .

CHAPTER THIRTY-TWO

Victoria's Diary
I hate this village. Can't wait to get away. Sometimes, I sneak up to the Big House and watch the Hartleys. They're so lucky. I wish I could be one of them.

Proving Lady Hartley's theory of the commoners wanting to be one of them, Victoria's fascination with the Hartley family continued over the next few pages and into her young womanhood:

I saw Lord David today. He went by in the motorcar with his school friends. He's grown quite handsome. I waved to them and his friends whistled. But Lord David didn't. There's a coldness in his eyes I wonder about . . . I s'pose all that business about his father. How can I get him to see me?

A few months later:

I saw him today and he SAW me! Lord David. Or David, as I shall now think of him. I didn't think much of his friends, 'specially that Mr. Cameron. He followed me out the back. Made beastly suggestions to me. I told him to sail his ship in other waters. He didn't like that but he smiled all the same.

April 7

I've a date with David today. He's driving me home from the club.

   Very kind of him.

June 21

Dinner with Davie, as I shall now call him, then dancing at the club . . . oh dear, I'll need more lessons from Miss Perony if I am to keep my man. For how can I ever fit into their world?

Three weeks later:

I'm working at Padthaway now.

   The fact amuses me, somewhat, but Soames doesn't like it. I think he's jealous. Jealous, jealous, jealous for Davie and I are so in love!

   I'm terribly happy. But Lady Hartley frightens me. Sometimes, I don't feel very safe here . . . the maids whisper, Mrs. Trehearn watches my every move. Something's not right and I don't trust Davie's mother. She has no heart and I swear Soames and she have some special plan to ruin our engagement for I caught him spying on me in London. Why can't he take no for an answer?

July 22

I told David today . . . about the child. It was a shock to me, too, but I needn't have worried. My Davie is honorable and he's proposed!

   Lady Hartley is outraged.

   Soames . . . I can't read. I think he knew it would happen. Best they both adjust to the idea. We're to marry as soon as possible, to avoid scandal.

I came to the week of the wedding. Holding the diary on my lap, I noticed the change of handwriting, the scratchy, indefinable letters and read the reasons behind it:

Had a shocking row with Davie today. Those dreadful rumors! Spun by all those who don't wish us to be together . . . Lady Hartley, Soames, and even Davie's friends. Cowards. They think that I, because I worked at the club, am a loose woman. I am not, I tell you, dear diary. I kept myself for Lord David and he knows it. The worst thing is that I saw doubt in my Davie's eyes today. He can't believe them truly, can he?

About the child? How could he?

I've written him a letter. I hope it works.

Then came the last page, the last few entries before her death, unspecified dates, tear-blotted paper, and odd entries here and there.

Went to London. Saw him. Went better than expected. Soames still jealous as a cat. Lady Hartley suspiciously kind. She gave me a beautiful perfume puffer and apologized for her earlier treatment of me. Dare I believe it? I don't trust her.

I'm so frightfully tired. Snapped at the maids and Lianne again. Didn't mean to . . . but the nerves, you know. Davie heard about it; Lianne must have told him. He came to my room. We had another row. His doubts disturb me. He's of the old school, proud, hates to be thought the cuckold. When there is no ground for him to do so! Oh, what am I to do? I can't tell him the reason I go to London. I can't allow anything to disrupt our marriage, not anyone, not even Connan. Dear Connan, he's always in need of money and thinks now my rich boyfriend will pay for everything. If only our dad had turned out to be whom we thought! I'll never forgive Mother for that.

As if my day could get any worse! I drank too much at dinner but I was angry . . . and ill. Feverish almost . . .

No . . . I can't rest. I feel very strange . . .

I don't know what I'll do. Can't trust David. I'm so scared . . .

I closed the diary and shut my eyes, letting her private testimony, her life, rest on my lap in perfect security. Victoria, the girl I'd seen lying there dead on the beach, sprang to life in my mind. I felt close to her, as close as I might be to a future heroine and her tragic end.

Walking back to Padthaway, I encountered Lianne.

"Did you read it? Do you see?"

I handed her the bag with the diary. "It should really go to Sir Edward, Lianne. I know you wish to protect your brother—"

"I'm going to destroy it," Lianne declared. "*Now.*"

She started running for the cliffs. Charging after her, I managed to grab her skirt. Losing the diary to a whim terrified me despite my desire to dismiss its contents for David's sake. "Let's wait," I pleaded, between breaths. "I didn't tell you before but I found a letter Victoria had written to your brother hiding inside a book in the library. He *knew* I'd found it and read it, and when we went to Stall's that day, he asked what he should do with it. I told him he'd have to hand it to Sir Edward. Don't you see, darling? Your brother's not afraid because he's *innocent.*"

She looked at me as if I were mad. "Why keep the diary? There's no need for it now."

"One shouldn't destroy an item belonging to the deceased, Lianne."

Considering the wisdom, she eventually handed the diary over to me. "You do what you think best with it, then. Just don't hurt Davie. Promise?"

I promised and we parted, she to Padthaway, and me to Ewe's

cottage with Victoria's diary pressing against me. It felt almost toxic against my skin and I knew I had to be rid of it. So I abandoned my track in favor of the one leading up to Castle Mor, and to Sir Edward.

Sir Edward accepted the diary with a solemn face.

"Thank you, Miss du Maurier. I couldn't have expected such honor from the Hartleys."

"Miss Lianne only meant to protect her brother," I said. "Do be kind to her."

"I shall," Sir Edward nodded, "but I have my duty. A duty that overrides friendship and landlords."

I watched his great eyebrows droop, then spring up again. "I have a duty, a power invested upon me by law, to uphold justice in this county and that includes justice for Victoria Bastion, however much her death is troublesome to the Hartleys."

Rubbing the diary across his robust stomach, Sir Edward groaned. " 'Tis no accident in my opinion, Miss du Maurier. Ricin is poison and I cannot believe Victoria administered such a substance to herself, can you?"

"No. I knew that she wanted to live," I said, thinking of her diary.

Sir Edward shook his head, grievous concern wavering in the orbs of his eyes. We stood on the landing by the door to his castle, or I should say, the Hartleys' castle.

"Would you like to see inside?"

Sir Edward must have noticed my wide-eyed and yearning look, for I'd glimpsed a huge candelabra and heavy tapestries adorning the thick stone walls. "It must be difficult," said I, never more at home than in a castle or historical landmark of some description, "to investigate your own landlord."

Ignoring my comment, Sir Edward pointed out the drawing room, the fireplace, and the other rooms of the restored medieval keep.

It was precisely what I'd expect of a proper detective, to reserve details of the case only for the purpose of catching the killer. Without him breathing a word, I understood the case had reached an impasse.

"Have you read the diary, Miss Daphne?"

"I have."

"May I ask your impressions?"

"My impressions . . . before I answer, may I ask you if Lord David showed you a letter Victoria had written him before she died?"

"I do have such a letter in my possession."

I nodded, elated that David proved a man of his word. He'd turned in the letter as duty dictated, just as I had my duty to submit her private journal. "My impressions are that Victoria had a secret of some kind. The entries with Soames you will find interesting, Soames and his jealousy."

"Ridgeway Soames, the cook?" Sir Edward seemed surprised. "But er, he and Lady Hartley—"

"May be lovers, but I believe Victoria and Soames knew each other quite well and in hiring her at Padthaway, he thought he'd have a chance with her."

"You're a woman. You understand girls better than an old man like me . . . do you think she and Soames were lovers? Carried on their affair at Padthaway until she swapped him for Lord David?"

Taking the diary from him, I showed him the relevant entry. "See, she says she 'kept' herself for Lord David."

"But any girl would say that," Sir Edward argued.

"I believe her. She was beautiful, yes, but that doesn't mean she was a wanton. Perhaps many have judged her cruelly, wrongly."

Sir Edward considered this, his hooded eyes revealing little. "Any other reflections? Does she mention Lord David and Lady Hartley?"

"Both, naturally. Lady Hartley terrified her, and there is the mention of bride gifts."

"Bride gifts?" Incredulous, Sir Edward's great eyebrows lifted. "I confess I am impatient to study this new evidence—thank you, Miss Daphne."

"It was simply the right thing to do," I said, and left Sir Edward to his deliberations, knowing this new evidence spelled doom for the entire Hartley family.

CHAPTER THIRTY-THREE

Partly out of guilt, I found myself at Padthaway the next morning.

"Miss Lianne and her ladyship are still abed," Mrs. Trehearn informed me, blank and expressionless as usual.

"Jenny Pollock?" I inquired.

"Miss Pollock should be awake at this hour. You will find her at the—"

"Yes, I know where to find her," I smiled, and strolled in the right direction, aware Mrs. Trehearn monitored my every move. I suddenly understood why Victoria felt so uncomfortable. *Mrs. Trehearn watches my every move.* If she watched every move, I thought, walking along the sleepy corridors, why did she choose to remain silent? Did she fear the loss of her job if she spoke against her employers?

She probably knew a great deal about the house and its secrets. A good housekeeper always did. However, discretion often played a part, and in this affair, it meant self-preservation. Mrs. Trehearn intended to preserve her illustrious position at Padthaway, as much as Lady Hartley meant to preserve her position as lady of the house.

"She came back, all right," Jenny said on seeing me. "Mrs. B. Demanding those clothes. Did ye hear of it?"

Settling down to a nice cup of fresh tea, I confessed I had overheard Lady Hartley and Lord David talking in the drawing room.

"Arguing, more like," Jenny huffed. "Well, she failed this time, Lady Muck. Lord Davie put his foot down and the clothes were sent to Bastion cottage."

"All those beautiful clothes," I whispered, a trifle disappointed. "They will be sold now, I suspect. And those furs . . ."

"Lady H is none too happy, for Davie paid for the whole lot," Jenny enthused, "but I s'pose the clothes should go back to the girl's mother for Lady Muck won't fit 'em, will she!"

"You don't think she wanted them for Lianne?"

Jenny's face took on a sad look. "I don't think my Lee Lee will be havin' a season. She'll do well if some nice man comes along and looks after her."

"Because of her illness? The one she inherited from her father."

"A lie and a fib that is!"

Not anticipating such intensity, I fumbled out an apology.

"Is that what *she* said, Lady Muck?"

"It's just what everyone says. Jenny, if you don't mind my asking, why do you stay here if you dislike Lady Hartley so much? I know there is David and Lianne—"

"More *my* babies than hers. *She* never cared about them, so I stay. I've always stayed. And I'll stay as long as my Lee Lee needs me. As long as I'm needed."

I glanced at my wristwatch. "Lianne doesn't usually sleep late, does she?"

"She had nightmares last night. She came here and I took her down to the kitchen, made her hot milk, then cuddled her till she slept again."

"She never mentioned her nightmares, poor thing. Are they . . . ?"

Jenny nodded. "How'd ye be if ye saw your own dad shoot himself?"

"Very disturbed," I answered. Eager to prevent a new bout of Jenny's morose reminiscing of the past, I asked if she knew where I could find the secret garden.

Her face turned white. "What did you say?"

"The secret garden. Lianne said it's David's project. Do you know where it is?"

Jenny's pallor deepened.

"Whatever is the matter, Jenny?"

I watched her shuffle to the window, to stare out upon her own little garden, and the flowers below. "How could he? How could he think to open it? The old place?"

I didn't know whether to remain silent or speak. I decided on the latter, interrupting her talking to herself. "Why? Do you have an objection?"

"I can't believe it . . ."

"Is the place cursed?"

Shaking her head, Jenny returned to her normal nonchalance. "Ah, we used to go there in the old days. I just wish my Davie had told me. He shouldn't keep secrets from Jenny."

Something in her eyes perturbed me, and I swept to my feet and to the door. "I'll go now, Jenny."

"Why didn't he tell me? Why didn't he tell Jenny?"

Her voice followed me outside as I tried to regain composure.

"Miss! Are ye all right, miss? Ye look lost!" Annie called from across the hall.

I made a conscious effort to remove Jenny's disturbing reaction from my mind. "Oh, I'm looking for Lord David's secret garden. I thought I'd wait there for Lianne. I heard she had a bad night last night."

"Aye, she did, poor thing, and I can show ye to the garden if ye like, miss. Oh dear." Her face fell. "Oops. I'm not supposed to know. Betsy told me not to say anythin'."

"About the garden? Then I'm like you, in trouble, for I just mentioned it to Jenny Pollock and she didn't look too happy to hear of it."

Annie, a kindred spirit, grinned. "Ye're safe, miss, and Mrs. T'll wallop me if she knew I took ye there. As for Jenny, don't know why she should be upset."

"I think it's because Lord David kept it a secret from her."

"Oh." Annie's mouth quivered. "Well, he's a grown man now, not a boy."

"Indeed, he is a grown man." I blushed, remembering our kiss in the library.

"And I hear he's taken with you, miss! Not that I should be sayin' such, so recent after . . ."

"Victoria." I said the name. "Annie, I have to ask you something. You know when you heard that argument between Lord David and Victoria, did you hear any man's name mentioned at all?"

Annie thought hard. "Lord Davie were so angry, maybe, for he didn't like her London visits and where she was goin' and she wouldn't say where she was goin' either. Two stubborn mules together, if ye ask me."

"You don't really think Victoria had an affair with another man and planned to plant the child on Lord David?"

"Oh, no, miss! It's true she had her pick of 'em males, even Mr. Soames got very cranky when she started to see Lord David, and I s'pose she liked to flaunt it a bit, but nope, miss, I think the babe were Lord David's and it's sad what happened to her."

"Who do you think murdered Victoria, Annie?"

Leaning across to whisper in my ear, she said, "If anyone wanted her out of the way, I'd say Lady H. But like Betsy keeps sayin', we're best not to talk of it."

I followed her lithe steps to the gardens outside, now more curious than ever as to Victoria's mysterious London journeys. Who did she meet there, especially on that final trip? *Went to London. Saw him. Went better than expected.*

Sunshine bathed my face, leading me to the peaceful serenity I loved here at Padthaway. How beautiful it looked outside, a lovely, still summer's afternoon, the green lawns a perfect setting for the stone mansion, the creeping wild roses climbing up the ancient walls. "This is the house," I said to myself, glancing over to hear the roar of the sea in the distance. "This is the house."

Intensely inspired, I nearly forgot Annie standing there, pointing to the place in the wall to the secret garden. "I think . . . I think I'll just sit here for a minute, Annie. Thank you."

"I'll let Miss Lianne know ye here, miss."

I nodded for I could not speak. A whole story forming inside my head, I sank onto the weathered stone seat to gaze up at the house. I imagined the hero, a tortured one worthy of the Brontës, an older man with a house and a dead wife. I pictured him brooding, accused of murder, even by his own silent servants.

He strolled into my sunshine, in a strangely pensive mood. Seeing me sitting there along the wall in the gardens, he made an obligatory effort to smile. "Making use of the morning light?"

"Lord David!"

"You sound surprised. This is my home, you know."

"Forgive me." I shook my head. "I must have been daydreaming."

"Dreaming up a future novel?"

"Your gardens are so beautiful," I said, motioning to the roses along the wall. "Look how they cling there, spiraling down amongst the wisteria with those alliums down the bottom. Ben certainly does a fine job. . . . I'm surprised he manages to do it all alone."

"Oh, he has his helpers." His face brightening at this compliment to his house, Lord David paused to smile. "We have a name for them. Ben and his merry weeders."

I laughed. "Weeding is an awful occupation, but I do envy you . . . owning a house as magnificent as this."

"You shouldn't envy us."

Standing there on the path, now relaxed and graceful, he viewed his house with new eyes. Boyish excitement replaced the former dark mood. "Ben and I are working on a secret garden. Would you like to see it?"

I glanced around for Lianne.

"If you've come to see my sister, she's not up yet."

"You heard about her nightmares last night? Is it to do with seeing her father die?"

Perhaps I shouldn't have said anything, for his face darkened and the brooding hero resumed.

"It's been hard for her," he said, "exposed to terrors at such a young age."

We spoke a little about his father's suicide.

"I didn't see the signs; I was shocked, like the rest of the world. He always appeared happy in his way . . . and then, suddenly . . ."

Observing his bewildered face, I wondered if he felt the same way about Victoria.

"Lianne's been under the care of a few doctors—some disastrous; she relates better to Jenny. Jenny keeps her steady, but one day she'll have to let go and let her find her own way."

I stopped him. "Before we go into the garden, I have a confession to make: Jenny knows about the garden."

I saw the flicker of concern in his eyes.

"Why were you keeping it secret from her? She seemed upset you hadn't told her."

"I wanted to surprise her. I wanted her to see it as it used to be— before my father died. We used to play inside as children. Jenny was always there, too."

I nodded, suppressing the desire to hug him. "Sometimes returning to a certain place is difficult. You should speak to her, though. Especially as I've blundered. I'm amazed Lianne didn't tell her. She seems to tell Jenny everything."

Again, his face shadowed and he asked that we not discuss Lianne any further. Oh no, I thought, he suspects his own sister.

My heart pounded. Lianne . . . had she found the poison hidden somewhere in the greenhouse and placed it in the perfume puffer? Lianne . . . had she followed Victoria, stumbling out to the cliffs, to make sure she died, to make sure she fell over the cliffs? Lianne . . . had she returned early the next day to look for the shoes? She was the first to see the body and I shivered, thinking back to that first day, back to Lianne's frightful eyes.

"This is my little project," Lord David murmured, his hand slipping through the hedges to unlatch a lever. "The door is this way."

I did not say Annie had shown me the way already. Weaving

through the heavy satin-leafed bushes, we ducked under the tiny hidden dome-shaped oak door.

Once inside, I let out a shrill sigh of awe and amazement. Walls laden with all kinds of creeping plants served to enclose a tiny bridge as the center feature, spanning a man-made pond, leading to a circular thatched cottage in the far back corner. "It's gorgeous!" I cried.

"Worthy of restoration," David echoed. "My father created it, but it was left to ruin after his death. He loved his place . . . and so do I."

And like a child, Lord David seized my hand to run across the pond bridge.

"There're fish down there, hiding under the lilies."

I squinted hard to find them, and yes, a big orange goldfish slithered between two lily pads. "You feed the fish?"

He nodded, drawing me away to point out the various shrubs and flowers. "My father collected all of these. This was his private little retreat. He was often here . . . alone."

Gazing at his face, warmed by the sunshine, I asked if he intended to keep it private.

"I am tempted, but that would be selfish of me. No, once it's finished, I want to open the whole house to the public."

"To the public? How does your mother feel about this?"

"She doesn't like it, but she'll like the money it will bring to the place."

I nodded, even though I couldn't see Lady Hartley warming to the idea of people roaming over her domain, despite the financial benefits.

"The cottage is still a ruin, but someday, I'll fix it."

We stepped inside, over the fallen beams amongst the wildness that grew there. I touched part of an old beam. "Would it cost much to renovate it?"

"Yes, and it's something that is not a priority at the moment."

His hand briefly spanned mine as it rested on the beam.

"Daphne, I know I shouldn't say this, but I can't stop thinking about you . . . after that kiss . . ."

He looked away, horrified and guilty that he could form an attachment so soon.

"It's just . . ."

"No, it's not just a kiss. You have to believe me, Daphne. I didn't kill her."

"No, but did your mother?"

Staring at the garden, he scratched his arm. "Oh, hell, I don't know. I don't know where the poison came from—"

"Mrs. Trehearn?"

"I've asked her. She swears she didn't have it."

"She may have told you and Sir Edward that, but do you believe her? Does her loyalty to you override her loyalty to your mother?"

He'd thought of all of this; I saw it edged in every line of his face. "I don't know. I just don't want you to think that I—"

"Could poison your bride?"

CHAPTER THIRTY-FOUR

I wanted to tell him then; I wanted to tell him about the diary.

His head hovered dangerously close to mine. "Do you believe me, Daphne? I have to know."

"Yes, I believe you," I murmured, closing my eyes as his hand reached out to cup my face.

I should have stopped him. I knew I should, but I let him explore my face, I let his fingers caress the length of my arm. Keeping my eyes shut, I let him kiss me again, a kiss so sweet and full of longing, I wanted it to go on forever.

Pulling away, I endeavored to find sanctuary in another part of the garden. My face still hot and flushed, I prayed for cool air to cool my emotions and my head. Perhaps to assist my plight and realizing he'd overstepped his own boundary, he began speaking of the next renovations to take place at the house. Leaving the garden, I nodded, scarcely listening to his plans for the tower.

"Did you show her? Did you show her the secret garden, Davie?"

I breathed a long sigh of inward relief as I watched Lianne chasing Jasper up the terrace steps.

"What did you think of it?"

Swirling around us both, Lianne's faith in me as her confidante and friend caused a sickness in my stomach. I felt sick, sick that I suspected her. How did she get the poison, though? Did she do it at her mother's direction?

The puffer. The puffer had all the answers. Oh, why, oh, why had I entrusted the perfume puffer to the major?

"I'm hungry." Lianne still skipped around us, merrily playing with Jasper. "Daphne can stay for lunch, can't she, Davie?"

Lord David cleared his throat. "Of course she may, if she wants to." Catching his sister by her waist, he smiled as she giggled. "How are you feeling now, Lee?" He pinched her nose. "No more nightmares?"

"No more nightmares," she replied, giving him a fierce hug before skipping off to lunch.

"I really should go," I began, "Ewe might be expecting me, and I don't want to impose."

"Nonsense," Lord David dismissed, frowning down at his riding coat. "I might change for luncheon. You know your way to the Green Salon, don't you?"

"That's unfair," I smiled. "You get to change whereas I do not. My mother would be horrified at my showing up at a grand house dressed like this."

He observed me with admiring eyes, looking over the full length of me. "I think you look fine."

But not beautiful like Victoria, I quibbled as we parted ways. How did he feel now that her room had been cleared out? Did he feel pain? Or relief?

"Thank goodness," Lady Hartley breathed upon seeing me arrive at the Green Salon. "My son has been rather testy of late. I didn't want to endure another *lecture*. . . . What is it, Trehearn?"

"You have a visitor, your ladyship."

I turned around to view her face, searching for clues. Mrs. Trehearn would have organized the clearing out of Victoria's room. Did she know I'd taken the perfume puffer, and the beads? How good a housekeeper was she? A bad one, I hoped, swallowing uneasily.

"A visitor!" Lady Hartley cried, inspecting the card. "Major Thomas Browning . . . don't believe I know him."

"Oh, I do!" Lianne snapped up the card. "Bid him entry, Trehearn, and if he hasn't lunched, set another place, please."

Astounded by her behavior, evidence of her infatuation for him, I answered all of Lady Hartley's questions. When and where we had met this Major Browning and what we knew of him. Exhibiting an interest in his possible connections, she stood when he arrived.

"Major Browning. You are very welcome."

Mrs. Trehearn, the efficient shadow, set another place for our guest and he joined us at the table. I lowered my head, my face blazing at his impudence. Why call at the house so early after an acquaintance, especially when it was to visit the family he warned me about?

"I just *had* to see your home." He charmed Lady Hartley with a smile. "Your daughter's description of its interior left me unable to put it off for another moment."

"I'm glad you came," Lady Hartley sprang to attention, examining his handsome face and correct attire. "We have so few visitors here. You've met Miss du Maurier, of course? Her father is very famous."

"Yes." The major's gaze sought mine. "And I had hoped to meet Lord David."

"My son will be along shortly."

"Then I am fortunate to have you three ladies to myself for a while."

I coughed, and the major leapt up to pour me a glass of water. Seeing him relax there on the settee opposite Lady Hartley, sipping his cider and chatting about this and that, I could have killed him. How dare he? What were his intentions? To befriend the family or to convict them? He certainly hadn't come here to see me, but at the first opportunity to whisper to me, he did so.

"I have news." His coarse whisper scathed my ear. "News . . . on our little experiment."

"Oh."

At that moment Lord David entered the room, and I moved toward the dinner table. Following suit, the major remarked upon the fine linen.

"Fine linen, sir?" I asked incredulously.

"David darling, Major Browning is visiting the area," Lady Hartley interrupted for introductions.

The men shook hands, Lord David wary, the major eager.

"The historical allure brought me here," the major teased to ease Lord David's mistrust. "The abbey treasure is a great one to guard, my lord."

Lord David did not register the joke.

"No, I come down every year to visit my uncle."

"Then you should have visited us before. Indeed, I had no *idea* someone of your quality frequented Windemere. Who is your uncle?"

"A lonely old fisherman. He lives in a . . . well, I'd say a *hut* on a hill not far from Castle Mor."

"Interesting," Lady Hartley beamed, and Lianne beamed with her. "You are always very welcome at Padthaway, Major."

His eyes shimmered toward me. "Thank you, my lady."

Reaching for my seat, I coughed, quickly reaching for my water glass. The major immediately expressed concern. I didn't want him acting so friendly to me in the presence of Lord David. I looked up at Lord David. He lifted a brow in query.

"I met the Major at Ewe's," I said. "Miss Perony, Major, have you seen her lately? You got along *so well* at Ewe's, I thought . . ."

"Miss Perony!" Lianne giggled. "She's old and ugly."

"Not ugly, *plain*," her mother corrected, smiling sweetly and preening for the major.

I nearly choked on my food. Lady Hartley left the major in no doubt of her interest in him. A replacement for Soames, I wondered?

The major stayed for afternoon tea, too.

"Intriguing courtyard," he remarked, as Lady Hartley linked

her arm through his to show him the room. "I am very curious about those Chinese vases. . . ."

Chinese vases! No, he was curious, *too* curious, about this entire case. Did he have a professional interest in it? Or was his interest purely ordinary, like Ewe Sinclair and the rest of us?

Lianne rushed to escort the major to the Chinese vases, pointing out other various items and their history amongst smiles and the occasional flirtatious giggles. Sickened by the scene, I couldn't wait for the whole affair to end.

It did, at the major's leisure I might add. He offered to drive me home and I had no choice but to go with him as I failed to think of an excuse quick enough. Walking home wasn't an option for it was raining and David retained his polite coolness in his farewells. Lady Hartley had been extremely warm, pressing the major's hand and inviting both of us for dinner the next evening, and Lianne curtsied and smiled.

"She's still waving," the major said as we motored down the drive.

I glanced back. "Why did you go there? You're no friend to them."

"Nor are you, submitting a private diary as evidence."

My mouth went agape. "How do you know about it? Why does Sir Edward talk to you and not me?"

"Because I called upon him with the results to the perfume puffer. He's running another test now . . . to be sure, but one thing you can be sure of, events are going to unfold rather rapidly now."

I sat in the car, frozen. I felt cold and guilty. I'd betrayed my friends and I felt especially guilty after Lord David and I kissed in the secret garden. "Events? Because of the puffer? What do you mean?"

Opening the door for me, he grinned. "You will see. No umbrella. You better run. I will pick you up tomorrow at six."

"She'll have her eye on him," Ewe predicted the next day. "Lady Hartley. Swappin' the peacock for the eagle."

"Who's the peacock?"

"Your Mr. Soames ye fancy is related in some way to Vicky."

Working outside in the garden was just the break I needed.

Ewe paused. "Ye never know. Ye may be right. Now I think of it, his face did look rather pinched at the funeral." She paused to instruct me on how to trim one of her precious hedges. "So the major's involved himself, too, has he? You watch. There'll be an arrest soon. Oh, how I wish I'd seen that diary! Must have been *ripe* with secrets."

"I hate to disappoint you but it wasn't what I expected. Those London visits . . . who could she be going to see?"

"It's Lady Hartley who did it," Ewe proclaimed, her eyes squinting into the distance. "Is that Connan Bastion I see on his bicycle?"

I peered into the distance. "I think it is." I got up quickly to brush my skirt. "I'll go see him."

"You'd better tell *him* about the diary," Ewe advised.

"I didn't want to say anything at first," I started, explaining how the diary and the perfume puffer came into my hands as he approached. "Sir Edward has them now and the major says there'll be an arrest soon."

Relief, grateful relief, washed over his face. "Ma will be pleased. Is it . . . will they do it?"

"Do what?"

"Arrest the Hartleys. I mean, they are the *rich* that get away with everythin'."

"Not murdering your sister." I pressed his hand.

He still did not believe me. "They'll pay the judge off. They'll get away with it."

"No, they won't, Connan. They can pay to have the best lawyer, but if the evidence is enough, your sister's killer will be brought to justice."

His violet eyes studied my face. "Miss Daphne, this is all your doin'. It'd never've happened if you hadn't come here."

I suppose it might not have, I congratulated myself. The beads still remained a mystery, though, so I asked Connan if he knew an

MSR. He said no, but he had remembered something about the London visits. "She had trouble with a bloke. She said she were scared of him. Tryin' to bribe her. She was worried about losin' Lord David." Hitting his head with his fist, he breathed out a long grieving sigh. "And I'm the idiot! Puttin' pressure on her to pay off me debts when she—"

"Had someone else to contend with? Someone sinister?"

"Yeah. S'pose that's it."

"Do you know where she went? Or where she met this person? Did she mention a name at all? *Think,* Connan. Think back to every word she said. She must have been upset."

"She were angry at me . . . and at him. No, she were angry at all of us, for not believin' her," he said. "Don't know what she meant by that."

"I think I do, but the London visits are important."

"I might be wrong," he said eventually, "but I think she might of said somethin' like Crow or Crowleys through it all.

"Thank you, Connan."

He cycled away and I resumed trimming the hedge. The action of cutting and snipping reminded me of Mrs. Trehearn. "The poison must have been in the house," I said to Ewe. "Mrs. Trehearn is lying to protect Lady Hartley. I wonder if Sir Edward now suspects her. . . ."

"Daphne!"

Lianne leaned over the fence. "I've come to get you."

"Now? For dinner? It's too early and the major's picking me up."

"But Mummy and I've got a surprise for you. The car's here now. Can she come now, Mrs. Ewe?"

Arching her brows, Ewe lifted her arms. "Ain't up to me, petal."

"Oh, please, Daphne, please. Mother expects you."

But I did not live under Lady Hartley's dominion, did I? For Lianne's sake, I went, though it was against my better judgment. I suspected Lianne's motives were vested in her feelings for the major.

My suspicions increased when her mischievous smile continued to Lady Hartley's room. Pacing along the open windows in her splendid room, her beribboned robe trailing behind her, she looked magnificent. A magnificent murderess, cool and unaffected by Victoria's brief intrusion into her world.

"Ah! I have a present for both of you. For tonight's gala, ladies, we must look our best. It appears Victoria had ordered two dresses as part of her wedding trousseau and instead of sending them back to the dressmaker, I decided to keep them. Jenny will make the appropriate adjustments—she can sew, you know."

I opened my mouth, horrified at the idea of wearing something of Victoria's. "Lady Florence, it's very kind of you, but I must—"

"No, you shall not, Daphne. I insist upon it, and if you are worried about my son, you needn't be. He knew nothing about these dresses and I thought the lavender would suit you very well."

Lavender. *Should I wear Victoria's lavender beads, too, my lady?* I thought to ask.

"Lianne . . . for you, the green." Tossing the dress to her daughter, she added, "See that Jenny adds a piece of lace to the top. It's far too low for a girl of your age."

The lavender dress, still wrapped in tissue paper, lay on my lap. Having no choice but to open it now, I did so, loving the feel of the soft satin.

"It shimmers like the moon," Lady Hartley grinned, "and you may borrow my amethyst set for the night." Raiding her dresser, she placed the box on my lap, too. "Now, off to Jenny, both of you."

Thus dismissed, Lianne and I carried our respective treasures to Jenny. "How do you feel about it?" I asked Lianne on the way.

"Weird" was her reply.

"Me, too. I don't think I can—"

"She'll be angry if you don't. Best we please Mother."

So we humored her ladyship, letting Jenny's deft fingers pin and make the needed adjustments. Victoria had a greater bust line than I; I had a slimmer waist, and the dress was far too long. Funny, I hadn't thought of her as tall when I saw her lying there on the beach.

"Don't like it," Jenny muttered again. "Wearin' the dead's clothes. No good."

"But they weren't actually hers yet," Lianne reminded for the fifth time. "None of us like it. Though"—she twirled in front of the mirror—"I do feel pretty in the green."

"It brings out ye pretty eyes," Jenny softened. "What're we goin' to do with that hair, though?" Clicking her tongue, she considered. "I think ye old enough to wear it up. Maybe Miss Daphne can help."

"Oh, don't keep calling me Miss Daphne," I said, tapping Jenny's shoulders. "You make me feel positively old."

It was a cheery afternoon, playing dress-up in Jenny's room, and she apologized for being "strange about the garden" the day before.

"It's all right, Jenny." I pressed her hand. "You don't have to apologize."

"I just thought he might have told me, that's all. Us having so many memories in that garden. Or Lee Lee."

"We didn't want to upset you," Lianne soothed as Annie and Betsy arrived to audition our final appearance.

Though they clapped their hands and said, "Oh, ye both look a beauty!" I still felt uncomfortable and annoyed with Lianne and Lady Hartley for disrupting my plan to drive with the major. I dreaded to think what he'd make of all this, and I had so many questions I'd hoped to ask him on the way.

Lianne twirled around, no doubt dreaming of the major. "Shall we go down now?"

"We'll watch ye go," Jenny smiled, proud.

Halfway down the stairs, adopting the gait of a royal princess under the amused eye of Jenny, Betsy, and Annie, Lianne paused.

"I forgot something. I'll meet you later."

We had decided to go down early to watch the major's arrival from the drawing room. Not wanting to sit lest I crinkle my dress, wanting to make a stunning impression for both David and the major's eyes, I decided to visit the *Beneficent Bride.*

The painting glowed there in the portrait gallery, illuminated against the darkened wall, the dim evening lights scarcely touching her face. A serene face, eyes dark, full of passionate unexplained mystery, her dainty hand coiled around the swing rope.

"Unforgettable, isn't she?"

The low murmur startled me.

Lord David approached from the other end of the corridor, a shadowy smile on his lips. "You were so intent. I was loath to disturb you."

My heart raced. It had a terrible habit of doing so whenever he entered a room.

"Is Lianne with you?"

"No," I swallowed, my heightened senses registering his slow advance, remembering how his arms felt around me, his lips on mine.

He laughed. "So you've managed to escape her. An amazing feat."

Leaning against the paneling, I permitted his gaze to make an assessment of my dress, praying he'd never learn the origin of it.

"New?"

I nodded.

He stepped back to admire. "The cut is perfect . . . and I see Mother loaned you her amethysts."

"Yes!" I smiled, my hand rising to caress the stones. "They're exquisite."

"No, *you* are exquisite."

"My lord!"

Now I had truly offended him.

"I understand. You wish to remove yourself from me because you suspect me."

"No, we are friends—"

"Friends," he echoed with distaste.

"More than friends," I amended, feeling the heat rise to my face. "That's why we must talk about her . . . Victoria."

He nodded, instantly cold. "What do you want to know?"

Taking a deep breath, I said what I'd planned to say next time we were alone. "I'm sorry about Victoria. I can imagine how difficult it must be losing the one you love. The love of your life. But I must know, what happened between the two of you?"

Staring ahead, the line of his jaw tensing, Lord David nodded. "Did I love her? I don't know if I know what true love is. I was enchanted by her." A low chuckle escaped his lips. "She used to call herself a 'changeling.' I suppose that's what she was . . . changeable."

I remained silent, thinking of her diary. I didn't find her changeable, but I suppose she may have presented herself to others differently.

"Do you want to know what happened that night?"

Without waiting for my reply, he went on, the tone of his voice tinged with a bitter sadness. "It started out a lighthearted affair between us, neither serious, or at least that's what I assumed. I saw her working at a club in London. My friends pointed her out and, jokingly, I asked her out on a date. She accepted and we did a few things together—films, shows, clubs, that sort of thing.

"I'd drive her home on the weekends. This became our pattern for a while, a pleasant dalliance we both enjoyed."

Afraid to turn my head to examine his reflective profile, I continued to stare at the painting, my mind painting the picture of their romance—the color, the gaiety, the excitement. "When did it change?"

"When she showed up here. She thought it a great joke . . . working in the kitchen. I didn't."

"How did she get the job?"

"Soames hired her. They knew each other from school or something. The two shared an odd history. I don't think he liked Victoria being here either."

"Or with you," I murmured. "He might have been in love with her."

I saw the thought had occurred to him.

"She fell pregnant?"

"Yes." He looked away, his face expressionless. "She said the child was mine. I believed her—now, I'm not so sure. I *wanted* to believe her but I kept hearing things . . . rumors. She begged me not to listen. She confessed she 'had a past' but that was done with and all that mattered to her was me and the child."

I listened to all this sadness and uncertainty, wishing I knew what to say. "You did the honorable thing. You were going to marry her."

"Yes, I was. The night she," he paused, "the night she *disappeared,* we had an argument before dinner. I made her cry. I felt wretched about it, but was glad we'd had it out. I still loved her, I still wanted to marry her, but at dinner she continued to persecute me by bringing up how distressing it was to have one's reputation scarred by malice. She meant to make a point: to me, to my mother. My mother and she clashed but Victoria was not herself that night. I put it down to drink, wedding jitters, the pregnancy, and our row. I suggested she go to bed. She got up and threw her glass of wine over me. I ran after her but she locked her door and refused to see me. I didn't see her until the next morning . . . when they found her . . ."

When *I* found her, Lianne and I, that fateful day.

Hearing noise down the hall, I paused to briefly touch his face. "I know you didn't kill her, David. Nor did she kill herself."

"I know," he whispered. "My mother . . ." He looked up, haunted, uncertain. "I made the mistake of discussing my doubts about the child with her. She'd heard tales from other ears, too. Soames, I suspect."

"What *was* Soames to Victoria? Do you know?"

"She called him her 'cousin' once. Mother was jealous, jealous of my bride, the woman she didn't approve of, stealing her place. I shouldn't have said anything to her. If I'd kept my mouth shut she might not have taken the action she did. Even now, she won't admit to it. *Prove* it, she says, and names Soames as the culprit because Victoria jilted him. *Soames* put the ricin in her dinner that night . . ."

The noise persisted.

He peered over my shoulder. "That will be Trehearn searching for us. We had best go."

They were all assembled in the dining room, each face registering surprise when David and I arrived together. Immediately detaching myself from his arm, I went to stand by Lianne.

The major chatted with Lady Hartley and I noticed her eyes kept flickering to the door, as though she expected—or feared—someone unpleasant to enter. To me, the major merely inclined his head, his quick eyes scanning my outfit.

To my surprise, the evening turned out quite enjoyable, just the five of us, and repairing to the courtyard for tea and cake, Lady Hartley ordered more bottles of champagne.

"What are we celebrating, my lady?" the major asked, jovial, not showing the least surprise when Mrs. Trehearn crept up to whisper in her ladyship's ear.

"A caller! Whoever can be calling at *this* hour?" Lady Hartley's demand echoed through the house. "Sir Edward, you say! And he wants to see *me*."

"Yes, my lady. And Lord David."

"Show him here, then."

Returning to her guests, Lady Hartley shrugged. "I shall have to speak to Sir Edward about his gross sense of decorum. One does not call at this hour. Whatever can he want?"

Sir Edward arrived, two policemen behind him.

"Forgive my intrusion, my lady, but I've come with a warrant."

"A warrant!" Lady Hartley shouted. "For who, pray? On what grounds?"

"For you, Lady Hartley. On the grounds of *circumstantial evidence* in the murder of Victoria Bastion."

"Evidence," she cried. "What evidence? If you need to arrest someone, arrest Soames. We all know there was something odd between him and Victoria. *Imagine.* The cook's girlfriend lands the lord of the house! How that must rile the man's pride and he's plenty of it—you only have to ask at the village."

"But Mr. Soames was in London at the time—"

"He *planted* it beforehand. He's a cook and he prepared all of Victoria's meals, probably slipped the solution taking up her morning tea. Oh, yes, he took tea to her sometimes, and I say on that last day he decided to avenge himself or, more accurately, his pride."

I glanced up at Lord David. He stood there, watching her, his eyes growing larger by the minute. "Mother, *please.*"

"I will not be accused of anything for I am innocent. Of course, I didn't *like* the girl—she wasn't good enough for my son—but I certainly did not poison her."

"Ah!" Sir Edward tapped his brow. "There is only one murderer in this room and it is you, my lady."

"Preposterous! How do you suppose I killed her? What proof do you have?"

"Proof of the poison ricin found in a perfume bottle you yourself gave to Victoria Bastion. Proof of Victoria's own words in her diary naming you as the giver of the gift and, more important, her fear of you. Fear that she would die. Fear that she would never become Lady Hartley because *you* didn't want her to be!"

I'd never seen Lady Hartley silenced before.

"I suggest, my lady," Sir Edward said, calm, but firm, "that you come with me now."

Staring at her empty champagne glass, she smiled. "The perfume bottle . . ."

Her tone sounded odd, whimsical.

"The perfume bottle," she murmured again.

"Traces of ricin were found inside that bottle," Sir Edward reiterated. "Who do you suppose put it there if not you, my lady?"

Bewildered, she looked at Lianne, me, and David. I could see her mind ticking, wondering who had found the perfume bottle. Lianne? Me? David? Trehearn? Annie? Betsy? Who had thought to turn it into the police?

Her gaze arrested me. She knew I'd done it. Her great spidery eyes stayed focused on me as she slowly left her chair and followed Sir Edward out of the door, keeping every ounce of her royal hauteur intact.

Lord David, pacing in the courtyard during Sir Edward's spiel, looked solemn, shocked, and pensive. Perhaps he, like the rest of us, thought Lady Hartley invincible and above the law.

Rubbing her eyes, Lianne went to David. "Where are they taking her?"

David drew Lianne to him. He said nothing, and she didn't ask again but instead looked at me. She knew I'd taken the perfume puffer, as I had given Sir Edward the diary.

She feared the future, as many in the district would, without Lady Hartley's rule.

"Don't worry," David said, "she'll be back."

CHAPTER THIRTY-FIVE

"Who are you, anyway? Clearly not just a major."

Grinning across at me in the car, Major Browning changed the gears. "Because you gave the perfume puffer to me, I'll let you in on a little secret. I work undercover, for Scotland Yard. 'When not at sea . . .' "

"You?!"

Now everything began to make sense. His coming to the area, his interest in the case, and his involvement in all of its details.

"The knights of justice thought Sir Edward needed a little help," he went on, amused at my continuing disbelief.

I recalled the possibility of another investigator looking into the case.

"I am still a *major*," he enforced.

"And a gentleman, no doubt. I suppose there is no 'uncle,' is there?"

"No," he laughed, "but if anyone's asking, George Filligan will say he is. I am, quite truthfully, staying at his humble abode by the sea."

I turned to him as we drove through the open gates of Padthaway. "You planned it, didn't you? You and Sir Edward."

He stopped the car and turned to me. "I am going to do something I never do."

"Which is?"

"Trust a woman."

He switched off the engine.

"Oh," I said.

"On a case."

"And I am the exception?"

"You are, Miss du Maurier. Without you, Lady Hartley would never have come with us."

"You still can't convict her, can you?"

"The fact will occur to her in the morning, and no, you are not completely right. We still might be able to convict her without a confession."

"If you're hoping she will give one, she will not."

"We will see."

He sounded mysterious. "You have a strategy in mind to catch her out, don't you?"

"How astute you are." He started up the engine again. "You had better be getting to bed, Miss du Maurier. Seen out in a parked car with a man of my reputation cannot be good, even though I know you *love* driving with me."

He laughed at my ashen face.

"Or is our erstwhile Lord David your favorite?"

My chat with David rose afresh in my mind.

"The man could not protect his own fiancée from his mother. He's weak."

"He is *not* weak," I defended. "He didn't know . . ."

"But he suspected. Is that what he told you? I know he's spoken to you. I can read your face like a book."

I sighed as we reached the village and he turned the lights down low on the car. "Yes, he told me everything."

"As he should if he is to start courting a new wife."

I glared at him. "How could you be so callous?"

"Because it's the truth, isn't it? He's kissed you, hasn't he?"

"No . . ."

"Word of advice. Don't lie. Your face is redder than Ewe's red roses."

Drat him. He was far too shrewd for my liking.

"What did he say? Your loverboy?"

"He is *not* my loverboy and I am far more interested in the mystery than men, thank you very much. How shallow do you think I am? If I wanted to protect him and his family, why would I have bothered to hand in the perfume puffer? The diary? The beads?"

"What beads? Did you find beads as well? What other evidence are you keeping from us?"

I realized then only Lianne, Ewe, and I knew about the beads. " 'To V, Love MSR,' it said. I asked everyone if they know who MSR is but nobody seems to know."

"MSR," he repeated. "How about Mostyn Summerville Ridgeway, also known as Soames, Ridgeway Soames."

"Cousins . . . yes," I said. Now her words began to make sense. Her fear of Soames alluded to a greater connection than a soured love affair. She feared his jealousy, his need to avenge his pride or, perhaps, her reversal of their "plan." The plan for her to marry Lord David, give birth to an heir, and steal Padthaway . . . "Cousins . . . it explains how Victoria got the job, and the picture in the paper—the likeness between the younger Bastion boy and Soames . . . I was right."

The major was amused. "You should work for us. You have a great mind, if a little . . . imaginative. We've interviewed Soames many times. Victoria always promised to marry him, since they were children. They kept their relationship secret because of his affair with Lady Hartley."

"They can't have been lovers. She said she kept herself for Lord David in the diary."

"Yes, I know. I read that entry, too."

"What does Soames say?"

"He says they had a romance but it never went beyond kissing. Victoria lost interest and both cousins wanted something better."

"You mean richer?"

"Exactly so. So one planned for Lady Hartley and the other—"

"Lord David," I whispered. "So Lady Hartley was correct—correct about Victoria. She was an adventuress. Yet her diary paints a very different picture."

"She may have had that original plan," the major concluded. "To marry a rich man, never expecting to fall in love with Lord David and that he would marry her. In saying as much, he wouldn't have married her without the baby."

"No, I don't think he would have either."

"Braving the mother's disapproval, Victoria knew she'd have to fight for her reputation. Everything was against her, unfortunately, and she made some unwise choices, choices that led to her death."

"What unwise choices? Do you mean the secret London visits? Whatever she was keeping from Lord David?"

He nodded. "One shouldn't keep secrets from one's fiancé. Not a good start to any marriage."

"I think someone was bribing her and she feared losing David over it—a man in her past, perhaps?"

He smiled. "I *do* think I'll recommend you for the service. She was very cautious in her London visits for I cannot track her beyond a hotel."

"Does 'Crow' or 'Crowleys' mean anything to you?"

"Crowleys? Yes, yes it does. It's a club, not a club for reputable ladies."

"Reputable," I murmured. "The last time I heard that word was from Bruce Cameron's lips at the wake. He said he saw Victoria at such a place. He must have meant Crowleys, too."

Amazed, he looked across at me. "Where did you hear of Crowleys?"

"From Connan Bastion," I said, proud.

"The devil . . ."

"Some people prefer talking to a woman. Perhaps I asked Connan the right questions."

"Perhaps I can learn a thing or two from you," the major conceded, and I left him feeling good.

A note arrived in the morning.

Ewe placed it under my door.

It was from the major.

> *Going to London today.*
> *Meet me at the crossroads at nine.*

I glanced at the time. Eight-thirty. I had half an hour to dress and reach the gate.

Abandoning any thought of breakfast, I readied myself, Ewe watching me with oversized owl eyes.

"Sir Edward did it! He really took her and she went with them? I thought they'd have to drag her out."

Lady Hartley being dragged anywhere did not fit into the scope of the probable. "They'll hold her for questions until she confesses."

"She won't confess," Ewe huffed. "Ain't the evidence enough?"

"The only fingerprints on the bottle belong to Victoria."

"She were clever then. I bet Trehearn mixed it up."

"So do I," I said. "But they won't speak. It's the wall of silence."

"No point protecting her now. They've got her."

Relieved to have achieved the near impossible, leaving Ewe who talked and talked and followed me halfway up the lane, I waited at the crossroads and at a quarter past nine, Major Browning's motorcar came speeding to a halt. Climbing in, I said, "Ewe thinks Mrs. Trehearn prepared the poison."

"Good morning to you, too," the major laughed, perusing my dismal morning outfit. "No time to dress? When I made such an effort?"

He had, too, shining there, newly shaven and smelling of cologne, his hair perfect and attired in a smart silver gray suit.

"What? Too formal?"

"Are we going to dine with the Queen?" Groaning at my ordinary day pants and black sweater, I started to smooth back my hair.

"No point. The wind'll blow it."

He was right, curse him. The only saving grace I possessed was the foresight to have brought along a comb in my handbag. And an umbrella. I'd been caught too many times in the rain recently.

"Mrs. Trehearn is the strangest creature I have ever encountered," the major began, grinning at the passing countryside. "Oh, Cornwall. Beautiful, isn't it?"

"We could have caught the train."

"Too rattly and there's nothing better than a *long* drive when such enchanting company is to be had."

He smiled across at me and I suggested he watch the road. "Mrs. Trehearn?"

"I tried my hardest to wrest a smile from her. A frown, *anything,* but she has what I never thought I'd find. A genuine stone face."

"Therefore she'd make a perfect liar. If the poison can't be traced and you have no fingerprints, Lady Hartley's lawyers will dismiss it."

"Victoria's diary is our greatest weapon, along with the housemaids' testimony. They all knew Victoria received the perfume from Lady Hartley."

"What is Lady Hartley saying?"

"Nothing. She refuses to speak to us without the presence of her lawyer, who, I understand, will be traveling down to Cornwall today from London as we are driving up."

I expected as much from Lady Hartley. "Why did she go so calmly last night?"

"There's a reason for it," the major replied elusively.

He refused to say more and, struggling to hold hair out of my mouth, I intercepted his little smirk. He loved to inspire defiance in me as much as he loved to drive fast, exhibiting his prowess at every bend and hill.

"You were very secretive about the diary, Daphne. Are you keeping abbey secrets from me, too? Or have you lost interest there?"

"The Victoria mystery is better. We have to find out who she met that day—the Wednesday she went to London—and if he's the same man she planned to meet the following week."

"The man of the diary?"

" 'Saw him. Went better than expected.' What do you suppose that means?"

"I don't know," the major replied, "but we will soon find out."

Skillfully navigating through the city traffic, he turned down several streets before parking the motorcar at the base of an old gray building boasting long glazed windows, green shutters, and antique balconies.

"It's a place where many clandestine events transpire. No place for a lady like you," he said, getting out the car.

"No place for a true gentleman either, I suspect."

"I never said I was a gentleman," he replied.

The club existed on the fifth floor, up a flight of narrow, winding stairs so steep I wondered how the inhabitants managed to climb down after their indulgences. A red carpet guided the last flight, leading up to a pair of double wooden doors bearing great lion-head handles and a stern-faced guardian. "Not open till twelve . . ."

The major slipped him a card and the white-suited man stood aside.

"Welcome to Crowley's," the major invited. "Try the barman. My attempts have failed so it's up to you."

I entered the club to the sound of a record playing, an Italian operetta, the cleaners looking up at our unexpected approach.

Spying the barman sprucing crystal glasses, a wizened old man well acquainted with life and its foibles, I sat down on a bar stool, a timid, lost smile on my face. "Hello, I know you're not open yet, but I'm wondering if you can help me. A lady used to come here . . . a tall, beautiful girl, dark hair, violet eyes—"

"Victoria Bastion. The murdered girl."

The curt directness put me off guard. "Why, y-yes . . . I am a friend of hers . . . she used to meet somebody here and I need to contact him. It's very important."

The wily old fellow smirked, his keen gaze monitoring a whistling Major Browning's casual forage about the room. Recognition sparked and caution set in, reflected by sharpening eyes and a gruff sneer.

"Oh, please, sir." I tried my damsel in distress appeal. "It's urgent I find this man. I have something of Victoria's to give to him."

My act must have succeeded for his eyes softened a little.

"The fellow you're after usually comes here at three . . . for his whiskey. Want to wait?" He pointed to a curved lounge area.

"No, but we'll be back. Thank you so very much." I patted his hand. "You're a very kind man."

"Well done." The major whistled once outside the door. "Your tactics do have their charm."

He was treating me as one would treat a partner. I liked the treatment, for it opened a new world for me, a world of research I could use in my writing.

"Have you thought of where to stay for the night yet?" Starting up the engine, he drove out of the building with a grin. "You can always stay with me."

"I'll stay with my family."

"What's your excuse for rushing to London for one night?"

"To collect my typewriter," I said. "My father bought me a new one."

He nodded, pleased. "Good. You can tell me what you plan to do with this typewriter on the way to lunch."

"Lunch!"

"Naturally, one has to eat."

CHAPTER THIRTY-SIX

The scarlet letters of Crowley's loomed before me.

Tucking a wisp of hair behind my ear, I paused on the landing and imagined Victoria's entrance to the infamous club.

Unlike my plodding arrival, I fancied I heard her quick, light step running up the stairs full of purpose and gaiety. On the landing, she stood still, her poise perfect, her figure a dream in her little red suit, a diamond-shaped feather hat and string of lavender beads gracing her beauty. Dancing off her wrist was a lady's purse, red and beaded, with a mirror and a tube of lipstick inside.

The doors to Crowley's swung open, the rigid-faced guardian charmed by her, all eyes drawn to this mysterious beauty traversing through the dimly lit private lounges. She drifted past the bar, bestowing a gracious smile to one admirer, and sailed toward the far back where a man waited under the shade of a greenish lamp.

I headed toward that lamp, alongside the major, toward a man of my father's age relaxing upon the armchair, his combed black hair splintered with gray, his facial structure of fantastic proportion, Roman almost, purple eyes dark, intense, changeable, eyes I'd seen before . . .

"Let me do this," the major hissed under his breath.

No formal greeting or introduction ensued. Commandeering the seat opposite the man, the major casually crossed his legs and ordered a drink. Opting for the end of the settee facing the two of them, I struggled to manage my nerves. Here was the man, the unknown tormentor Victoria feared. Searching his face, I had my answer. "You're her real father, aren't you?"

The halting whisper left my lips before I could stop it.

I dared not look at Major Browning.

Robbed of his anonymity before he chose to publicize it, Victoria's father smiled, an elusive smile of wary caution. "How'd ye know?"

"The eyes . . . I found her on the beach."

"I thought Miss Hartley found her."

"We found her together," I explained, undaunted, ignoring any silent reprimand from the major. Despite his theory, I felt this was the way to proceed. Natural, open, unmilitary.

"And you're the girl from the papers—Miss du Maurier, isn't it? Allow me to introduce myself. Elias Wynne."

His accent sounded faintly Welsh but I wasn't sure.

"I follow everything Lord David does," Elias said as he winked at me, "ever since me daughter become engaged to the man."

I thought of Victoria's unrelenting search for her true father, her need to find him. Once she succeeded, how did she feel?

Elias chuckled, reinforcing the instinct of distrust creeping up my arm. A vulnerable Victoria, at last finding her father, wanting desperately to recapture the love and affection she'd missed throughout her life, now understanding why she always seemed merely tolerated at home. She must have opened her heart to the man sitting before me, and invited him to share her new life. Her new life with Lord David, as Lady Victoria Hartley, mistress of Padthaway.

Oh yes, it all became so clear to me. Elias's selfish gratification upon discovering he had a beautiful daughter, a gratification that transformed to opportunistic gloating when she announced her wedding plans, and his shock at her death, came into warped view.

"You're trying to blackmail Lord David now, aren't you, Elias? Just as you did your daughter."

Swilling his glass of whiskey, the major ordered another round of drinks.

"I fancied gettin' to know me daughter a bit. What's wrong with that? Besides, she wanted me round for *safety* reasons. Were plannin' to meet me here after her weddin'. Proves she were murdered."

I bristled at the horrific vision of this creature showing up at Padthaway, plundering through the house, demanding to see her ladyship and Lord David. Had Victoria seen Elias this way, as he truly was? I had to find out. "Mr. Wynne, did your daughter invite you to her wedding?"

Now the truth emerged. He couldn't hide the fact.

"No, she didn't, did she? She didn't want you in her life. And when the blackmail attempt failed upon your daughter's death, you decided to blackmail Lord David. Were you successful?"

"Were I successful?" he barked, laughing. "I'd say *more* than successful, for he paid a pretty penny for me to keep me mouth shut. For *I* know."

"What do you know, Elias?" The major refilled the man's beer.

"I know she were murdered, pure and simple. I seen it with me own eyes."

"Liar. You're too drunk to ever find your way to Padthaway."

He shrugged. "Maybe so, but I've got a letter. A letter from me Vicky. In it, she wrote it might be awhile till she can next see her dad and give him a bit of money. I didn't like that note so I, Elias the drunk, if ye please, gets on a train and goes down to Cornwall to see me girl, see me girl get wed, was me plan."

"When did you arrive?"

"On the night of her murder. For on me way to this grand place . . . it were late, I stopped by the pub first, got directions, then went along the sea to the place. Didn't expect to see me girl out there on the cliffs, did I?"

The major and I exchanged an incredulous glance. "You saw her? On the night? Did she see you?"

"Nope, she did not, for she had company."

I didn't like the way he said "company." "Do you mean a man?"

"I mean," his eyes narrowed, "her murderers."

"Murderers?" the major and I echoed, astonished.

"That's what I said and what I saw, me, Elias, with me own two eyes . . . *two* of 'em, yep, two. One, me future son-in-law."

"And the other person you saw was a girl, wasn't it, Elias? Did you see them kill her?"

The major asked the questions now, for I felt too ill to do so. I kept seeing David's face. No, I could not believe it.

"They must of, for she were dead on the beach the next day, weren't she?"

"If Victoria was in trouble, why didn't you go to help her? What happened, Elias?"

Elias now grew quiet, his reddened face betraying his embarrassment. "I tried to get to me Vicky. I tried. But I'd drunk too much beer and threw up. I must have passed out for I remember nothin' till the morning."

"Did you see Victoria dead?"

He nodded, his face grim. "I saw her shoes. And then I looked over . . ."

"And saw the dead body," the major finished. "Why did you scally away then, Elias? Why didn't you report it? I think I know why. You thought you'd turn Victoria's death to your advantage. You thought you'd blackmail Lord David instead and make more than a pretty penny. You gave yourself away before, Elias, when you mentioned he'd been paying you. Paying you to stay quiet! A *chief* witness in your own daughter's murder."

Elias didn't like the denunciation. "What were I to do, then? She was dead so why not make a buck out of it?"

"Elias, you're going nowhere until you make a full statement, here and now. I hope at some stage of your life you regret your actions for they lack all common decency."

———

"The shoes are important," I said on the road back to Cornwall the next morning.

"Lord David is the next target," the major replied, "and I leave him to you, Miss Daphne du Maurier. If he trusts you, he'll confess to you."

I doubted his theory, as much as I doubted my own ability to face the family now, after hearing Elias's story.

I went, though; I had no choice as Lianne had called for me.

"Where'd you go?"

Fresh from her bath, Lianne tugged the robe of her dressing gown.

"You were gone *all* day. Ewe says you went to London."

"Yes, I went to get a typewriter."

"I can't believe you went to London without me!"

Sighing, I shook my head, and sat down on the bed. "I fear you're going to be very angry with me. I went with the major. He asked me to go . . . to see if we could discover any more about the man Victoria went to meet in her diary."

"So you didn't go to get a typewriter. You went off to find out who this person is. Well, did you succeed?"

I nodded.

"Who is it?"

"Victoria's father."

"Her father . . ."

The word sounded foreign on her lips. "Funny. I never thought Victoria had a father."

"He wasn't a nice one. He was blackmailing her. I have to speak with your brother."

"What do you need to speak to me about?" Lord David entered Lianne's bedchamber, carrying her ribbon in his hand. "I found this on the terrace."

"Oh, thank you! It's my *favorite* ribbon. Daphne's been busy, Davie. She went to London. Met Victoria's father."

"Did she?"

Lord David's eyes turned suddenly dangerous.

"Y-yes," I stammered. "Elias is a nasty person. Wouldn't surprise me if *he* murdered Victoria."

I hoped to allay the growing suspicion in his face, but it didn't work.

"There's a painting I want to show you, Daphne. Lianne, you stay here for the moment."

"All right." She smiled her merry smile, whistling, quite oblivious to my fear.

We reached the top of the stairs. Searching for any sight of Annie, Betsy, or even Mrs. Trehearn, I attempted to appear calm.

"This way," Lord David gestured down.

"Where are we going?" I said in a small voice.

He did not reply, and I prayed for Annie or Betsy to turn a corner and find me, to save me from this madman.

I soon found myself staring up at the *Beneficent Bride*.

"The lost bride," he murmured. "You have developed a very singular interest in what happened to my lost bride, haven't you, Daphne?"

I felt numb. The voice didn't sound like Lord David's. It sounded like a stranger's.

"Why did you not come to me with the diary?"

"You said your mother did it," I breathed, afraid to look into his eyes. "Has she confessed?"

"Confessed?" He laughed.

"Yes, for she went with Sir Edward willingly. I thought . . ."

"She has no need of confession, for *I* killed Victoria. Why else do you suppose she went to jail? To protect *me.*"

I stopped to peruse his face. "You believed she was meeting a man in London, didn't you? A lover? You also thought she and Soames planned to plant a bastard on you. Is that why you chose to get rid of her by poison?"

A flicker of amusement crossed his face. "I am innately curious how you deduced all of this. What did Elias really say?"

"He was blackmailing you because he saw you and Lianne with

Victoria on the cliffs that night. Which one of you did it? What happened? Lianne hid the shoes, didn't she? Victoria's shoes."

Heaving a deep sigh, one verging on regret, he stared up at the painting. "I will finish the story I began in front of this painting. For you, Daphne, for you. I am a man and I will not allow my mother to suffer for a crime I committed."

"You followed Victoria to London a few times, didn't you? You watched her go into the club, thinking she met a lover there, the father of her child."

"Yes." Silently, he touched the face of the bride in the painting with his finger. "She was beautiful, like a doll. But I couldn't trust her. She had not told me about Soames, and I found out. Her necklace fell off one day—the clasp opened. She swore Soames and she had never been lovers but I didn't believe her."

"She was a virgin when she came to you. She said so herself in her diary."

"Was she," he whispered, a haunting pallor creeping into his face. "I couldn't tell; we'd drunk too much that first time."

"She *was* innocent," I maintained. "But she should have trusted you. She tried to handle everything herself—Soames, Connan, her father—but she only served to feed your doubts."

He nodded, a faint smile appearing on his lips. "You do care for me, don't you, Daphne? You justify things for me."

"I can't justify murder, David. That's why you've written your confession, haven't you? To release your mother?"

He nodded again. "When I saw her sacrifice herself for me so willingly, I knew the truth would come out. Besides, I am tired of people bleeding me. Elias is only one. Death or jail for me is a release, a haven."

"What happened? You bought the poison or did Mrs. Trehearn mix it for you?"

"A friend of mine gave me the poison."

"Bruce Cameron?"

"We were at the club, drinking. I started talking and by the end of the night, the poison ended up in my pocket. I took it home. I saw the perfume bottle on her dresser and simply slipped it inside. That was after the argument when she taunted me about the baby. We made up before dinner though, and I went to her room to get the bottle, but it had disappeared . . ."

"You were too late. She'd sprayed herself with the poison, its lethal inhalation worsening through dinner."

"Yes."

"Then she fled to her room, not knowing the reason for her sickness, maybe thinking it had to do with the baby and emotional distress, and decided to go for a walk. She felt heated, maybe. She collected her shoes and walked out to the cliffs. Why did you follow her? You knew she was going to die, didn't you?"

"I was hoping to save her, but she ran so crazily. When I caught up to her she just stood there, her black hair blowing in the wind, and laughed at me. 'You poor fool, David,' she said. 'Can't you see I want to be alone?' She ordered me to go and stood on the edge of the cliff, peering over. 'Why do I feel so ill?' she kept saying, and I asked her if she'd used the perfume spray. She looked at me then, a queer kind of look. I saw the notion of poison occurring in her eyes and it surprised her so much she stumbled and fell. Fell straight down to the sea, and to this day I don't know if she meant to do it or whether it was an accident."

"She died thinking it was your mother who had poisoned her. Not you."

"That's why I won't allow my mother to suffer for the crime. If I were truly callous, I'd leave her to her fate. Better she returns, though, and better I hang since I cannot escape my destiny."

"What destiny is that?"

"Madness. Just like my father. Go now, Daphne. Go now before I hurt you. Break the news to my mother . . . if you would."

"I will," I promised, and hastened out of the house.

CHAPTER THIRTY-SEVEN

"The house of death," Ewe chorused, long silent after the dramatic turn of events.

"I hear Lady Hartley has reinstalled herself supreme back at Padthaway," Miss Perony said. "I heard she fired Soames *and* Mrs. Trehearn."

"Wants a fresh start. Changes servants like linen," Ewe muttered.

"She will mourn the loss of her son," Miss Perony whispered. "I still can't believe Lord David could do that. Every time I saw him, he always appeared so charming and circumspect. Will he really hang for murder, Major?"

"It depends on the jury."

"I heard you delivered the news to Mrs. Bastion," Miss Perony went on.

I thought of the beads, the beads I'd dropped into Mrs. Bastion's lap. She thanked me when the major and I left, the major elaborate in his praise of my help during the case.

I did not return to the abbey. Upon hearing the news of Lord David's arrest, I had been summoned home, and coming home with this tale contented me more than discovering ancient scrolls.

The mood at Padthaway was of a house in mourning.

Lady Hartley, Jenny, Betsy, Annie, and Lianne commiserated in the courtyard. I imagined they had all stood outside to watch Lord David being taken away, never to return.

Lady Hartley was furious with me. She blamed me for the loss of her son.

"*You*. You did it all. When we did nothing but *befriend* you, you turned out to be a viper in the bosom."

In her grief, Lady Hartley had turned on everyone, hence Soames and Mrs. Trehearn's prompt dismissal.

I walked past Mrs. Trehearn's study on my way out, eager to catch a glimpse of the room where the strange woman had spent most of her days. To my disappointment, the room shone new and clean, but for the housekeeping journal left on the table. I knew I shouldn't have taken it, but curiosity overcame me.

"What have ye there?" Ewe spotted me when I returned to the cottage, book under my arm. "Get a lashin' from her ladyship?"

"Yes," I smiled, "and I've borrowed Mrs. Trehearn's house-keeping journal. I'm going to my room to read it."

Mrs. Trehearn's housekeeping journal I discovered to be a meticulous notation of household affairs, extending back twenty years, amazingly detailed. Records on everything from the price of eggs to new linen.

Flicking through the early dates, I stumbled upon one circled entry:

October 21 £300 Dr. Castlemaine, Penzance

This was a peculiar entry, for that was a great deal of money back then for a doctor's visit. Was the appointment for Mrs. Trehearn or for some other staff member? It must be for some household affair or it wouldn't have been featured in this book.

The circle emphasized its importance. Other amounts weren't circled, only this one.

Penzance and Dr. Castlemaine . . . another country drive in order, Major Browning?

He thought I was mad.

"I might be," I sighed, "but I have two days left and what else am I to do? I can't rest now that I've got a taste for mystery."

He lifted an amused brow at the delivery of my logic. "I've learned to trust your instincts. I'll take you then. Are you ready now?"

Seeing me enter the car with the book on my lap, the major gave me a surreptitious glance. "So, what have you pinched there, Sherlock?"

"It's Mrs. Trehearn's housekeeping journal." Opening the book in my lap, I perused the entries. "Two pounds for sugar . . . six for meat . . ."

"Fascinating reading."

"It's this one—'October 21 £300 Dr. Castlemaine, Penzance.' Twenty-odd years ago."

"I fail to see the significance."

So intent in my further examination of the journal, I failed to hear him.

"Where do you think to find this Dr. Castlemaine?"

"I don't know." Listening to the putting engine, a sound I found oddly soothing, I prepared for the long journey. Pity I hadn't thought to bring coffee and biscuits. Alerted to hunger, my stomach rumbled in protest and mortified, I twisted my head away.

"Ah, hunger breeds irritability, and we can't have Sherlock's mind working bald. I suggest we make a stop at a charming seaside village."

A break sounded wonderful.

"If that suits you and your schedule, Sherlock."

I no longer bothered to roll my eyes at the Sherlock quips. He seemed determined to use it, it amused him, and one must amuse one's driver. I did, however, send him a sweet smile. "It suits me perfectly, *Thomas*."

To my chagrin, he grinned. "I like the way 'Thomas' sounds on your lips . . . want to take the wheel later?"

He did enjoy vexing me, didn't he?

"Unless, of course, you *can't* drive."

"I can so!"

"Excellent. I knew I was correct in that assumption."

I endured thirty more minutes of his assumptions regarding my character. By the time we reached the village, I was ravenous. Promising the best Cornish pasties and strong coffee, the major guided me inside the humble wayside inn, conveniently isolated, I noticed on arrival.

"Don't worry," he smirked. "If I planned a rakish abduction, I'd have chosen a better location to conduct the affair. I do have singular knowledge in that department, you know."

"I'm sure you do." While we waited for breakfast, served by a gracious, plump farmer's wife, I upbraided him for sending me into Padthaway alone. "I am lucky. Lord David could have killed me, too."

"That's unlikely." He refused to look even slightly remorseful. "Besides, you're a resourceful girl. You would have found a way to escape."

"You are no gentleman," I retorted.

The rain started two minutes after we climbed back into the car and arrived at the next crossroad.

"Cornwall," the major chuckled, "and its changeable weather."

Cornwall and its changeable weather. Padthaway, the house of a thousand mysteries, its changeable seasons.

"Dreaming up another story?"

"Just a headache. Are we nearly there yet?"

"Almost."

As we entered the thriving city, a bustling town once alive with pirates, thieves, and smugglers, the rain began to subside. The air outside the car was cool and I shivered.

Taking off the sweater under his jacket, the major wrapped it firmly around my shoulders and drew me into the nearest pub, where an open fire called my querulous, shaky limbs.

"You sit down. I'll make the inquiries," the major directed.

I smiled my thanks, attuned to the plethora of noise surrounding me.

"Aw, ye're in luck today, Mister. Mister Brown, was it? Casper, I am, and used to live right above that fancy doctor. He had rooms— all private ones. I had to use the back steps."

"Do you remember the street name, Casper?"

"Aw, call me Casp. Me friends do and I'll take ye there if ye like. It's only a few blocks away."

Walking down seemingly endless lanes of slimy, treacherous cobbles, we arrived at the site of a building.

A demolished building.

Casper cursed. "I don't believe me eyes! It's gone . . ."

Detecting a black-caped man strolling across the street, the major left us to gape at the dirt mound.

"No joy there," he called back, betraying a little glumness. "Any ideas, Daphne? Casper?"

Wracking his half head of hair, Casper's foul breath exploded. "I know! Mrs. Tremayne! If ever a snoop. She knows everybody's business. Been here for centuries."

It was only a mild exaggeration. Mrs. Martine Tremayne lived across the street, at number fifty-nine. Sprightly for a seventy-two-year-old, and sharper than a thistle, the wizened eyes made a quick summary of our likely trio. Gripping her broom like a weapon, she listened to the reason for our call.

"Castlemaine, eh? Ye'd best come in . . . No, not you, Casper Polwarren. Get ye back to the pub."

Casper Polwarren, suddenly the proud owner of a five-pound note slipped to him by the major, was more than happy to comply.

Mrs. Tremayne's ground floor, mercifully, failed to exhibit that old smell. The other usual relics existed, several tiny tables, dusted lace curtains, photo frames, last decade's cushions, worn but well tended furniture.

Invited to sit down, she sped off to fetch a newspaper clipping of some sort. The major and I shared a look of amusement. Ewe Sinclaire had a soul mate.

"Here, read this."

Huddled together on Mrs. Tremayne's couch, we examined the

black-and-white face of a European man, bald and slim, and the title below it.

DOCTOR EXPOSED
Since the burning down of his building,
further details have emerged regarding
the doctor's *secret* clients . . .

"He'd take them in," Mrs. Tremayne huffed. "Fancy types wantin' to get rid of their babes. They paid well, ye see. We plain folk with our sniveling noses don't even tinkle to the likes of him . . . snooty pig he were."

"Look here"—I showed the major—"they've printed his entire appointment book, listing all the names."

"That's why I kept the clippin'," a proud Mrs. Tremayne declared. "Ye don't throw away things like that. A copper found it on the street, half burn out it were, but still readable. He got greedy. Sold it to the papers and lost his job, but I'm sure he got a goodly sum for it."

I'm sure he did, too, recognizing one or two of the names. Some were skillful abbreviations or alterations to conceal identities, but the shrewd Dr. Castlemaine had noted the true names in a small column to the side, directly under the monetary amount.

Balking at the exorbitant sums, the major lifted a brow. "I am obviously in the wrong industry."

A lucrative clinic of scandalous proportions. "Whatever happened to the doctor?"

"Ha! Lost his mind, he did, and there were never a more fittin' punishment for the likes of him. Thinkin' himself so smart. You'll find him at Doreen's nursin' home up yonder, but it's really a nuthouse for droolin' nutters."

Drooling nutters. Smiling at the colloquial phrase, I ran my finger down the names and dates until a name flashed before me, a curious name. "Hearn!"

Hearn for Trehearn? I quickly looked to the side notation. *300 pounds, Jenny Pollock, took dead child.*

I must have half choked for the major thumped my back.

"Know her, do ye?" Mrs. Tremayne sniggered.

"Yes, she's a nurse in a household where I've stayed."

"Humph! She won't have been the first. Caught the eye of the lord, did she? Sent off here to squash the scandal?"

The clipping fell to my lap. Jenny Pollock, the pretty nursery maid with the children . . . Jenny and Lord Hartley. Like a diamond shower, everything sprinkled into place. I suddenly remembered her defense of him: *He weren't mad, or if he were, it was she that sent him that way.*

What had Lady Hartley said of their discreet arrangement? She had her affairs and her husband had his, extending among the household staff, as was often the case in large households. She must have turned a blind eye to it until Jenny became pregnant!

A pregnant nursery maid must have been a source of irritation to the lady of the house, especially if her husband loved Jenny. Was that a possibility?

"A simple carte blanche, of sorts," the major decreed, dismissing my theory. "The problem solved with the hasty removal of the goods."

I sent him a look of reproach.

"Well, it's true." He failed to display adequate repentance. "You can't have the illegitimate playing with the legitimate, can you?"

A good point, a point I found very disturbing. "We have to get back to Padthaway."

CHAPTER THIRTY-EIGHT

The long, winding drive to Padthaway, the silent mansion, filled me with a sense of dread.

Shaken of now another secret, a secret the house wished to reveal to me, I absorbed the warnings of the gusty wind, the naked branches strewn of their leaves, their skeletal fingers encroaching upon the drive.

Then a burst of beauty. Padthaway, gracing the grassland. *My* Padthaway, standing proud, ready to receive me.

"Do you want me to drop you here?" the major asked.

"Yes, I must talk to Jenny alone. You keep Lianne occupied."

He grinned. "A pleasant occupation . . . are you sure you can handle this?"

"Oh, please." I exited the car with a huff and hurried up to the house.

Going around the back way, I spotted Annie in the hallway and asked for Jenny's whereabouts.

"Oh, Miss D, she's in her garden last time I saw her."

"Thank you, Annie."

Watching her go, I thought it would take the servants a long time to grow used to the place without Lord David.

None more so than Jenny.

I feared her reaction.

Putting aside her garden spade, she wiped her hands on her apron. "Different now Trehearn's not here. Lady Muck's interviewin' butlers now. Got a new cook, too. Mrs. Lockley. We all like her."

"That's good," I said, drawing out one of her garden chairs. Heeding the major's warning, I acted normal on arrival, chatting, mentioning my recent drive with the major.

"Oh, where'd ye go?"

"Penzance."

She dropped the spade. "Oh, and what were ye reason for going there?"

She was nervous.

"Jenny, don't be afraid. I know about the baby, *your* baby. The one Dr. Castlemaine took from you."

Turning red at the name, she drifted to the chair opposite me.

"Please talk to me," I implored. "I'm your friend. I'm here to listen to you and *your side* of the story."

"Does the major know about it?"

I couldn't lie to her. "Yes, he does. I asked him if I could see you first."

She nodded, grimly accepting she now had to divulge the story she'd kept hidden for so many years.

"I were thirteen when I came to his house," she began, "young, full of silly dreams. I came to nurse little baby David." A fond smile tempered her lips. "What a sweet thing he were . . . he took to me and I to him. We were two little happy peas, livin' in our own world. Oh, I had to answer to the head nurse and all, but most of the time, me and baby David were alone. The mother didn't want 'im. She'd only poke her head in every now and then, hear the progress report, and go back to her parties. She never wanted to hold him."

"But the baby didn't suffer," I said softly. "You gave him plenty of love."

Her face softened. "Aye, I did. Me whole heart."

"I can see you both," I smiled, "little David, perfect, and you,

Jenny, pretty Jenny with the golden hair and blue eyes. I can see why Lord Hartley fell in love with you."

Her eyes froze at the mention of his name.

"Tell me about him, Jenny. Did he treat you kindly?"

Silently walking further down that closed tunnel, she eventually responded. "He were a strange one, his lordship, but he loved visitin' the nursery. *He'd* pick up the child, nurse 'im, and the babe adored him. He were unhappy . . . unhappy with *her*. Outside, he were different, but in the nursery, he were meek as a lamb."

"He started to come more regularly," I proceeded, "you and he . . . in the secret garden . . . a happy little family."

A capricious smile touched her lips. "Aye, it were like that, I s'pose. A play family for him."

"But you didn't mind. You loved him and he was good to you."

She nodded. "Passionate lover he were, but gentle, ever so gentle. Never once did he lay a finger on me or speak nasty."

"But outside he behaved differently."

Forced to nod again, she succumbed to the beauty of her memories, the love, the kindness, the happiness.

"When did Lady Hartley find out, Jenny?"

Startled out of her trance, she shivered. "We hid it from her. Terry said we must be careful of her and we were . . . for years. Mrs. T and the head nurse, they knew. Went to Mrs. T for me herbs . . ."

"But then you fell pregnant, even *on* Mrs. T's herbs."

"Aye. When her ladyship carried Miss Lianne, I found out I were expectin', too, to me horror. After all these years . . ."

"How did Terry react?"

"*She* said he had to give me up. She'd not have his *bastard* in the house. But Terry didn't want to give me up. He started to go a little crazy. He always did when he were confused. He *hurt* people."

"But never you, Jenny. Never you."

A tear rolled down her face. "I never got to say good-bye to him. They drove him to shoot himself. I just wish they'd let me say good-bye . . ."

"But they didn't. Just as they didn't let you keep your child. They packed you off to Penzance."

The horror of the locked memory opened with force. "I did it . . . to keep me job. And if it weren't for Lee Lee, bless her heart, *madam* would've sent me packin'. But she couldn't stomach the screamin' child. Nobody could. She were left to me . . . I calmed her. Only me."

Which explained her deep bond with Lianne. "What happened to your baby, Jenny? The baby you took from Dr. Castlemaine's?"

Crazed eyes greeted me again, followed by a curiously slow smile, ominous in nature, eerie, unlike the Jenny I knew. "I wanted to keep her. I tried to, but it were too late. *He* killed her and I took my little girl with me. I placed her in a safe place. . . ." Her gaze slowly turned to the herb garden.

I shuddered. "It must have been very hard. How you must have hated Mrs. T and Lady H for what they'd done to you . . . you had David and Lianne, but you couldn't forget what they'd done, could you, Jenny?"

"No!" Flying out of her chair, Jenny's hands seized my neck. "Just as I can't forgive you for hurtin' my Davie boy. He'll die, die, die, because of you!"

Her crazed eyes obstructing my vision, I desperately tried to loosen her grip on my throat. I couldn't breathe . . . and felt nauseous, faint . . . dizzy . . .

Then relief. The major's strong arms enclosing me, Lianne restraining the frenzied Jenny.

"It's all right, Jenny," Lianne soothed. "Daphne did the right thing. You always told me to do the right thing, and it was Davie that gave himself up. You lost your baby, but you have me. *Your* Lee Lee, always."

Jenny nodded, and as I watched Lianne hold and rock her, I came to appreciate the close bond they shared and the full reason for Lianne's nightmares. Seeing her father shoot himself and die before her eyes, and later, to see David, the brother she adored, the brother she would do anything to protect, convicted of murder.

"Forgive me." Jenny gazed at me, getting up, a little embarrassed over her behavior. "I don't usually . . ."

"I know." I pressed her hand.

She nodded and disappeared inside for a moment or two.

Upon her return, she dangled something before the major. "I s'pose I don't need to hide these now, do I?"

Clutched in her hand were the sandy bottoms of a pair of shoes.

Victoria's shoes.

CHAPTER THIRTY-NINE

"Jenny knew. Lianne had seen David do it. She had followed her brother out to the cliffs that night. Jenny protected them both by hiding the shoes in her room."

"A fitting end," Ewe declared. "I always knew one of 'em Hartleys did it. Just didn't know which one."

"We have Miss du Maurier to thank for Jenny and the clue of the shoes," the major said, tipping his hat to me. "Nobody would think twice about it, but our Miss Sleuth remembered the shoes . . . and that conversation on the cliff whilst picnicking with Jenny and Lianne."

"She's a bright lass." Ewe smiled at me fondly. "Even if she does scuttle off when she's supposed to stay with me!"

"And the other clues," I prompted the major. "Admit it, you and Sir Edward were lost. You needed me."

"We did."

It was a simple and genuine praise, without mocking, and I confess I felt rather proud, too.

LONDON HOUSE, *SOME MONTHS LATER*

The gloomy pathway beckoned. She paid no attention to its dilapidated state, neither seeing nor hearing the

windstorm brewing around her. Such was her state
of mind as she progressed toward her destination,
knowing this was the last time—

"Daphne!"

Jostled out of my chair, I typed the last sentence. My finger still poised on the full stop, I ripped out the page and gleefully reviewed those last beaming words.

"Daphne! Are you ready? We're late."

Jeanne and Angela were groaning in the hallway. Unconcerned with their panicky prompting, I dressed, taking one last look at the bleakness of the day outside. Hamstead in London failed to compare with my beloved Cornwall. I missed seeing the water, feeling the fresh sea air on my face. I missed the boats gracing the harbor and most of all, I missed those frightful days at Padthaway.

"You *cannot* wear that to a luncheon with Winston Churchill."

I smiled at Angela's deadpan face. "I certainly can and I will. In any case, nobody shall notice me."

"Doing the usual, are we? Sitting in a dark corner, taking notes about everybody."

"At least she does it *mentally* these days," Jeanne cried behind her, ever cheerful. "Here's your hat, Daph."

Our parents waited for us outside. Father, presenting his usual dashing image, and Mother, graceful, conscious of the time, and frowning over my hasty appearance.

"Daphne, dearest, you ought to take more care. I know there are no obscure Lord Davids to tempt you at political luncheons."

"You never know," Angela grinned, delighted at the thought of making new influential connections. "Perhaps your Major Browning will show up. He seems to have friends in high places."

"Oh, I believe he's away at sea," my mother echoed, lowering her voice to a modest whisper, "and after that one call in Fowey, we never heard from him, did we, Daphne dearest?"

I wished she would stop preempting the major's lack of interest. That one call, a mere friendly follow-up one, obligatory after those horror-filled days at Padthaway, had spurred her to think of him as a possible future husband for me.

"Better watch out," Angela warned. "I might take an interest in the dashing major if you don't."

"The major's promised to take me sailing when he comes back," Jeanne piped in, full of faith.

"When he comes back?" my mother lamented. "When*ever* will that be?"

My father rolled his eyes. "You women, always ready to spear a man. Paint on a smile now because we're here."

The luncheon party commenced.

Spotting a willowy tree outside Sir Winston's mansion, I slipped the notebook out of my reticule. I had two letters to write. One to Ewe, and one to Lianne. I'd not forget Lianne needed a friend now, especially as it appeared likely her brother would hang for murdering Victoria Bastion.

"Hello, old girl."

I smiled up to see J. M. Barrie usurp a seat beside me. "Are we in camouflage? I hope so. I simply can't abide political mumbo jumbo, can you?"

I watched him try to hide, albeit unsuccessfully, behind a palm leaf, and laughed. I loved Uncle Jack for his eccentricity and penchant for Brussels sprouts. I said I didn't spy any of his favorite vegetables on the table fare this day and he gave me a woebegone look. "Woebegone, dismal . . . I found a new word the other day, Uncle Jack. Lugubrious . . . for a gloomy, cheerless character, and I know exactly the person who fits it. Mrs. Trehearn, except I'll have to call her something else, won't I?"

"How about Danvers?" he reflected behind his palm branch, his fingers splaying across in horror. "Oh, hide me, there's the chancellor and he's after a signing. Trouble is, I can never get away. . . ."

So we camped out, the two of us, for a good hour or so until

Father found us and roused us back to normal land. Mother was most put out, but, of course, she sent Uncle Jack a charming smile.

I was grateful to go home to Cornwall.

To the house at Ferryside, to my room overlooking the river, my writing desk, the boats in the harbor . . .

Putting aside Ewe's letter, where she recounted all of the local Windemere news, including Lianne doing well and taking up Jenny's love of monograms, I gazed out the window.

I thought of Padthaway. I thought of all the people, the faces, the long, winding drive up to the gracious mansion, a white-faced Mrs. Trehearn waiting at the door, the corridors leading to the west wing and that magnificent room, crazy old Ben snipping at his hedges in the garden . . . and an idea for a novel burned within me, deep and irrepressible.

I sat down to write.

A boat in the harbor drifted toward me, its name elusive but for the first letter.

A monogram . . . large, scrawling, distinctive.

A monogram . . . beginning with *R*.